Susanna Gregory was a police officer in Leeds before taking up an academic career. She has served as an environmental consultant, doing fieldwork with whales, seals and walruses during seventeen field seasons in the polar regions, and has taught comparative anatomy and biological anthropology.

She now lives in Wales with her husband, who is also a writer, and is the creator of the Thomas Chaloner series of mysteries set in Restoration London.

Also by Susanna Gregory

The Matthew Bartholomew Series

A PLAGUE ON BOTH YOUR HOUSES
AN UNHOLY ALLIANCE
A BONE OF CONTENTION
A DEADLY BREW
A WICKED DEED
A MASTERLY MURDER
AN ORDER FOR DEATH
A SUMMER OF DISCONTENT
A KILLER IN WINTER
THE MARK OF A MURDERER
THE TARNISHED CHALICE
TO KILL OR CURE
THE DEVIL'S DISCIPLES
THE KILLER OF PILGRIMS
MYSTERY IN THE MINSTER

The Thomas Chaloner Series

A CONSPIRACY OF VIOLENCE
BLOOD ON THE STRAND
THE BUTCHER OF SMITHFIELD
THE WESTMINSTER POISONER
A MURDER ON LONDON BRIDGE
THE BODY IN THE THAMES
THE PICCADILLY PLOT
DEATH IN ST JAMES'S PARK

A VEIN OF DECEIT

Susanna Gregory

sphere

SPHERE

First published in Great Britain in 2009 by Sphere
This paperback edition published in 2010 by Sphere
Reprinted 2010, 2011, 2013, 2014

A CIP catalogue record for this book
is available from the British Library.

ISBN 978-0-7515-3915-8

Typeset in New Baskerville by Palimpsest Book Production Limited,
Falkirk, Stirlingshire
Printed and bound in Great Britain by
Clays Ltd, St Ives plc

Papers used by Sphere are from well-managed forests
and other responsible sources.

MIX
Paper from
responsible sources
FSC® C104740

Sphere
An imprint of
Little, Brown Book Group
100 Victoria Embankment
London EC4Y 0DY

An Hachette UK Company
www.hachette.co.uk

www.littlebrown.co.uk

For Liz and Edmund Betts

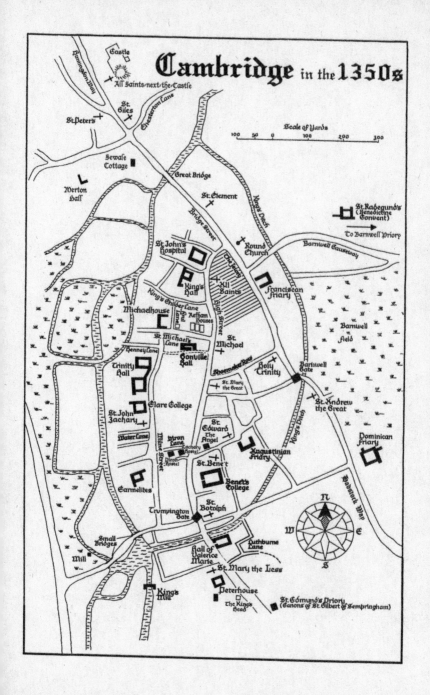

PROLOGUE

August 1357, Haverhill, Suffolk

It was a glorious summer afternoon, with fluffy white clouds flecking an impossibly blue sky, trees whispering softly in a gentle breeze, and the lazy sound of bees humming among the hedgerows. Cows lowed contentedly in the distance, and the air was rich with the scent of ripe corn and scythed grass.

There had been a fierce heatwave earlier in the year, followed by torrential rains that had devastated farmland all over the country. Fortune had smiled on the parish of Haverhill, though: its crops had survived the treacherous weather, and the harvest was expected to be excellent – its villagers would not go short of bread that winter, and the fat sheep dotting the surrounding hills indicated they would not be short of meat, either.

But the three men who stood around the little tongue of exposed rock in the middle of the wood saw none of this plenty: their minds were on another matter entirely.

In the centre of the trio was Henry Elyan, lord of the larger of Haverhill's two manors. He was a slim, elegant man who took considerable pride in his appearance – he loved clothes, and spent a lot of money ensuring he was never anything less than perfectly attired, from his fashionable hat to his stylishly pointed shoes. His weakness for finery exasperated his wife, who was always reminding him that while Elyan Manor was not poor, it was not exactly wealthy, either, and they had a duty to their tenants to use their profits more wisely than frittering them away on extravagancies.

'Are you sure, Carbo?' he asked of the man on his left. 'You cannot be mistaken?'

Carbo gave one of his peculiar smiles, the kind that made Elyan wonder whether it was wise to place so much trust in the man – it was common knowledge that he was insane. Of course, Carbo had not always been out of his wits. He had been a highly respected steward for many years, and his descent into madness had been fairly recent. No one knew why he had so suddenly lost his mind, although Elyan did not accept the widely held belief that grief for a dead mother had tipped him over the edge. He was sure there was another explanation, although he could not imagine what it might be.

'I am not mistaken,' Carbo said in an oddly singsong voice. 'It was God who brought me to this place and told me what lies beneath. And God is never wrong.'

The last of the three men was Elyan's neighbour, who owned Haverhill's second, smaller manor. Hugh d'Audley was thin, dark and pinched, and everything about him suggested meanness and spite. Elyan had never liked him, but money would be needed to exploit Carbo's astonishing find, and d'Audley was the only man in the area who might be in a position to lend some. So Elyan had set aside his natural antipathy towards the fellow and was trying his damnedest to be pleasant.

D'Audley, however, was sighing impatiently, making no attempt to hide the fact that he thought his time was being wasted. 'Of course Carbo is mistaken! He is deranged, and you are a fool to set stock by anything he says.'

'Coal is God's most special gift to the world,' chanted Carbo, kneeling to rest a reverent hand on the narrow

2

thread of dark rock he had found on his seemingly aimless wanderings. If he was offended by d'Audley's curt words, he gave no sign. 'He calls it black gold. Black gold.'

D'Audley rolled his eyes, and Elyan despised him for his stubborn inability to look past Carbo's lunacy and see what might lie beyond. He felt like grabbing the man and shaking some sense into him. Did he not know that coal seams were unheard of in Suffolk, so finding one in Haverhill was a fabulous piece of luck? And Elyan knew, with every fibre of his being, that it was going to make him rich – that he would never again have to listen to his wife carping on about the price of fine linen, or begrudging him the cost of his soft calfskin shoes. The prospect of such unbridled luxury made him giddy, and it was only with difficulty that he brought his attention back to the present.

'How do *you* know about coal and mining so suddenly?' d'Audley was demanding of Carbo. 'You have lived in Haverhill all your life, so how can you possibly claim expertise about minerals?'

'God told me,' replied Carbo distantly. 'He explained about the black gold.'

'You see?' said d'Audley, turning rather triumphantly to Elyan. 'The man is addled!'

Elyan did not reply. The copse in which Carbo had found the lode was dense with brambles and alder, and no one had bothered to forge a path through the prickly tangle before. There had to be some reason why Carbo had done it, so perhaps God *had* guided him there. Or was d'Audley right, and grubbing around in the undergrowth was just something madmen did?

'It is very fine,' crooned Carbo, ignoring d'Audley as he stroked the rock. 'The best black gold.'

'Actually, it is not,' countered d'Audley. 'I used the bucketful you gave me last night, and it smoked and spat like an old kettle. Good coal burns quietly and cleanly, but this stuff is rubbish.'

'Perhaps it was just wet,' suggested Elyan, refusing to let d'Audley's sour humour spoil his burgeoning hopes. 'But regardless, it will make us wealthy – assuming you want to be part of it, of course? I shall need money to excavate, and if you invest, you will share the profits.'

'But I am not convinced there *will* be profits,' said d'Audley, looking disparagingly at the thin line of crumbling black rock.

Elyan shrugged, feigning indifference to his neighbour's scepticism. Unfortunately though, mining was expensive, and he could not finance such a venture alone; he needed d'Audley's help.

'It is your decision,' he said with studied carelessness. 'I asked you first because you are my friend, and I wanted you to share my good fortune. But if you are not interested, I shall approach Luneday instead – he knows a good opportunity when he sees one.'

He would do nothing of the kind, of course – the lord of neighbouring Withersfield Manor was only interested in pigs, and was unlikely to spend money on anything else. But d'Audley hated Luneday with a cold, deadly passion, and was blind to reason where he was concerned.

'Wait,' snapped d'Audley, as Elyan started to walk away.

Elyan smothered a smirk before he turned; just as he had predicted, d'Audley was appalled by the notion that Luneday might benefit from a venture he himself had rejected. 'Wait for what?'

'Wait for me to mull it over,' replied d'Audley sullenly. 'I cannot make such a decision on the spur of the moment. I need time to think about it.'

'Then do not take too long,' warned Elyan. 'I want to begin operations as soon as possible.'

They both turned when Carbo started to sing. The ex-steward was lying on top of the seam, treating it to a popular ballad about love and devotion. D'Audley's eyebrows shot up, and Elyan took his arm and pulled him away before Carbo's antics lost him an investor.

'My wife is well,' he said pleasantly, flailing around for a subject with which to distract d'Audley. 'After twenty years of marriage, Joan and I had all but given up hope of an heir, yet our baby will be born in December.'

'Congratulations,' said d'Audley flatly, and Elyan realised, too late, that this was not the subject to win d'Audley's good graces. If he, Elyan, were to die childless, then d'Audley was one of three parties who stood to inherit his estates. A child would change all that and, unsurprisingly, d'Audley had not greeted the news of Joan's pregnancy with any great delight.

'Yet who knows what the future might bring,' Elyan gabbled on, cursing himself for his thoughtless tongue as he struggled to make amends. 'Joan is old to be having a first child, and the midwife says it will be a miracle if she delivers a healthy son.'

But d'Audley was not listening. He was staring at a nearby holly bush, eyes narrowed. 'Is that a foot I see poking out from under those leaves?'

Elyan looked to where he pointed, then strode forward for a better view. Carbo began muttering to himself, rocking back and forth on his heels as he watched the two Suffolk lordlings with eyes that were too big in his pale, thin face. Elyan reached the bush and gingerly pulled back the branches, careful not to snag his beautiful russet-coloured tunic. A body lay beneath, half buried in leaf litter. It was that of a young man, who wore a black tabard over his shirt and hose. A reddish-brown stain on his chest indicated he had been stabbed or shot with an arrow.

'That is academic garb,' said d'Audley, stepping back smartly, and covering his mouth and nose with his sleeve. The weather was hot, and the corpse was far from fresh. 'He must belong to one of the Cambridge Colleges – a student, perhaps. What is he doing here?'

'I have no idea.' Elyan was horrified. 'He cannot have come to spy on my coal, because the only people I have told about it are my wife, my clerk, my grandmother, Gatekeeper Folyat . . .'

He trailed off, uncomfortably aware that this was a considerable list – and Folyat was a notorious gossip. Unfortunately, the gatekeeper had caught him crawling about in Haverhill's bramble-infested woods and Elyan had felt compelled to offer him some explanation; he did not want his villagers thinking he was as mad as Carbo.

'Have you told any scholars about the seam?' asked d'Audley.

'No.' Elyan hesitated. 'However, my clerk went to Cambridge last week. Perhaps he—'

But d'Audley was not interested in what Elyan's clerk might have done. 'This lad has been murdered,' he declared, glancing around him uneasily. 'Stabbed or shot. We had better hide the body before anyone sees it.'

Elyan gaped at him. 'What? But surely, we should contact the Sheriff, and—'

'No!' D'Audley's voice was loud and harsh. 'The last time a Sheriff visited Haverhill, he liked it so much that he declined to leave, and we were obliged to feed him and his retinue for nigh on a month. I am not squandering money like that again, so we shall shove this boy in the ground and forget we ever set eyes on him.'

'I will fetch a spade,' said Elyan, after a moment of silent deliberation. His inclination had been to argue – to do what the law expected of him – but d'Audley had a point:

entertaining Suffolk's greedy Sheriff *had* been expensive, and he would rather they spent their resources on excavating what the mine had to offer.

'And then we had better deal with Carbo,' said d'Audley, gesturing to where the madman was humming to himself, eyes closed. 'It is obvious that he is the killer, and he should be locked away before he turns on one of us. We should summon his brother, and—'

'It is not obvious at all,' interrupted Elyan, startled. 'He may be a lunatic, but there is no harm in him. However, that sinister Osa Gosse has taken to haunting our parish of late, and he will commit any crime for the right price. It is far more likely that *he* killed this young man.'

D'Audley regarded him with an unreadable expression. 'Perhaps this corpse is a sign – a warning that I should be wary of joining your venture. So *you* can bury it: this is your land, so it is your problem, not mine. Watch the mud on your fine clothes, though. It stains.'

And with that, he turned on his heel and stalked away. Elyan watched him go with an expression that verged on the murderous.

CHAPTER 1

October 1357, Cambridge

The scream echoed along Milne Street a second time. Doors were opening, lights flickered under window shutters, and voices murmured as neighbours were startled awake. Matthew Bartholomew, physician and Doctor of Medicine at the College of Michaelhouse, broke into a run. Folk were beginning to emerge from their houses, asking each other why Edith Stanmore was making such an unholy racket in the middle of the night. The noise was coming from her house, was it not?

It was cold for the time of year, and Bartholomew could see his breath pluming in front of him as he sprinted along the road; it was illuminated by the faint gleam of the lamp his book-bearer, Cynric, was holding. There was rain in the air, too, spiteful little droplets carried in a bitter wind that stung where they hit. He glanced up at the sky, trying to gauge the hour. Other than the disturbance caused by the howls, the town was silent, and the velvety blackness indicated it was the darkest part of the night, perhaps one or two o'clock.

'What is happening?' called one of Milne Street's residents, peering out of his door. It was Robert de Blaston the carpenter; his wife Yolande was behind him. 'Who is making that awful noise? Is it your sister? I can see from here that her lamps are lit.'

Bartholomew sincerely hoped it was *not* Edith howling

in such agony. She was his older sister, who had raised him after the early death of their parents, and he loved her dearly. Stomach churning, he forced himself to slow down as he negotiated his way past Blaston's home. The recent addition of twins to the carpenter's ever-expanding brood meant they had been forced to move to a larger property, and he was in the process of renovating it; the road outside was littered with scaffolding, wood and discarded pieces of rope. Bartholomew's instinct was to ignore the hazard and race as fast as he could to Edith's house, but common sense prevailed – he would be no use to her if he tripped and knocked himself senseless.

'It is not Edith – it is a woman in labour,' said Yolande, seeing his stricken expression and hastening to reassure him. Bartholomew supposed she knew what she was talking about: the twins brought her number of offspring to fourteen. 'Edith must have taken in a Frail Sister.'

Bartholomew faltered. A lady named Matilde had coined that particular phrase, as a sympathetic way of referring to Cambridge's prostitutes. He had been on the verge of asking Matilde to marry him, but had dallied too long, and she had left the town more than two years before without ever knowing his intentions. It had been one of the worst days of his life, and even the expression 'Frail Sisters' was enough to make him reflect on all that his hesitancy had caused him to lose. But he came to his senses sharply when he blundered into some of Blaston's building paraphernalia and became hopelessly entangled.

'There are more Frail Sisters than usual,' Yolande went on, watching her husband try to free him – a task not made any easier by the physician's agitated struggles. 'Summer came too early and spoiled the crops, so a lot of women are forced to earn money any way they can.'

Another cry shattered the silence of the night. In desperation, Bartholomew pulled a surgical knife from his medical bag and began to hack at the rope that had wrapped itself around his foot. He could not really see what he was doing, and the carpenter jerked away in alarm.

'I cannot imagine why you are in such a hurry,' Blaston muttered, standing well back. 'You are not a midwife, so you are not obliged to attend pregnant—'

'He is different from the other physicians,' interrupted Yolande briskly. 'The Frail Sisters trust him with their personal ailments, because Matilde said they could.'

Suddenly, Bartholomew was free. He began to run again, aiming for the faint gleam ahead that represented his book-bearer's lamp. Cynric, of course, was far too nimble to become enmeshed in the carpenter's carelessly strewn materials. There were two more wails before the physician reached Edith's house, and without bothering to knock, he flung open the door and rushed inside.

Edith's husband, Oswald Stanmore, was a wealthy merchant, and his Milne Street property was luxurious. Thick woollen rugs were scattered on the floor, and fine tapestries hung on the walls. Not for him the stinking tallow candles used by most people; his were beeswax, and gave off the sweet scent of honey. A number were lit, casting an amber glow around the room. They illuminated Edith, kneeling next to someone who flailed and moaned. The rugs beneath the patient were soaked in blood; there was far too much of it, and Bartholomew knew he had been called too late.

'Thank God you are here, Matt!' Edith cried when she saw him. Her face was pale and frightened. 'Mother Coton says she does not know what else to try.'

Bartholomew's heart sank. Mother Coton was the town's

11

best midwife, and if she was stumped for solutions, then he was unlikely to do any better. He knelt next to the writhing woman and touched her face. It was cold and clammy, and her breathing was shallow. He had been expecting someone younger, and was surprised to see a woman well into her forties. Her body convulsed as she was seized by another contraction, and the scream that accompanied it was loud enough to hurt his ears.

'It is getting worse,' said Edith in a choked voice. '*Do something!*'

'She took a potion to rid herself of her child,' explained Mother Coton. She was a large, competent person, whose thick grey hair was bundled into a neat coif. 'Pennyroyal, most likely.'

'No,' objected Edith. 'I am sure she—'

'I know the symptoms,' interrupted Mother Coton quietly. 'I have seen them hundreds of times. She brought this on herself.'

'But Joan *wanted* this child,' cried Edith, distressed. 'She had all but given up hope of providing her husband with an heir, and was delighted when she learned she was pregnant.'

Mother Coton declined to argue. She turned to the physician. 'Can you save her? You snatched Yolande de Blaston from the jaws of death after I told her family to expect the worst. God knows how – witchcraft, probably. Will you do the same for this woman?'

'I cannot,' said Bartholomew, hating the dismay that immediately flooded into Edith's face. It upset him so much that he barely registered why Mother Coton thought he had been successful with Yolande; he was used to people assuming his medical triumphs owed more to sorcery than book-learning and a long apprenticeship with a talented Arab *medicus*, but he did not like it, and usually made a point of telling them they were mistaken. 'I can only ease her passing.'

'No!' shouted Edith, beginning to cry. 'You must help her. Please, Matt!'

Her tears tore at his heart, but she was asking the impossible. He began to drip a concentrated form of poppy juice between the dying woman's lips, hoping it would dull the pain and make her last few moments more bearable.

'I have never seen this lady before,' said Mother Coton to Edith, while he worked. 'And I know most of the pregnant women in Cambridge. Is she a visitor?'

Edith nodded, sobbing. 'We were childhood friends, although I have not seen her for years – not since she married and left Cambridge. We met by chance in the Market Square two days ago, and she has been staying with me since. She came to buy ribbons for the baby clothes she plans to make.'

'Then I am sorry for your loss,' mumbled Mother Coton, in the automatic way that suggested these were words uttered on far too regular a basis.

'Is Joan's husband staying here, too?' Bartholomew asked. 'If so, we should summon him.'

'He is lord of Elyan Manor, in Suffolk. But he did not come with her to shop for baby baubles – he stayed home.' Edith's hands flew to her mouth in horror. 'Oh, Lord! What will *Henry* say when he learns what has happened? He will be distraught – Joan said this child means a lot to him.'

'She came alone?' asked Bartholomew, surprised. Suffolk was a long way away, especially for a woman at such an advanced stage in her pregnancy.

'She came with her household priest, who had business with King's Hall. He is staying at the Brazen George.'

13

Edith clambered quickly to her feet. 'I shall send a servant to—'

'It is too late,' said Bartholomew, as Joan's life-beat fluttered into nothing. 'I am sorry.'

Edith stared at him, and any colour remaining in her face drained away. 'Then she has been murdered,' she declared in an unsteady voice. 'Do not look at me in that disbelieving way, Matt. I have never been more sure of anything in my life.'

Bartholomew was used to losing patients – he had been a physician for many years, and was the first to admit that the field of medicine was woefully inadequate, even among the most dedicated and skilled of practitioners – but that did not mean he found it easy. Even when he did not know the victim, there were grieving friends and kin to comfort, and dealing with death was the part of his profession he most disliked. He led Edith to a bench, and held her in his arms while she wept.

'She was my oldest friend,' she whispered, heartbroken. 'We spent all day picking ribbons for her baby. Then we ate just after sunset, and sat laughing about old times. How can she be dead now?'

Bartholomew had no answer. He glanced up, and saw Mother Coton was still with them. He had sent his book-bearer to fetch a bier, while two maids were swabbing the blood from the floor, so she was not lingering to be helpful. It took him a moment to realise she was waiting to be paid.

Fees were usually the last thing on his mind on such occasions, and it was a constant source of amazement to him that others felt differently. He could not pay her himself – Mother Coton's charges were princely and he was far from rich – so he was obliged to interrupt Edith's tearful reminiscences and remind her of her obligations. Fortunately, the need to address practical matters forced Edith to compose herself. Wiping her eyes, she took a key from a chain around her neck and unlocked a chest.

'I do not care what your experience tells you, Mother Coton,' she said, handing over several coins with a defiant glare. 'Joan did *not* take something to end her pregnancy.'

The midwife made no reply, although her expression said she thought Edith would accept her diagnosis in time. Bartholomew was inclined to agree: Joan's symptoms matched those of an attempt to abort. Of course, Edith's testimony suggested Joan was happy with the prospect of motherhood, but it was not unknown for women to change their minds, and Joan was old for a first pregnancy – perhaps she had not wanted to risk dying in childbirth.

One of the maids picked up Joan's cloak, intending to lay it over the body. As she did so, a little pottery jar dropped out. Had it landed on the flagstones, it would have shattered, but it fell on a rug, then rolled under the bench. Bartholomew bent to retrieve it.

'A tincture containing pennyroyal,' he said, after removing the stopper and sniffing the contents. He poured a little into his hand, then wiped it off on his leggings. 'Not the herb, but the oil, which can be distilled by steaming. It is highly toxic.'

Mother Coton nodded her satisfaction at being right. 'It is the plant of choice for expelling an unwanted child.'

'Then someone gave it to her,' said Edith firmly. 'She did not take it of her own volition.'

Mother Coton looked as if she might argue, but then raised her shoulders in a shrug, and when she spoke, her voice was kinder than it had been. 'You should rest now, Mistress Stanmore. It has been a long night, and things will look different in the morning.'

One of the maids escorted her out, while the other took away the blood-soaked rugs and finished cleaning the floor. She was efficient, and it was not long before all evidence of traumatic death had been eradicated – with the exception of the cloak-covered corpse. Edith stared unhappily at it.

'Where is Oswald?' Bartholomew asked, realising for the first time that his brother-in-law had not made an appearance. Stanmore was solicitous of Edith, and although theirs had been an arranged marriage, they were touchingly devoted to each other.

'Lincolnshire. He told you at least twice that he was going, and asked you to look after me.'

'Did he?' Bartholomew was appalled to find he could not remember. Term had just started, and he had been saddled with more students than he could properly manage. He was struggling to cope. Of course, that was no excuse for failing in his obligations to his family.

'Yes,' she replied. 'Otherwise he would have ordered me to stay at our manor in Trumpington, where he thinks isolation will keep me safe. He does not like the notion of me being in town alone.'

'Then I have let him down,' said Bartholomew guiltily. 'I have barely seen you since term began.'

She shot him a wan smile. 'It was what I was hoping. I do not want a protector breathing down my neck, and the servants are here. So are the apprentices. And then Joan came . . .'

'You say she was visiting Cambridge?' asked Bartholomew, sensing her need to talk.

Edith nodded through fresh tears. 'She was my closest friend when we were children. Do you not remember her? Our favourite game was to dress you and the dog up like twins.'

16

Bartholomew raised his eyebrows. 'It seems to have slipped my mind.'

'She has not changed.' Edith's smile was distant. 'We still laugh at the same things, and she was so happy to be giving her husband an heir. She thought she was too old to conceive.'

Bartholomew would have thought so, too. 'It is unusual to be pregnant for the first time at her age.'

Edith's thoughts were miles away, and she did not hear him. 'She joked with your colleague Wynewyk in the Market Square – she persuaded him to choose the colour of the ribbon she was buying, and their witty banter attracted quite a crowd. They were flirting, making people laugh.'

Bartholomew regarded her askance. 'I sincerely doubt it! Wynewyk prefers to flirt with men.'

'Well, he was doing it with Joan today,' said Edith stiffly. 'They were very funny.'

Bartholomew did not want to argue with her. 'Why was she staying with you, if you had not met for so many years?'

'Her husband does business with King's Hall, and sent his priest there to draft some agreements. She decided to travel with him, to shop for baby trinkets. She was going to lodge in the Brazen George, but when we met by chance in the Market Square I decided she would be more comfortable here, with me. But someone still managed to kill her . . .'

'No one killed her,' said Bartholomew gently. 'And if you say she wanted this child, then we must assume her death was an accident – she took the pennyroyal by mistake. Her pregnancy was obviously well along, so no apothecary would have prescribed it. She must have bought that tincture herself, without realising it would harm her.'

Edith sniffed, then nodded, although he could see she was not convinced. He supposed she did not have the energy to debate the matter; it was very late, and he knew from the amount of spilled blood that the battle to save Joan had raged for some time before he had been summoned.

'We ate supper and talked a while,' said Edith unhappily. 'Then she went to bed, while I stayed up, sewing Oswald a new shirt. Not long after, she stumbled into this room, and there was blood . . . I wanted to call you, but she said she needed a midwife. Perhaps I should have ignored her wishes . . .'

'Mother Coton knows what she is doing. You did the right thing.'

Edith sniffed again, then looked up when there was a soft tap and the maid answered the door. 'Here is Cynric, and he has brought three of your pupils to carry Joan away. He is a thoughtful soul.'

Bartholomew's book-bearer had been with him since he was an undergraduate, and was more friend than servant – and wholly indispensable. As he watched Cynric usher the students inside, he thought, not for the first time, what an ill-matched trio his apprentices were. Valence was tall, fair and amiable; Risleye was short, dark and sly; while red-haired Tesdale was one of the laziest lads he had ever encountered.

'Valence is a pleasant young man,' said Edith, regarding them critically. 'But I cannot imagine what possessed you to accept Tesdale and Risleye. Surely, nicer lads applied for the honour of being taught by you? Moreover, I thought Risleye was Master Paxtone's protégé, so why have you been lumbered with him?'

'He is a good student,' replied Bartholomew. But he could see from Edith's expression that this was not enough

18

of an answer to satisfy, and because he was sorry for her distress over Joan, he pandered to her curiosity. 'Paxtone said he was unteachable, and asked me to take him instead. It happens sometimes – a tutor and a pupil finding themselves incompatible.'

'I imagine *you* think Risleye is unteachable, too,' said Edith, indignant on her brother's behalf. 'But I doubt Paxtone will consent to take him back again. It was unfair to foist such a fellow on you. Risleye is a horrible creature – spiteful, greedy and opinionated.'

She was right: Bartholomew *was* finding Risleye something of a trial. The lad was devious, argumentative and arrogant. However, he was also conscientious, intelligent and eager to learn, virtues that might turn him into a decent physician one day; and, Bartholomew thought, if Risleye knew his medicine, then his odious personality was irrelevant.

'And Tesdale is almost as bad,' Edith went on when he made no reply. 'His sole purpose in life seems to be devising ways to shirk his duties. And he has a nasty temper.'

Bartholomew started to object, but stopped when he realised she was right about Tesdale, too: the lad *was* hot-headed, and was always the last to volunteer for any tasks that needed performing. But he also possessed a gentle, confident manner that patients liked, which was enough to make Bartholomew determined to do his best by the lad – the plague had left a dearth of qualified physicians in England, and he felt a moral responsibility to train as many new ones as possible. However, his resolve was tested when Tesdale shoved past the maid and, without so much as a nod to Edith, began to hold forth.

'It was not me, sir,' he declared without preamble. 'Risleye is lying.'

'I am not,' declared Risleye, fists clenched angrily at

19

his side. 'My essay on Galen *has* been stolen. The thief waited until I had added the finishing touches, then broke into my private chest and made off with it.'

'You are wrong, Risleye,' said Valence softly. 'And this is not the right place for—'

'He thinks *I* took it, because I am too lazy to write my own,' interrupted Tesdale resentfully. 'But I would not touch his stupid essay with a long pole.'

'These three were the only ones awake,' muttered Cynric to Bartholomew, apparently feeling some explanation was needed for his choice of bier-bearers. 'I shall know better next time.'

'I was awake because my work is stolen,' snapped Risleye, overhearing. 'Michaelhouse is full of thieves, and it is not safe to close your eyes there.'

'You lost it,' countered Tesdale angrily. 'It will turn up in the morning and—'

'Oh, yes!' snarled Risleye. 'After someone has copied all my ideas, to pass off as his own.'

'Stop,' ordered Bartholomew sharply, seeing Edith's distaste at the clamouring voices in the place where her friend lay dead. 'Help Cynric, and remember why you are here.'

'Because you want us to shift a cadaver?' asked Risleye, frowning his puzzlement at the remark.

'Because he wants us to take his sister's friend to the church,' said Valence quietly. 'Which we must do with the minimum of fuss, to avoid unnecessary distress.'

'Very well,' said Tesdale with a huge yawn. 'And then we should go home – I am exhausted.'

Edith watched in distaste as Risleye, Cynric and Valence lifted Joan on to the bier. Tesdale did not help, and confined himself to issuing instructions. 'I cannot imagine how you put up with them,' she said.

There were times – and they were becoming increasingly frequent as term went on – when the physician wondered the same thing.

'You are needed at Michaelhouse,' said Cynric to Bartholomew, as he and the students carried the body out of Edith's house. 'Wynewyk is ill.'

Bartholomew was surprised – his colleague had seemed well enough earlier. Leaving Cynric and the students to deal with Joan, he hurried back to the College, his footsteps echoing hollowly along the empty lanes. He was not sure how much time had passed since he had arrived at his sister's home, but it was still dark and there was no sign of daybreak.

He knocked on the gate and was admitted by Walter the porter, who greeted him with a scowl. Recently, a prankster had relieved Walter's beloved pet peacock of its tail, and because the incident occurred shortly after Bartholomew had given a lecture on superstitious beliefs – including one that said peacock feathers could cure aching bones – Walter held the physician personally responsible.

'How long until dawn?' Bartholomew asked pleasantly. He disliked discord and wanted peace.

'How should I know?' snapped Walter. 'Do you think I have nothing better to do than watch an hour candle burn?'

The physician did not feel like berating him for his insolence – and Walter's surly rejoinders were likely to wake half the College if he tried – so he headed towards Wynewyk's room without another word. As he walked across the yard, he looked around at the place that was his home.

Michaelhouse was a medium-sized foundation, and

part of the University at Cambridge. It boasted a handsome hall, two accommodation wings that joined it at right angles, and a range of outbuildings. All were protected by a high wall and a gatehouse that contained the porters' lodge. Unfortunately, time had taken its toll, and the College was starting to look decidedly shabby. Moss and lichen grew over its roofs, most of which leaked, and its honey-coloured stone was in desperate need of scrubbing. The courtyard was a morass of churned mud, mixed with the fallen leaves from a scrawny cherry tree.

It currently housed about sixty students, more than could comfortably be taught by its Master and eight Fellows. One reason they were overworked was because one of their number, Father William, was on a sabbatical leave of absence – which everyone knew was a nice way of saying he had been exiled to a remote part of the Fens for being a zealot. Bartholomew missed William, although he was not sure why: it was certainly not for his dogmatic opinions and argumentative personality.

Wynewyk lived in the same building as Bartholomew, the older and more leak-prone of the two accommodation wings. Like all Fellows, he shared his chamber with students, and it was a tight squeeze at night when they all spread their mattresses on the floor. Bartholomew stepped over the slumbering forms, straining his eyes in the darkness to make sure he did not tread on any. Wynewyk had lit a candle, but he had muted the light with a shade, so as not to disturb his room-mates.

'Thank you for coming, Matt,' he whispered. He was a small, neat man who taught law. He had been at Michaelhouse for about three years, and Bartholomew liked him and considered him a friend. 'I have been feeling wretched all night, although I cannot imagine why

22

– my stars are in perfect alignment, so I should be in fine fettle.'

'What did you eat at supper?' Bartholomew asked, to change the subject. Unusually for a physician, he placed scant trust in the movements of the celestial bodies, but this was a controversial stance, and he took care to keep his opinion to himself; rejecting the ancient and much-revered art of astrology would result in more accusations of witchcraft, for certain.

'The same as you: bread and cheese. I also had a mouthful of posset, but there were nuts in it, and I have an aversion to them, so I spat it out. My tongue still burns, though.'

The posset had contained almonds, but supper had been hours ago, so any reaction Wynewyk might have experienced from his brief contact with them should have been past its worst. Bartholomew examined his colleague, but could find nothing wrong except a reddening in the mouth. He prepared a tonic of soothing herbs that would help him sleep.

'Where have you been?' asked Wynewyk. 'You took ages to come. Were you out?'

Bartholomew nodded absently as he worked. 'Seeing a friend of Edith's, but I was called too late.'

'Dead?' asked Wynewyk uneasily. He crossed himself. 'Then I hope you have better luck with me.'

'You are not going to die,' said Bartholomew, helping him sit up so he could sip the remedy. 'You will be perfectly well again tomorrow.'

'Have any of your patients heard news of Kelyng?' Wynewyk asked, pushing away the cup when the physician put it to his lips. 'You promised you would find out.'

Kelyng was Michaelhouse's Bible Scholar, who had failed to arrive when term had started. He owed a fortune in unpaid fees, and even the salary he earned from reading the scriptures aloud during meals had failed to reduce the debt to a reasonable level. It would not be the first time a student had elected to abscond rather than pay, and Bartholomew, like the other Fellows, thought Kelyng had done so. Kind-hearted Wynewyk was rather less willing to believe the worst of the lad.

'They saw him leave Cambridge in August,' replied Bartholomew, 'but no one has seen him since.'

Wynewyk grimaced at the unhelpful news, and began to drink the medicine. 'Did you hear what happened yesterday?' he asked between sips. 'I had a run-in with that horrible Osa Gosse. He accused me of trying to seduce him.'

'And did you?' asked Bartholomew, knowing that while Wynewyk was usually discreet, there were occasionally misunderstandings in his quest for willing partners.

'No!' Wynewyk sounded horrified. 'He is a revolting fellow – a liar and a thief. You look as though you have not heard of him, which amazes me. He is an inveterate felon, always being accused of some crime or other. He hails from Clare in Suffolk, but has recently taken up residence in our town.'

'How do you know him?' asked Bartholomew curiously. Wynewyk owned a great weakness for ruffians, but he usually drew the line at criminals.

'Everyone knows him – or everyone who does not wander around with his mind full of medicine, at least. I had the misfortune to make his acquaintance about a week ago, when he spat at me. I objected, and he drew a dagger. Fortunately, Paxtone of King's Hall saw what was happening, and shouted for help. Gosse's servant was killed when the Carmelite novices rushed to my rescue.'

'I know who you mean,' said Bartholomew in understanding. Besides being a physician and a Doctor of Medicine, he was also the University's Corpse Examiner, which meant he was obliged to provide an official cause of death for anyone who died on University property. The man in question had been stabbed on land belonging to King's Hall, so Bartholomew had been asked to give a verdict.

'I wish Gosse would go back to Clare,' said Wynewyk unhappily. 'He blames me for the death of this servant, even though I was not the one who knifed him.'

'You should rest,' said Bartholomew kindly. Talking about the incident was agitating Wynewyk, and he would not sleep if his mind was full of worry.

'Thank God for Paxtone,' said Wynewyk fervently. 'He saved my life. I never thought much of him until recently, but he is a decent soul.'

'Yes, he is,' agreed Bartholomew, although he was surprised to hear Wynewyk say so – Wynewyk rarely fraternised with men from other foundations, because he believed it created issues of loyalty. Many academics agreed, and confined their circle of acquaintances to within their own College or hostel. But Bartholomew did not see any problem, and had a number of friends outside Michaelhouse, Paxtone among them.

Wynewyk seemed to know what he was thinking. 'You are astonished I should befriend anyone from King's Hall. But Paxtone and its Warden, Powys, are erudite men. I like them.'

Bartholomew let him talk, and gradually Wynewyk's eyes began to close. The physician waited until his colleague's breathing became slow and even, then crept from the room.

* * *

There was a slight lightening of the sky in the east, which told Bartholomew it would not be long before the bell rang to summon Michaelhouse scholars to their dawn devotions. He was tired, though, and the prospect of even a short nap was appealing, so he walked to his chamber, and began the tortuous business of stepping over sleeping students in the dark. There were seven of them, most pleasant, intelligent lads determined to become good physicians. Risleye had wanted to join them, eager to share his teacher's chamber rather than be farmed out elsewhere, but the others had united to keep him out. Bartholomew thought they probably could have squeezed him in, but had not objected too loudly when Risleye had been told to lodge with one of the other masters.

He reached his bed and lay down, but the moment he closed his eyes, Tesdale began to whimper, caught in a nightmare. He knew from experience – Tesdale had bad dreams most nights – that waking caused the lad distress, and that the episodes usually ended of their own accord anyway. However, the noise was not conducive to falling asleep, so Bartholomew decided to put the time to good use by reading instead. He could not do it in his chamber, lest the light disturbed those who were managing to sleep through Tesdale's moans, so he went to the library. This was a corner in the main hall that comprised a few shelves and three lockable chests. The tomes were either chained to the wall, or secured inside the boxes, depending on their value and popularity; books were expensive, and no foundation could afford to lose them to light-fingered scholars.

He began to read *De proprietatibus rerum* by Bartholomaeus Angelicus, refreshing his memory of the text he was going to teach that day. It was not long before he became engrossed, and when the bell rang to wake the scholars for morning mass, he was surprised to find the time had passed so quickly. Reluctantly, he closed the book, and walked down the stairs and into the yard.

It was another cold, gloomy day, with clouds thick and heavy overhead. It was windy, too, and autumn leaves swirled around until they made soggy piles in corners. He breathed in deeply, relishing the clean scent of damp vegetation. He whipped around in alarm when he heard a sound close behind him, but it was only Cynric. The Welshman prided himself on his stealth, and was always sneaking up on people with the clear intention of making them jump out of their skin.

'I saw that woman – Joan – and your sister in the Market Square yesterday,' the book-bearer said. The expression on his dark face was sombre. 'It does not seem right that she should be walking and laughing one moment, then dead the next. Do you think someone cursed her?'

'No,' said Bartholomew, struggling for patience. Cynric always looked for supernatural explanations to matters he did not understand, and while the physician was used to it after so many years, he still found it exasperating. 'She swallowed pennyroyal. That is what killed her.'

'Mother Coton said Joan wanted rid of the child,' Cynric went on. 'But in the Market Square yesterday, she seemed all eager for motherhood – she was choosing ribbons, and making enough show about it to gather an audience.' He shook his head, as if the ways of the world were a mystery to him.

'Did you see her buy anything other than ribbon?' asked Bartholomew, idly wondering how she had come by the pennyroyal. The apothecaries would not have sold it to her – the Church was not very understanding of merchants who let women buy the means to destroy their unborn children.

Cynric raised his eyebrows, amused. 'A rich woman in

27

a market? Of course I saw her buying other things, boy! And she paid me to carry them all to your sister's house, so I know for a fact that there were a lot of them. But she went nowhere near an apothecary, if that is what you are really asking. Are you going to church dressed like that, by the way?'

In the growing light, Bartholomew saw his clothes were bloodstained from kneeling next to Joan. He needed to change. He hurried to his room, smiling greetings to his colleagues as he passed. They nodded back, some grumbling about the rain, others more intent on discussing a debate on Blood Relics that was due to take place the following week.

He ducked into his chamber – stepping over Tesdale, who was always the last up – and quickly donned fresh clothes. His hat had blown into a puddle the previous day, and he had forgotten to take it to the laundry, so it was still filthy. Annoyed with himself, he slapped it against the desk a few times, to beat off the worst of the muck, then jammed it on his head, hoping no one would notice its sorry state. Once he had given his boots a quick rub with the cuff of his shirt, he was ready.

There were still a few moments left before Master Langelee would lead the College in procession to St Michael's Church for morning prayers, so he unlocked the door to the cupboard-like room where he kept his medical equipment, to check the progress of a goose-grease salve he was making. It was thickening nicely, and would soon be ready.

He was about to leave when a ring-mark on the work-bench caught his eye. He frowned, because he had spent some time polishing it the day before – hygiene was important when making substances that were to be ingested, and he was always scrupulous about it. He

supposed one of his students must have spilled something, then neglected to clean it up. However, his list of
potential culprits was short; some of the ingredients he
kept in the room were dangerous, so only the most senior
pupils were allowed access. And, after a jape involving an
'exploding' book the previous week, only Risleye and
Tesdale were currently permitted inside – the rest were
banned until they had proved themselves mature enough
to be trusted.

He bent to inspect the mark more closely, then jerked
back in alarm when he caught the distinctive aroma of
poppy juice. He stared at it in horror. It was one of the
substances no student was allowed to use without his
supervision, placed on a high shelf that was off-limits to
all and sealed in a container marked with a warning
cross of red ink. He looked up at the shelf, and was
uneasy to note that someone had been fiddling there:
the pots had been moved so their labels no longer faced
the front.

He stood on a stool and began to hunt for the poppy
juice. When he found it, he opened the jar and looked
inside. It was about half full. He was relieved – if Risleye
or Tesdale *had* included some in a remedy they had
prepared, then they had not taken very much. Of course,
he would have to speak to them about using it at all; it
was far too dangerous to be doled out by lads who were
not yet qualified.

He began to replace the jars in their proper order, but
there was an ominous gap. Bemused, he searched the
other shelves, but it did not take long to confirm his suspicions: the pennyroyal was gone.

'Hurry up, Matt, or you will be late.' It was Brother Michael,
the University's Senior Proctor and one of Michaelhouse's

masters of theology. The portly Benedictine was also Bartholomew's closest friend. That morning, his monastic habit was covered by a handsome fur-lined cloak, his flabby jowls had been scraped clean of whiskers, and his lank brown hair was smoothed down around a perfectly round tonsure. He was immaculate, and Bartholomew felt poor and shabby by comparison.

'My pennyroyal is missing. I know I had some – I used it to treat a festering ulcer a few days ago.'

Michael tugged his cloak around his ample frame, as if he thought it might ward off unpleasant images as well as the cold. 'Perhaps you finished it,' he remarked, without much interest.

'There was some left. I know there was.'

Michael saw his concern and frowned uneasily. 'It is dangerous? Poisonous?'

'I lost a patient to pennyroyal last night. Two, if you count her unborn child.'

Michael's frown deepened as Bartholomew told him what had happened. 'Are you saying *your* supply killed this woman? That one of your pupils—'

'No!' It was too dreadful a possibility to contemplate. 'Joan was a visitor, so cannot know my students. It must be coincidence, although . . .' Bartholomew trailed off, uncertain what to think.

'Are you sure it is missing? Perhaps it is simply mislaid.'

'It has gone,' said Bartholomew worriedly. 'I cannot recall *exactly* how much was left . . .'

'Shall I ask Langelee to excuse you from church while you continue to look for it? I suppose I can be prevailed upon to perform your duties. After all, it will only be the fifth time I have assisted at mass since the beginning of term because you have been too busy with patients to do it yourself.'

'Three physicians are not enough to look after a town the size of Cambridge,' objected Bartholomew defensively. 'Especially now Robin of Grantchester has stopped his work as surgeon. Paxtone, Rougham and I are overwhelmed by the number of people wanting help.'

'Yes, but Paxtone and Rougham have the sense to decline new cases,' said Michael tartly. 'You physick anyone who summons you.'

'What would you have me do? Refuse them and let them suffer?'

Michael sighed. 'No. But let us hope Valence, Risleye and Tesdale elect to practise here when they graduate next year. Then there will be six physicians. Of course, while Valence will be a boon, the same cannot be said for the other two. Tesdale is too lazy, and Risleye is so lacking in anything resembling human kindness that it would not occur to him to dispense charity.'

Bartholomew nodded, but his attention had returned to his missing medicine. Both Tesdale and Risleye had borrowed the storeroom key from him that week, but neither should have used pennyroyal, so what had happened to it? Had Tesdale taken it for another student jape? Risleye would not have done, because he had no sense of humour. But Bartholomew had been furious the last time his pupils had abused his trust, and he doubted any would risk doing it again. He did not often lose his temper, and he knew his anger had alarmed them.

He followed the monk outside, locking the door behind him and wondering who else might have had occasion to raid his supplies. He knew about the healing properties of pennyroyal – it was good for stomach pains, dropsy and cleaning ulcers – but did it have non-medical applications, too? Cynric had been known to 'borrow' materials for cleaning his sword, while Agatha the laundress was willing to try anything in her ongoing war against moths. He supposed the disappearance of the pennyroyal was not necessarily sinister, although the notion that anyone could wander into the storeroom and help himself to whatever he pleased was disturbing.

It was cold and wet in the yard, and his students had taken refuge in the porters' lodge. The slow-witted Librarian, Rob Deynman, was with them. Deynman had been a medical student himself, until the College had offered him a 'promotion' in order to prevent him from practising on an unsuspecting public. They looked around as Bartholomew approached, and he saw they were all grinning, except Risleye whose face was infused with rage.

'Tell him, sir,' Risleye cried, outraged. 'Tell Valence that garden mint should not be given to teething children, because it is a herb of Venus, and so stirs up bodily desires. That is bad for babies.'

'I said it can be used to remedy colic,' corrected Valence patiently. 'I did not say you should feed it to brats in the kind of quantity that will drive them wild with lust.'

His cronies laughed, and Risleye flushed even redder, clenching his fists.

'I knew a man who ate an entire patch of mint once, in the hope that it would make him lusty,' said Deynman, ever amiable. 'He was obliged to remain in the latrine for the next two days, and his wife was deeply vexed.'

The students laughed again, but Bartholomew was not in the mood for levity. 'Did any of you use concentrated poppy juice in a remedy this week?' he demanded. 'Or take any of my pennyroyal?'

'You told us not to touch the stuff on the top shelf,' said Risleye virtuously. 'And I *never* disobey orders. Tesdale does, though.'

'All I took this week was some yarrow to treat Dickon Tulyet's cold,' said Tesdale, shooting his classmate a weary look. 'Why? Have you lost some?'

Bartholomew scratched his head. Perhaps the stain on the workbench *had* been there when he had polished it the day before; he had been preoccupied with all the teaching he was due to do, so his mind had not been wholly on the task in hand. And the pennyroyal? There was no explanation or excuse for that: it had gone, and that was all there was to it.

Once prayers had been said, and breakfast served, eaten and cleared away, Michaelhouse's masters and their students gathered in the hall for the morning's lessons. Bartholomew spoke on *De proprietatibus rerum*, the author of which listed a number of herbs and their uses, and although pennyroyal was on the physician's mind to begin with, he had all but forgotten about it by the time the noonday bell rang some hours later.

He was hoarse from trying to make himself heard. Wynewyk had declared himself indisposed, so Master Langelee had taken his class instead, and as he knew nothing about law, he had passed the time by talking about local camp-ball ratings instead – he was an avid camp-ball player, and loved nothing more than a vicious scrum in which it was legal to punch people. The ensuing discussion had grown cheerfully rowdy, and Bartholomew had not been the only one struggling to teach over the racket.

Langelee was a burly man, with muscular arms and a thatch of thick hair, who looked more like a warrior than the head of a Cambridge College. Before becoming a scholar, he had worked for the Archbishop of York, and there were details about his previous life that Bartholomew still found unsettling. But his rule was just and fair, and his Fellows were satisfied with his leadership. One of the most astute things he had done was to delegate his financial responsibilities to Wynewyk, who had a good head for figures and an unerring eye for a bargain.

'Lord!' muttered Michael, coming to join the physician and casting a venomous look in the Master's direction as the students clattered out of the hall. 'That was tiresome. My theologians were not interested in camp-ball when we started out this morning, but they are gripped by it now. They tell me Langelee's exposition of leagues and points was far more interesting than Holcot's *Postillae*.'

'No surprise there,' murmured Bartholomew, collecting the wax tablets his lads had been using, and stacking them in a cupboard.

Michael's expression hardened. 'Well, your class was not exactly enthralled by whatever ghoulish subject you had chosen, either: Tesdale could not stop yawning, Valence was staring out of the window, and even Risleye's attention strayed. I hope Wynewyk is better by this afternoon, because I am not in the mood for another bawling session.'

'Ask Langelee to lower his voice, then.'

Michael grimaced. 'I did – he told me he was practically whispering as it was. But the real problem is not him, it is the number of students we are trying to teach. We were stupid to let him enrol all those new pupils last Easter, because none of us can cope. Even with Thelnetham and Hemmysby newly installed as Fellows, we struggle. And all the money is gone, anyway.'

'What money?' asked Bartholomew, bemused.

'The money we raised by accepting these additional fee-paying scholars. It has all been spent, and our coffers are emptier now than ever. We discussed it at the last Fellows' meeting.'

'Did we?' Bartholomew did not remember.

'You spent the whole time writing. Foolishly, we thought you were taking notes, and only learned later that you were penning a remedy for gout. You are lucky the rest of us care enough about your College to pay attention.'

Bartholomew watched the servants begin to arrange the hall for the noonday meal. Trestle tables were assembled, and benches set next to them. Cynric stoked up the fire, while scullions carried dishes from the kitchens to the shelves behind the serving screen. They did not smell very appetising – poor food was just one economy forced on them by Michaelhouse's ailing finances.

'I met Edith when I went out for a little proctorial business earlier,' said Michael, seeing the physician had no answer to his charge. 'She is pale, but seems to be coping with her friend's death.'

'You did not mention my missing pennyroyal, did you?' asked Bartholomew anxiously. 'She is sure to put the two "facts" together, and it took me a long time to convince her that Joan was not murdered. I do not want to give her a reason to rethink.'

'Of course not,' said Michael impatiently. 'However, it does seem odd that Joan spent the day buying baby ribbons, then swallowed a substance to rid herself of her child the same night.'

'Perhaps the ribbons were a ruse, to conceal her true intentions. A cover, in other words.'

'And then she killed herself, too?'

'And then died because she was unsure of the dosage,' corrected Bartholomew. 'But regardless of what happened, it is not our concern. She is not a scholar, and Edith's house is not University property. *Ergo*, it is outside the

Senior Proctor's jurisdiction, and we are busy enough, without making more work for ourselves.'

'It would be my jurisdiction if it was your pennyroyal that ended up inside her,' retorted Michael.

'That is unlikely,' said Bartholomew, although not without a degree of unease. 'Pennyroyal is not rare or unusual – it grows everywhere. And the oil can be distilled by anyone with a pot and a fire.'

Michael was unconvinced. 'I dislike coincidences, and here we have a dangerous substance going missing from your storeroom – a place that is basically inaccessible to anyone but Michaelhouse men – and a woman dying of ingesting some of the stuff the very same night.'

'But I do not know when it disappeared,' objected Bartholomew. He really did not believe that the two events could be connected – how could a stranger like Joan know anyone in a closed, monastic-style foundation like Michaelhouse? – but there was a cold, unsettled feeling in the pit of his stomach, even so. 'There is nothing to say it was the same day she died.'

Michael scowled at him. 'You are splitting hairs and missing my point – which is that it has gone, and you have no idea where. And you are sure your students did not take it?'

'They say not, and there is no reason to doubt them.'

'Then it was stolen by someone else,' concluded Michael.

'But, as you have just pointed out, no one outside Michaelhouse has access to my storeroom.'

'Then I recant that statement. We often have visitors, and there are always tradesmen arriving with deliveries. Meanwhile, we pay our servants a pittance, which means they do not stay long and owe us no loyalty. I barely know some of the staff these days. Perhaps one of them took it.'

'I keep the door locked at all times.'

'Rubbish! You often leave it open while you run to the library to check a reference or fetch water from the kitchen. Besides, locks can be picked. And if this pennyroyal oil is as dangerous as you claim, then I am perturbed by the notion that it is unaccounted for. I want answers, Matt – not only as your friend, but as Senior Proctor, too.'

'But who would want to harm Joan?' asked Bartholomew, unhappy with the way the conversation was going. 'She has not lived in Cambridge for years, and no one here knows her.'

'Then you had better question your students again.' Michael's expression turned from severe to worried. 'But do it discreetly. That business earlier in the year has not been forgotten yet, and your reputation is . . .' He waved a plump hand, unable to find the right words.

But Bartholomew knew what he meant. A magician-healer called Arderne had raised doubts about his abilities in the spring, and this had been followed by a frenzy of superstition in the summer, during which many of his patients had been quite open about the fact that they believed he was good at his job because he dabbled in sorcery. They did not care, as long as he made them well, but that was beside the point: it was unsafe for a member of the University to be seen as a practising warlock. Bartholomew had kept a low profile since then, shying away from controversy, but people seemed unwilling to let the matter rest, regardless. He hoped it would not dog him for the rest of his life.

'You will have to find it,' Michael went on. 'The pennyroyal, I mean. It cannot stay missing, not if it has the power to kill.'

'And how am I to do that?' asked Bartholomew tiredly.

'Besides, as I told you, it is not rare or unusual – lots of homes keep a supply of it.'

Michael regarded him worriedly. 'If you say so, but I have a very bad feeling about this.'

So did Bartholomew, although he was reluctant to admit it, even to Michael.

That afternoon, Bartholomew conducted a thorough search of his storeroom. The missing pennyroyal was not there, although the hunt did warn him that he was running alarmingly low on a number of essential ingredients. He sent Tesdale, Valence and Risleye to the apothecary to replenish them, using most of his October wages to do so. When they returned, he summoned all his students to the hall.

'*I* did not take the pennyroyal,' declared Risleye angrily, before the physician could tell them what he wanted to discuss. 'I never touch anything on that top shelf, although I think such a precaution is unnecessary at this stage of my training. I do not see why *I* should be penalised, just because everyone else took part in that silly joke with the igniting book.'

'I did not take it, either,' said Tesdale, alarmed when he saw he was the only other suspect. 'And nor do I leave the room unattended.'

'Yes, you do,' countered Risleye spitefully. 'You never remember all the ingredients you might need for a remedy, and often have to go out to fetch something.'

'Well, you are guilty of that, too, Risleye,' said Valence, who had been the ringleader of the exploding-book incident. 'You left the door wide open the other day, when Walter tripped over his peacock and you went to help him up. And you were gone for ages.'

'That was different,' flashed Risleye. 'An emergency.

I bandaged his grazed arm really carefully, but then he refused to pay me. It took me a while to argue my case.'

Bartholomew was aghast. 'You charged one of our own servants for medical treatment?'

'Of course,' replied Risleye, unabashed. 'He was a patient and I cared for him. That equals a fee.'

'Give it back,' ordered Bartholomew. He cut across Risleye's indignant objections. 'Have any of you let anyone else in the storeroom?'

The assembled students shook their heads, and Bartholomew sighed when he saw his interrogation was not going to provide him with answers. And he could hardly berate Risleye and Tesdale for leaving the storeroom unattended when he was guilty of doing the same thing himself.

Unfortunately, their combined negligence meant that virtually anyone could have slipped in and stolen the oil. But who would want it? And who would know what it was capable of doing? He supposed the answer to the second question was obvious: the red cross on its jar warned students that it could be harmful, so anyone with a modicum of sense would know the pot held something to be used with caution.

'Perhaps the thief did not want pennyroyal,' suggested Valence, voicing what Bartholomew was already thinking. 'You keep far more potent items than that: henbane, dog mercury, cuckoopint.'

'And poppy juice,' added Risleye. 'People are always asking me to give them poppy juice, because it makes them feel happy.'

'And do you oblige?' asked Bartholomew, thinking of the stain on the bench.

Risleye was outraged. 'Of course not! The last time I touched it was days ago, when I helped you prepare that pain remedy for Isnard. You were hurrying me, and would not answer questions, which was wrong, because my education is far more important than the well-being of some non-paying rogue.'

Bartholomew *had* rushed Risleye, because Isnard's need was urgent. Had haste resulted in a spillage that was overlooked and not cleaned up? Yet there was something about Risleye's denial that made the physician uneasy – he had caught Risleye out in lies before. Or was he allowing personal dislike to cloud his judgement?

'If the thief came for something else and ended up with pennyroyal, then it means he cannot read,' said Tesdale, rather pompously. 'Every jar is clearly labelled, after all. Perhaps we can assume it was filched by a servant. Or by one of the men who came to mend the roof.'

Bartholomew was not sure what to think, and only knew he had been inexcusably careless. If it transpired that his pennyroyal *had* found its way to Joan, he was not sure Edith would ever forgive him. And she would have every right to be angry.

By the time he had finished the interrogation, a number of people had sent word that they needed to see him. Medical training at universities was largely book-based, but he wanted *his* students to see real diseases and wounds, too, so he usually took the more senior pupils with him when he went to tend patients. In the past, this had meant two or three lads, but Langelee's decision to accept more scholars, along with Paxtone's inability to teach Tesdale, meant he currently had eight. It was an absurdly high number, and clients tended to be alarmed when they all trooped into the sickroom. Because of this, he had been compelled to devise a rota, which was unsatisfactory for a number of reasons.

'I got landed with a case of toothache last time,' whined

40

Risleye. 'And Tesdale got the venery distemper. Now I get toothache *again*, while he has a strangury. It is not fair!'

'I will exchange my bloody flux for your strangury, Tesdale,' offered Valence. 'And then Yaxley will take the bloody flux in return for his rhagades. You have not had rhagades yet.'

'Lord!' muttered Bartholomew, listening to the haggling in distaste.

He set off before they could involve him in it, leaving them to scurry to catch up. They pursued him in a gaggle, drawing attention to themselves with their lively good humour – except Risleye, who remained sullen. Then, when they reached the house of a patient, two would detach themselves from the mob and follow him inside.

He rarely rushed consultations, always trying to ensure both patient and pupils understood exactly what he was doing – although the students itched to be done with the mundane cases and on to the more interesting ones. As a result, the visits filled the rest of the day, and by the time they returned to Michaelhouse, it was dark and they had missed supper.

'I do not care,' said Risleye smugly. 'I have fine bread and fresh cheese in my room, so *I* will not starve.'

He strode away without offering to share, and Bartholomew thought it no surprise that he was unpopular. Not all his classmates could afford the luxury of 'commons', and would go hungry that night. Fortunately, the rest were better friends, and agreed to a pooling of resources.

'It will be better than College food,' crowed Tesdale gleefully, on seeing the fine fare that was going to be available to him that night. 'The meals are terrible these days – no meat, and peas galore.'

Bartholomew could only nod agreement. The situation

would not have been so bad if Agatha – College laundress and self-appointed overseer of the kitchens – knew how to render pulses more interesting. But she only boiled them to a glue-like consistency, and when the Fellows complained, she retaliated by sending some very nasty concoctions to their table; she was not very good at accepting criticism. The previous noon had seen cabbage mixed with a variety of fish-heads.

'I am sorry I was careless with the storeroom door, sir,' said Tesdale, when the other students had gone. 'But do not worry about the pennyroyal. There will be an innocent explanation for it.'

'Such as what?' asked Bartholomew.

Tesdale shrugged. 'Cynric says it puts a lovely shine on metal, so perhaps one of the servants took it to buff the College silver. Or, as it has a strong but not unpleasant aroma, perhaps someone filched it to sweeten the latrines or to drop into his wet boots. Its loss is not necessarily sinister.'

Bartholomew sincerely hoped he was right.

During the evenings, it was the Fellows' wont to gather in the comfortable room called the conclave, next to the hall. Candles and lamps were lit after dark, and on cold nights there was a fire in the hearth. Some Fellows read, some marked exercises prepared by students, and others enjoyed the opportunity for erudite conversation. The atmosphere was always convivial, which was something they all treasured – academics, being blessed with sharp minds, often had sharp tongues to go with them, and many members of other Colleges were barely on speaking terms. Michaelhouse, though, was a haven of peace, and although there were disagreements, they were rarely acrimonious.

When Bartholomew arrived, the room was unusually empty. Wynewyk was still unwell, Langelee was out, and

Father William was languishing in the Fens. He sat at the table, and was pleasantly surprised to discover that Michael, unhappy with the supper Agatha had created, had provided his colleagues with something edible instead.

'She gave me a beetroot, Matt,' explained the monk, his green eyes full of righteous indignation. 'A hard, barely cooked one. It was reclining in a dish of melted butter, with a soggy leek for garnish.'

Bartholomew took a slice of meat pie. 'Did you send it back?'

'Only after he had drained the butter into a cup, and quaffed it,' replied Suttone, a plump Carmelite who fervently believed that the plague would return at any moment. 'I wish I had thought of that. I like butter, and there was a lot of it.'

Bartholomew felt slightly queasy. 'Where is Langelee?' he asked, to change the subject.

'Dining at King's Hall,' said Michael with a grimace. 'He found out what Agatha planned to give us, and hastened to make other arrangements. He should have warned us, too.'

'*I* warned you,' said Clippesby. He was a Dominican friar who taught theology and grammar. The College cat was in his lap, and he held a frog in one hand and a mouse in the other. 'The wren saw what Agatha had cooked, and I came immediately to tell you. But you ignored me.'

'That wren is unreliable,' retorted Michael. It was widely accepted that Clippesby was insane, although he had been at Michaelhouse long enough for his colleagues to overlook all but his most brazen idiosyncrasies. 'If you had heard it from the peacock, I might have been more willing to listen.'

The two newest Fellows sat near the window, and Bartholomew was disconcerted to note that Thelnetham was filing Hemmysby's nails. It was a curious thing to be doing, especially as Hemmysby was not very interested in personal appearances. He was a quiet theologian, who divided his time between Cambridge and Waltham Abbey, where he held a lucrative post.

Thelnetham, on the other hand, *was* interested in what he looked like, and was never anything short of immaculate. He was a brilliant Gilbertine, an expert in both canon and civil law, and a demon in the debating chamber. Like Wynewyk, he had a penchant for male lovers, although where Wynewyk was discreet, Thelnetham sported brightly coloured accessories to his religious habit and indulged in flamboyantly effeminate conversation. The students liked him, because his lectures were boisterously entertaining, although he could be brutally incisive, too.

'What are you doing?' Bartholomew asked him.

'Hemmysby's nails,' replied Thelnetham, as if the answer were obvious. Bartholomew supposed it was, and realised he had asked the wrong question. Thelnetham smiled, and elaborated anyway. 'They are a disgrace, and a man is nothing without smart nails. You always keep yours nice, which is considerate, given that you use them for clawing about in people's innards.'

Bartholomew winced at the image. 'I do nothing of the kind.'

Thelnetham wagged his file admonishingly. 'Now Robin the surgeon no longer practises his unsavoury trade – for which we all thank God – you are free to hack and saw to your heart's content. You should be careful, though. Physicians are not supposed to demean themselves with cautery.'

'Leave him alone, Thelnetham,' said Michael mildly. 'Robin's retirement means all the Cambridge physicians are forced to dabble in surgery these days. Even Paxtone is obliged to bleed his own patients, although word is that he is not very good at it.'

44

Bartholomew was astonished to hear this. He knew Paxtone was a firm believer in the benefits of phlebotomy, but he had not imagined him to be enthusiastic enough about the procedure to open his patients' veins himself. The King's Hall physician disliked getting his hands dirty, and preferred his treatments to revolve around the inspection of urine and the calculation of personal horoscopes.

'There, I have finished, Hemmysby,' said Thelnetham, sitting back in satisfaction. 'You now have fingers any lady would be proud to own. Can I tempt anyone else to a little beautification?'

'Not if you turn us into girls,' said Suttone in distaste. 'That nasty Osa Gosse mocked me today, shouting that my habit was womanly. I cannot have feminine hands, or he may do it again.'

'Very well,' said Thelnetham, slipping the rasp into the enormous purse that hung at his side. He turned to Bartholomew. 'Has Wynewyk spoken to you about Tesdale yet?'

'No,' replied Bartholomew warily. 'Why? What has he done?'

'His nightmares,' explained Thelnetham. 'He cries and whimpers, and not all of us are heavy sleepers like you. He wakes us up. You must talk to him, find out what is causing these night-terrors.'

'I have tried. But he denies there is a problem, and I cannot force—'

There was a sharp knock on the door, and Cynric burst in. His face was pale and his hands were shaking badly. Bartholomew regarded him in alarm – the book-bearer was not easily disturbed.

'It is Master Langelee.' Cynric took a deep, steadying breath. 'He has been murdered.'

CHAPTER 2

Bartholomew raced out of Michaelhouse, medical bag banging at his side. It was raining heavily, and the night was dark, so it was difficult to see where he was going. He tripped twice, but did not slow down – he could not, not when his stomach churned in horror at Cynric's news, and all he wanted was to reach Master Langelee as quickly as possible. He was so agitated that he was only vaguely aware of Michael puffing along behind him; Cynric ran at his side.

'The Master was just leaving King's Hall when he was attacked,' panted Cynric. 'Tobias, their porter, saw it happen, and thinks Osa Gosse is responsible.'

It was not far to King's Hall, Cambridge's largest, richest and most powerful College, and when Bartholomew arrived, there were three people in the street outside it. The first was its head, Thomas Powys. Powys had been Warden for years, and Bartholomew knew he must be good at his job, or the King, who loved to meddle in the College's affairs, would have replaced him. The second was Tobias the porter, who held a lamp. And the third was Langelee, lying motionless on the ground. Bartholomew felt sick, appalled to be losing yet another colleague to the violence that erupted so often in the little Fen-edge town.

'I sent for you as soon as I saw it happen,' said Tobias, moving forward with the lantern when Bartholomew skidded to a halt and knelt to examine his fallen comrade. He sounded horror-stricken. 'I could not believe it.'

'What happened?' gasped Michael, resting his hands on his knees as he struggled to catch his breath. It had been a hard sprint for a man of his girth.

'A vicious little villain stepped out of the shadows and stabbed him,' replied Tobias, shaking his head incredulously as he spoke. 'Master Langelee was twice his size, so it was like David and Goliath. I am amazed Gosse had the courage to tackle someone with *his* reputation.'

'What reputation?' asked Powys. He was a pleasant man, with long teeth, dark eyes and a stoop.

'As a dirty fighter,' explained Tobias. '*I* would not have taken Master Langelee on, and I am a professional soldier.'

'Are you sure it was Gosse?' demanded Michael. 'You saw his face?'

'No,' admitted Tobias reluctantly. 'It was dark. But who else could it have been? It was only ever a matter of time before he went from theft to murder.'

'If only Paxtone had been home,' said Powys shakily. 'He might have been able to save Langelee. But he is dining with Doctor Rougham at Gonville Hall – and now it is too late!'

'Langelee told me he was coming here tonight,' said the monk. His face was pale in the gleam of the lamp, and his voice was not quite steady. Like Bartholomew, he was fond of the Master, despite Langelee's myriad idiosyncrasies. 'Why did you invite him?'

'He invited himself,' said Powys, wringing his hands miserably. 'Because Michaelhouse was having beetroot. I told him it was late – that he should not stay to help us drink yet another cask of wine – but he said he could look after himself. I should have insisted he leave sooner. This is *my* fault!'

'It is no one's fault,' said Bartholomew. 'And he is—'

'It is one thing to murder students,' whispered Michael.

47

There was a catch in his voice, and his eyes were moist. 'But this is our Master, and I will not rest until—'

'He is not dead, Brother,' interrupted Bartholomew. 'He is in a stupor.'

A startled silence greeted his words.

'But that is impossible!' exclaimed Tobias, the first to find his voice. 'He has no heartbeat.'

'He does,' said Bartholomew. 'But you probably could not feel it because he is wearing a leather jerkin under his tabard. There is a deep gash in it, though, which suggests someone meant him harm.'

Michael peered at the slash. 'So, he *was* attacked?'

Bartholomew nodded. 'I imagine the impact knocked him off his feet, and once he was down, the wine took over. He does tend to drink a lot when he is in other Colleges.'

'He certainly indulged himself this evening,' averred Powys, after crossing himself, and breathing a brief prayer of thanksgiving. 'Far more than usual. In fact, it appeared as though he was *trying* to drink himself into oblivion. I suppose I should have stopped him, but it goes against the grain to deprive a guest of hospitality.'

'So he is in a drunken slumber?' asked Cynric, to be sure. 'We have been upset for nothing?'

Michael pointed to the damage on Langelee's jerkin. 'It is not nothing, Cynric. Someone intended him to die, and would have succeeded, were it not for his armour. However, just because the attempt failed does not mean it will be forgotten. I *will* have this villain under lock and key!'

'Do you think it has anything to do with Langelee's work for the Archbishop?' asked Powys, glancing around uneasily. 'He made a lot of enemies then, if his stories are to be believed.'

'I suspect those enemies know the difference between a blade catching on hard leather, and a blade sliding into flesh,' said Michael wryly. 'So I doubt this has anything to do with his past.'

'His purse is missing,' said Bartholomew, pointing to where it had been cut from Langelee's belt. 'Perhaps it is just a case of theft.'

'Gosse is a thief,' pounced Tobias. 'He *must* be the culprit. The man I saw was small and wiry, and Gosse is small and wiry. Of *course* he is the villain! How can you even think otherwise?'

But Bartholomew was reluctant for conclusions to be drawn without proper evidence; attempted murder was a capital offence, and it would not be the first time an innocent man had hanged just because he owned a dubious reputation. And Tobias's testimony was weak, to say the least.

'But if Gosse is such an experienced thief, then why did he attack Langelee?' he asked reasonably. 'Our Master is a formidable opponent, even when drunk, so why not wait for an easier victim?'

'That is a good point – one I shall address when Gosse and I enjoy an informal chat tomorrow,' said Michael. He shivered as the wind blew a flurry of raindrops into his eyes. 'Meanwhile, we had better carry poor Langelee home, before he drowns.'

Bartholomew had witnessed Langelee drunk on many occasions, but never to the point where he was quite so deeply insensible. It was worrying, so he decided to monitor him through the night, sending his own students off to sleep in the hall. He wrapped Langelee in blankets, and placed a bucket near his head. Then he sat at his desk and began to read the essays his students had written – all except

Risleye, who still claimed his had been stolen. When the night-watch announced it was three o'clock, Langelee woke with a start.

'Where am I?' he demanded, looking around blearily. 'Am I ill? I feel sick.'

'An excess of wine can do that to a man,' replied Bartholomew dryly, watching him reach for the pail. 'Do you remember anything of what happened?'

'I recall Warden Powys giving me cheaper brews once he thought I was too inebriated to notice.'

'He said you made a concerted effort to drink yourself stupid. Why? Has something upset you?'

'I am Master of a College,' replied Langelee flatly. 'Of course something has upset me: money. We do not have any, and I have nigh on a hundred mouths to feed – students, Fellows, commoners, servants. I was a fool to have taken on those new pupils last Easter, because they have transpired to be more of an expense than a source of revenue.'

Bartholomew was bemused. 'But you have been concerned about funding for years. What is different now?'

'I cannot talk about it,' said Langelee miserably, turning away. 'Not to you, and not to anyone. The burden is mine alone to bear.'

Bartholomew would have been content to leave it at that, because he had no wish to become acquainted with the sort of business that could drive a resilient, insensitive man like Langelee to drink. But friendship compelled him to persist.

'You do not have to worry alone. All the Fellows will help, especially if it concerns the College.'

'It *does* concern the College,' whispered Langelee, his expression agonised. 'But I cannot . . .'

'Perhaps we should talk tomorrow,' suggested

Bartholomew gently, when Langelee closed his eyes and seemed unable to continue. 'When you are less overwrought.'

'Overwrought,' echoed Langelee bitterly. 'That is a kinder word than drunk. And you are right: I did set out to drown my sorrows this evening, although it was a waste of time. They still plague me, only now I have a raging headache to go with them.'

Bartholomew handed him a dose of the tonic he often dispensed to those who had overindulged. 'We were appalled when we heard you had been attacked,' he said. 'We thought you were dead.'

'Attacked?' Langelee frowned, cup halfway to his lips, then understanding dawned in his eyes. 'God's blood! You are right! Someone emerged from the shadows and tried to stab me! Christ! I might have forgotten, if you had not jogged my memory.'

'If whatever is worrying you is going to lead to murderous ambushes, then you should not keep it to yourself,' said Bartholomew, concerned for him. 'Some of us may be able to help, especially Michael.'

Langelee gazed at him in confusion. 'You think the assault on me is connected to my problem?'

'Without knowing the problem, it is impossible to say,' replied Bartholomew, supposing the Master's wits must still be muddled, for the question was an inane one. 'Did you see anything that might allow us to catch the culprit?'

Langelee's face creased into a scowl as memories began to resurface. 'I saw someone – a skinny devil – lurking in a doorway, and when I walked past, he cowered away. I thought that was the end of it, but then I heard footsteps and the scoundrel was on me before I could act. I saw the flash of a knife and managed to turn, so the blade caught my armour. Then I heard him running away.'

'Did you see his face?'

Langelee shook his head. 'I thought it was Osa Gosse at first, but he has a distinctive odour, and I have been trained to notice that sort of thing. It was not him. I think it was a scholar.'

Bartholomew eyed him warily. 'Are you sure?'

'No, I am not sure,' snapped Langelee testily. 'I shall have to think about it. However, my purse seems to be missing, and as I am sure *you* did not steal it, it seems I was the victim of a robbery. Forget I mentioned scholars. I am unwell, and fever is making me spout nonsense.' He raised the cup and downed the tonic, evidently aiming to emphasise the current fragile state of his health.

'Rest now and talk to Michael in the morning,' said Bartholomew kindly. 'The Senior Proctor does not like it when masters are stabbed. Especially his own.'

In a demonstration of his extraordinary capacity for recuperation, Langelee sat up the following morning and announced that he felt fighting fit. He was pale and his eyes were bloodshot, but he seemed otherwise unscathed, either by the attack or by the amount of wine he had swallowed. There was not even a bruise where the knife had hammered home.

He rang the bell for the daily procession to church, not caring that it was rather earlier than usual. Yet even though he tried to be his usual gruff and boisterous self as his colleagues emerged from their rooms and hurried to fuss over him and ask him questions, there was a reserve in his replies that was out of character. Michael noticed it, too.

'What is wrong with him?' he asked of Bartholomew. 'He pretends nothing is amiss, but I am the Senior Proctor and I know the difference between lies and truth.'

'Perhaps he is embarrassed,' suggested the physician.

52

'A camp-ball hero, knocked to the ground and almost stabbed by a fellow everyone agrees was petite. It must be humiliating.'

'Wine,' said Thelnetham, shaking his head disparagingly as he and the other Fellows came to join them. 'It turns grown men into weaklings. Of course, that is just the way I like them—'

'Hush!' urged Wynewyk reprovingly. He also looked better that morning, finally recovered from his malady. 'That is not the sort of remark that should be bawled at volume.'

'Is it not?' drawled Thelnetham. There was a merry twinkle in his eyes that said he was teasing. 'I do not see why. It lets us all know where we stand. Or lie.'

'Yes, but we are about to go to mass,' objected Wynewyk prudishly. 'We should not be thinking about venal matters – at least, not until after breakfast.'

Thelnetham laughed, and flung a comradely arm around the lawyer's shoulders. 'Very well. Then we shall resume our discussion immediately after we have devoured our coddled eggs.'

Wynewyk recoiled at his touch, and struggled free. 'Please! Not here!'

'Where then?' asked Thelnetham mischievously. 'The hall? Or do you have a particular tavern you frequent? I know they are forbidden to scholars, but I am sure *you* do not always obey the rules.'

'Leave him, Thelnetham,' warned Bartholomew, taking pity on his friend. 'He has not been well.'

'I apologise,' said Thelnetham, effecting a gracious bow, although amusement still lingered in his eyes. 'I shall leave my friendly jousting until he is ready for it, then.'

'Thank you, Matt,' said Wynewyk weakly, when Thelnetham had gone. 'I am not in the mood for his banter

53

today. Almost losing Langelee was distressing, and I had bad dreams all night.'

'So did Tesdale,' said Michael ruefully. 'He howled like a Fury, and it took Valence ages to settle him down. I thought he was going to wake the Pope in Avignon, he yelled so loud.'

'Poor Tesdale,' said Wynewyk worriedly. 'Something is bothering him, and I wish you would find out what, Matthew. It is probably money, because he owes Michaelhouse rather a lot of it.'

'I will ask him again,' promised Bartholomew. 'But he always denies there is anything amiss, and I cannot force him to confide.'

'Well, please try,' said Wynewyk. 'Kelyng suffered from night-terrors, too, and now he has disappeared. I would not like to think we have failed a second unhappy student.'

'Kelyng has *not* disappeared,' said Michael firmly. 'He has decided to abscond. It is not the first time a lad has elected to run away rather than pay what he owes, and I doubt it will be the last. If I had incurred Kelyng's level of expenditure, I might flee, too.'

They processed to the church, where Suttone officiated at the morning mass, and Bartholomew assisted. It was over in record time, because Suttone was eager to hear details of the Master's brush with death. Flattered by the Carmelite's demands for the full story, Langelee declared that talking was permitted at breakfast that day – meals were normally eaten to the sole sound of the Bible Scholar's droning voice, although Kelyng's absence made this difficult – then treated the entire College to a lively and improbably colourful account of his adventures. It was rather different to the version related by Tobias and Powys, and failed to mention the amount of wine he had swallowed or the drunken slumber that had followed, but his audience sat in spellbound silence until he had finished, anyway.

'Well, we are glad you survived,' said Suttone warmly, rubbing his hands together as the servants began to put bowls of food on the table. 'None of *us* want the post of Master.'

'I would not mind,' said Michael, poking in distaste at something that appeared to be a mixture of scrambled eggs and parsnips. 'But only if Wynewyk continues to manage the finances, which is the tedious part. The rest would be fun.'

'I might resign and let you do it,' said Langelee heavily. 'God knows, it is a thankless task.'

Bartholomew raised his eyebrows in surprise. He had never heard the Master talk about stepping down before, and could see that Michael was alarmed by the notion that his flippant remark might have been taken seriously. The monk might have harboured ambitions in that direction once, but since then he had carved himself a niche as the University's most influential scholar – the man who told the Chancellor what to do, and who made all the important decisions. Accepting the Mastership of Michaelhouse would represent a considerable demotion, and Bartholomew doubted the monk would do it – especially as he had once confided that his next post would be either abbot or bishop.

'Do not make any hasty decisions, Master,' advised Michael quickly. 'Especially as you are probably still shocked after last night's episode. Give yourself time to recover before—'

Langelee waved a dismissive hand. 'Last night's episode was nothing. I have experienced far worse in games of camp-ball – and not just on the field, either. Why do you think I have taken to wearing a boiled-leather jerkin?

Because some teams will do anything to win, and good players like me are never safe from sly attacks in the street. But I had better say a final grace, because I have a great deal to do today, and I am sure you do, too.'

He had intoned no more than two lines before he faltered, having apparently forgotten the words. As it was a prayer he used regularly, Bartholomew peered around Michael's bulk to regard him in alarm, wondering whether he had bumped his head when he had fallen and was not in his right wits. Langelee made a vague gesture to indicate that his scholars were dismissed, then left the hall.

'What is wrong with him?' demanded Suttone, when he had gone. 'He is not himself today.'

'Do you think it is malnutrition, from the terrible food we have been given over the last few weeks?' asked Michael. 'He is a large man, and will not thrive on this sort of muck for long.'

Bartholomew glanced sharply at him, wondering if he was making a joke. Langelee *was* a large man, but Michael was considerably bigger.

'It might be,' agreed Suttone, who also boasted an impressive girth. 'I know I am wasting away.'

'I am exhausted,' declared Michael, flopping into a fireside chair in the conclave that evening. All the Fellows were there. Bartholomew, Suttone and Wynewyk were at the table, preparing lessons for the following day, Thelnetham and Hemmysby were reading a Book of Hours together, and Langelee was sitting by the window. He was gazing into the courtyard below, although it was dark outside and he would not be able to see anything. Clippesby was at his feet, playing with the College cat.

'Why are you exhausted, Brother?' asked Wynewyk courteously, when no one else seemed interested and the monk was beginning to look annoyed by the lack of response. Bartholomew forced his thoughts away from his work when he realised he was being rude.

'For several reasons,' replied Michael. 'I spent all morning teaching, and all afternoon questioning Gosse about the attack on our Master last night. Then I visited the apothecaries and asked whether they had sold any pennyroyal recently.'

Bartholomew regarded him guiltily. He had meant to make that enquiry himself, but too many patients had demanded his services that day, and he had had no time. 'And had they?'

'They say not, but I am not sure whether to believe them. They have lied to me in the past.'

'Pennyroyal?' asked Thelnetham, bemused. 'Why would you want to know about that?'

'Matt is interested in it,' replied Michael vaguely. He glanced at Langelee, who was still staring out of the window. 'Is anyone curious to know the outcome of my encounter with Gosse?'

'I am,' said Wynewyk, when Langelee made no reply. 'What happened?'

'He does not live alone,' began Michael. 'He has a sister, although you would not think they were related to look at them; he is small, while she is enormous. She is reputed to be a witch – although people tend to say that about anyone they do not like.'

'They say it about Matthew,' Thelnetham pointed out. 'But he is very popular – among the lower class of citizen, at least. He is heartily reviled by persons of quality, of course.'

'That is untrue!' declared Wynewyk hotly, while Bartholomew regarded the Gilbertine in surprise. He knew not everyone approved of the way he practised medicine,

57

but he had not been aware that he was 'heartily reviled'. 'He is very highly regarded among the town's burgesses.'

'Only because they are afraid to antagonise his brother-in-law,' said Thelnetham acidly. 'Oswald Stanmore is a powerful man, and no sane merchant wants to incur *his* displeasure.'

'Gosse's sister is named Idoma – not a lady I would like to meet on a dark night,' Michael went on, cutting across Wynewyk's retort. Bartholomew's unorthodoxy was one of few subjects on which the Fellows could not agree, and there was almost certain to be a quarrel if they pursued it. 'I do not recall when I last met a more unpleasant pair, and I am glad I took plenty of beadles with me.'

'You did not fight them, did you?' asked Thelnetham with a moue of distaste. 'Blood is so difficult to remove from one's habit.'

'I would not know,' replied Michael, regarding him askance. 'I am usually careful not to spill any, especially my own.'

'Did Gosse confess to attacking the Master?' asked Wynewyk.

'No,' replied Michael. 'He claims he was in the Cardinal's Cap when Langelee was ambushed, and the landlord confirms this. Unfortunately, the tavern was busy, and the landlord cannot say whether Gosse was there *all* night. And the Cardinal's Cap is not far from King's Hall.'

'Langelee said it was a scholar who attacked him,' said Bartholomew. 'Not Gosse and—'

'Forget the matter, Brother,' said Langelee, turning from the window at last. 'It *was* a scholar, but it will transpire to be someone who does not want me to play in the next camp-ball game – some cheating villain from one of the rival teams. Pretend it did not happen.'

'I most certainly shall not,' declared Michael, horrified.

'An attempt was made to kill the Master of my College, and that is unacceptable. I will unmask this villain and he shall answer for his crime.'

'Then do it after you have eliminated the annoyance represented by Gosse,' said Langelee tiredly.

Bartholomew frowned. 'What annoyance?'

'Several Colleges have been burgled recently,' explained Langelee. 'We all know Gosse is responsible, and the other heads of houses are beginning to ask why the Senior Proctor lets him roam free, doing as he pleases.'

'Because my hands have been tied,' Michael snapped. 'Apparently, Gosse visited the town a few years back, and was convicted of theft. But he appealed the sentence, and clever lawyers got him acquitted. Then he sued, and Cambridge was forced to pay him a substantial sum in damages. The Mayor and his burgesses have informed me that it will not happen again.'

'You mean you have been ordered not to challenge him?' asked Suttone, shocked. 'He can do what he likes, and you must let him, lest he demands more compensation?'

Michael nodded, his expression dark and angry. 'He has already hired himself a lawyer, and knew exactly how not to incriminate himself when I interviewed him.'

'What lawyer?' demanded Thelnetham, indignant on behalf of his legal colleagues. 'No one in the University would have anything to do with such a low scoundrel.'

'He is a Suffolk man, apparently,' replied Michael. 'Probably someone from Clare, which is Gosse's home. I did not meet him, but he had briefed Gosse well. I came away feeling as though I had been bested.'

'This Gosse sounds horrible,' said Hemmysby. 'But I had never heard of him before last night.'

'Neither had I,' said Bartholomew. He opened his book again, not very interested in felons. Ambitious criminals were always invading the town in search of easy pickings, but they did not last long; Michael or Sheriff Tulyet usually ousted them before they did too much harm.

'He *is* horrible,' replied Michael grimly. 'And so is his sister, who is said to be insane.'

'I am said to be insane, too,' remarked Clippesby from the floor. 'But that does not make it true.'

'Well, it is true in Idoma's case,' said Michael. 'She twitched, blinked and flexed her fists the whole time I was there, giving the impression that it would take very little to send her into a frenzy of violence. I am not easily unnerved, but there was something about her that unsettled me profoundly.'

'They are not like normal felons,' agreed Suttone. 'They are higher born, more intelligent and far more devious. I am glad it is not my duty to tackle them.'

Thelnetham was unimpressed by the situation. 'Your hands may have been tied by the burgesses, Brother, but what about the Sheriff? Why does he not act?'

'He is in London, explaining to the King why our shire is so expensive to run,' replied Michael. 'Constable Muschett is in charge – a man who would not challenge a goose. He openly admits that Gosse frightens him *and* that he has no intention of doing anything that might see him sued.'

'Bastards,' snarled Langelee suddenly, standing abruptly and stalking towards the hearth. He took a wild kick at the poker, which flew against the wall and ricocheted off, landing with a crash that made all the Fellows jump. The cat hurtled under the table in alarm.

'My!' drawled Thelnetham, wide-eyed. 'Do we feel better now?'

'No, we do not,' snarled Langelee. 'We shall feel better when we have broken his neck.'

'Why would we . . . would *you* do that?' asked Bartholomew uneasily, wondering what had precipitated the burst of temper. 'You said Gosse was not the man who attacked you.'

'No, but he has committed other crimes,' said Langelee darkly. 'And do not look at me like that, because I am not telling you anything about it. You will be angry. All of you will be angry.'

'What has he done?' demanded Michael. 'If it is something to do with the College, we have a right to know. We will probably find out anyway – this is no place for keeping secrets.'

Langelee swallowed hard. It was a moment before he spoke, and when he did, his voice was choked with emotion. 'Two days ago, I left the Stanton Cups in the hall by mistake – unattended. Someone stole them.'

His colleagues regarded him in horror. The Stanton Cups were a pair of beautiful silver-gilt chalices, bequeathed to Michaelhouse by its founder, Hervey de Stanton. They were normally kept in a locked chest in the Master's room, but Langelee believed such treasures should be used regularly, for everyone to see and appreciate, so they were often out. It was an attitude Bartholomew applauded, although their loss was a serious blow.

'They were taken from the hall?' asked Bartholomew. 'Then why did no one see the thief? It is seldom empty. Students, Fellows or servants are always there.'

'Because the cups went missing when we were all at that debate in Peterhouse,' replied Langelee wretchedly. 'And the servants were picking apples in the orchard. I suspect the culprit saw us leave then slipped in when Walter was looking the other way.'

'Why do you think Gosse is responsible?' asked Michael. His voice was flat and low, and Bartholomew looked at him sharply, suspecting he was more angry with Langelee for his carelessness than the burglar for his audacity.

'Because both Suttone and Clippesby told me – independently – that Gosse was loitering around the College the morning the cups went missing. And later, Thelnetham reported seeing him running down the High Street with something tucked under his cloak.'

'Yes, I did,' agreed Thelnetham, horrified. 'But I did not know it was the Stanton Cups!'

'And I did not know Gosse was contemplating theft,' added Suttone, equally appalled.

'I did,' said Clippesby. He was under the table, trying to soothe the cat. 'The ducks guessed what was being planned, but Walter declined to put their warning to good use by being more vigilant.'

The Dominican's odd habit of sitting quietly in the shadows while he communed with nature meant he was often witness to incidents no one else saw. Unfortunately, his eccentric way of reporting them meant he was rarely taken seriously. Bartholomew was not surprised Walter had declined to act on intelligence provided by birds.

'Why did you wait so long before telling us?' demanded Michael of Langelee. 'I am Senior Proctor. I have a right to know about crimes committed in my own College.'

'Because I hoped to get them back on the quiet,' explained Langelee. 'I went to Muschett, but he said that since no one actually *saw* Gosse make off with them, we cannot accuse him of theft. We—'

'But that is outrageous!' exploded Michael, temper breaking at last. 'Those cups are worth a fortune. If Gosse took them, it is our prerogative to reclaim them.'

'Not according to Muschett,' said Langelee. 'Believe me, there is nothing I would like more than to punch Gosse until he gives them back. But Muschett said that would be seen as an attack by the University against a layman. He feels the Stanton Cups are not worth the riot that is sure to follow.'

'He is probably right,' acknowledged Suttone, cutting across the spluttering reply Michael started to make. 'Gosse may be a criminal, but there are many who would side with him against the University. And without Sheriff Tulyet to keep them in order, there might well be bloodshed.'

'But we are talking about the Stanton Cups!' protested Thelnetham, shocked. 'Does Muschett seriously expect us to ignore the fact that this lout has stolen our most valuable treasure?'

'*Now* do you see why I was reluctant to confide in you?' asked Langelee, accusing in his turn. 'You have reacted just as I predicted you would.'

'Oh, do not worry,' said Michael bitterly. 'I do not want a riot. However, I shall keep a close eye on Gosse, and pounce with all the weight of the law if I catch so much as a glimmer of silver gilt.'

'I wonder if he took my pennyroyal, too,' mused Bartholomew. But then he shook his head. 'No, he cannot have done, because my storeroom would have been locked when we were at the debate.'

'Unless one of your careless lads left it open,' said Michael savagely. 'And as far as I am concerned, we have no idea *what* Gosse did when he roamed here unattended.'

As soon as it was light the following day, Michael left the College to investigate the Stanton Cups' disappearance, but it did not take him long to learn that Langelee was right: Gosse's curious activities around the time of the theft were circumstantial, and there was no indisputable evidence to link him with the crime – and certainly none convincing enough to allow a search of his house. Bartholomew doubted the monk would find anything anyway: too much time had passed, and the chalices would either be hidden in a safe place, or sold.

'It is hopeless,' said Michael despairingly, when he and the physician met in the hall for the noonday meal. 'Constable Muschett, the Mayor and all the burgesses joined together and expressly forbade me to investigate – they do not usually tell the University what to do, but it is different this time. They are presenting a united front because they still resent the fine they were obliged to pay the last time Cambridge tackled Gosse. I wish to God Dick Tulyet were here.'

'It *is* a pity the Sheriff is away,' agreed Bartholomew. 'But being angry will not bring our chalices back. It is better to devise a way to prevent Gosse from burgling anyone else.'

'How can I, when I have been ordered to stay away from him?' shouted Michael, banging a plump fist on the table in frustration. Several students eased away, not wanting to be close when the Senior Proctor was in a temper. 'Well, all I can say is that I hope he robs these cowardly officials, because then they might feel differently. Of course, Gosse is too clever for that – he knows who is protecting him, and chooses his victims with care.'

'The Blood Relic debate is a week on Monday,' said Bartholomew. 'Virtually every scholar in the University will be there – we have been looking forward to it for weeks now.'

'So?' snapped Michael. 'What does that have to do with anything?'

'It will mean a lot of empty Colleges and hostels,' explained Bartholomew patiently. 'And if Gosse invaded Michaelhouse when everyone was out, then—'

'Then he will almost certainly be planning something for then,' finished Michael. His eyes gleamed, and some of the fury went out of him. 'You are right! And I shall be ready for him. Thank you, Matt. You have made me feel considerably better, good physician that you are.'

Because it was Saturday, Bartholomew could finish teaching early, so he set his students some astrological calculations to keep them occupied and out of trouble, then went to visit his sister. Although he did not believe in the power of horoscopes, he still taught his pupils how to calculate them: they would not pass their disputations if he ignored that part of the curriculum, and he had no desire to be accused of corrupting their minds with unorthodox theories.

He found Edith making preserves in the kitchen, and the sweet scent of fruit filled the house – apples and plums from the garden, and the last of the blackberries from the hedgerows.

'The harvest was dismal this year,' said Edith, wiping her face with the back of her hand. It was hot in the room, with several huge pots bubbling furiously over the fire. 'I usually make three times this amount – half for us, and half for Yolande de Blaston's brood. They will be disappointed.'

'I thought you would have gone back to Trumpington by now,' said Bartholomew. He had been in the process of stealing an apple from one of the jars, but her words stopped him: he had no wish to deprive Yolande's children.

'You mean after what happened to Joan?' Edith gave a wan smile. 'I considered it, but Trumpington is lonely without Oswald, and I will only dwell on what happened. I am better off here.'

65

'I am sorry I could not help Joan.'

'You did your best. That priest never did appear, by the way.'

Bartholomew gazed at her blankly. 'What priest?'

'The one she came here with – Neubold. We sent for him to give her last rites, but he never arrived. I made enquiries at the Brazen George, where he was lodging, but the landlord said he has not been back to his room since the night Joan died, although he paid for it until the end of the week.'

Bartholomew shrugged. 'Perhaps he finished his business early and decided to go home.'

'And abandon the wife of his employer without saying a word?'

Bartholomew was uneasy. 'What are you saying? That he is implicated in Joan's death?'

Tears welled in Edith's eyes. 'I am *sure* she did not take the pennyroyal deliberately, Matt. I know Mother Coton thinks Joan's joy at being with child was a ruse, so she could rid herself of it without suspicion, but she is wrong. I spent three days with Joan – I would have seen through such an act.'

Bartholomew was not sure she would. Edith was an honest, uncomplicated soul, and expected others to be the same. Her open nature was one of the things he loved about her, because it was not something he often encountered in the University, where men had been trained to prevaricate.

'Then it was an accident – she took something she thought would help the baby,' he said, feeling a sharp twinge of guilt when he thought about his missing supplies. 'But she was misinformed.'

'I cannot imagine how she came by pennyroyal. The apothecaries would not have sold her any.'

'Perhaps she brought it with her.' Bartholomew thought, but did not say, that if she had, then it indicated premeditation, and Joan's few days of so-called happiness with Edith were indeed a cover for the crime she had been intending to commit.

He changed the subject, knowing they would argue otherwise, and began to talk about the forum on Blood Relics that was due to take place in nine days' time. It was not a topic that greatly intrigued him, but the University was on fire with it, and some of the enthusiasm had seeped into him. He found he was looking forward to hearing some of the best minds in the country – Michael's among them – hold forth on the matter.

'I made you a cake,' said Edith, passing him a neatly wrapped parcel when he paused for breath. Blood Relics did not interest her at all. 'It contains the last of the almonds from our garden.'

'Thank you. I had better be going. The Saturday Debate is due to start soon.'

'The *Saturday* Debate?' Edith frowned. 'I thought you said this event was to be Monday week.'

'The Blood Relic colloquy is on Monday. But the Saturday Debate is the weekly discussion at Michaelhouse, instigated by Thelnetham to keep our students off the streets. The Fellows kept avoiding them, so Langelee made them mandatory. I have missed the last two because of summonses from patients, and my colleagues will think I am shirking if I do it again.'

'Can you spare a few moments more?' asked Edith, rather tearfully. 'Joan's husband made arrangements to collect her body from St Mary the Great today, and I should talk to him. Will you come with me? I would rather not go alone.'

* * *

St Mary the Great was Cambridge's biggest and grandest church, used by the University for events too large for the debating halls – such as discussions about Blood Relics. That day, loud voices rang from the Lady Chapel where Joan lay, and Bartholomew saw that quite a deputation had arrived to claim her earthly remains. Two men and an elderly woman stood side by side, watching the verger and half a dozen servants struggling to load the body into a sturdy box for transport home.

'Which one is Henry Elyan?' whispered Bartholomew. 'Joan's husband?'

Edith regarded him askance. 'The one wearing black, of course, to show he is in mourning. Do you know nothing of the latest courtly fashions?'

Bartholomew did not, but it was clear that Elyan was well versed in such matters. The cut of his black clothes indicated they were expensive, and his gipon, or tunic, was decorated with more buttons than the physician had ever seen on a single garment. His handsome shoes were made from soft calfskin, and the jewellery that glittered at his throat and on his fingers was exquisite.

'It is a pity you could not save her,' Elyan said bitterly, after Edith had introduced her brother and given a brief account of what had happened. Elyan's eyes were red, indicating he had been weeping. 'She was very dear to me, and so was her child – my heir. Their deaths are a terrible shock.'

The elderly woman stepped forward. She was tall for her age, and voluminous skirts swirled around thick, practical travelling boots. A veil covered her head, but several strands of white hair had escaped to hang rakishly down the sides of her leathery cheeks. Sharp blue eyes indicated a person of character, who was used to having her own way.

68

'I am Agnys Elyan,' she announced. 'My grandson and I are grateful for your efforts. Joan often talked about her happy childhood here, and we are glad she died among friends.'

'Her death was unnecessary,' said Elyan. His voice was unsteady. 'She came to buy ribbons for our child – she should not have died purchasing ribbons.'

'No, she should not,' agreed his grandmother gently. She reached out to touch his arm, a self-conscious gesture of sympathy that caused him to look away quickly, a sob catching at the back of his throat. She turned to Bartholomew and Edith, speaking to give him time to compose himself. 'Joan was fit and well before she left, and we were horrified to learn about this horrible accident.'

'Accident?' asked Edith.

Bartholomew felt like jabbing her with his elbow, but suspected Agnys would notice and demand an explanation. He held his breath, hoping Edith's question would not lead the Haverhill folk to wonder whether there was more to Joan's death than they were being told. It would do no one any good if they clamoured murder – and Bartholomew was sure it was nothing of the kind.

Agnys nodded. 'Constable Muschett told us how she had swallowed a potion to strengthen the babe. We were appalled, because she was very careful about what she ate and drank. But I suppose even cautious women make mistakes.'

'Her mistake cost me a much-loved wife,' said Elyan in a muffled voice. He stood with his back to them, scrubbing surreptitiously at his eyes. 'Not to mention an heir twenty years in the making. Of course, this assumes it was her fault. For all I know, someone gave her this poison on purpose.'

'Pennyroyal is not poison,' said Bartholomew, thinking guiltily about the loss of his own. 'It is—'

'Pennyroyal?' echoed Agnys in disbelief. 'I sincerely doubt she drank that! I taught her about herbs myself, and she was well aware that pennyroyal is not for expectant mothers.'

'You are right,' said Edith, before Bartholomew could stop her. 'Joan did *not* take it on purpose.'

'What are you saying?' demanded Elyan, whipping around to regard her intently. 'If she would not have taken it of her own volition, and she was too sensible to have swallowed it by accident, does this mean she was forced to imbibe it against her will? She was *murdered*?'

'Of course she was not murdered,' said Agnys, before Bartholomew could say the same thing. 'But there are many elixirs with fanciful names that make no mention of the nature of their contents. She must have bought one that promised health and vitality, and the seller neglected to—'

'That is murder,' said the third member of the visiting party, entering the discussion for the first time. He was small and dark, with short black hair that was plastered to his head like a greasy cap. Spindly red-clad legs poked from under a purple gipon, giving him the appearance of a predatory insect.

'I agree, d'Audley,' said Elyan coldly. 'Any apothecary or physician giving pregnant women pennyroyal is guilty of murder, as far as I am concerned. And he deserves to hang for his crime.'

'Stop it, both of you,' ordered Agnys sharply. She glared at d'Audley. 'And you can keep your nasty opinions to yourself. No one asked you to accompany us to Cambridge, and I, for one, wish you had not. You have been nothing but trouble – complaining all the time.'

70

D'Audley did not like being admonished like a naughty child. He drew himself up to his full height, eyes flashing with indignation. 'I am lord of a Suffolk manor, and I shall not be berated—'

'Oh, be quiet, you silly little man,' snapped Agnys, regarding him with utter disdain before turning her back on him. She addressed her grandson, taking his hand in hers. 'Joan's death was an accident, Henry, so let us leave it at that. There is no evidence of foul play, and you will only distress yourself further if you start making unfounded accusations.'

'But she swallowed pennyroyal,' said Elyan stubbornly, pulling away from her. 'And I want to know why. How could she do such a thing? Could she not taste it?'

'It must have been disguised,' said Edith quietly. 'Perhaps with honey or wine. I am sure she did not know what she was drinking.'

'Quite. So it was an accident,' said Agnys, in the tone of voice that suggested the discussion was over. 'But the servants have finished now, and Joan is in the box. Go outside and help them put her on the cart, Henry, and then let us be away from this sad place. I want to be home by this evening.'

'I will help you, Elyan,' said d'Audley, with the air of a martyr. 'And then we shall visit Constable Muschett together and order him to mount an enquiry into this grave matter.'

'You will do no such thing,' snapped Agnys, although her grandson looked as if he thought it a very good idea. 'It is none of your damned business. Help Henry with the coffin, if you will, but we shall speak no more of murders and enquiries – unless you want to ride home alone. But I would not recommend it – the roads are hardly safe.'

D'Audley shot her a look of such loathing that Bartholomew was unnerved. Agnys glowered back,

71

unabashed, and it was d'Audley who looked away first. He turned on his heel and stalked out. Elyan followed, and it was not long before the physician and his sister were alone with the old lady.

'I am sorry if I upset them,' began Edith apologetically. 'But—'

'They will survive,' stated Agnys grimly. 'Although in the case of d'Audley, I might wish otherwise. But I am sorry *you* have been subjected to all this sorrow. You have been more than kind.'

'Is there anything more we can do?' asked Bartholomew, before Edith saw in Agnys a sympathetic ear and tried to convince her that Joan's death was suspicious. 'Fresh horses, perhaps, or the loan of a sturdier cart?'

'Thank you, but we will manage. Did Joan . . . say anything before she died?'

'Anything about what?' asked Edith, bemused.

'About her child,' replied Agnys vaguely. 'About Haverhill.'

'A great deal,' replied Edith. An expression of unease immediately flitted across the old woman's face, although Edith did not notice and chattered on blithely. 'She said she had never been so happy, and was looking forward to being a mother with all her heart.'

Agnys's relief was palpable, although she struggled to mask it. 'I am glad she died contented.'

'That was an odd remark,' said Edith, when Agnys had followed her grandson and neighbour outside, and she and Bartholomew were alone again. 'What did she mean?'

'She is terrified that Joan might have swallowed pennyroyal deliberately, and loves her enough to want her buried in a churchyard, not a suicide's grave. Why do you think she is so insistent that it was an accident and that there must be no investigation?'

'But it was *not* an accident,' protested Edith. 'And she *should* know that Joan was murdered.'

'She was not murdered,' said Bartholomew tiredly. 'There is no evidence—'

'There is no evidence it was an accident, either,' interrupted Edith, beginning to walk away from him, wearing the determined face that told him argument would be a waste of time. 'I know what I believe, and nothing you can say will convince me otherwise.'

Bartholomew left Edith with the guilty sense that he was deceiving her: that he should confess that her friend had died from a dose of the same kind of herb that was missing from his storeroom. But he knew it would achieve nothing other than to fuel her suspicions, and he was almost certain now it was *his* pennyroyal Joan had swallowed anyway. As he had told Michael, it was not a rare or unusual plant, and women often kept some dissolved in vinegar, as a remedy against swooning. Perhaps she had swallowed some of that, either by accident or design.

He was so engrossed in his thoughts as he walked home that Paxtone of King's Hall was obliged to prod him in order to gain his attention.

Paxtone was a portly physician, whose ample bulk was perched atop a pair of ludicrously slender ankles; Bartholomew was always expecting them to snap under the weight, and never knew what to say when his colleague complained of aching feet. Paxtone was not a talented practitioner, for he refused to act on any theory that had not been penned by ancient Greeks, but he was a decent teacher, and no one had a better grasp of Galen and Hippocrates.

That morning, he was with Warden Powys and another King's Hall Fellow named Shropham. Shropham had been in Cambridge long before Bartholomew had joined the University, but was one of those mousy nonentities who was hard to remember. He was older than his two colleagues, but his demeanour towards them had always been deferential. He was slightly built, with large, sad eyes and hair of an indeterminate colour, somewhere between brown and grey.

Wynewyk was with them, which Bartholomew thought was odd – the Michaelhouse Fellow rarely befriended scholars outside his College. But then he recalled Wynewyk saying he enjoyed intellectual discussions with King's Hall. It did not appear that their discussion was intellectual that day, however: he and Powys were laughing fit to burst, Paxtone looked aggrieved and Shropham dismayed.

'Matthew can resolve this,' said Paxtone stiffly. 'Because the debate has turned absurd.'

'It has,' agreed the Warden, wiping tears from his eyes. 'I have not laughed so much in years.'

Paxtone grimaced, then turned to his fellow physician. 'We are debating whether knives keep their sharpness if you leave them pointing northwards at night.'

Bartholomew failed to see what could be amusing about such a topic, or why Paxtone should be so obviously irritated by it. 'Yes?' he prompted warily.

Paxtone pursed his lips as he glared at Powys and Wynewyk. 'And this pair *will* insist on guffawing every time I posit a notion – they say I am employing *a posteriori* reasoning to argue a baseless superstition. It is Shropham's fault: he does not believe my contention that blades self-sharpen under certain conditions.'

Shropham's expression was one of abject mortification. 'I am not saying you are wrong, Paxtone,' he said, in something of a bleat. 'I merely remarked that I tried leaving my dagger in the way you suggested, and it was still blunt the following morning.'

'Then you did not aim it directly north,' declared Paxtone. He took a small knife from the pouch he carried at his side. It was identical to the ones Bartholomew used for surgery. 'Look at mine. You could shave a pig with this.'

'Why would you want to do that?' asked Powys innocently. Wynewyk smothered a snigger.

'It *is* sharp,' acknowledged Shropham, ignoring them as he ran a tentative finger along the edge. 'And I am not questioning whether the trick works for you. I am only saying that I tried it, and it failed to work for me. I do not suppose you chanted a spell at the same time, did you?'

'A *spell*?' squawked Paxtone, so loud in his horror that Shropham cringed. Wynewyk and Powys dissolved into more paroxysms of mirth, although Bartholomew could not help but notice that the humour did not touch Wynewyk's eyes; there was an odd expression in them, which could only be described as bleak. He wondered what was going on. 'Spells are for witches and heathens, but *I* am a *physician*!'

Bartholomew pulled his attention away from Wynewyk when he realised Paxtone was being inconsistent. 'Believing knives retain their sharpness when they point north is hardly scientific,' he pointed out. '*Ergo*, it is not unreasonable to assume you invoke charms—'

'There is a wealth of difference between a natural phenomenon that hones metal, and magic,' countered Paxtone curtly. 'I am *not* superstitious.'

'What about you, Bartholomew?' asked Powys, struggling to bring his amusement under control. 'Do you sharpen your knives by leaving them pointing northwards at night?'

'No,' replied Bartholomew. 'I use a whetstone.'

'Well, I suppose you would,' said Shropham. 'You use

yours for cautery, and I imagine slicing into a man's entrails with blunt blades would be unpleasant for all concerned. You, of all people, will want to be assured of a keen edge.'

'Shropham has won this debate, Paxtone,' said Warden Powys, before Bartholomew could inform them that he was *not* in the habit of slicing into entrails with sharp knives – at least, not as long as other viable options were available. 'His empirical test nullifies your contention.'

'Good steel needs less whetting than cheaper metal,' said Wynewyk kindly, seeing Paxtone's vexed expression. 'So, perhaps we should conduct a series of experiments using different alloys. Personally, I think the debate is still in progress.'

'I did not mean to cause trouble, Paxtone,' said Shropham, eyeing his colleague uncomfortably. 'You are almost certainly right – I must have mis-aimed my knife. I would not have mentioned the matter at all, but it is my job to prepare the quills for the students' examinations, and—'

'You take things too seriously, Shropham,' said the Warden, flinging a comradely arm around his Fellow's shoulders. 'You are a scholar, so you are supposed to be argumentative – there is no need to apologise because you question someone else's ideas. Look at Bartholomew – he does it all the time, even to medical theories that have been accepted as proven fact for hundreds of years.'

Bartholomew watched the three King's Hall men walk away, and supposed his attempts to be uncontroversial had not been as successful as he had hoped.

'Ignore him, Matt,' said Wynewyk, seeing his dismay. 'He was only trying to make Shropham feel better – he does not really think you are an incurable nihilist. Incidentally, the Saturday Debate has been postponed for an hour because Langelee needs to finish something. He would not say what, but he has been in his office all morning. Perhaps he is devising a way to reclaim the Stanton Cups.'

'I hope not. He is not subtle, and any plan he develops is almost certain to be violent.'

Wynewyk looked alarmed. 'Do you think he would consider hurting someone, then?'

'To reclaim valuable heirlooms for his College? Yes, of course! You know what he is like as well as I do. He is an avid player of camp-ball, for a start – and the only purpose of camp-ball is to legitimise a lot of thumping, punching and kicking.'

Wynewyk crossed himself. 'Do not be late for the debate, Matthew. Our Master has been in an odd mood all week, and I would hate to see this violence unleashed on you.'

When Bartholomew arrived home, he was unimpressed to find his students involved in a quarrel about Risleye's lost essay. It had still not been found, and Risleye wanted to search his classmates' possessions. They were outraged by the notion, and had presented a united front against him.

'If you were innocent, none of you would mind,' Risleye was shouting. He was near tears.

'It does not exist,' jeered Tesdale provocatively. 'You only claimed it was stolen, so you would be excused from handing it in.'

'Lies!' howled Risleye. 'But I *will* recover it, no matter what it takes. I will come at night, while you are all sleeping, and look then.'

'You will do no such thing,' ordered Bartholomew, not liking to imagine the commotion that would ensue should Risleye attempt what he threatened. He was almost certain to be caught, and the resulting rumpus would wake the entire College. 'You cannot have forgotten all these brilliant ideas so soon. Write them out again.'

'And make sure you keep them safe this time,' gloated Tesdale, delighted that Risleye had effectively lost the argument.

'Enough,' said Bartholomew sharply. 'I cannot believe how petty you have all become of late. What is wrong with you?'

'It is not *me*,' objected Risleye. 'It is *them*. I am not the one who made the book explode—'

'But you knew about it, and did nothing to stop us,' countered Valence. 'Complicity is—'

'For God's sake!' cried Bartholomew, supposing he would have to find ways to keep them away from each other until the disputation started, to give tempers a chance to cool. 'You are like a lot of children. Risleye, go to Yolande de Blaston and collect the forceps I left behind last week. Meanwhile, Tesdale can scrub that stain off the workbench in the storeroom.'

'Scrub?' echoed Tesdale, appalled by the prospect of physical labour. '*Me?* Let Valence do it – he is more junior than I.'

'But it is my birthday,' objected Valence. 'I need to cut up the cake I bought, to distribute to my *friends* during this afternoon's debate.' He shot Tesdale a look that said he would not be getting any.

Bartholomew ignored them both. 'The rest of you can visit patients and report back to me on their health. Valence, you can have Isnard.'

'Not Isnard!' groaned Valence. 'He will want to sing to me again. I cannot imagine why Brother Michael let him back into the Michaelhouse Choir, because he cannot carry a tune.'

'None of them can,' said Tesdale. 'But they think that if they bellow at the top of their lungs, no one will notice. And it is true, by and large. I never realised before that something can simply be too loud to hear. Why is that, sir? Is there a physiological—'

'The cleaning materials are in the kitchen,' interrupted Bartholomew, knowing perfectly well that lazy Tesdale was trying to sidetrack him in order to avoid the chore he had been set. 'You had better make a start, or you will miss the debate.'

Shooting each other resentful glances, the students shuffled past him, rolling their eyes or grimacing when he allocated them particularly awkward or garrulous customers. He did not care. The sick would appreciate the attention, and it would do his pupils no harm to learn that life as a physician was not all interesting diseases and challenging wounds.

'Is that a cake?' asked Michael, arriving just as the last pupil had been dispatched to see Chancellor Tynkell. The lad would not have a pleasant time of it, as Tynkell had an aversion to any form of personal hygiene. Bartholomew often wondered how Michael, who was fastidious, could bear to spend so much time in the man's pungent company.

'Edith gave it to me,' he said, moving to prevent the monk from unwrapping it. 'I am going to take it to the debate, for the Fellows to share. The students have one of their own, apparently.'

Michael pulled a disagreeable face. 'Edith's cakes are wasted on our colleagues. Clippesby is too fey to appreciate what he is eating, while Suttone is getting fat and should avoid rich foods.'

Bartholomew glanced sideways, and thought Michael was a fine one to be talking. The monk had lost some weight the previous year, but his fondness for bread, meat and lard-drenched Lombard slices meant he had regained most of it.

'A silver paten was stolen from Peterhouse this morning,' Michael went on when there was no response. All the while, he watched the cake with eagle eyes. 'It was Gosse, of course, but he managed to do it without being seen. I spent hours questioning students, Fellows and passers-by, but no one saw anything useful.'

'Then how do you know Gosse is responsible?'

'Because I defied the town worthies, and questioned him anyway. He loved the fact that I am certain of his guilt but can do nothing about it. He *claims* he was at a religious meeting in St Giles's Church when the theft took place.'

'Perhaps he was. Did you ask the vicar?'

'Of course, but it was one of those ceremonies where the place was packed and people came and went at will. Gosse *was* at St Giles's, but no one can say whether he was there the *whole* time. And those who might know are too frightened to talk. It is frustrating, knowing the identity of a culprit but being powerless to act.'

'He will make a mistake eventually, or steal in front of a witness who is not afraid to speak out.'

'Yes, but how many more heirlooms will we lose in the meantime?' demanded Michael bitterly. 'It is his lawyer who is to blame. Neubold.'

Bartholomew frowned. 'Neubold? That is the name of the priest who accompanied Joan to Cambridge, then failed to come and give her last rites.'

Michael shrugged. 'Joan hailed from Suffolk, and so does Gosse. Perhaps Neubold is a common name there. Or perhaps this priest dabbles in criminal law to supplement his stipend.'

'What about the attack on Langelee?' asked Bartholomew. 'Have you solved that yet?'

'No, but come with me to my office in St Mary the Great,'

said Michael, giving the cake one last, covetous glance before making for the door. 'My beadles have found a witness, and he has agreed to meet me there. It will not take long, and we shall be back in time for the Saturday Debate.'

CHAPTER 3

The witness to the attack on Langelee transpired to be a thin, beak-nosed Dominican with wild eyes and filthy robes. He stank, and Bartholomew did not think he had ever seen hands more deeply ingrained with dirt. He wondered why Prior Morden, the head of the Cambridge Black Friars, had not ordered him to bathe. The man was a hedge-priest – an itinerant cleric with no parish of his own – but the fact that he wore a Dominican habit meant Morden would have some control over him.

'Tell me what you saw,' ordered Michael, indicating that the friar should sit on a bench – a handsome piece of furniture that matched his exquisitely carved desk. Bartholomew surveyed the room's tasteful elegance and understated wealth, and wondered how long Michael would obey the order to leave Gosse alone. The monk had not risen to such dizzy heights by letting himself be bullied, or by following instructions he thought were foolish.

'It was dark that night,' replied the friar with a peculiar smile. 'As dark as the finest coal. Coal is a glorious substance. It shines like gold. Black gold.'

'Right,' said Michael warily. 'What is your name?'

'I have many names, but I like the one God gave me best – Carbo. It is Latin, and means—'

'Coal,' said Michael. 'Yes, I know. Now, about the incident near King's Hall on Thursday . . .'

'I saw a small man step from the shadows with a knife. He stabbed a big man, then ran away.'

'Did you recognise the small man?' asked Michael hopefully. 'Or do you know his name?'

'No.'

The priest gesticulated as he talked, and Bartholomew noticed that the movements of one hand were less fluid than the other. He kept tilting his head to one side, too, shaking it, as if to clear his ears of water. The physician wondered what was wrong with him.

'Can you describe this attacker?' Michael was asking.

Carbo breathed in deeply, and an uneasy expression crossed his face. 'Can you smell garlic?'

'Garlic?' queried Michael, startled. 'No. Unless Agatha put some in my midday pottage . . .'

'There!' exclaimed Carbo, snapping his fingers and beaming. 'It has gone! All is well again.'

'I am glad to hear it,' said Michael, regarding him askance. 'But you were about to describe—'

Carbo closed his eyes, and began to speak in a curious, chant-like manner. 'The man I saw. A youth or small man. Well dressed. Scholar's uniform. Neat hair. Good boots – black, like coal.' His eyes snapped open again, and he grinned broadly. 'Coal is a marvellous thing, although it brings out the worst in people. Do you not agree?'

Michael blinked. 'I have never given it much thought, frankly. Is there any more you can tell us? This was an attempt on a man's life, and we are eager to catch the culprit, lest he tries it again.'

'I can tell you he should have darkened his face with coal-dust, because then I would not have seen him loitering in that doorway, waiting for his prey. He would have been invisible.'

'Do you think Langelee – the big man – was his intended victim?' asked Michael.

'Yes – he let other folk pass unmolested, and only made his move when the big man came. He knew who to kill. Can you smell garlic? I smell garlic.'

'Lord, Matt!' exclaimed Michael, when Carbo had been sent on his way with money for a decent meal. 'He is as mad as Clippesby. What is it about the Dominican Order that attracts lunatics?'

'You should speak to Prior Morden about him,' said Bartholomew, concerned. 'He is obviously ill, and should not be wandering about on his own. He needs care and attention.'

'Very well. Do you think we can trust his testimony?'

Bartholomew shrugged. 'He confirmed what Langelee said – that the culprit wore academic garb.'

Michael was thoughtful. 'His description of the culprit's neat hair does not sound like Gosse, either – Gosse is virtually bald. So perhaps this is one crime of which he *is* innocent. But speak of the devil, and he will appear, because there is Idoma.'

'Who?'

'Gosse's sister. Folk say she is a witch, but only because they are afraid of her. Obviously, it is easier to be frightened of a witch than admit to being intimidated by an ordinary woman.'

Bartholomew studied Idoma as she approached, and supposed she was an impressive specimen. She was taller and broader than most men, and many of his younger students would have been proud to boast a moustache like hers. Her hair was bundled under a wimple, but the tendril that escaped was jet black. It matched her eyes, which were oddly expressionless, and reminded him of a shark-fish he had once seen off the Spanish coast. The similarity was enhanced when she opened her mouth to speak, revealing two rows of sharp, jagged teeth. And

Suttone had been right when he claimed she was a cut above the average villain, too – she carried herself with an aloof dignity that indicated she was no commoner.

'Lost any more chalices recently, Brother?' she asked gloatingly.

'Why?' asked Michael coldly. 'Which ones has your brother stolen now?'

'You cannot make that sort of accusation,' said Idoma, stepping forward threateningly. Michael held his ground, so they were eye to eye. 'Our lawyer says so.'

Michael smiled without humour. 'But your lawyer is not here, is he, madam? What did Gosse do with my College's cups? If they are returned, I *may* be persuaded to speak at his trial – the one that is a certainty, given the number of crimes he commits. A word from me may see him escape the noose.'

'Do you have proof with which to accuse him?' Idoma asked, unblinking eyes boring into his.

Watching them bandy words, Bartholomew found it was easy to imagine her sitting over a cauldron, chanting spells to rouse demons from Hell. Then he grimaced, aware that he was allowing himself to be influenced by popular bigotry. Of course she was not a witch, any more than he was a warlock. It was not her fault she looked the part. Or was it? She did not *have* to wear long black skirts, and nor did she have to cultivate an aura that oozed malevolence.

'I have no evidence to trap him yet,' said Michael, softly menacing in his turn. 'But it is only a matter of time before I do. You can tell him that, if you like.'

Idoma inclined her head. 'We shall see. And now, if you do not mind, I have better things to do than talk to you. Get out of my way.'

Bartholomew was surprised when the monk obliged.

He watched her stride away, noting how most pedestrians and some carts gave her a very wide berth.

'Damn!' breathed Michael, shaking his head. 'I did not mean to move, but I could not stop myself. It is those peculiar eyes of hers. There is something very eerie about them, and I felt myself powerless to resist her. It was uncanny – and disturbing, too. Perhaps she *is* a witch.'

'She is not. And her eyes are only striking because they do not reflect the light. *That* is what lends them that flat, impenetrable expression. There must be some unusual pigment in the iris, which—'

'There is more to it than that – Idoma has an evil charisma about her. So does Gosse. But they will not be free to burgle and rob their way through the town for much longer in the misguided belief that they are untouchable, because I meant what I said. I *will* catch them.'

Bartholomew nodded. 'But be on your guard from now on, Brother. If the tales about Gosse and Idoma are true, then they represent a formidable adversary.'

There was a hard, cold gleam in Michael's green eyes. 'But so do I, Matt. So do I.'

When Bartholomew and Michael returned to the College, the monk immediately laid claim to Edith's cake. The physician tended to be absent-minded about such matters, and Michael did not want to sit through the Saturday Debate with nothing to eat. He whisked it away for cutting up.

Because Bartholomew's pupils were still occupied with the tasks he had set them his chamber was empty, so he took the opportunity to spend a few moments with his treatise on fevers. He had started writing it several years before, as a concise guide for students. It was now several volumes long, and he still had not finished everything he wanted to say. He picked up his quill, but had penned no more than a sentence when there was a tap on his door. It was Langelee.

'The Stanton Cups,' said the Master without preamble. 'Their loss is a terrible blow to us all.'

Masking his frustration that he was not to be permitted even a few moments to himself, Bartholomew set down his pen and leaned back in his chair to give the Master his full attention. 'We will miss them when we celebrate special masses, but we have other chalices.'

'True,' acknowledged Langelee. He sat heavily on the bed. 'But even so . . .'

Bartholomew glanced out of the window when the bell rang to announce the debate was about to start. Scholars began to troop towards the hall, some enthusiastically and others dragging their feet. The occasions were popular with the brighter students, who did not mind Thelnetham calling on them to argue a case at a moment's notice, but they were dreaded by those who were less articulate.

'We had better go,' he said, when Langelee did not seem to have anything else to add. He closed his books and put the lid back on the inkwell.

'The topic today is whether a man should be allowed to marry a goat,' said Langelee gloomily.

Bartholomew regarded him in disbelief. 'Are you sure? Suttone usually vetoes that sort of subject – there is only so far he allows Thelnetham to go in his quest to amuse.'

Langelee shrugged. 'Perhaps I misheard. It is probably whether goats should be allowed to wed each other. Or perhaps goats have nothing to do with it. I did not pay much attention, to be honest.'

'I see,' said Bartholomew, not seeing at all. He stood,

and indicated that Langelee should do likewise, so they could leave. 'If the subject is contentious, we will be needed to calm—'

But Langelee remained where he was. 'Please sit down. I have something to tell you – something only you can help me resolve.'

Reluctantly, Bartholomew returned to his seat, supposing he had made the offer of a sympathetic ear two nights before, so now he had no choice but to honour it. However, he sincerely hoped the confession would not turn out to be anything too alarming, perhaps involving Langelee's former life as the Archbishop's spy, or a romantic tryst with someone else's wife. Scholars were forbidden relations with the town's women, but Langelee tended to ignore that particular rule.

'We had better wait until the debate has started,' said Langelee, standing to lean out of the window and look into the yard. 'I would rather no one knows what we are doing.'

Bartholomew's misgivings intensified. Langelee held his breath when Michael thundered down the stairs from his room above. The monk pushed open the door to ask whether Bartholomew was ready, and Langelee pressed himself against the wall, so as not to be seen. His shadow was clearly visible, though, and the physician knew from Michael's amused smirk that he had seen it.

'I will come in a while, Brother,' said Bartholomew. 'There is something I need to finish first.'

'I will make your excuses to Thelnetham, then,' said Michael. He carried Edith's cake, but there were crumbs on the front of his habit. He winked at his friend, made the kind of gesture that said he wished him luck, and left.

When the last of the scholars had entered the hall and

the door was closed, Langelee turned to the physician. 'This is difficult, and I am not sure where to start. As you may have guessed, it is not just the loss of the Stanton Cups that is bothering me.'

'Take your time,' said Bartholomew kindly, seeing the distress in Langelee's face. Whatever was troubling the Master was clearly serious; he did not think he had ever seen him in such a state.

Langelee reached inside his tabard and produced a slender, leather-bound book and a pile of parchments. When he passed them to Bartholomew, his hand shook.

'The College accounts,' said Bartholomew, recognising the tome. He was puzzled. 'Can you not make them balance? I thought you had delegated that task to Wynewyk.'

'I have,' said Langelee. 'And you know why: a Master's duties are onerous, and managing the finances for such a large foundation takes a lot of time. Wynewyk is good with figures, so it seemed sensible to pass the responsibility to him. It leaves me free for more important College business.'

'What is wrong, Langelee?' asked Bartholomew gently, seeing he would have to do some coaxing unless he wanted to be there all day. 'What do you want to tell me?'

'Go over the accounts. Do not demand explanations or ask me questions – just assess what you see, and let me know what you think. I shall sit here quietly until you have finished.'

Bartholomew regarded the endless rows of tiny, neat figures with dismay. 'But Wynewyk keeps very detailed records of all our transactions. It will take me ages to—'

'I do not care. I will not say a word until you are done. Do not rush – take as long as you need.'

'Perhaps you should go to the debate,' suggested

Bartholomew, not liking the notion of the Master looming behind him as he worked. He imagined there would be all manner of sighs and impatient rustles if Langelee thought he was taking too long, despite his assurances to the contrary.

'I do not want to leave them,' said Langelee, nodding at the book and the pile of documents. 'I will stay here, if you do not mind.'

'Where do you want me to start?' asked Bartholomew, a little helplessly. 'These records go back more than a decade – before the plague.'

Langelee opened the book to a specific page. It was dated a year before, roughly where Langelee's bold scrawl gave way entirely to Wynewyk's neat roundhand. Before that, both had made entries.

'There,' he said, stabbing a thick forefinger at the record for the previous November. 'That was when I decided I trusted him so completely that I stopped checking his sums. They were always right, anyway.'

Bartholomew regarded him uneasily. 'What are you saying? Wynewyk would never—'

'Just look at the figures,' interrupted Langelee shortly. 'And then we will talk.'

By the end of the afternoon, Bartholomew had been through the accounts so many times that the columns of figures were beginning to swim before his eyes. He leaned back and flexed his aching shoulders. There were a number of conclusions that could be drawn from the complex calculations in the book and the documents that lay in front of him, but none made him happy.

First, it was possible that Wynewyk had made a series of honest mistakes. But Bartholomew felt there were too many errors to be attributed solely to careless arithmetic.

Second, it could be argued that Wynewyk had been promoted beyond his abilities, and that the discrepancy between what the College should have owned, and what was actually in its coffers, was down to incompetence. But Wynewyk was intelligent, and the physician did not see him as inept.

And third – although Bartholomew was loath to believe it – Wynewyk could have been lining his own pockets at Michaelhouse's expense.

'Well?' asked Langelee. As good as his word, he had remained silent the whole time. He had paced to begin with, but an irritable glance from the physician had made him sit again, and then he had either looked at the pictures in Bartholomew's medical books, or dozed on the bed. Now he was uncharacteristically grave. 'Is there an innocent explanation for why we are short of thirty marks?'

Bartholomew did not reply. He stood, and pushed the window shutters further open, feeling the need for fresh air. A cold breeze blew in, billowing among the parchments on the table and sending some to the floor. Neither scholar moved to retrieve them. The physician leaned against the stone mullion and gazed across the courtyard. It was deserted, and the only thing moving was Walter's tailless peacock, which was scratching in the mud for food.

'Please,' said Langelee in an uncharacteristically strangled voice. 'You must tell me what you think. Are we thirty marks short? Or have I missed something?'

'You have not missed anything,' replied Bartholomew. He closed the shutters, thinking this was a discussion they had better have with the window barred against possible eavesdroppers. Frequent bellows of laughter from the hall showed that the debate was still in full swing, but he did not want to take the chance that someone had left early. 'Thirty marks have gone astray.'

'My next question is how,' said Langelee unhappily. '*How* has such a vast sum disappeared?'

'Through some cunning manipulation.' Bartholomew spoke reluctantly, not liking what he was saying. 'A quick glance at the records suggests all is in order, and it is only when you work through them carefully that these . . . these *inconsistencies* are apparent.'

Langelee massaged his eyes wearily. 'Your assessment coincides with mine. So what shall we do? Confront him, and demand to know what the hell he thinks he is doing? Or shall we inform the Senior Proctor, and let there be an official investigation?'

'Wynewyk is not a thief,' said Bartholomew, his thoughts in turmoil. 'He will have a reason for doing what he has done, and you should give him the opportunity to explain himself.'

'What *reason*?' Langelee sneered the last word. He began to pace, the agitation that had been in control earlier now erupting. 'What *reason* gives him the right to steal thirty marks?'

Bartholomew spread his hands, trying to think of one. 'Perhaps he has invested in a scheme that will make the College a profit eventually.'

'Then why conceal it so slyly?' demanded Langelee angrily. 'He knows we do whatever he recommends – he could suggest we invest in the moon, and we would do it. We *trust* him.'

'Yes,' said Bartholomew firmly. 'We do. So all we need to do is talk to him, and ask what is going on. You are agonising over nothing.'

'I am agonising over thirty marks,' countered Langelee. 'A fortune.'

'What made you suspicious in the first place?' asked Bartholomew, after a silence in which both men reflected on how much more pleasant life in Michaelhouse would have been with an additional thirty marks. They would not have had to endure such dreadful food, for a start.

Langelee sat on the bed again, as though pacing had sapped his energy. 'Experience. I dealt with some very treacherous villains for the Archbishop of York, and it taught me how to recognise them. I had Wynewyk marked for a scoundrel from the beginning.'

Bartholomew did not believe him, thinking it was easy to express reservations with the benefit of hindsight. 'Then why did you accept him as a Fellow?'

'Because I hoped he would use his aptitude for deceit to benefit us,' snapped Langelee. 'God knows, we need something to give us an edge over Cambridge's venal tradesmen.'

'That is a dreadful thing to admit! We do not want a reputation for unfair dealings. The University is unpopular enough as it is, without courting trouble by cheating those who do business with us.'

'They would cheat us, given the chance,' Langelee flashed back. 'And a reputation for honest trading would make us the target of every thief in the shire. It is better to be crafty and slippery.'

'God's teeth!' breathed Bartholomew, shocked. He tried to bring his thoughts back to Wynewyk. 'But if you knew he was a thief, why did you entrust him with Michaelhouse's money?'

'Because I did not think he would cheat *us*. I kept a close eye on him for two years, as he steered us from poverty to prosperity. Eventually, I decided he could be trusted, and spent less time checking his work. And in

November, I stopped altogether. It was a terrible mistake, but I thought two years was enough to gain a man's measure.'

'It *is* enough,' said Bartholomew. 'In fact, I am so sure Wynewyk would never hurt us that I am willing to wager anything you like on there being an innocent explanation.'

'I hope you are right, I really do. And if he refunds our thirty marks, I may be prepared to listen to his excuses. However, if he has spent it on himself, then he can expect my dagger in his gizzard.'

'We shall talk to him as soon as the debate is over,' said Bartholomew, not entirely sure that Langelee was speaking figuratively. That was the problem with having a Master whose previous occupation had involved so many insalubrious activities. 'He will put your mind at rest.'

'He will lie,' predicted Langelee despondently. 'You will believe him, and I will be alone with my suspicions once more. I chose to confide in you because you are faster at arithmetic than the others, but I should have approached Michael instead. He is less inclined to see the good in people.'

Selfishly, Bartholomew wished Langelee *had* lumbered Michael with the burden of confronting a colleague with accusations of dishonesty. He was about to recommend that they made a list of all the questionable transactions they had found, when there was a knock at the door. It was Cynric.

'There has been an incident,' he said tersely. 'In the hall.'

'Another fight?' asked Langelee wearily. 'I thought I had made my views clear about that: if someone cannot win his point with words, then he must go outside to throw his punches. We are scholars, not louts, to be brawling in our own hall.'

'No one was fighting,' said Cynric. He was subdued, and Bartholomew was assailed with the conviction that something was very wrong. 'And everyone was so intent on listening to Clippesby explain why goats make good wives that no one realised what was happening until it was too late.'

'Too late for what?' demanded Bartholomew, coils of unease writhing in the pit of his stomach.

'For Wynewyk,' said Cynric. He looked down at his boots, reluctant to continue.

'Wynewyk?' echoed Bartholomew, unable to avoid shooting Langelee an anxious glance.

'He is dead,' explained Cynric softly. 'I think he died laughing.'

That wintry afternoon, a fire had been lit in the hall, but Bartholomew's breath still plumed in front of him as he hurried towards the dais, where a tight knot of Fellows and students had clustered around their stricken colleague. When he saw the physician and the Master enter, Thelnetham detached himself from the throng and hurried towards them, white-faced and shaking.

'It has been a horrible week,' he blurted, 'what with bad weather, poor food and the loss of the Stanton Cups, so I chose a silly subject to cheer us up. But I never meant for . . .' He trailed off.

Langelee regarded him warily. 'Never meant for what?'

'Never meant for Wynewyk to laugh so hard that he died,' finished Thelnetham in an appalled whisper. 'I did not even know such a thing was possible.'

Wynewyk was sitting at the high table, although he had slumped across it, as if he had grown bored with the debate and had fallen asleep. Bartholomew wondered if he was playing a prank, albeit one in poor taste, for his colleagues were distressed. All around, voices were raised, some in horror and others in disbelief; the babble quietened as he and Langelee approached.

'Clippesby was postulating the merits of goat wives,' explained Michael, as the physician bent to examine the fallen Fellow. The monk's face was very pale. 'And I was opposing him. But if I had thought for a moment that our ridiculous banter would lead to . . .'

Despite Wynewyk's restful pose, Bartholomew could see he was dead even before he felt the absence of a life-beat in the great veins of the neck. The lawyer's face was an unnatural shade of blue, and his eyes were half closed, staring at nothing.

Premature death was no stranger to members of the University – besides fatal brawls, there were accidents, suicides and a whole gamut of diseases – but it was still rare for it to occur quite so unexpectedly. Wynewyk was no more than thirty, and had been in good health. Bartholomew turned to his book-bearer.

'Fetch a bier, Cynric. And escort the students from the hall – they do not need to see this.'

'You mean he *is* dead?' Langelee looked appalled. 'But he was all right when I saw him earlier this afternoon.' He lowered his voice. 'Do you think he died because of . . . you know?'

Bartholomew was not sure what to think, and for a moment could do no more than stare at the man who had been his friend. He recalled the times he and Wynewyk had sat reading in companionable silence in the conclave after the others had gone to bed. And the times they had filched an illicit jug of wine from the kitchens, while Wynewyk had confided his concerns for his elderly father or waxed lyrical about whichever rough soldier had most recently captured his fancy.

'In August, he went to visit family in Winwick,' said Suttone. The Carmelite was near tears. 'We all missed him, even though he was only gone for a week. What shall we do now he is gone for ever?'

Bartholomew had no reply, and watched numbly as Cynric ushered the students from the hall. They were reluctant to go, not because they were ghoulish, but because they did not want to leave the reassuring presence of the senior scholars. Tesdale was crying, and Valence was trying to comfort him. By contrast, Risleye was excited, arguing that he should be allowed to stay so that he could learn from the case. Bartholomew appreciated the young man's desire to expand his medical knowledge, but his behaviour was inappropriate. He glared at him, and Risleye slunk out without another word.

'What happened?' he asked, when they had gone. 'Did Wynewyk say he felt unwell?'

'Not that I heard,' replied Michael, still ashen. 'I was just refuting Clippesby's contention that goats like a year's betrothal before committing themselves to wedlock, when Suttone began to yell.'

'The sudden clamour frightened us,' added Clippesby, his peculiar eyes wide and intense. 'We all leapt to our feet, to find him staring at Wynewyk as though he were a ghost.'

Suttone crossed himself. 'What happened, Matthew? Is it the plague? I have been saying for years that it will return, but I did not expect it to manifest itself in Wynewyk. There are far more sinful—'

'He was laughing,' said Michael, curtly cutting across him. 'Thelnetham's chosen topic was absurd, and Wynewyk found it very amusing. He chortled all afternoon.'

'He did,' confirmed Hemmysby quietly. He dabbed his eyes with the sleeve of his habit. 'In fact, I thought he was

97

drunk, because his hilarity seemed out of proportion to the humour of the situation.'

'He did not *seem* drunk,' said Thelnetham. He hesitated. 'Or did he?'

'What did he drink – and eat – at the noonday meal?' asked Bartholomew.

Everyone looked at Hemmysby, with whom he usually shared dishes. The theologian shrugged and wiped his eyes again. 'He drank watered ale. And he ate pea pottage, like the rest of us.'

'And at the debate, he had wine and Edith's cake,' added Michael. He grimaced. 'In fact, I think he ate mine, too, because when I came for a bite it had gone, and I do not recall finishing it.'

'He would not have taken cake,' said Bartholomew. 'He had an aversion to almonds, and knew to avoid them. Where is the wine?'

Michael handed him the empty jug. 'But there cannot be anything wrong with it, because it came from the barrel that served the whole College. It was not the best brew I have ever sampled, and some of the students said it tasted bitter, but none of *us* are dead.'

Bartholomew inspected Wynewyk again, looking in his mouth and at his neck, and wondering whether his excessive giggles had been a response to Langelee discovering the inconsistencies in the accounts. Had he guessed what the Master had found, and an attack of fright or conscience had led to the strange laughter and then his death? But the physician had never heard of such a thing happening before, at least, not outside popular stories.

He wondered what Langelee would do now. His choices were to make Wynewyk's activities public, or allow them to die with their perpetrator. Either way, Michaelhouse would lose thirty marks. Absently, he picked up the goblet from which Wynewyk had been drinking. It was empty, but there was nothing to suggest foul play – no odd aromas or residues in the bottom.

'He was not poisoned,' said Michael quietly, seeing the line Bartholomew's thoughts had taken. 'No one has any reason to harm Wynewyk.'

Bartholomew was careful not to look at Langelee. 'Who poured the wine?'

'Tesdale,' replied Thelnetham. 'It should have been me, because I am the most junior Fellow, but I was presiding over the debate, so I paid Tesdale to do it in my stead.'

'It was a kindness,' said Hemmysby, smiling wanly. 'Thelnetham is quite capable of pouring wine and presiding at the same time, but Tesdale is poor, and Thelnetham was being thoughtful.'

Thelnetham flushed uncomfortably. 'Nonsense! The truth is that I was afraid this cheap brew might stain my habit – and I have a rather important date with a certain young man tonight.'

Michael shook Bartholomew's arm. 'I know your appointment as Corpse Examiner has exposed you to more murder than is normal for a physician, Matt, but you must not allow it to lead you to see evil in *all* untimely demises. Sometimes, men just die.'

'I suppose it might have been a seizure,' acknowledged Bartholomew, although he was not sure what to think. None of the other Fellows knew about the inconsistencies in the accounts so could have no reason to harm Wynewyk, while Langelee had an alibi in Bartholomew himself. And even if the Master had arranged for an accomplice to feed his errant Fellow some toxic substance, it would have been difficult to target his victim without poisoning the rest of the College, too.

'Of course it was a seizure,' said Langelee sharply. 'What else could it be? But here is Cynric with the bier, so we should take Wynewyk to the church. The sooner he is there, the sooner we can start to think about arrangements for his burial.'

'Oh, Lord!' whispered Suttone, distressed by the notion. 'I suppose it does fall to us to organise the ceremonies. However, it will take several days to—'

'We shall inter him tomorrow,' interrupted Langelee tersely. 'We can hold a requiem mass later.'

Michael's eyes narrowed. 'Why the hurry, Master?'

'Because I want our students to resume their normal routine as soon as possible – and we cannot afford a grand funeral, anyway. Our coffers are empty.'

'And there is the crux of the matter,' said Suttone bitterly. He bent down and tugged Wynewyk's purse from its belt, shoving it fiercely at Langelee. 'Perhaps you might care to see whether he has enough to pay for his own rites, Master.'

'That is a good idea,' said Langelee, either oblivious to or uncaring of the fact that Suttone was being facetious. He tipped the purse's contents into his hand, ignoring the looks of shocked distaste that were exchanged between his Fellows. 'A few pennies and a rock.'

'A rock?' asked Bartholomew, startled. 'What kind of rock?'

Langelee tossed it to him. 'One with sharp edges and crystals.'

'A charm,' said Cynric, who knew what he was talking about when it came to matters superstitious. He set the bier on the floor, and peered over Bartholomew's shoulder. 'Men often carry stones like that for luck or protection. It is quite normal.'

'Perhaps he bought it to ward off seizures because he

100

knew he was susceptible to them,' suggested Clippesby. He looked away. 'It is a pity the wretched thing did not work.'

Cynric and Langelee lifted Wynewyk on to the stretcher, then Suttone, Clippesby, Thelnetham and Hemmysby began to pray over the body. Bartholomew went to stand in the library, so as not to distract them. Langelee and Michael followed him there.

'You have told me in the past that people often die of natural seizures, Matt,' said Michael softly. 'Yet you seem oddly reluctant to accept that this is what has happened to Wynewyk. Why?'

'Because of what he knows,' explained Langelee, when he saw Bartholomew was not sure how to reply. He proceeded to give a brief account of what they had discovered, and Bartholomew was not surprised when the monk refused to believe it.

'You can look for yourself,' said Langelee tiredly. 'All the Fellows can. There is no point in keeping it secret now. Damn Wynewyk! How could he do this to us? To his friends?'

'I can see why his death set warning bells jangling,' said Michael to Bartholomew. 'It *is* a suspicious combination of events. But is there any tangible evidence to suggest foul play?'

'No,' said Langelee, very firmly. 'I imagine what happened is that his guilty conscience killed him. And the laughter was hysterical, because he knew he was on the verge of being exposed.'

'I will never believe that of him,' said Bartholomew angrily. 'Never.'

'Matt?' prompted Michael, still waiting for an answer to his question.

'When I looked in his mouth, I could see from his teeth that he *had* eaten some of Edith's cake. He should not have done: it was full of almonds, and he had an aversion to those.'

'You mean the cake gave him this seizure?' asked Michael.

Bartholomew raised his hands in a shrug. 'It might have done. Or the almonds caused him to choke. He usually spat them out when he realised what he was eating, but his wild laughter suggests he might have had more wine than usual. Perhaps it made him incautious.'

'I have no idea what you are telling me,' said Michael impatiently.

'I am saying that I do not know what happened, Brother,' snapped Bartholomew, distress and shock making him uncharacteristically testy. 'Perhaps the almonds did induce a seizure. Or perhaps he would have had one anyway. However, he knew he was supposed to avoid nuts, so why are they on his teeth? Did he eat the cake *knowing* what would happen?'

Michael regarded him warily. 'You think he guessed what Langelee was doing, and killed himself? I do not think that is very likely. Suicides do not spend their last moments laughing their heads off.'

'His aversion was not a secret,' said Bartholomew, rubbing a hand through his hair as he tried to make sense of it all. 'Perhaps someone knew what would happen if he were to eat the cake, and plied him with it deliberately.'

'Well, it was not me,' said Langelee, when monk and physician looked at him. 'I am no killer. Well, not of my colleagues, at least.'

The abrupt nature of Wynewyk's demise preyed heavily on Bartholomew's mind, and he could not stop himself from wondering whether one of his colleagues had become suspicious of something Wynewyk had said or done, and had conducted his own survey of the accounts. The books were always available for Fellows to inspect, and thirty marks was an enormous sum of money.

He walked to his room and found Valence, Risleye and Tesdale there. Risleye was trying to draw his classmates into wagering on the outcome of Langelee's next camp-ball game, but the other two were pale and subdued, not in the mood for chattering about sport. Risleye became exasperated when he saw his attempts to cheer them up were not working.

'We are all upset about Wynewyk,' he said irritably. 'But sitting here, all gloom and misery, is doing no one any good. Come to the kitchens – Agatha will sell me a jug of ale, and I shall share it with you.'

'But *I* served him wine,' said Tesdale, beginning to cry again. 'His death might be my fault.'

'It is not your fault,' said Bartholomew gently. 'Why should you think such a thing?'

'Because he had such a lot of it,' sobbed Tesdale. 'He is usually abstemious, but he kept draining his goblet today. I took care to refill it, because he has always been kind to me and I wanted to return the favour: if he was of a mind to get himself tipsy, then I was going to facilitate it for him.'

'Are you saying he was drunk?' asked Bartholomew.

'Perhaps that is why he laughed so much,' suggested Valence, before Tesdale could reply. 'The disputants were not *that* funny, and I thought it odd at the time that Wynewyk should cackle so.'

'He was not drunk,' said Tesdale, although he did not sound certain. 'Merry, maybe. But he was a good man. I struggled to pay my fees last term, so he gave me more time to raise the money. And he sometimes shared his commons with me.'

'Perhaps he liked the look of you,' suggested Risleye baldly.

'Enough of that sort of talk,' snapped Bartholomew, knowing Wynewyk would never engage in an inappropriate relationship with a student, especially one from Michaelhouse.

Risleye objected to the reprimand. 'But he *did* like men – it was no secret. I am not maligning him – merely offering an explanation for his munificence. And you can say what you will, Tesdale, but Wynewyk was *not* generous – his tight hold on the College purse strings is testament to that.'

'Well, he was generous to me,' mumbled Tesdale. He sniffed, then regarded his classmate hopefully. 'Did you mention sharing a jug of ale?'

Bartholomew left them, and walked aimlessly along the High Street, craving time alone to think. He heard someone calling his name, and turned to see Michael waddling after him.

'How could you even *think* of wandering off after what has just happened?' the monk demanded angrily. 'Surely you must know I still have questions to ask?'

'I am sorry,' said Bartholomew unhappily. 'I thought I had answered them all.'

Michael scowled. 'I want to speak to you without Langelee giving his opinion every few moments. I still cannot believe what he said about the accounts. I will inspect them myself tonight, but I want your views first. Are you sure he is right?'

'Quite sure. We gave Wynewyk free rein to buy everything the College needs – food, cloth, pots, fuel, stationery. Most of the entries show he paid impressively low prices for them. Except for three commodities purchased from

Suffolk, where he paid ridiculously high ones: wood, coal and pigs.'

Michael's face was pale. 'This is dreadful! We all trusted him – he was our friend. But this is no place to be talking. Come to the Brazen George with me. We both need a drink.'

The Brazen George was Michael's favourite tavern. Such places were forbidden to scholars, on the grounds that ale, students and townsfolk were a volatile mix and likely to result in trouble, and his beadles were always on the lookout for academics who thought the rules did not apply to them. Being caught resulted in hefty fines. Michael, however, did a good deal of University business in taverns, and had declared himself exempt from this particular statute. Punishing others for what he enjoyed himself made him something of a hypocrite, but he did not care enough to change his ways.

He led the way to the small chamber at the back of the inn, which the landlord kept for his exclusive use. It was a pleasant room, with real glass in the windows and a fire in the hearth.

'It will be a bad winter,' predicted Taverner Lister, bringing not just ale, but roast venison and a dish of apples, too. Michael's eyes glistened: it was better fare than anything he was likely to be offered at Michaelhouse. 'Folk will starve when the snows come.'

'A number of my patients say the same thing.' Bartholomew watched the monk tie a piece of linen around his neck to protect his habit from splattered grease. He wondered how Michael could bring himself to eat after what had happened. 'Bread is already expensive.'

'Then eat well while you can,' suggested Lister. 'Because this time of plenty will not last.'

'Lord!' exclaimed Michael, when he had gone. 'He can be a gloomy fellow sometimes.'

'I refuse to believe Wynewyk was cheating us,' said Bartholomew, taking one of the apples and playing with it listlessly. 'So there must be another reason why this thirty marks is missing. Do you have any idea what it might be?'

Michael began feeding, and was silent for so long that Bartholomew was beginning to think he had forgotten the question. 'Blackmail,' the monk said eventually.

Bartholomew gazed at him. 'Wynewyk was not the kind of man to harbour dark secrets.'

Michael regarded him soberly. 'How do you know? No matter how we look at it, he took thirty marks. This has shocked us, which implies we have no idea what kind of man he was.'

'I know he was no thief,' persisted Bartholomew stubbornly. 'And Langelee will feel terrible when we uncover the truth and Wynewyk is exonerated. However, I accept your point that Wynewyk's failure to tell us what he was doing suggests he was more enigmatic than we realised. What do you think someone could have been blackmailing him about?'

Michael tapped a bone on the edge of the platter as he thought. 'He preferred men to women, but that was common knowledge, so no one could have threatened to make it public. And he confined himself to older men – rough, soldierly types – so there is no question of an inappropriate seduction.'

'Perhaps it is something to do with his academic work,' suggested Bartholomew. 'He devised a new and controversial theory.'

Michael laughed, genuinely amused. 'You are the only Michaelhouse Fellow who indulges in that sort of thing, and Wynewyk was an uninspired scholar, to say the least.

He did not even have any interesting ideas about Blood Relics – and everyone likes to hold forth about those. Indeed, I am worried about the debate on the subject that is due to take place Monday week.'

'Why?' asked Bartholomew, bemused.

'Because too many clever men with novel theories have been scheduled to speak, and—'

'Then what else could Wynewyk have been blackmailed about?' demanded Bartholomew. He did not care about the debate. 'If Wynewyk was a dull scholar, and his private life was an open book?'

Michael rubbed his flabby jowls. 'I really have no idea. But if there is anything insalubrious in his life, we shall find it, you can be sure of that. Now, tell me more about his death.'

'You know as much as I do. He swallowed nuts, which he should not have done, and Tesdale thinks he was drunk. Perhaps he ate the nuts because his wits were befuddled with wine, and his death was an accident. Or maybe he did it deliberately, because it was an easy way out of whatever predicament he was in. Or perhaps someone fed him something toxic earlier in the day and he was dying before the debate started, which would explain his odd behaviour. Or maybe it *was* a seizure.'

'In other words, the possibilities are accident, suicide, murder or natural causes,' concluded Michael dryly. 'That is hardly helpful, Matt.'

'I cannot draw conclusions from evidence that is not there.'

'Then we must find some,' determined Michael. 'I want you to inspect Wynewyk's body again. I know pawing the corpse of a friend will be distasteful to you, but we have no choice.'

*   *   *

107

Wynewyk had been taken to the Stanton Chapel in St Michael's Church, where he occupied the parish coffin. The chapel, named for the College's founder, was a pleasant, airy place adjacent to the chancel, with delicate windows and tasteful paintings on the walls. Niches on either side of the altar contained statues, one of the Virgin Mary and the other of St Michael. They looked down with flat stone eyes, although Bartholomew had always thought their expressions inexplicably sad. Perhaps they did not like the number of Michaelhouse scholars who had lain dead in front of them.

The physician forced himself to begin his examination. Obviously, there were no wounds to find, because Wynewyk had died in a room full of witnesses and someone would have noticed if he had been injured. Even so, he went through the motions – assessing his colleague for marks of violence and disease, trying to ascertain whether there might be something less obvious that had brought about the sudden death of a healthy man. He spent a long time examining the mouth, even tipping the head back, to assess the throat. It was slightly swollen.

'Some people have aversions to specific substances,' he said, more to himself than Michael, who was sitting on a nearby tomb trying not to watch, 'which cause the neck tissues to swell. This prevents air from entering the lungs, so the victim suffocates. However, Wynewyk's throat does not appear to be dangerously inflamed . . .'

'So what are you saying?' demanded Michael, when the physician trailed off.

'Wynewyk knew nuts were dangerous for him, so why did he eat them? Even drunk, I cannot imagine him being so recklessly careless.'

'So you think it was suicide?' pressed Michael.

'No,' said Bartholomew. 'Suicide means accepting that

108

he did something untoward – something that warranted a brisk exit from the world. And I refuse to believe that of him.'

'So, we are left with murder, accident or natural causes. What do you make of his giggling? Would he have been able to laugh so heartily, if he was struggling to breathe?'

Bartholomew shrugged helplessly. 'Clearly, he *did* laugh, because you heard him. I suppose it might have been a hysterical reaction brought about by a shortness of breath.'

'I am not sure about this nut theory,' said Michael, after a moment of silence. 'It smacks of deviant thinking on your part, and I do not want attention drawn to your heterodoxy. I prefer our original diagnosis: that he died laughing – a seizure. It will be better for everyone – including Wynewyk – if we agree on a verdict of natural causes.'

'You mean we should lie?' asked Bartholomew coolly.

'I mean we keep our fears and suspicions to ourselves until we have sufficient evidence to make them public.' Michael gazed at their colleague's cold, waxen face, then released an anguished cry that made the physician jump. 'Lord Christ, Wynewyk! How could you *do* this to us?'

When they had finished their dismal business in the church, Michael went to tackle the accounts, but Bartholomew did not feel like going with him. Nor was he inclined to visit the conclave, which would be full of talk about Wynewyk, or his room, where his students might ask for a medical explanation for what had happened. Normally, he encouraged his pupils' willingness to learn, but he was not equal to it that evening. He told the monk he was going to see a patient, and set off along the High Street.

It was dusk, although there was not the merest glimmer of colour in the western sky, where the sun had set behind a bank of thick clouds. It was cold, too, and people scurried along with their heads down, reluctant to be out. Traders hauled their carts homeward, wheels squelching and hissing in the mud that formed most of Cambridge's streets. A musician played a haunting melody on a pipe, hoping to be tossed coins by passers-by, but Bartholomew wished he would play something a little more cheerful. The tune was so sad that he felt his throat constrict, and he was forced to take several deep breaths when an image of Wynewyk's face sprang unbidden into his mind.

He glanced at King's Hall as he passed, seized by a sudden desire to discuss his nut theory with a fellow physician – someone who would understand what he was talking about. Medicine was not an exact science, and the longer he practised, the more he realised he did not know, so it was always good to air new ideas with colleagues. Paxtone was not an ideal choice for debates, because his experience was narrow and so was his mind, but he was better than Rougham of Gonville Hall. Making up his mind, Bartholomew headed towards the College that was Paxtone's home.

He hammered on the gate and was admitted by Tobias the porter. As he was being escorted across the yard, they were intercepted by a thin, mouse-like man wearing King's Hall's blue tabard. As usual, it took Bartholomew a moment to recall Shropham's name, for the diffident lawyer never did or said anything to make it stick in his mind.

'I shall conduct our visitor to Paxtone's quarters,' Shropham said to Tobias. 'Gosse was loitering around earlier, and I would rather you stayed by the gate.'

'You think he might burgle King's Hall?' asked

Bartholomew, as Shropham led the way to the handsome suite of rooms on the top floor where Paxtone lived. It did not sound very likely: not only was the College built like a fortress, but many of its scholars were the sons of nobles, who had been trained to wield swords and shoot arrows. Gosse would have to be insane to risk an invasion.

'Probably not, but you cannot be too careful. I am sorry about Wynewyk, by the way. I saw your book-bearer carrying his corpse to the church and he told me the news. Your poor College is not having much luck this term; first you lose Kelyng the Bible Scholar, and now Wynewyk.'

'Kelyng is not dead,' objected Bartholomew. 'He just decided not to return for his final year because it would have meant paying a massive debt for past fees.'

'I see,' said Shropham. He smiled sadly. 'But I shall miss Wynewyk. He was a fellow lawyer, and was always laughing at something.'

Bartholomew glanced at him sharply. 'Laughing?'

His tone startled Shropham, who backed away with his hands in the air, apologetic for having said something out of turn. 'I only meant that he was a cheery sort of fellow, but if you say I am mistaken, then that is fair enough. I am sure he was perfectly sombre.'

'He was not sombre, either,' snapped Bartholomew. He disliked sycophants, and recalled with distaste Shropham's habit of never contradicting anyone. It was a curious trait for a scholar: they had been trained to argue, and were usually delighted to do so.

Shropham was becoming flustered. 'Perhaps he was both – merry sometimes, and grave the rest of the time. A man of contrasts. Yes, that must be it.'

'Actually, he was very even tempered,' countered Bartholomew, a little testily.

111

'Yes, he was that, too,' gushed Shropham, somewhat desperately. 'Very even tempered.'

Bartholomew smothered his irritation, knowing Shropham was only trying to make conversation; he was just not very good at it, and had chosen a subject that was too raw for idle chatter.

'You teach law?' he asked, deciding they might do better if they discussed something else.

'Yes,' replied Shropham. 'Except when I teach the Trivium – grammar, logic and rhetoric.'

'I know what the Trivium is,' said Bartholomew. He grimaced at his abrupt tone and wondered what it was about Shropham that seemed to be bringing out the worst in him. He struggled to make amends, forcing himself to smile. 'Which parts of it do you teach?'

'All of it,' replied Shropham. 'The other masters ask me to take their classes, and I do not like to disappoint – you know how senior scholars hate wasting their time with basics.'

'But *you* are a senior scholar,' Bartholomew pointed out, bemused. 'You have been here for years – before me, and long before Paxtone. You should not be saddled with the Trivium.'

'Perhaps I should not,' said Shropham, blushing furiously. 'But when friends approach me for assistance it seems churlish to refuse.'

'Right,' said Bartholomew, suspecting he was abominably abused by his so-called friends.

'Here we are,' said Shropham, opening Paxtone's door with obvious relief.

Paxtone's two light, airy chambers – one for teaching and the other for private use – overlooked the water meadows, and saw some spectacular sunsets. That day, however, the shutters were closed, and a fire was blazing

112

in the hearth, filling the private room with a warm, amber glow. The floor was of wood, but woollen rugs were scattered across it, and the walls had matching hangings, all selected with impeccable taste. Unlike Michaelhouse, not all King's Hall Fellows were obliged to share their accommodation with students, and Paxtone paid a hefty rent to ensure his continued privacy.

'He is teaching,' whispered Shropham, pointing through the door that linked the two chambers; three lads could be seen sitting on stools at Paxtone's feet. They were listening to his analysis of Galen's views on almonds as an astringent. 'He is one of the most inspired tutors in the College. Do you lecture on Galen, Doctor Bartholomew?'

'Of course,' replied Bartholomew, startled by the question – and by the notion that the staid Paxtone should be considered inspired. 'It would be impossible not to, because his theories are cornerstones of traditional medicine.'

'Then I must come to hear you some time. I am sure you will be equally good.'

Bartholomew frowned as Shropham fussed around him, ensuring his cloak was hung up neatly and that he was satisfied with the state of the fire. The lawyer was so determined that Paxtone's guest should sit in the chair by the hearth that he gave him a rather enthusiastic shove that saw him topple into it. Bartholomew winced when something dug into his leg.

'Is it yours?' asked Shropham, watching him pull a small knife from under his thigh. 'It fell out of your bag as you sat?'

'As I was pushed,' muttered Bartholomew. Shropham's obsequiousness was grating on his nerves. He took a deep breath and forced himself to be gracious. 'It looks like one of mine, but it is actually Paxtone's. We both use these plain steel blades, because they are easy to clean.'

'Perhaps he left it there to sharpen it – pointing north, so it will hone itself.' Shropham took it from him and set in on a shelf. 'Is this true north, do you think?'

'Move it to the left a little.' Bartholomew had all but forgotten the curious debate Paxtone had been airing with his colleagues earlier that day, and experienced an acute stab of grief when he recalled Wynewyk's amusement. He swallowed hard, and pursued the subject of knives in an effort to push the memory from his mind. 'Paxtone and I buy them from the same forge. They are the perfect size for delicate surgery and—'

'Paxtone would never demean himself by doing surgery,' interrupted Shropham indignantly. Then he blushed when he saw he had been insulting, and began to gabble in an effort to make amends. 'Not that surgery is degrading, of course, but he uses *his* blades for more lofty purposes.'

'Such as what?' asked Bartholomew innocently. The question was a little wicked, because Paxtone was forced into 'surgery' because Robin of Grantchester was no longer available to do it for him. It was likely therefore that the King's Hall physician *did* use his knives for cautery.

Shropham swallowed uneasily. 'Such as peeling fruit and paring his nails. Not sharpening quills, of course, because I do that for him.'

'Really? And what do his students do, while you perform these lowly tasks?' Bartholomew had not meant to sound rude, but the words were out before he could stop them. And he genuinely wanted an answer, bemused as to why a scholar of Shropham's seniority should act as servant to his equals.

But Shropham did not take the question amiss. 'I would not trust that rabble to see to his needs. And it is a great pleasure to serve a fine man like Paxtone.'

114

'I see,' said Bartholomew, deciding he had better not pursue the subject any further. It was too bewildering, and he had had a long and distressing day.

'He will not be long,' said Shropham, leaning forward to pat a cushion into place. 'Here is a psalter to occupy you while you wait. Unless you would rather I kept you company? There is nothing more important than ensuring Paxtone's acquaintances are properly looked after.'

'I see,' said Bartholomew, wondering whether Paxtone had acquired himself a jealous lover. But Paxtone had always seemed rather asexual, and on the few occasions when he had mentioned a preference, it was usually for Yolande de Blaston. 'I will read, thank you.'

Shropham bowed his way out of the room, and his footsteps clattered down the stairs.

'Christ!' breathed Bartholomew, when the man had gone. 'He is stranger than Clippesby!'

Bartholomew listened to Paxtone's lecture through the door for a while, but it was a basic one, delivered at a very early stage in his students' studies, and he knew he would learn nothing from it. He was not in the mood for perusing psalters, either, so he went to the books in Paxtone's private library, intending to read what Galen had written about nuts – and about men who laughed themselves to death.

The tomes were stored in a wall-cupboard, and Bartholomew had been told in the past that he could browse through them whenever he liked. He opened the door and began to read the titles, impressed by the extent of his friend's collection: books were hideously expensive.

He grabbed Galen's *On Temperament*, but could not find what he wanted to know, so he started to look for Aristotle instead, knowing the philosopher had addressed a number of curious medical questions. He did not recall laughter or nuts being among them, but it had been some time since he had studied the texts carefully, and he did not trust his memory.

He found the book he wanted and started to tug it out, but a small bag in front of it fell to the floor. There was a skittering sound as several pebbles rolled out. With a sigh, he knelt to retrieve them. They were some sort of white crystal, and he supposed they were a mineral deemed to possess a particular healing property. He had always been sceptical of such claims – for example that rubies could protect a person from plague – and assumed most sensible physicians thought the same. Of course, Paxtone was not always sensible where medicine was concerned.

'What are you doing?'

The sound of his colleague's voice so close behind him made Bartholomew jump. He had not noticed that Paxtone had stopped teaching and had come to see what was going on.

'Looking for Aristotle,' explained Bartholomew, slipping the last of the stones inside the bag.

'I see,' said Paxtone flatly, taking it from him and replacing it on the shelf. He bent to lock the cupboard with a key that hung on a string around his neck. 'And did you find it?'

'Yes – but I might look in Avicenna, if I cannot find what I want in Aristotle,' replied Bartholomew, somewhat puzzled by his friend's frosty manner.

'Then let me know when you need it.' Paxtone gave a pained smile. 'I shall not be long now.'

Bartholomew could only suppose Paxtone had been dabbling in something of which he was slightly ashamed

– perhaps a foray into folk medicine – and wanted to keep the matter quiet. But he did not dwell on the matter for long, because his mind was too full of Wynewyk.

He sat in the chair, and opened the Aristotle, but could find no mention of nuts, although there was a good deal about humour being good for the health. There was, however, nothing to suggest that it might bring about death, unless in delirium. Bartholomew frowned as he considered the notion. Had Wynewyk been delirious?

'They have gone at last,' said Paxtone, coming to flop into the seat opposite. 'They are full of questions, and I thought I would never prise them out. How is Risleye? Is he settling in with you?'

Bartholomew wondered why he should ask, given that the relationship between master and pupil had been acrimonious enough for both to want a transfer. 'He seems to have made himself at home,' he replied cautiously, unwilling to admit that he was finding the young man 'unteachable', too.

'He is a good boy, who learns quickly,' said Paxtone with a smile. 'He will be no trouble.'

'He must have been trouble, or you would not have asked me to take him on.'

Paxtone waved an airy hand. 'He is young and opinion-ated, while I am old and opinionated. It was not a good combination. Did Shropham offer you any wine?'

'No,' said Bartholomew. 'But I am sure he would have done, had I hinted that I was thirsty.'

Paxtone winced. 'Yes, I am afraid he does have a tendency to fawn. I cured him of a strangury, you see, and since then he has attached himself to me like a devoted dog. It is irritating, but he has his uses. You seem distracted, Matthew. Is something wrong?'

117

'You know how some folk have aversions to particular foods, which make them sick or give them rashes. Have you ever heard of a violent reaction to nuts?'

'No. However, nuts are not poisonous, and if you have a patient who claims to have been rendered unwell because of them, then I suggest you look to some other form of toxin.'

Bartholomew rubbed his eyes. 'Then is it possible for a man to laugh himself to death?'

'Of course, just as it is possible for a person to die of sadness.' Paxtone walked to the table, and filled two cups with wine. 'Unhappiness may cause a person to forget to eat, or render him susceptible to an imbalance of humours. It is very easy for emotions to bring about a death. But this seems a curious topic for a practical man like you. What has spurred this particular interest?'

'Wynewyk is dead,' replied Bartholomew. It was not easy to say the words, and they sounded unreal to his ears. 'He died eating a cake with nuts in it. While laughing.'

Paxtone's jaw dropped in horror. 'Oh, the poor man! How dreadful!'

'I do not suppose you would look at him, would you? To see if you can spot anything amiss?'

'Absolutely not!' exclaimed Paxtone with a shudder. 'You know I dislike handling corpses.'

Bartholomew did know, but had forgotten. He turned to another question. 'Wynewyk was with you earlier – you were debating how to sharpen knives. Did he complain of any illness or pain?'

'He seemed well enough to me.' Paxtone drained his wine, and when he set the goblet on the hearth, his hand was shaking. 'This is a shock. Poor Wynewyk! He told me he was thinking of purchasing some new law books this coming week.'

118

Bartholomew thought uncomfortably of the Michaelhouse accounts. 'Expensive ones?'

Paxtone shrugged with the carelessness of a man who never had to be concerned with such matters. 'I imagine so. However, Risleye told me that Wynewyk summoned you on Wednesday night. What were his symptoms then? The ailment may have been a precursor to his death.'

'It is possible,' acknowledged Bartholomew, wondering why Risleye should have been reporting such matters to his old teacher; he had been under the impression that they could not stand the sight of each other. 'He said he had sipped an almond posset, and mentioned a burning mouth. It led me to assume that even a small taste of nuts was capable of creating an imbalance of his humours.'

'And this is how you devised your theory about nuts being poisonous?' mused Paxtone. 'You think he ate more of them, and they killed him?'

'I have come across similar cases in the past. It is rare, but not unknown.'

'I suppose your Arab master taught you this,' said Paxtone, rather disparagingly. 'However, the ancient Greeks do not mention it, and it sounds a bit far-fetched to me.'

Bartholomew realised he was foolish to have imagined that Paxtone might help him. He liked the man, but he should not have come expecting a proper medical debate. He stood, thinking they were wasting each other's time, but Paxtone indicated that he should sit again.

'You said Wynewyk was laughing when he died?' Paxtone spread his hands. 'Then *there* is your cause of death. I put it to you that it was a seizure, induced by an excess of choler.'

'You are probably right,' said Bartholomew tiredly. 'The swelling in Wynewyk's throat might have been caused by a number of factors. I suppose nuts are not necessarily responsible.'

'It is always hard to lose a colleague,' said Paxtone kindly. 'But I can think of far worse ways to go than laughing myself to death.'

'Does laughter always equate with happiness?'

'Well, no,' said Paxtone. 'Hysterical cackles can mean quite the reverse – implying a person is distressed. You must have seen how easily smiles turn to tears in some of our more impressionable students, especially around the time of their disputations. However, you should not—'

Their discussion was interrupted by a sharp knock at the door, and Tobias entered.

'Constable Muschett is ailing again,' he said apologetically. 'He needs to be bled.'

Paxtone's face registered his distaste, and he turned to Bartholomew. 'I do not suppose you . . .'

'No,' said Bartholomew firmly. 'Phlebotomy is a procedure that carries more risk than advantage, as I have told you before.'

'The ancient Greeks disagree,' retorted Paxtone curtly. 'It is very beneficial, and I advise all my patients to have it done three times a year. Unfortunately, now Robin the surgeon is unavailable, I am obliged to do it myself. But there is no need for you to leave, Matthew. Stay and read my Aristotle. I will not be long, and we shall resume our discussion when I come back.'

Bartholomew had no wish to return to Michaelhouse, and was more than happy to sit in Paxtone's peaceful chamber. He did as his friend suggested, scanning Aristotle in search of any report of a man dying of laughter. He was on the verge of falling asleep when there was a knock on the door and Tobias entered again, this time with Cynric at his heels.

'I thought you might be here,' said the book-bearer. He sounded relieved. 'Brother Michael needs you. There has been a fight, and one of the brawlers is dead. You are needed to tend the wounded.'

CHAPTER 4

Bartholomew knew from experience that people injured in fights often fared better if he reached them before anyone else attempted to 'help'. It was frustrating to see a man die because he had been given all manner of potions to drink, but no one had bothered to stem the flow of blood. He ran down the stairs, and met Paxtone halfway up. The King's Hall physician was wiping his hands on a rag.

'Messy business, phlebotomy,' he said sheepishly. 'Thank God I wore an apron. What are you—'

'Brawl,' replied Bartholomew tersely. 'Will you come?'

He did not wait for a reply, but was aware of Paxtone turning to follow and was grateful; another pair of hands was invariably useful on such occasions. However, the portly physician could not hope to keep up with the rapid pace set by Cynric, and soon fell behind.

The book-bearer led the way to the Market Square. Night had fallen, bringing with it a drenching drizzle that seeped through cloaks and trickled down the backs of necks. It was miserable weather, and Bartholomew wished he was home in front of the fire. Others did not feel the same way, though, and a sizeable circle of onlookers had gathered at the scene of the incident.

Near the front, with the best view of what was happening, were a man and a woman. There was a space between them and the rest of the crowd, as if no one wanted to get too close. Idly, the physician wondered why – both were well

122

dressed, covered in jewellery and looked respectable – until he recognised Idoma.

'Osa Gosse and his sister,' muttered Cynric, nodding towards them. 'I suspect most of their finery belongs to someone else – not that their victims would dare complain, of course.'

Bartholomew regarded Gosse without much interest as he passed, more concerned with reaching the injured. A brief glance told him that the man causing such consternation was short and compact, quite unlike his hefty sibling. However, he shared her dead, shark-fish eyes and malign demeanour, and there was something in his confident, arrogant stance that indicated he was a cut above the average villain. Bartholomew was not amused when the fellow grabbed his arm, jerking him to an abrupt standstill. Cynric tried to come to his rescue, but was blocked by Idoma's substantial bulk.

'Your University has something I want,' said Gosse. He spoke softly, so no one else would hear. 'And I shall have it, no matter what it takes. It will be easier for everyone if you just give it to me.'

Bartholomew wrenched free. He had no idea what the man was talking about, but he was not about to engage in a discussion when there were people who needed his help. He took a step away, but a heavy hand fell on his shoulder and spun him around. This time, it was Idoma manhandling him.

'How dare you walk away!' Her eyes were cold and hard, and Bartholomew did not think he had ever seen a more malevolent expression. 'My brother is talking, so you will listen.'

'Tell your colleagues,' ordered Gosse, leaning close and treating the physician to a waft of bad breath, 'I *will* have what is rightfully mine, or the streets of your fine town will run with blood.'

More irritated than intimidated, Bartholomew pushed Gosse away from him. The man's eyebrows shot up in astonishment that someone should dare fight back. Then Cynric managed to dodge around Idoma and stood next to his master, hand on the hilt of his long Welsh hunting knife. Idoma started to reach for Bartholomew again, but stopped when Cynric's blade began to emerge from its scabbard.

'I do not like you, physician,' she whispered, pointing a finger at Bartholomew in a way he supposed was meant to be menacing. Then she turned and began to shoulder a path through the onlookers. Most people moved before she reached them.

'That is unfortunate for you,' said Gosse with a sneer, before turning to follow her. 'Because bad things happen to people my sister does not like.'

'You want to watch that scum, boy,' said Cynric uneasily, once the pair had gone. 'She is a witch, while he is a vicious devil, who would think nothing of slipping a dagger between your ribs.'

'Cynric is right,' gasped Paxtone, who had finally caught up. 'They are not folk you should have as enemies, Matthew. It would have been better to give them whatever it was they wanted.'

'But I do not know what they wanted. Other than for me to be frightened of them – which I am not.'

'Really?' asked Paxtone, impressed. 'Because they terrify *me*. However, if you go out on errands of mercy during the night from now on, I recommend you carry a sword. It is common knowledge that you are a skilled and deadly warrior, so you should be able to fend them off.'

Bartholomew gaped at him, not liking the notion that he, a man of healing, should have acquired a reputation for the military arts. He had certainly done nothing to warrant it. 'I am not a—'

124

'He was not very good before we went to France last year,' said Cynric, pleased by what he saw as a compliment. 'But then we fought in the battle of Poitiers, and he got a lot of practice.'

'Matt!' came Michael's urgent voice. 'What are you doing? I need you here.'

Bartholomew broke away from Paxtone and Cynric, and hurried to where Michael was waiting. The monk's latest deputy, Junior Proctor Cleydon, was there, too, a competent but nervous man who was anxiously counting the days until his term of office expired. He had told Bartholomew on several occasions that he did not think he would survive that long, given that the post was dangerous – and the arrival of Gosse and his formidable sister had done nothing to quell his unease.

It took Bartholomew no more than a moment to assess what had happened: a knife fight between two men. One lay on the ground with the weapon still embedded in his middle, while the other perched uncomfortably on an upturned crate and clutched his left arm with his right hand. Blood flowed between his fingers. Seeing immediately that the prone man was more in need of a priest than a physician, Bartholomew went to the one who was sitting. Michael's beadles – the men who kept order in the University – seemed to be more interested in the corpse than the survivor, so the body was well lit, but the injured man sat in shadows.

'I need a torch,' Bartholomew said, cutting away the victim's sleeve. When the lamp arrived, he focused on his work, aware that he needed to stem the bleeding as quickly as possible.

Meanwhile, Paxtone crouched next to the second victim, although his examination was confined to what he could see: he disliked handling corpses, and went to considerable lengths to avoid doing it. His aversion was based on the superstitious notion that touching bodies enabled poisonous miasmas to pass from the dead to the living. The belief reminded Bartholomew of the 'healing stones' in Paxtone's room, and his colleague's strange insistence that knives sharpened magically when they were left pointing north. Still, he supposed, what else could he expect from a man who thought the movements of remote planets had an impact on the health of an individual?

'There is nothing I can do here,' Paxtone announced after a moment. 'The fellow is quite dead, and there can be no dispute about the cause: a dagger in the stomach.'

'In the liver,' muttered Bartholomew, wishing anatomy was not forbidden in England. He was sure even Paxtone would benefit from knowing the precise locations of various organs.

'It is Carbo,' said Michael.

Bartholomew spared a brief glance at the body, and saw it was indeed the half-mad Dominican friar.

'Did you speak to Prior Morden about him?' he asked, not surprised Carbo had met an untimely end. He had seemed incapable of looking after himself, and the fact that he had seen Langelee attacked attested to the fact that he wandered about after the curfew had sounded.

'Morden was out when I visited the Dominican Friary,' said Michael. Then his voice became bitter. 'I was supposed to go back there this evening, but I let other matters distract me.'

Bartholomew could only surmise that the monk had not enjoyed his time with the College accounts.

'It hurts,' whispered the injured man weakly. Bartholomew looked up sharply, because the voice was familiar. As usual, it took him a moment to recognise the nondescript features, but his astonishment at the man's identity was nothing compared to Paxtone's.

'Shropham?' gasped the King's Hall physician. 'What in God's name are *you* doing here?'

'He is here murdering Dominican priests,' replied Cleydon when Shropham made no reply. 'He stabbed Carbo.'

There was a stunned silence when Cleydon made his announcement, the only sound being the crackle of torches and the low-voiced grumbles of onlookers as they tried to resist being moved on by beadles. The reek of burnt pitch filled the air, along with the stench of rotting vegetables from a nearby costermongery. The rain carried its own aroma, too, of fallen leaves, frost-touched grass and the swollen river; it reminded Bartholomew that winter was approaching with all its inherent miseries – cold feet, leaking roofs, ice in the latrines, and the kind of fevers that claimed the old and the weak.

'No!' exclaimed Paxtone, when he had recovered from his shock. 'Fellows of King's Hall do not go around murdering Dominican priests or anyone else.'

'I thought it was—' began Shropham. He swayed, and Bartholomew indicated that Paxtone and Cynric were to support him.

Fortunately, the injury was clean, and should heal quickly; Shropham would experience some pain and stiffness, but the prognosis was good. Then he glanced at the man's haunted face, and wondered whether it would matter. Shropham, like all scholars, had taken religious orders that would protect him from the full rigours of secular law, but the murder of a priest was a serious matter, and the Dominicans might call for him to be hanged.

'You had better tell me what happened, Shropham,' said

127

Michael, when he saw Bartholomew had finished suturing, and only bandaging remained. 'If you feel well enough.'

'He does not,' said Paxtone immediately. 'He needs to go home, where he can recover from this dreadful ordeal. It cannot have been easy, watching a priest slaughtered.'

'No,' agreed Shropham weakly.

'Are you saying you did not kill him?' asked Michael. 'That someone else is responsible?'

'That is not possible, Shropham,' said Cleydon quietly. 'You and Carbo were the only ones here when we happened across you. And you cannot deny that the knife poking from his belly is yours: you have none, and he holds his own in his dead hand.'

'I am not sure . . .' began Shropham. He swallowed. 'Perhaps he had two – and killed himself.'

Bartholomew regarded him uncertainly. The explanation was feeble, to say the least.

'Come, Shropham,' cried Paxtone, equally appalled. 'You must have more to say for yourself than that! Someone else was here, someone Cleydon missed in all this dark and rain. You were coming to this priest's aid because you saw him being attacked by ruffians.'

'Gosse,' suggested Cynric helpfully. 'He was here a few moments ago.'

'I cannot remember,' said Shropham dully. 'Perhaps Carbo fell on the knife by mistake.'

'Not from that angle,' said Bartholomew, who had seen enough wounds to be able to distinguish the more obviously deliberate from the accidental.

'Self-defence, then,' said Paxtone, sounding desperate as he appealed to his colleague to save himself. 'The Dominican was deranged, and did not know what he was doing. Priests often become unhinged if they spend too long fasting. It is a medical fact.'

'He has a point,' said Bartholomew to Michael. 'Carbo was not rational when we met him. He did not seem dangerous, but ailments of the mind often take unpredictable courses.'

'I do not know whether the Dominican was the type to starve himself for prayers,' said Shropham. 'I am not saying you are wrong, Paxtone – indeed, you are *never* wrong – only that I cannot verify it.'

'So, the priest was a stranger to you,' said Paxtone, refusing to give up. 'He approached you without saying who he was, and you struck out to protect yourself. It was an accident.'

'I am not sure,' said Shropham tiredly. 'Did you see those quills I left for you, Paxtone? They are the best out of the whole batch I sharpened today.'

Paxtone regarded him in disbelief. 'How can you be thinking about such matters now? Do you not see the seriousness of the situation? You are accused of murder!'

Shropham hung his head, and tears slid down his cheeks. Michael and Cleydon pressed him with more questions, but he refused to answer.

'Is there any reason why he should not be incarcerated, Matt?' asked Michael eventually, exasperated by the lack of co-operation. Like Bartholomew, he had been ready to give Shropham the benefit of the doubt, but the evidence of his guilt was overwhelming, and his bewildering silence was doing nothing to help. 'This wound will not kill him?'

'Let me take him home,' begged Paxtone. 'I promise he will not escape.'

'No,' said Bartholomew, not liking the notion of Shropham roaming free. He had read of cases where someone had committed murder then remembered nothing about it, and did not want Paxtone to be Shropham's next victim. 'Michael can lock him in the documents room in St Mary the Great. It is warm and dry, but secure.'

Paxtone was dismayed, and barely listened to Michael telling him the crime was as straightforward as any he had seen: Shropham's weapon was embedded in Carbo, and the Junior Proctor himself was able to say there was no one else in the Market Square when the victim was attacked. Shropham would almost certainly be found guilty of murder.

'I refuse to believe it,' said Paxtone, white-faced with horror as Cleydon led the prisoner away. 'Shropham has been in Cambridge for decades and has never shown any propensity for violence before. Why should he start now?'

'I wonder why he would not talk to us,' mused Bartholomew. 'It is almost as if he wants us to think he is guilty.'

'He was a soldier once,' said Cynric, who had been listening to the discussion from the shadows. When he spoke, everyone jumped, because they had forgotten he was there. Bartholomew knew he should not be surprised: since the year they had spent travelling overseas together, the Welshman had grown bold about offering his opinions where he thought they were needed. 'He fought in Scotland. Afterwards, he came here and became a lawyer.'

'Being a warrior does not make him a killer,' said Paxtone, while Bartholomew wondered whether King's Hall would have kept Shropham's military past quiet, had Cynric not revealed it.

'Of course it does,' countered Michael. 'That is what warriors do: they kill people. But why do *you* think he resisted your attempts to exonerate him?'

'Because he is injured,' snapped Paxtone. 'And shock has robbed him of his wits. When he recovers, he will provide you with an explanation that will make you sorry you doubted him.'

'Your loyalty commends you,' said Michael quietly. 'Did you ever meet this Dominican? Carbo?'

'Of course not,' replied Paxtone, turning to look at the dead man with distaste. 'I do not fraternise with hedge-priests. However, look at the cuffs on his sleeves – the Cambridge Black Friars do not wear theirs like that. *Ergo*, he is a visitor, which means Shropham has no reason to harm him. Fellows of the University do not go around stabbing strangers.'

'My experience as Senior Proctor tells me otherwise,' said Michael sombrely. 'I do not suppose you can throw any light on the matter, can you, Matt?'

Bartholomew crouched next to Carbo, grateful the beadles had finally ousted the ghouls, so he no longer had an audience. Carbo was no cleaner than he had been when they had met him in St Mary the Great, and his face was thin to the point of being skeletal. The physician was not surprised Paxtone assumed he had been fasting, and wondered if he was right.

'He died of a single knife wound that penetrated his liver,' he said, rinsing his hands in a rain-puddle before standing. They felt oily from touching the priest's habit, and he would have to scrub them before he went to bed. 'It would have killed him fairly quickly.'

'I had better go and tell Warden Powys what has happened,' said Paxtone. He sounded near tears. 'He will doubtless want to talk to you about keeping Shropham in King's Hall until we prove his innocence – which I am sure we will.'

'He cannot imagine a colleague being capable of murder,' said Michael, watching Paxtone waddle away. 'But Cleydon virtually watched the whole thing happen, and he has no reason to lie.'

* * *

131

Bartholomew woke later than usual the following day, because his students were aware that he had been out late and had taken care not to disturb him when they rose. He was a heavy sleeper at the best of times, and might not have stirred until noon had Michael not taken it upon himself to do the honours by hurling open the window shutters and clapping his hands.

'Shropham had a comfortable night,' the monk reported, sitting at the desk while Bartholomew tried to rally his sluggish wits. He cocked his head as a bell began to chime. 'Langelee is almost ready to lead us to church for Sunday prayers, so you had better get up or you will be late.'

The physician clambered out of bed, hopping across the icy flagstones on bare feet as he made for the bowl of water Cynric left him each night. He washed and dressed quickly, listening to Michael describe all he had done that morning. The monk made it sound as though he had been up for hours while his friend had been sleeping the day away.

'Is Shropham showing any sign of fever?' he asked, straightening his tabard as he followed Michael across the yard. They were the last to arrive, and Langelee immediately led his neat phalanx of scholars through the gate and up St Michael's Lane.

'None that I could see,' replied Michael, taking his usual place at Bartholomew's side. Something felt strange about the procession – a change in something deeply familiar – and Bartholomew was momentarily confused when he glanced behind him to see Thelnetham next to Clippesby, where Wynewyk normally walked. 'He is subdued, and refused the food my beadles took him, but that is understandable. Unfortunately, he still refuses to talk to us.'

'I will examine him again today,' said Bartholomew, trying to concentrate on what the monk was saying as grief

132

for Wynewyk washed over him. 'Perhaps he will tell me what happened.'

'I doubt it, but you are welcome to try. So is Paxtone, Warden Powys and anyone else who will make him understand that declining to co-operate with the Senior Proctor is not a good idea. Even a half-baked explanation will only result in exile, given that he can claim "benefit of clergy", but maintaining this ridiculous silence might well see him hanged.'

The Sunday mass was an unusually gloomy affair, and Bartholomew was not the only one who kept glancing at the spot where Wynewyk had always stood. Some of the younger students cried, and the physician was obliged to escort several home early. Risleye, Valence and Tesdale accompanied him, the latter two clearly struggling to control their own distress.

'Still,' said Valence, attempting a smile, 'at least he died happy. I would not mind going like that when my time comes – surrounded by friends, and laughing fit to burst.'

'Perhaps he did,' said Risleye with wide eyes. 'Burst, I mean. Perhaps his innards exploded, because of all the choleric humours that bubbled when he was so full of mirth. It is a pity we cannot anatomise him, because I would like to test such a hypothesis.'

For the first time ever, the physician found himself grateful that anatomy was illegal.

'Hippocrates says laughing is good for you,' said Tesdale. 'He says nothing about it making you explode.'

'I suppose you might be right,' conceded Risleye, then added rather salaciously, 'There was no blood. If Wynewyk had exploded, there would have been pots of blood.'

'Enough,' said Bartholomew sharply, aware that the graphic discussion was upsetting the younger students. 'He died happy, so let us say no more about it.'

'*Did* he die happy?' asked Risleye. 'Personally, I thought his guffaws had a strangely brittle quality to them – as if he did not really think the debate was funny, but could not help himself.'

'I said, enough!' snapped Bartholomew, although he found Risleye's observation an uncomfortable one. If Wynewyk had been agitated, then perhaps he *had* eaten the nuts deliberately, fearing his days of manipulating the accounts were numbered. Or was Bartholomew wrong to doubt his integrity?

'There is the breakfast bell,' said Valence, brightening at the prospect of food. 'It is Sunday, so perhaps there will be egg-mess, like there used to be before Wynewyk tightened the purse strings.'

'You cannot blame him for that,' objected Tesdale. 'It is hardly his fault that food prices have risen and students are slow in paying their fees – or run off without paying at all, like Kelyng. He did his best with what he had. Still, some egg-mess would be nice . . .'

The other students followed him to the hall, but Bartholomew did not feel like eating whatever Agatha had concocted, certain that eggs would not feature in it. And Risleye's remark about Wynewyk's 'brittle' laughter had unsettled him. He went to Langelee's room instead, and spent the time reassessing the College's finances. Surely he could find something to prove Wynewyk innocent?

When the meal was over, Michael came to find him. He saw what Bartholomew was doing, and cleared a space on one of Langelee's benches. Then he sat down and raised questioning eyebrows. Reluctantly, Bartholomew shook his head.

'I have uncovered nothing new. Just confirmed what we already knew – that the questionable transactions are for three commodities bought from Suffolk: coal, wood and pigs. But I am sure Wynewyk was not cheating us, Brother. There *must* be an explanation that will exonerate him.'

'So you keep saying. But I went through most of his personal papers this morning and found nothing to indicate what that explanation might be.'

'Then we must look harder. My students need to hear Theophilus's *De urinis* before I can give my next set of lectures, and Risleye has offered to read it aloud to the others. That means I am free to help you unravel this mess – and clear Wynewyk's name.'

Michael was pleased. 'And in return, I shall help you hunt down your lost pennyroyal. I know it pales into insignificance when compared to Wynewyk, but it is still a toxic substance, and I will feel happier when we have satisfied ourselves that it did not end up inside Joan.'

'I do not believe it did. Indeed, the more I think about it, the more I am convinced that there could not have been much left when I finished making the ulcer salve. Of course, it does not take much to kill a person . . .'

'Well, the more *I* think about it, the more I am afraid that it might have been stolen at the same time that something else went astray,' said Michael. 'Namely the Stanton Cups.'

Bartholomew frowned. 'Why would Gosse take pennyroyal? I own far more expensive substances than that – and far more dangerous ones, too. Foxglove, mandrake, poppy juice . . .'

'Even if he can read, he was probably in a hurry, and grabbed whatever he could reach.'

'Should I talk to him about it, warn him of its dangers?'

'That would be tantamount to accusing him of theft, and he will go crying to his lawyer about slander. Besides, if he does have it, your warning may encourage him to

135

feed it to someone he does not like. No, Matt. We must devise another way to ascertain whether he is the culprit.'

Bartholomew nodded acquiescence, although he was unsure whether or not to be concerned. *Was* his pennyroyal in Gosse's hands? Or had someone from Michaelhouse taken it to help with some innocent task, and was now too frightened to own up? The physician rubbed a hand through his hair, and turned to yet another cause for concern.

'Do the other Fellows know about the missing thirty marks yet?'

'Langelee told them after breakfast. Predictably, they are all very upset.'

'We could talk to Wynewyk's friends,' suggested Bartholomew. 'They may know what he—'

'*We* were his friends. He had acquaintances from other foundations – such as Paxtone and Warden Powys from King's Hall – but his *friends* were here, at Michaelhouse.'

Bartholomew tapped the accounts book with his pen. 'The inconsistencies only arise when he made purchases from Suffolk. As far as I can tell, he paid a total of eighteen marks for coal, seven for wood and five for pigs. But none of these supplies have been received.'

'I reached the same conclusion, and so did Langelee. Then I went back through the receipts and found the names of the three Suffolk men with whom he did business. Did you do that?'

Bartholomew shook his head. 'I just studied the figures.'

'The largest amount was paid to a man called Henry Elyan of Haverhill, who—'

'Elyan?' echoed Bartholomew, startled. 'But he is Joan's husband.'

'The woman who died of pennyroyal?' asked Michael. 'What a curious coincidence!'

Bartholomew's thoughts were reeling. 'Is it coincidence? Elyan came to collect his wife's body on Saturday, which is the same day that Wynewyk died.'

Michael considered the matter, but then shook his head. 'I am as bemused by this strange happenstance as you are, but it cannot be relevant. It is impossible that Elyan is involved in whatever happened to Wynewyk. First, he cannot have gained access to our College, and second, he is a stranger to our town, so not in a position to hire someone else to do it for him. Besides, I thought we had agreed that Wynewyk died of a seizure brought on by laughter.'

'We did not agree – *you* decided that was what we were going to tell people. However, the truth is that I have absolutely no idea why Wynewyk died. But to return to Elyan, do not forget that his wife travelled here with their household priest – Edith told me Neubold represented Elyan in his business dealings with King's Hall. In other words, he is not as much a stranger to Cambridge as you think.'

'He is, if he sends Neubold to do his work,' Michael pointed out. 'But we shall bear the possibility in mind. Meanwhile, there is another connection, too – Gosse's lawyer is also called Neubold. Of course, we do not know if it is the same man.'

Bartholomew frowned. 'If they *are* one and the same, then it raises another question – namely, why did a respectable lady elect to keep company with the kind of man who has felons as clients?'

'According to what Edith told me the day after Joan died, Joan simply took advantage of an opportunity to travel. She also said that Neubold failed to come when Joan was dying. That is odd.'

'Perhaps Joan was not the only one with friends here,'

suggested Bartholomew, wondering whether Neubold had taken the opportunity to avail himself of a Frail Sister; prostitutes were not very readily available to priests in small villages, and Neubold would not be the first cleric to take advantage of what a large town could offer.

The notion of Frail Sisters reminded Bartholomew of Matilde, and he tried to imagine what she would have said, had she heard of what Wynewyk stood accused. She had been fond of Wynewyk, and Bartholomew was sure she would have defended him.

'. . . message did not reach Neubold in time,' Michael was saying as the physician wrenched his thoughts away from two people he had loved and lost. 'Although I doubt Elyan was pleased when he learned Neubold had failed his wife. But we are moving away from the real point here, which is that Wynewyk wrote in our accounts that Elyan sold him coal.'

'But we do not burn coal. Did he mean charcoal? He uses the Latin *carbo*, which can mean either. And there is yet *another* coincidence: the Dominican whom Shropham killed was named Carbo.'

'I once had a black horse called Carbo, and so did two of my sisters,' said Michael tartly. 'If you start seeing links between the name of a mad priest and the items Wynewyk bought, we will never get to the bottom of this mess, because we will be distracted by irrelevancies. Besides, Carbo was not the man's real name.'

'No. It sounded as though it was one he had picked for himself,' Bartholomew agreed.

'Actually, he claimed God gave it to him. But to return to more important matters, the accounts tell us that Wynewyk made large payments to two more Suffolk men, as well as Elyan: d'Audley for wood, and Luneday for pigs.'

'D'Audley?' Bartholomew was growing confused. 'He is

138

Elyan's friend, who came with him to collect Joan's body and take it home.'

But Michael was not listening. 'It makes no sense,' he said, his voice a mixture of hurt and frustration. 'Wynewyk must have known he would be caught eventually, so why did he do it?'

'That is what we are going to find out,' vowed Bartholomew. 'He will have had his reasons.'

'I do not know what to think. On the one hand, I feel betrayed. On the other, I cannot help but feel you are right, and there must be an explanation. It makes me sympathetic to King's Hall, though: none of them believe Shropham is a killer, although the evidence says otherwise. Visit him, Matt. Now, this morning. Persuade him to tell you why he is putting his colleagues through this nightmare.'

Shropham had been moved to the proctors' gaol, a small, cramped building near St Mary the Great, and although it was not the festering hole used to secure prisoners in the castle, it was a dismal place nonetheless. When Bartholomew was shown into Shropham's cell, the King's Hall man was sitting disconsolately on the edge of a wooden bed. He had been provided with blankets, although he had made no effort to wrap them around himself. Bartholomew did it for him, after he had inspected the wound and found it healing well.

'It will be sore for a few days,' he said. 'And you will have to favour it for a while, until the muscles mend. Do you want anything to ease the pain?'

'I want something that will kill me,' whispered Shropham, looking at him for the first time since he had arrived. 'Something that will allow me to slip away without causing any more trouble.'

There were a number of ways a prisoner could take his own life in prison – he could hang himself from the bars on his window, cut himself with the knife provided for slicing up his meat, or drown himself in the water left for drinking and washing – and the fact that Shropham had not tried any led Bartholomew to conclude he was not serious.

'It would be a lot easier if you just told the truth,' the physician said practically. 'Carbo was not in his right mind, and while that does not give anyone the right to kill him, it might go some way towards explaining what happened. Your situation is not as hopeless as you seem to think.'

'It is,' said Shropham miserably. 'Brother Michael will put me under oath, and if I make up a tale to exonerate myself, I shall have to do it with my hand on the Bible. My immortal soul . . .'

'I said you should tell the truth, not lie,' objected Bartholomew. 'You must have a reason for what you did, so tell Michael, and let him help you.'

'No,' said Shropham in a low voice. 'I would rather die than . . . Are you sure you cannot give me something to end it all? It would be for the best.'

Bartholomew left feeling slightly soiled. Patients had pleaded with him to end their lives before, but they were usually dying of painful diseases, so their demands were understandable. He had never been asked to provide an easy way out for someone reluctant to tell the truth, and he had not liked it.

He was lost in thought as he walked down the narrow lane that led to the High Street. Shropham did not seem like a cold-blooded killer, but Bartholomew struggled to remember him each time they met, which underlined the fact that he really did not know him at all. For all he knew,

Shropham was a seasoned assassin, and this was just the first time he had been caught.

He glanced up when he saw a flicker of movement in the shadows ahead of him, then stopped when two figures materialised. They were Gosse and Idoma. Bartholomew sighed. He was not in the mood for a set-to with felons.

'Well?' Gosse asked, nonchalantly drawing his dagger and using it to clean his fingernails. 'Did you pass my message to your colleagues? About handing over what is rightfully mine?'

'It slipped my mind,' replied Bartholomew. 'Partly because I have no idea what you were talking about. What do we have that you think is yours?'

'Do not lie,' said Idoma, fixing him with her peculiar eyes. Involuntarily, he took a step backwards. Michael was right: there was something unpleasantly charismatic about her, something that had compelled him to move against his will. 'You know perfectly well what my brother means.'

'I assure you, I—' he began.

'Perhaps he is telling the truth,' said Gosse to his sister. 'One can never tell with scholars, slippery creatures that they are. But that is no excuse for failing to act as my messenger.'

He brought his gaze back to the physician, who slid his hand inside his medical bag and let his fingers close around his childbirth forceps. They were reassuringly heavy. The implement had been a gift from Matilde, and he wondered what she would say if she knew he used it more often as a weapon than he did to assist pregnant women. He was sure she would not approve, and rightly so.

'But we shall give him another chance,' Gosse was saying softly. 'Because we are generous.'

Idoma scowled, and Bartholomew was under the

141

impression that she had hoped for a more violent end to the encounter. He recalled the rumour that she was insane, and thought the tale might well have some basis in fact; that day, everything about her bespoke barely suppressed aggression, from the odd twitching of her ham-sized hands to her peculiar eyes.

'Give it back,' she snarled. 'Just tell them that.'

'Give what back?' asked Bartholomew, tightening his grip on the forceps.

'Someone will know,' replied Gosse enigmatically. 'And you can tell that monk something else, too. He will make no more disparaging remarks about us. If he does, he can expect to hear from our lawyer.'

'He is not the only one to associate you with certain . . .' Bartholomew decided at the last moment that 'crimes' would not be a wise choice of words '. . . certain *incidents*, and—'

'Then you can pass them the same message,' declared Gosse. 'To keep their slanderous opinions to themselves. But we have wasted enough time here, Idoma. Come.'

He spun on his heel and stalked away. Idoma watched him go, and when she turned back to the physician, there was a curious and far from pleasant expression on her face. Bartholomew forced himself to meet her eyes, fighting a deeply rooted instinct that clamoured at him to take to his heels. It was Idoma who looked away first. Unhurriedly, she turned and began to follow her brother. For someone so bulky, she had an uncannily light tread, like a large predator. Bartholomew leaned against the wall the moment she had passed out of sight, aware that his heart was racing furiously.

He asked himself what it was about the pair that had inspired such a reaction – he was not a timid man, and they had not said or done anything overtly frightening.

142

Had he been wrong to dismiss the notion that Idoma dabbled in witchcraft? Or were they just two powerful bullies who knew how to use the force of their personalities to good effect? Regardless, he was glad they had gone.

Michael's eyes narrowed when Bartholomew told him what had happened, and the physician was hard pressed to stop him from assembling his beadles and going to tackle the Gosses there and then.

'They did nothing wrong,' said Bartholomew. 'Other than exude an air of menace, and I do not think that is illegal. If it were, you would be obliged to arrest yourself, because it is an art you have honed to perfection when dealing with recalcitrant undergraduates.'

Michael grimaced. 'That is different – I am on the side of right and justice. The Gosses are not.'

'How many burglaries have you attributed to them now?' asked Bartholomew, changing the tack of the subject slightly.

'Seven – all in the wealthiest Colleges and hostels. But there is not a single witness, which means they are both cunning and skilful. Unfortunately, they are confining themselves to the University; the townsfolk have not had to suffer their depredations. And the burgesses intend to keep it that way, which is why they are making it difficult for me to investigate.'

'You think they have an agreement?' asked Bartholomew uneasily. 'That the Gosses will restrict themselves to scholars' property, as long as the town keeps *you* in check?'

'I do,' said Michael. 'Constable Muschett virtually told me as much. Normally, I would treat his orders with the contempt they deserve, and go after the Gosses as I see fit. But he has the backing of *all* the burgesses, and I cannot antagonise them *en masse*, especially as Dick Tulyet is not

143

here to calm troubled waters. There are too many delicate trading arrangements at risk.'

Bartholomew was not very interested in commerce. He began to think about Gosse's mysterious words. 'What does he want from us? He kept saying we have something that is rightfully his.'

Michael raised his hands. 'How can the University have anything that belongs to thieves from Suffolk?'

Bartholomew returned the gesture. 'Scholars travel, Brother. And some of them hail from Clare – the home of the Gosses is a large settlement, complete with castle and priory.'

'I know that, but I checked our registers, and no one currently enrolled in the University comes from there. There were three last year, but they have left. I can state, quite categorically, that we have no association with Clare at the moment.'

'Then what did Gosse mean? What does he want from us?'

'You may be looking for logical answers where there are none to find. As I have told you before, Idoma is not quite sane – her demand may be the product of a deranged mind.'

Bartholomew regarded the monk doubtfully. 'I am not so sure, Brother. I was under the impression that she *and* Gosse think we have some specific item that they believe belongs to them. Neither sounded confused to me.'

Michael waved a dismissive hand. 'Well, we do not have it, whatever it is. I have already asked all seven Colleges and hostels whether any of their members have been to Clare recently, but none have. I repeat: there are *no* connections between these felons and their Cambridge victims.'

'Perhaps you had better pass their request to our colleagues, anyway,' suggested Bartholomew. 'Or they may corner someone else – someone who does not carry child-birth forceps in his bag, and who might be rather more intimidated by them.'

Michael agreed. 'Very well. You know, Matt, I have met many scoundrels since becoming a proctor, some of them extremely dangerous. But I do not think I have ever encountered anyone who unsettles me to the same extent as Idoma. There is definitely something sinister about her.'

Bartholomew frowned. 'There is, but I cannot decide what. It cannot just be her shark-fish eyes; there is something else, too. Could it be that she is extremely large?'

'Possibly. I grabbed one of her arms when I interviewed her once, and it was like gripping iron – she is strong as well as sizeable. You should steer clear of her and Gosse from now on. I have my beadles to protect me, but you are often out alone.'

'You think they could best me?' asked Bartholomew, smiling. 'A deadly veteran of Poitiers?'

'It is not funny,' said Michael sternly. 'You are a fool if you underestimate the threat they pose.'

'I do not underestimate them. But equally, I will not let them unnerve me again – it is what they want, and I do not intend to play that game. But Wynewyk is more important than them, and it is time to bury him. Come, or we will be late.'

The weather suited the occasion as Michaelhouse's scholars gathered outside the church. The clouds were a dense, unbroken grey, and rain fell in misty veils, blown this way and that by a determined wind. In their uniform black cloaks and tabards they formed a sombre group as they processed to the grave, accompanied by no sound except the tolling of a bell. Once there, Bartholomew listened to the sorrowful, moving eulogy delivered by Clippesby, and found

145

himself inventing all manner of improbable explanations that would see Wynewyk absolved of any wrongdoing. When Clippesby had finished, the servants lowered the coffin into the ground.

'He might as well be buried at sea,' muttered Thelnetham – the drizzle had formed a deep puddle at the bottom of the grave. 'Still, perhaps it will serve to quench the fires of Hell, because that is where he is bound. God does not approve of men who cheat their colleagues.'

'We should wait until we have all the facts before condemning him,' said Bartholomew coldly. Thelnetham was a relative newcomer, so what right did *he* have to judge Wynewyk?

'If you say so,' replied Thelnetham, adjusting the hood of his Gilbertine habit to keep the rain from his eyes. 'But if he was innocent, why did he go to such lengths to conceal what he was doing?'

'This is neither the time nor the place for such a discussion,' chided Langelee, raising a hand to prevent the physician from responding. 'Save your opinions for the Statutory Fellows' Meeting tomorrow afternoon, where the matter will be aired in full.'

A number of people, including Chancellor Tynkell, a contingent of soldierly ex-lovers from the castle, and a small group of scholars from King's Hall, had come to pay their respects at Wynewyk's graveside. Hospitably, Langelee invited them back to the College for wine and honey cakes. Among the guests was Warden Powys.

'Thank you for tending Shropham last night, Bartholomew,' he said quietly. 'It is a dreadful business, and I agree with Paxtone that there will be some rational explanation for what has happened. I have known Shropham for years, and he has never been violent before.'

'He is malleable, though,' said Bartholomew. 'He told

me he runs errands for the rest of you – teaching classes you dislike, sharpening your quills . . .'

'He is not *made* to do those things,' said Powys, a little defensively. 'He pesters us until we agree to let him. We do not feel entirely comfortable with it, but it seems to make him happy. And we are all busy men, so you cannot blame us for taking advantage of what is freely offered.'

'Why does he do it?' asked Bartholomew. It was odd behaviour for a senior scholar.

'I really have no idea. And it has been going on for so long that I no longer give it any thought.'

'Did you ever meet the Dominican he killed? Carbo?'

Powys grimaced at his choice of words. 'No, I had never seen Carbo before. And I took several Fellows to view his corpse in the Black Friars' chapel today, but they did not know him, either. Prior Morden says Carbo is not one of his own people, so he must be a visitor. *Ergo*, there is no reason for Shropham to have . . .' He waved his hand, not sure how to describe what had occurred.

'If there is an explanation, Michael will find it,' promised Bartholomew, seeing the unhappiness in the Warden's face, and sympathising. It was how he felt about Wynewyk.

'I visited Shropham earlier,' said Powys miserably. 'But he declined to talk to me. What is wrong with him? Could he have a brain fever?'

'He does not seem ill,' said Bartholomew doubtfully. 'Just tired and sad.'

Powys's expression was pained. 'Paxtone may have to contest your opinion about that, if the Black Friars clamour for him to be hanged. The murder of a priest is a serious matter, and a plea of insanity may be the only way to save him. We do not want him executed.'

Bartholomew watched him move away, wondering to what lengths he would go to save his colleague. Would

Michaelhouse do the same for Wynewyk? Would a tale be invented to explain the missing money, which would absolve him from any wrongdoing? He rubbed his head, and wished with all his heart that Wynewyk was alive to explain himself.

When the guests had gone, Langelee decided the rest of the day was to be dedicated to lessons, despite the fact that it was Sunday, when learning was usually suspended.

'We must resume the semblance of normality as soon as possible,' he said, looking around at his Fellows and ignoring the fact that teaching on the Sabbath was not normal at all. Then, in one of his legendary leaps of logic, he added, 'I do not want it said that Wynewyk was the victim of foul play.'

'Why would anyone say that?' asked Michael suspiciously.

'Because Bartholomew informed Paxtone that Wynewyk was poisoned,' Langelee replied, shooting the physician a pained glance. 'Warden Powys just told me.'

'I said nothing of the kind,' objected Bartholomew indignantly. 'I mentioned Wynewyk's aversion to nuts, but Paxtone said it was excessive hilarity that carried Wynewyk away: he thinks it brought about a fatal imbalance of humours.'

'And which of these two theories is correct?' asked Suttone worriedly.

'I do not know,' replied Bartholomew. 'I thought the almonds had killed him at first, but perhaps Paxtone is right and it *is* too outlandish a—'

'He died of a seizure brought on by laughter,' said Michael firmly. He glared at the physician. 'It is what we agreed, and it is what we shall tell anyone else who asks.'

'Well, he had a lot to laugh about,' said Langelee bitterly. 'Thirty marks successfully stolen.'

'Perhaps God struck him down,' suggested Thelnetham.

'I imagine He does not approve of thieves who gloat over their spoils, especially ones who do it in front of their victims.'

'I do not believe that,' said Clippesby, bending down to pick up the College cat, which had come to wind itself around his legs. 'Wynewyk did not steal from us – he was our friend. And, if it is not too much to ask, I would rather no one voiced uncharitable thoughts about him until Brother Michael has proved his innocence. Which I know he will.'

'Our students are waiting,' said Langelee, bringing an abrupt end to the discussion. 'We shall take their minds off this dismal occasion with lessons, and Michael can resume his enquiries into Wynewyk's crimes tomorrow.'

It was late by the time the Master decided the students had been taught enough that day, by which point their heads were spinning and their masters were exhausted. Agatha had cooked pea pottage for supper, but it was full of peculiar lumps – she claimed they were apple, but they were hard and tasteless, and Bartholomew suspected they were the cattle fodder that had mysteriously gone missing the previous week.

'Wynewyk has a lot to answer for,' muttered Michael, glowering at his bowl. 'We made good money from the sale of Sewale Cottage last summer, and we also have a tidy income from renting out the shops we bought from Mistress Refham. We should be living like kings, not eating this slop.'

'And that is something we should have thought about weeks ago,' said Bartholomew tiredly. 'The quality of food has been declining for months and Agatha is always saying she does not have enough money to make ends meet. We should have guessed far sooner that something was amiss.'

149

Michael glowered at him. 'I hope you are not suggesting that it is *our* fault Wynewyk stole from us? That had we been more vigilant, it would not have happened?'

Bartholomew shrugged. 'Why not? It is true. We all noticed the decline in the quality of meals, and we all complained. But none of us bothered to investigate.'

'That is complete and utter nonsense!' exploded Michael, loudly enough to draw disapproving glances from his colleagues. Talking at meals was overlooked if done discreetly, but yelling was not. He lowered his voice. 'It did not occur to me to investigate, because it did not occur to me that a colleague – a man I liked and trusted – would cheat us.'

'Enough, Bartholomew,' said Langelee, when the physician opened his mouth to reply. 'I told you at the churchyard – save your opinions for the Statutory Fellows' Meeting tomorrow. Our students have long ears, and I do not want them overhearing something we would all rather they did not.'

He had a point, and Bartholomew did not want Wynewyk to become the subject of scurrilous rumours. He turned his attention to the pottage and found himself glad the rigours of the day had robbed him of his appetite, because it was almost inedible and certainly lacking in any nutritional benefit. He was not the only one who toyed listlessly with it until the servants took the dishes away.

When Langelee had said a final grace in his appalling Latin, which, as usual, entailed leaving out words he did not like the look of or substituting for them ones of his own devising, the Fellows adjourned to the conclave, leaving the hall to the students. Neither gathering was very merry.

'I will ask the rats about the accounts, Brother,' offered Clippesby. Bartholomew could see a whiskery nose protruding from the Dominican's sleeve, and hoped he had not brought one to the conclave. He did not mind most of Clippesby's 'friends', but he drew the line at rats. 'They have an eye for figures, and will prove Wynewyk was doing no wrong.'

'You think everyone is good, Clippesby,' said Michael. He made no comment about the rats' fiscal abilities – he had learned it was best to leave such declarations unchallenged, because acknowledging them invariably resulted in a rash of theories and remarks that should have seen the Dominican incarcerated for his own safety. 'But the world is a wicked place.'

'People are wicked,' corrected Clippesby. 'Animals are not. Incidentally, the spiders did not see anyone steal your pennyroyal, Matt. You asked me whether I knew anything about it.'

'Lord!' breathed Thelnetham. He was still not used to Clippesby, and found him unsettling. 'You talk to spiders? I thought you confined yourself to creatures with fur or feathers.'

'Spiders have fur,' averred Clippesby. 'Next time you meet one, have a closer look.'

Thelnetham shuddered and made no reply.

Bartholomew was usually tolerant of Clippesby's idiosyncrasies, far more so than the other Fellows, but he was not in the mood for them that night. He made his excuses to Langelee, and left the College. He was worried about his sister, and wanted to make sure she had not mounted her own investigation into Joan's untimely death.

'I cannot stop thinking about her,' said Edith without preamble when he arrived. She was sitting by the fire, shivering, even though the room was hot. 'She *was* murdered. Why will you not believe me?'

Bartholomew regarded her unhappily. 'You have let her husband's claims unsettle you. Elyan was upset and angry, and said things he did not mean. You heard what his grandmother—'

'He is right to be suspicious. Someone gave Joan pennyroyal, encouraging her to drink it by saying it would strengthen her blood or some such nonsense. She took it in good faith, and died for her trusting nature.'

'But she did not know anyone in Cambridge,' Bartholomew pointed out reasonably. 'Other than you. Why would she drink a potion offered by a stranger?'

Edith glared at him. 'If *you* gave me a tonic, telling me it would benefit my well-being, I would swallow it without question. So would any of your patients, whether they are intimately acquainted with you or not.'

'You think a physician hurt her?' Bartholomew was shocked. 'Paxtone or Rougham? Or me?'

'Of course not, but there are plenty of other folk who dabble in matters of health – witches, wise-women, midwives, apothecaries and even priests. Perhaps one of them did it.'

'But why? Joan came to Cambridge to buy ribbon. Surely she cannot have made enemies—'

'*She* did not have enemies. But Elyan might have done – perhaps someone wanted to ensure he never had his heir.'

'So the culprit followed Joan all the way from Haverhill, with the express purpose of damaging her unborn child?' asked Bartholomew doubtfully. 'That does not sound very likely.'

'Or perhaps the priest did it,' Edith went on, ignoring him. 'Neubold. Why else would he fail to come to her deathbed? Because *he* killed her!'

'Easy,' said Bartholomew, thinking she was letting her

imagination run riot. 'No one killed Joan, and there will be a perfectly rational explanation for the absence of this cleric.'

'How do you *know*?' demanded Edith angrily. 'You have no idea what kind of life Joan lived in Haverhill. She and Elyan might have accrued some *very* dangerous foes.'

'Did she mention any?'

'No,' admitted Edith. 'But perhaps she was oblivious to the malice they bore her. She was a kind, loving person, always eager to see the good in people. She even said nice things about Osa Gosse, and we all know he does not deserve it.'

'She knew him?' asked Bartholomew uneasily, thinking about Michael's notion that Gosse might have stolen the missing pennyroyal.

'She recognised him as an inhabitant of Clare, which is not far from Haverhill, apparently. They exchanged words.'

'Hostile ones?'

'No. It was mostly pleasantries about the weather and Cambridge's pretty churches, but then Gosse began to hint that he wanted her to buy *him* some Market Square trinkets – for his sister, he said. He is not poor, and I did not see why she should buy him anything.'

'Then what?' asked Bartholomew, when she paused.

'It does not matter,' said Edith, looking away. 'You have enough to worry about.'

'Then what?' repeated Bartholomew.

Edith sighed. 'I shall tell you, but it really was nothing, and I do not want you doing anything you might later regret. Gosse and Idoma frighten me, and—'

'Edith!' said Bartholomew, exasperated. 'What happened next?'

Edith sighed a second time. 'I took her arm and pulled her away, to bring an end to the discussion. Gosse objected,

presumably because he thought Joan was about to capitulate, and he . . . found a way to express his disappointment.'

'How?' asked Bartholomew, feeling anger begin to boil
inside him. It was one thing for Gosse to corner him in
secluded alleys, but another altogether to pick on his
beloved sister.

Edith took his hand. 'It was nothing, Matt. He grabbed
a handful of mud and threw it. But it contained pebbles,
and hurt when it struck my head.'

'He lobbed stones at you?' demanded Bartholomew, fury
erupting. He stood abruptly, with the wild notion of racing
out to find Gosse there and then, and showing him what
happened to thieves who dared harm Edith.

'Pebbles,' she corrected. She indicated he was to sit again
while she finished her tale. 'I complained to Constable
Muschett, but he said there was nothing he could do
because there were no witnesses. But there *was* a witness
– Valence saw what happened.'

'My student?' asked Bartholomew, startled. 'He
mentioned none of this to me.'

'I ordered him not to, because I knew how you would
react. Meanwhile, Muschett said Valence did not count as
a witness, because of the Stanton Cups – he thinks
Michaelhouse will go to any lengths to get them back,
including accusing Gosse of other crimes, to discredit him.'

'Muschett thinks we are dishonest? That we would lie?'
Bartholomew was offended.

'I shall be glad when Sheriff Tulyet comes home,' said
Edith, ignoring his questions. '*He* will not be intimidated
by Gosse. Did you know the Frail Sisters often see Gosse
prowling the streets at night? And that the next day there
is always a burgled College or hostel? It is obvious he is
the culprit, but everyone is too timid to challenge him.'

'Because he won a lawsuit against the town,' explained

Bartholomew, deciding not to ask how she was acquainted with what prostitutes did. He was sure her husband would not approve if she had decided to take up where Matilde had left off, and act as their advocate. 'The burgesses were obliged to provide compensation, and no one likes paying the villain who stole from them. I imagine most people would rather stay low until he moves on.'

'I do not blame them – and I do not want *you* tackling him over what I have just told you, either. I mean it, Matthew. And if I hear you have disobeyed me, I shall be very angry.'

Bartholomew smiled, recalling similar words issued when he had been a child. He was no longer six years old, but he still did not want Edith angry with him.

She smiled back, then patted his hand. 'But to return to Joan, I doubt Gosse is the one who harmed her, because I cannot imagine *he* knows what pennyroyal can do.'

'What about Idoma?' asked Bartholomew. He closed his eyes, and wished he had not asked. He wanted Edith to think she was wrong about Joan, and the way to do it was not by posing questions that would make her reassess what she knew of the Gosse family.

'She is too stupid to know about poisons,' replied Edith with a dismissive sniff. 'But *someone* harmed Joan – I am sure of it. And I am tempted to ride to Haverhill and tell Elyan so.'

'Please do not,' begged Bartholomew. 'If you are right, then Joan's killer will not be very happy to see you, and you will put yourself in danger.'

'But I cannot sit here knowing that my oldest friend is dead by foul means, and do nothing about it,' cried Edith, eyes filling with tears. 'It is not right!'

'I will ask Michael to investigate,' promised Bartholomew. The monk would not appreciate being volunteered for such a task, but the physician did not know how else to stop her. 'He needs to speak to Elyan anyway, because Wynewyk bought coal from him.'

He did not tell her that most of the transactions appeared to be illegal on Wynewyk's part, and that the money passed to Elyan – if it was ever received – was for goods that had never been delivered.

Edith was silent for a while. 'Very well,' she said eventually. 'If Elyan does have enemies who might strike at him through his pregnant wife, then Michael is the man to see justice done.'

CHAPTER 5

The following day was wintry, with low clouds in the sky and a biting cut to the wind. Bartholomew was summoned in the small hours by a patient who had poisoned himself by drinking a lot of bad ale. When Isnard the bargeman had recovered enough to be left, the physician returned to the College, hoping to snatch a little sleep before the day began, but Cynric was waiting with a message from Chancellor Tynkell, who had one of his stomach upsets – something the physician felt would not happen if the man washed himself occasionally.

Afterwards, as he was near, he decided to visit Shropham in the proctors' gaol, and found himself glancing around uneasily as he walked. Then he recalled how Gosse had thrown stones at Edith, and half wished the felon would appear, so he could mete out a little justice with his fists. He was not normally prone to violent urges, but he hated the thought of anyone harming his sister.

'Living in the elegant comfort of King's Hall has made me soft,' said Shropham, looking up when Bartholomew was shown into his cell. 'I do not think I have ever been so cold. Will you give me something to make me sleep? Poppy juice, perhaps? I will need a lot of it, because—'

'No,' said Bartholomew firmly. He knelt next to Shropham and examined his arm. It was healing fast and cleanly, although Shropham did not greet the news with much pleasure. 'You have spent two nights in captivity now. Surely, it is time to tell Michael what happened?'

'I *have* told him. I do not remember – it was dark and difficult to see.'

'Well, which was it?' demanded Bartholomew archly. 'If you cannot remember, how do you know it was dark and difficult to see?'

'It was night,' replied Shropham flatly. 'It is always difficult to see at night.'

'Did you know Carbo?' asked Bartholomew, recalling that Shropham was a lawyer, so trying to catch him out was likely to be a waste of time – he would know how to weasel his way out of any careless slips of the tongue.

'No, but I saw him gazing at King's Hall on several occasions.'

'Gazing?' echoed Bartholomew curiously. 'Why would he do that?'

'I have no idea, and neither will my colleagues. They do not fraternise with hedge-priests, as I am sure they have said. But please do not ask me anything else, because I do not want to talk about it.'

'Let Michael help you,' urged Bartholomew, seeing the man's inner agony. 'It is obvious something is badly amiss, so tell him what he needs to know and let him investigate the matter.'

Shropham opened his mouth, and for a moment Bartholomew thought he was going to capitulate. But then his lips set in a grim line, and he shook his head. 'There is nothing to say. But I am very cold, and my arm aches. Give me something to ease the pain. Something strong.'

Bartholomew made an innocuous tonic of feverfew and mint, and asked the beadles to give the prisoner more blankets. He also warned them to watch him, although he doubted Shropham would kill himself with any of the means currently at his disposal. Did that mean he would not stab a priest, either? Bartholomew was not sure what

158

to believe, and walked slowly back to Michaelhouse, wondering what dire secret Shropham carried – and whether King's Hall shared it, and was willing to let him hang rather than have it made public. College loyalty ran deep, and it would not be the first time a Fellow had sacrificed himself to protect the foundation he loved. He found himself thinking about Wynewyk, who had been devoted to Michaelhouse, and became even more convinced that his colleague would never have done anything to damage it.

When he arrived home, he was startled out of his morose reverie by Risleye and Tesdale, who were arguing over who was to read *De urinis* to their classmates that morning. It entailed work, so Tesdale thought Risleye should do it, while Risleye was protesting that he had done the honours the last time.

'While you two have been squabbling, Deynman has pre-empted you.' Bartholomew indicated the hall with a nod of his head. Through the window, the Librarian could be seen, pacing back and forth with a book in his hand. Deynman was not a gifted academic, and the physician dreaded to think of how he was mangling the text, no doubt rendering it all but incomprehensible.

Tesdale beamed. 'Good! Reading is *such* a chore, and—'

'It is not good at all,' interrupted Bartholomew. 'I asked one of you two to do it.'

Risleye grimaced. 'It is not our fault he sneaked in. He gave up medicine when he became Librarian, so he is not supposed to teach. He knows reading to the juniors is our responsibility.'

'He does,' agreed Tesdale. 'But he cannot accept that he is no longer your student. He often asks for access to your storeroom. We refuse, but he sometimes slinks in when we are not looking.'

Bartholomew stared at him. 'Why would he do that? And why have you not mentioned it before?'

Tesdale shrugged. 'He declines to say – he merely informs us that he is Librarian, and thus immune to interrogation by students. And I did not mention it before because I forgot until now.'

Bartholomew supposed he would have to speak to Deynman and demand to know what he thought he was doing. He could not imagine why the Librarian should want to take pennyroyal, but with Deynman, anything was possible.

'Go to the hall and make sure he reads the correct passages,' he said tiredly. 'And if he fails, I am holding you two responsible; if you had not been bickering, he would not have stepped into your shoes.'

'That is unfair!' cried Risleye angrily. 'It is not our fault that—'

'We will do our best,' said Tesdale, jabbing his less-prudent classmate with his elbow. He blew out his cheeks in a sigh. 'It will not be easy to wrest the tome from him, though – he likes books.'

Michael had heard Bartholomew's voice from his room upstairs, and came down to speak to him. He pulled a disagreeable face as he watched the two pupils walk away.

'It seems to me that virtually anyone can get inside your storeroom,' he said reprovingly. 'You claimed originally that it was just Tesdale and Risleye, but now we learn Deynman has been there, too – and he was "promoted" to Librarian specifically to keep him away from toxic medicines.'

There was no defence to the accusation, and Bartholomew saw he would have to be a lot more careful about his security arrangements in future.

'I visited Shropham,' he said, changing the subject before

the monk could admonish him further. 'He is recovering well, but still refuses to explain what happened on the night Carbo died.'

'Carbo,' mused Michael. 'We still know nothing about him, other than the fact that he was a Black Friar who was not in his right mind. It is time we remedied the situation, so we had better visit the Dominican Friary – see what Prior Morden has managed to learn about the fellow. Are you ready?'

Bartholomew looked out of the window without enthusiasm. It was raining again. 'Now?'

'Yes, now! There is a mystery surrounding this priest's murder, and I mean to find out what it is. I refuse to let Shropham hang, just for the want of a little probing.'

'You think Shropham is innocent, then?'

'There is insufficient information to allow me to judge,' replied Michael pompously.

'I thought you said this was as straightforward a case as any you have seen.'

'I have changed my mind.' Michael's expression was haughty. 'And I need your help, because I am feeling overwhelmed. Besides Carbo's murder, I am expected to explore Wynewyk's transgressions, find Langelee's attacker, devise a way to retrieve the Stanton Cups, and locate your lost pennyroyal.'

'I am investigating the pennyroyal myself.'

'But not very effectively, for you still do not know what happened to it, and it has been four days since you noticed its disappearance. Do not look sour, Matt. It is true.'

Feeling somewhat chastened, Bartholomew followed him across the sodden courtyard to the gate. He was surprised to see Walter using the thicker, heavier of the two bars to secure it – the porter usually favoured the lighter one during the day, as it was easier to handle.

'It is to keep Gosse out,' Walter explained. 'I am not having him in *my* College again.'

'Do you think he might pay us another visit?' asked Bartholomew, surprised.

'Yes I do – he got the Stanton Cups last time, so he probably thinks there are other rich pickings to be had,' said Walter grimly. He bent down to pick up his peacock, rubbing its head with a calloused finger. It crooned at him, and Bartholomew saw the affection between them was mutual. 'I reckon he stole my bird's tail, too. For a long time, I assumed *you* were the culprit, because you said in a lecture that peacock feathers can cure aching joints. But now I begin to wonder.'

'I mentioned a superstitious belief to that effect,' corrected Bartholomew, not for the first time. 'But then I went on to explain how there is no evidence that it works, and—'

'Gosse would think nothing of hurting a bird,' interrupted Walter, lost in his own bitter reflections. 'He came to Cambridge because Sheriff Tulyet is away, you know. He would not have dared show his face if our Sheriff were here.'

'Then you will just have to rely on the Senior Proctor to see justice done,' said Michael grandly, brushing a speck of mud from his elegant cloak.

Walter looked him up and down disparagingly. 'I suppose we will,' he muttered. 'God help us.'

To reach the Dominican Friary, Bartholomew and Michael had to pass through the guarded entrance to the town known as the Barnwell Gate, then travel along a road called the Hadstock Way. And after the village of Hadstock, Bartholomew thought as they walked, the highway went on to Suffolk, where Elyan and d'Audley lived.

162

'I told Edith you would look into Joan's death,' he said, recalling his promise to his sister. 'I know you are busy, but it was the only way I could stop her from mounting her own investigation.'

Michael was mystified. 'I thought you said it was an accident or suicide. Or has Edith learned that you were careless, and wants to know whether it was *your* supplies that killed her friend?'

Bartholomew winced. 'She believes Joan was provided with pennyroyal by someone who meant her harm – or to deprive Elyan of his heir. I think she is wrong, but . . .'

'But you would rather I meddled with a distant landowner's dangerous enemies than your sister,' finished Michael flatly. 'Very well. I shall tell her enquiries are under way – which they are, because I want to know exactly who has been in your storeroom. I do not like Risleye.'

Bartholomew regarded him uneasily, uncomfortable with the juxtaposition of the two remarks. 'You think he took it?'

'Two days ago, I would have said no one at Michaelhouse is a thief, but Wynewyk's treachery has given me pause for thought. And I have been wary of Risleye ever since Paxtone foisted him on you. He said he could no longer teach the lad because of irreconcilable personal differences, but I am sceptical; you do not abandon a bright student when one more year will see him graduate.'

Bartholomew was not sure where the discussion was going. 'You think Paxtone sent Risleye to Michaelhouse for a reason other than teaching?' he asked, bemused. 'Such as what?'

Michael shrugged. 'To spy. Risleye told Paxtone that Wynewyk summoned you for a cure on Wednesday night. Now why would he do that, if they find each other's company so objectionable?'

'It would have been a casually passed remark when they happened to meet in the street,' replied Bartholomew, regarding him askance. 'It is hardly enough to warrant accusations of espionage!'

'If they like each other enough to exchange gossip, then why did Paxtone part with Risleye in the first place?' demanded Michael. 'And do not say Michaelhouse has nothing Paxtone could possibly want, because it has you: he has always been jealous of your success.'

'Lord, Brother!' breathed Bartholomew, stunned by the turn the conversation had taken. 'You have been Senior Proctor too long, because you see intrigue where there is none. I imagine he gives daily thanks he is *not* me, with my destitute patients, over-full classes and unconventional theories.'

'Well, just bear my warning in mind,' said Michael coolly. 'And if it transpires that Paxtone *did* send Risleye to you for reasons other than education, then do not say I did not warn you.'

They walked in silence through a soggy, dripping landscape. To their left lay the boggy expanse of Barnwell Field, in which a flock of grey-brown sheep grazed, jaws working rhythmically as they watched the scholars pass. To the right was the fetid snake of the King's Ditch. When they reached the powerful walls of the Dominican Friary, Michael knocked on the gate and asked to see the Prior.

Prior Morden was tiny, with legs and arms in perfect proportion to his elfin torso. He was sitting at a table in his handsome solar, chair loaded with cushions to raise him to a functional height; Bartholomew recalled his sister making similar arrangements for him when he was a child. Morden's legs swung in the space below the seat, clad in minute knee-high boots.

'I have learned nothing new, Brother,' he said, wincing

as the monk threw open the door so hard that the latch hit the wall with an ear-splitting crack. 'I still do not know who Carbo was, or where he came from. I assume that is why you are here? To ask me about him?'

Michael plumped himself down on a bench, heavily enough to make it tip. He squawked in alarm as it threatened to deposit him on the floor, flailing his arms in a wild attempt to regain his balance. To his credit, Morden did not laugh, although Bartholomew saw an amused twinkle in his eyes, which was suppressed the moment the monk recovered his composure and began to glare.

'We have a number of questions,' said Bartholomew, before the monk could accuse Morden of deliberately placing unstable furniture where unwary guests might use it. The charge would probably be justified, because the Black Friars were notorious for indulging their slapstick sense of humour. Bartholomew did not mind, and had always liked Morden, but Michael considered him a buffoon, and his manner towards the diminutive Prior often verged on the contemptuous.

'Fire away, then,' said Morden amiably, sliding off his chair and landing with a slight thump. He walked across the room and filled two goblets from a jug. 'I shall do my best to answer, but do not hold your breath. As I said, I have met with scant success.'

'Did Carbo hold a post in Cambridge?' Michael accepted the proffered goblet, and downed the contents in a single swallow. Then he gagged. 'God save us, man! What is this? It is not wine.'

'It is a little something my brethren and I enjoy on cold mornings,' replied Morden, and if he thought the monk's response was entertaining, he hid it well. 'Fermented parsnip juice.'

Michael shoved the goblet back at him with distaste.

'I thought you were being hospitable, but now I feel as though my innards are being scoured with drain cleaner.'

'It will do you good,' said Morden ambiguously. 'And the answer to your question is no: Carbo did not hold a post in Cambridge. He was an itinerant, as far as I can tell – a wandering preacher who follows the road. It is odd that a respectable man like Shropham should want to kill him.'

'I am not sure he did.' Michael shrugged at the Prior's surprise. 'As you say, it is an odd thing for a scholar of King's Hall to do, and I feel there is something we are not being told.'

'Shropham is holding out on you?' asked Morden, his interest piqued.

Michael nodded, frowning as he assembled his thoughts. 'He could have argued self-defence, or claimed that the real culprit ran away before my Junior Proctor arrived on the scene. But instead he refuses to speak. I cannot imagine what kind of secret is worth his life: he may very well hang if we let matters lie.'

'Perhaps that is what he wants,' suggested Morden. 'Some folk find shame difficult to handle.'

'Shame?' queried Michael. 'What are you talking about?'

'Perhaps he has done something to embarrass King's Hall, and sees death as the only honourable recourse. He is certainly the kind of man to sacrifice himself for his College – he is always trying to ingratiate himself by performing menial tasks for his colleagues, after all.'

'If he is that devoted, he would not have done anything to discredit King's Hall in the first place,' Bartholomew pointed out.

'We all make mistakes,' said Morden. 'It would not be the first time a good man has erred.'

'Is Shropham a good man?' mused Bartholomew, more

166

to himself than the others. 'I have known him for years but I have no idea what he is really like.'

'Yes, I believe he is essentially decent,' replied Morden. 'At one point, he was considering taking major orders, and we spent several weeks discussing it. In the end, he decided to remain a secular, which disappointed me. He would have made a fine Dominican.'

Michael's expression suggested that a fine Dominican did not necessarily equate with a decent man, but he said nothing, and moved to another subject. 'So what *have* you discovered about Carbo?'

'We have been unable to ascertain his origins, despite summoning all Black Friars within a ten-mile radius to come and look at him. The cuffs of his habit are odd, though, and the style is unfamiliar to us. They suggest he hails from somewhere distant, perhaps London or Norfolk.'

'What about Suffolk?' asked Michael.

Morden raised his tiny eyebrows, surprised by the question. 'Yes, possibly. Other than that, all we have are guesses. His habit was patched and frayed, which *may* imply he took holy orders some time ago. Of course, it might also mean he inherited a second-hand robe from another priest.'

Michael stood. 'Drink your parsnip juice, Matt, and let us go and inspect this hapless fellow.'

Bartholomew swallowed the concoction, feeling a strong but not unpleasant burn as it made its way to his stomach. He experienced a moment of agreeable light-headedness, followed by a sensation of warmth all over his body. Morden was right: the beverage did dispel the chill of winter.

Bartholomew and Michael followed the Prior across the yard, to the chapel in which Carbo's body was being stored. It had been washed and dressed in a clean habit, ready to be laid to rest as soon as the proctors released it. While

Bartholomew began his examination, Michael regaled the Prior with details of the upcoming Blood Relic debate. The monk was looking forward to the occasion, eager to show off his prowess as a disputant; Morden, by contrast, was dreading it, afraid he might be called on to say something, thus exposing his poor grasp of the subject in front of the whole University. He had never been a gifted academic.

'Have you had any word from Kelyng?' Morden asked, more to change the subject than to elicit information about Michaelhouse's missing Bible Scholar. 'He was thinking of becoming a Dominican, too, and I was disappointed when I learned he had failed to return for the start of term.'

'We suspect he was intimidated by his unpaid fees,' replied Michael. 'It is a pity, because he was an excellent student, and might have gone on to great things. And I do not mean by becoming a Black Friar, either – I mean by making contributions to philosophy.'

'Or camp-ball,' countered Morden waspishly. 'He was Langelee's student, and your Master would much rather study game strategies than Aristotle.'

'Perhaps Carbo was not a priest at all,' said Bartholomew, to prevent Michael from responding with a retort that might lead to a spat. It was true that Langelee preferred sport to lessons, but Morden was hardly the person to be making snide remarks about it. 'Maybe he found or was given the Dominican habit, and wore it because he was a beggar who had nothing else.'

'And your evidence for such a suggestion?' asked Michael.

'This,' replied Bartholomew, pushing the lank black hair from Carbo's forehead to reveal a pink scar that curved around towards the left temple.

'So he suffered a cut on his head at some point,' said Michael, bemused. 'What of it?'

'From the colour of the scarring, I would say it happened in the last two years or so. And it was a serious injury – there is a depression of the skull beneath, suggesting a healed fracture. People with damage to the front of their heads often exhibit the symptoms we saw: an inability to communicate, strange behaviour, paralysis of the limbs. One hand moved jerkily, if you recall.'

'Not really,' said Michael, unconvinced. 'But—'

'Then there was the way he kept shaking his head, as if to clear his ears.' Bartholomew was disgusted with himself for not making the diagnosis when Carbo was alive. 'Hearing a persistent ringing sound is another symptom. So is confusion about smells – he asked twice if we could detect garlic. I should have understood immediately what was wrong with him.'

'But why does all this make you think he was not a Dominican?' asked Morden, puzzled.

'Because your Order would have taken better care of a member who had lost his senses after such an injury,' said Bartholomew. 'He would not have been allowed to wander the country alone, without food or shelter. And poor Carbo is badly malnourished.'

'It is possible, I suppose,' conceded Michael, although he sounded doubtful. In his mind, there was nothing unusual about a poorly fed, half-mad Dominican. 'However, Shropham must have killed him for a reason, so I suspect he was more than just a vagrant.'

'Carbo witnessed Langelee being stabbed,' began Bartholomew tentatively. 'Do you think he was killed by our Master's assailant – perhaps to keep the culprit from being identified?'

'Shropham attacked Langelee as well as Carbo?' asked Morden, regarding him in confusion.

'Of course not,' said Michael. 'And Carbo was killed two

169

days *after* the assault on Langelee, when he had already been interviewed about what he had seen – it would have been like locking the stable door after the horse had bolted. *Ergo*, I do not think the two incidents are connected.'

Bartholomew reconsidered. 'Then perhaps he witnessed a different event – one Shropham did not want him sharing with anyone else.'

'Shropham is not the kind of man to resolve awkward situations with violence,' objected Michael, and the physician saw he was beginning to persuade himself that there was going to be an exculpatory explanation for what had happened – one that would see Shropham exonerated.

'He might if it were to protect his College,' averred Morden. 'And I understand it was his knife that was embedded in Carbo's belly.'

'True,' acknowledged Michael. 'But let us not forget that Carbo had a dagger, too – despite the fact that friars are not supposed to carry weapons – and it was in his hand when my Junior Proctor found him. That suggests a fight, not an ambush. Where *is* Carbo's blade, Morden? Do you have it, or did it go astray amid all the confusion?'

The Prior opened a wall cupboard, and handed the monk a sack that contained Carbo's few possessions. There was his frayed habit, a pair of ancient boots, an empty purse and the dagger. The knife was made of base metal, and was stained with blood, although whether it was Carbo's own or Shropham's was impossible to say.

Bartholomew unrolled the habit and inspected it, noting the huge stitches that repaired a tear in the hem. An ungainly patch had been attached near the hip, too. Yet when Bartholomew looked on the inside of the garment, the material was sound – the patch was not there to mend damage. Frowning, he looked closer, and realised its real purpose was to act as a place in which to conceal a

170

document; he could feel parchment crackling under his fingers. Prior and monk watched with interest as he slit the stitches to retrieve it.

'That is cunning,' said Morden admiringly. 'No one would ever think of investigating a patch. Well, no one who is not a Corpse Examiner, that is.'

'What is it, Matt?' asked Michael eagerly. 'A secret message?'

'A letter,' replied Bartholomew, spreading the document on the table. It was thin and friable, as though it had been read and reread until it was almost worn away. The words were faded, and the ink had run, but it was still just about legible. 'From someone's mother.'

'Whose mother?' demanded Michael. 'Carbo's?'

Bartholomew shot him a look that asked how he was supposed to know. 'And there is something else here, too. A piece of coal.'

Michael took the rock from him. 'Perhaps it is ballast, to stop his habit from flying up in the wind and revealing his nether-garments. I sew pieces of metal into my hems for the same purpose.'

'It is too light to prevent embarrassing revelations,' said Morden, studying it as it lay in Michael's palm. 'Perhaps it is an amulet. Many folk believe certain stones hold magical or healing powers.'

'Carbo kept mentioning coal when we interviewed him,' Bartholomew pointed out. 'And his name is Latin for the stuff. He must have developed a fetish for it, so I do not think we should read too much into finding a lump of it in his clothing.'

'Let me see the letter,' ordered Michael, elbowing Bartholomew out of the way. The light was good, but the monk still squinted. 'Damn people and their tiny writing! Read it aloud, Matt.'

Bartholomew obliged. '*My Son and Friend. God's Greetings*

171

and wishes of Good Health from your Loving Mother. The Withersfield Pigs are strong and Fine this year, and I wish you could See them, for I think they would make you Well again. I think of you Always.'

'Is that it?' asked the Prior, disappointed. 'A message about pigs from a doting dam? I would not think it worth-while to hide such a thing. Why not carry it openly?'

'Perhaps it is code,' suggested Michael hopefully, picking it up and turning it this way and that. 'There must be some reason why it was concealed.'

'You both know friars are not supposed to hoard mementoes from their past lives,' Bartholomew pointed out. 'So it is not really surprising that Carbo hid this one.'

'True,' Morden sighed, beginning to head for the door. 'But interesting though this is, I must return to my duties. If I do not order more fuel today, my brethren will freeze in the coming winter – and it promises to be a hard one. You can see yourselves out.'

Michael opened his mouth to object – he had no wish to be abandoned with a corpse – but closed it when Bartholomew began to speak. The physician's attention was on the letter.

'Withersfield,' he said thoughtfully. 'One of Wynewyk's odd transactions was with Withersfield. It is in Suffolk – the next village to Haverhill, where Elyan lives.'

Michael nodded. 'Wynewyk bought pigs from a Withersfield man called Luneday – beasts which also happen to be the subject of this curious missive. Does this mean there is a connection between Wynewyk's dealings and Carbo's murder? That makes no sense!'

Bartholomew frowned. 'No, it does not. However, just because we do not understand the association does not mean we should dismiss it. After all, both Wynewyk and Carbo died on the same day – Saturday.'

But Michael shook his head. 'We have no evidence that the two of them ever met.'

'We have no evidence they did *not* meet, either, and you have always distrusted coincidences. Here we have a murdered priest carrying a piece of coal and a letter mentioning Withersfield, while Wynewyk bought pigs from Withersfield and coal from Haverhill – the latter from Elyan, whose wife Joan is also dead in unusual circumstances.'

Michael shook his head again, denying the relevance of the connections Bartholomew was making, but there was a glint in his eye that indicated he was intrigued by the possibilities.

'It is a pity we cannot tie Gosse into this, too,' the monk said. 'Then we would solve all our problems, and a good many people would be grateful to us.'

'Give it time,' said Bartholomew, thinking about Edith's contention that Gosse had lobbed stone-laden mud at her and Joan. 'You never know.'

'There is only one thing we can do,' argued Michael, speaking at the Statutory Fellows' Meeting that afternoon. They were discussing what should be done about the missing thirty marks – wisely, Langelee had postponed any formal discussion of Wynewyk's activities until the first rush of indignation had passed and his Fellows were in more reflective frames of mind. 'We must conceal our erstwhile colleague's thievery at all costs.'

The Master was presiding over the assembly. He toyed restlessly with his sceptre, a hefty piece of brassware that symbolised his authority: it was tapped on the table in front of him to announce the beginning and end of official gatherings. Suttone and Hemmysby, who sat nearest to him, flinched as it was tossed recklessly from hand to hand, while Thelnetham had already moved, making it clear *he* was not going to be brained by Langelee's agitated fidgeting. Meanwhile, Clippesby was more interested in the hedgehog in his lap than in anything his colleagues were saying, and Bartholomew was struggling to stay awake after spending so much of the previous night with patients.

'Why must we hide what Wynewyk did, Brother?' asked Hemmysby, calm and reasonable. 'What can be gained from dissembling? Surely it is better to be truthful?'

'Being truthful would make us a laughing stock for trusting our coffers to a villain,' Michael pointed out tartly. 'The other Colleges would never let us forget our gullibility.'

'That is true,' agreed Suttone. 'No good can come out of making this public.'

'Wynewyk did one decent thing, though,' said Thelnetham. 'He died – he fell on his sword, as the Romans would have said. Of course, it would have been polite to leave us with an explanation.'

'Wynewyk was not a thief,' said Bartholomew, for at least the fourth time since the meeting had started. Clippesby nodded agreement, but the others merely rolled their eyes or shook their heads. 'I cannot imagine why you are all so ready to condemn him.'

'We are ready to condemn him because the evidence says we should,' snapped Thelnetham. 'I do not think I have ever encountered a more clear-cut case of a man defrauding his friends.'

'Thelnetham is right, Matt,' said Michael, more kindly. 'Wynewyk's death *is* convenient for all concerned. It means he is not obliged to suffer our hurt indignation, and we are free to deal with his crimes as we see fit – which is by ensuring that no one outside this room ever comes to hear about them. It sounds callous, but his demise is a blessing in many ways.'

Bartholomew tried not to look at Langelee. The Master's previous life as the Archbishop of York's henchman meant he was used to finding permanent solutions to sticky problems, and while there was no evidence that he *had* taken matters into his own hands, Bartholomew did not understand why – or even how – Wynewyk had died, and was confused and unhappy about the whole affair.

Unfortunately, Langelee guessed what he was thinking, and an offended expression crossed his face. 'You suspect I had something to do with his end! Well, I did not. If I had, we would not be sitting here talking about his misdeeds, because you would know nothing about them – I would have kept them from you, so you would never know I had a motive for his murder.'

Thelnetham frowned as he tried to grasp the convoluted logic. He shrugged when he found he could not, and turned to Bartholomew. 'I do not think the Master harmed Wynewyk, Matthew – not when he has the most to lose from this death.'

Langelee's eyes narrowed in suspicion. 'I do? And why is that, pray?'

'Because you are the one who gave him the keys to our coffers. Now he is roasting in Hell, *you* bear the responsibility for what he did – his wicked betrayal of our College.'

Langelee scowled, and the sceptre was tossed a little higher. 'As I recall, we all voted for him to take over the finances. It was a joint decision.'

'Yes, but it was on the understanding that he would discuss everything with you first,' said Michael. 'By relinquishing all control, as you did, you virtually invited him to defraud us.'

'I disagree,' said Bartholomew hastily, seeing Langelee's face darken. 'We all trusted Wynewyk, and I still think we were right to do so. There will be an explanation—'

'Oh, there will be an explanation,' interrupted Thelnetham bitterly. 'And I can tell you what it is right now: Wynewyk was a greedy dog who feathered his own nest at our expense.'

'Then where is the money?' demanded Bartholomew, resenting the fact that Thelnetham was so eager to condemn Wynewyk; he was, after all, the Fellow who had known him for the least amount of time. 'It is not in his room, because you have all searched it.'

'He gave it to a friend,' Thelnetham snapped back. 'One of his lovers. God knows, I like the company of a gentleman myself, but at least I do not favour ruffians. I was appalled by some of the louts he entertained – men *I* would not have deigned to notice.'

There was an uncomfortable silence, and Bartholomew was not sure whether the observation said more about Wynewyk's choice of partners, or Thelnetham's unappealing snobbery.

'Well, I do not believe it,' said Clippesby eventually, setting the hedgehog on the table and scratching his hands. Bartholomew recalled reading somewhere that hedgehogs were full of fleas, and felt himself grow itchy. 'Wynewyk's dishonesty, I mean. Could it be poor accounting? His arithmetic was lacking?'

'Unfortunately not,' replied Michael. 'He definitely used College money to purchase goods we never received. For example, since August he has passed Henry Elyan eighteen marks for coal.'

'But we never use coal,' Suttone pointed out, puzzled. 'And eighteen marks is enough to fuel a furnace – which we do not have.'

'Exactly,' said Michael. 'And he gave Hugh d'Audley, Elyan's neighbour, seven marks for wood.'

'That is a lot of timber,' mused Thelnetham. 'But our

sheds are virtually empty, and he told me only last week that we need to fill them before winter sets in. He said he was worried about where the money would come from, and I was sympathetic. What a scoundrel!'

'And finally,' said Michael, 'he paid Roger Luneday of Withersfield five marks for pigs.'

'Are there any other irregularities?' asked Suttone.

'One or two,' replied Michael. 'But the payments to Elyan, d'Audley and Luneday make up the bulk of the missing money. Those transactions total thirty marks.'

'Does anyone know these men?' asked Thelnetham. 'I have never heard of them.'

'I met Elyan and d'Audley when they came to collect Elyan's dead wife,' replied Bartholomew. 'I do not know Luneday, though. Do you think they were blackmailing Wynewyk for—'

'You are grasping at straws,' interrupted Thelnetham curtly. 'No one was blackmailing him. However, it would not surprise me to learn that he did not provide these Suffolk men with anything – that he has been pocketing the money for himself.'

Uncomfortably, Bartholomew recalled Paxtone's tale about Wynewyk's plan to buy new law books. But he did not believe the two could be connected, and stubbornly pushed it from his mind.

'Perhaps he chose Haverhill and Withersfield because they are so far away,' suggested Suttone tentatively. 'They are difficult to visit, so it will not be easy to verify what is going on. If I am right, I imagine he was horrified when Elyan arrived in Cambridge to claim a dead wife.'

'Hah!' exclaimed Thelnetham triumphantly. '*Now* I understand what happened.'

'What?' asked Langelee warily, when the Gilbertine paused for dramatic effect.

'Think about it for a moment,' said Thelnetham. 'Elyan collected Joan's body on Saturday, which is the day Wynewyk died. So, I put it to you that our felonious Fellow spotted Elyan in town, and was terrified that he was about to be exposed. He attended the debate, but was so agitated that he began to laugh wildly – and this false hilarity brought on the seizure that killed him.'

'It is medically possible, I suppose,' conceded Bartholomew, when everyone turned to look at him. 'But—'

'Damn the man!' cried Langelee suddenly, bringing his sceptre down with such force that splinters flew. All his scholars jumped in alarm, and Hemmysby, who was closest, put his head in his hands and made a whimpering sound. 'How could he leave us in such a wretched mess?'

'Because he was a selfish brute,' said Thelnetham, before anyone else could speak. 'And I am glad he is dead, for we are well rid of him. But we should not squander any more of our precious time debating what happened to him, because I, for one, do not care. We should concentrate on deciding what to do about our missing thirty marks.'

'Oh, I know how to resolve that,' said Langelee, inspecting the damage to the table with a puzzled frown, as if he could not imagine how it had happened. 'Michael and Bartholomew will go to Suffolk, meet Elyan, d'Audley and Luneday, and ask if they have our money. And if they do, they will demand it back again.'

That evening, Bartholomew went to visit Isnard the bargeman, to see whether he had recovered from the bad ale that had made him so sick the night before. He took Risleye, Valence and Tesdale with him, because the rota said it was their turn, although they were not very pleased – they were hoping to win a rather more interesting case.

'I made a few enquiries about your missing pennyroyal,' announced Risleye, as they walked along the towpath towards Isnard's house. 'You were alarmed when you first learned it had gone, but you have paid it scant attention since, and it is too important a matter to neglect.'

Bartholomew felt his jaw drop. The lad was right: he should have spent more time assessing what had happened to the stuff – but it was not for a student to scold him about it, and he was on the verge of issuing a sharp reprimand when Valence spoke.

'Your "enquiries" are nothing of the sort, Risleye. They are accusations without foundation.'

'They are conclusions based on logic,' Risleye flashed back. He turned to Bartholomew. 'I have deduced that a servant is responsible. They have free access to every part of the College, and some of the substances in your room are worth a lot of money.'

'Servants would not steal from a master,' countered Tesdale. Then he frowned. 'Would they?'

'Sadly, some people will do anything for money,' said Risleye. He glanced archly at his classmate. 'Including you, Tesdale, so do not look so shocked. I know who made a whole two shillings from the sale of a remedy that had peacock feathers as a key ingredient.'

'That was you?' asked Bartholomew, dismayed.

'No, it was not!' declared Tesdale, but his face was red and he would not meet his teacher's eyes. 'I would never touch that nasty, greasy creature. It bites, for a start.'

'You wore gloves,' flashed Risleye. 'I saw you.'

'How could you, Tesdale?' cried Valence, appalled. 'That poor bird! How *could* you?'

Bartholomew closed his eyes, and supposed he would have to apologise to Walter for mentioning the superstitious cure, thus encouraging a callous student to profit from it.

'They will grow again,' said Tesdale sullenly. 'No harm was done – and it was an experiment, in the name of science. I wanted to conduct an empirical test, to ascertain the efficacy of—'

'You wanted the two shillings,' interjected Risleye. 'And you cannot—'

'Stop,' said Bartholomew tiredly. 'If you persist in squabbling, you can go home.'

'Really?' asked Risleye keenly. 'Does this mean we can claim the next case on the rota instead, then? It must – we have not seen Isnard yet, so this "visit" cannot count.'

'Not so fast,' ordered Bartholomew, as all three young men started back the way they had come. 'I want you to take a sample of Isnard's urine, and assess whether you think he needs more charcoal to balance his excess of yellow bile.'

The students rolled their eyes, but followed him to the bargeman's riverside cottage without further complaint. Isnard had made a miraculous recovery, given that he had been so wretchedly sick the night before. He was up and talking to Yolande de Blaston, who was known to supplement the family income by working as a Frail Sister. Bartholomew often wondered whether she might not have had fourteen children had she confined herself to the marriage bed.

Yolande was cooking something over the hearth, although the rumpled bedcovers suggested she had provided her professional services first. Bartholomew marvelled at the bargeman's capacity for regeneration, certain such violent vomiting would have laid most other men low for days.

'Good evening, Doctor,' smiled Yolande. 'Would you like some stew? It contains real meat – something Michaelhouse rarely sees these says, according to Agatha. She says you are destitute.'

'You seem better, Isnard,' said Bartholomew, ignoring the remark. He had gone out to escape College affairs, and did not want to discuss them with Yolande.

'Much better,' affirmed Isnard with a contented grin. 'I am a little weak, but Yolande knows how to cope with a fellow's temporary shortcomings. She is far more inventive than the other whores.'

'Even though the twins are not long born, I am forced to work again,' explained Yolande, while Bartholomew hoped she would not notice the way the students were sniggering at the bargeman's blunt confidences. She had a fiery temper. 'Food is dear, and we are worried about the winter.'

'I will help,' offered Isnard. 'Especially if you do *that* again. I have never experienced anything quite like it. It is expensive, of course, but quality always costs, does it not, Doctor?'

'I suppose it does,' said Bartholomew, wondering what she had done.

Isnard seemed to think he knew anyway, because he addressed the three pupils. 'Never think you can keep secrets from your master, because he can read your innermost thoughts.'

'Can he?' asked Tesdale uncomfortably. He blushed furiously, and Bartholomew supposed he had allowed his imagination free rein as the bargeman had waxed lyrical about Yolande's talents.

'Oh, yes,' said Isnard. 'If I tell him I was in church when I was in a tavern, he always knows.'

Bartholomew tended to know about Isnard's drunken revelries because either they were the talk of the town, or he reeked of ale; there were certainly no uncanny abilities involved. But he saw his students would learn no new medicine now the bargeman was on the mend, so he

181

indicated they could go. Risleye had the audacity to wink conspiratorially on the way out, clearly of the opinion that they were being dismissed so the physician could learn what Yolande had done for Isnard. Bartholomew did not know whether to be amused or irritated by the presumption.

'I was sorry to hear about Wynewyk, Doctor,' said Yolande, when the students had gone. She ladled stew into three bowls, and indicated that Isnard and Bartholomew were to join her at the table; evidently, her contract with the bargeman entailed being fed for her labours. 'He was a good man, although he was never one of my regulars – I only saw him occasionally.'

'Did you?' asked Bartholomew, startled. 'I thought he preferred men.'

'Oh, he did,' said Yolande. 'But we all like a bit of a change from time to time.'

To stop himself wondering whether Wynewyk had financed his frolics with Yolande by cheating Michaelhouse, Bartholomew concentrated on the stew instead. It was delicious, and he realised how much he missed decent food. Matilde had been an excellent cook, and had often fed him when the College was going through one of its lean phases. As usual, thoughts of his lost love deprived him of his appetite. He set down his spoon.

'I have never heard of anyone dying of laughter before,' said Isnard, grabbing the physician's bowl and finishing it himself. 'Does Brother Michael not think Wynewyk's death suspicious?'

'It brought on a seizure,' explained Bartholomew hastily, aware that Isnard and Yolande were both rather keen on gossip. 'It is sad when it happens to a man in his prime, but it is not unknown.'

'It is odd he talked to that priest, though,' said Yolande. 'Now *he* is dead, too.'

'What priest?' asked Bartholomew.

'The Dominican,' replied Yolande. 'He called himself Carbo, although it was not his real name.'

Isnard looked interested. 'Do you know his real name? Only Brother Michael came to ask if I knew it yesterday, and I wish I could have told him. I like helping the man who conducts my choir.'

'*Your* choir?' asked Yolande, amused. Then she frowned as a thought occurred to her. 'Can my husband join? He cannot sing, but the free bread after rehearsals would be very welcome.'

'I will speak to Brother Michael,' promised Isnard grandly. 'I am sure there will be a place for Robert among the tenors. They cannot sing, either, so he will be in good company.'

Bartholomew had no doubt at all that Blaston would be accepted, regardless of his musical abilities or lack thereof. Michael had a soft heart when it came to the poor, and it was common knowledge that the choir's entire membership comprised men and boys – and even a few women – who desperately needed the post-practice refreshments. It was not common knowledge that he often paid for the victuals himself, however.

'Tell me about Carbo and Wynewyk,' prompted Bartholomew.

'I saw them chatting together,' obliged Yolande. 'They were with Powys, Shropham and Paxtone from King's Hall. Do you think Shropham killed Carbo, by the way? I do not – he is too meek.'

Bartholomew's thoughts were a chaotic jumble as he tried to make sense of what she was telling him. 'The King's Hall men said they had never met Carbo.'

'Then they were not telling you the truth,' said Yolande firmly. 'Although they were talking like acquaintances who meet by chance, not like friends. I was touting for business, hoping Paxtone might hire me, and I edged quite close to them – close enough to hear what they were saying. They were going on about the weather and the price of coal. It was rather stilted, actually.'

'Did Shropham look as though he knew Carbo? asked Bartholomew. 'Address him by name? Or did Wynewyk?'

'Not that I heard. Later that day, I saw Wynewyk with your sister's friend, too – Joan. He was flirting with her in the Market Square, and they were laughing over ribbons.'

Bartholomew was about to say that Wynewyk would not have flirted with a woman, but then he recalled Edith telling him the same thing. And there was Yolande's earlier testimony to take into account – that Wynewyk liked the company of a lady on occasion. It made Bartholomew question how well he really had known his colleague, despite all the time they had spent confiding in each other.

'Carbo and Joan travelled here together from Haverhill,' Yolande was saying.

'Carbo was Elyan's priest?' asked Isnard. 'Then I *do* know his name! It is Neubold – Carbo Neubold, perhaps. I met him in the Brazen George, and we chatted for a while. You had better tell Brother Michael right away, Doctor. He is going to be pleased with me.'

'He is,' agreed Bartholomew, although the discovery raised more questions than answers. How could Elyan have employed such a fellow to represent him to King's Hall? Or place his heavily pregnant wife in such hands? Of course, it explained why Joan was so eager to stay with Edith: Carbo had reeked, and would not have made for pleasant company. And that was before the lingering symptoms of his head injury were taken into account.

184

'Carbo – it suits him better than Neubold – gave Paxtone some lovely little rocks,' said Yolande chattily. 'Paxtone told me they ease the pain of childbirth, so I filched one when he was not looking.'

'You stole from him?' asked Bartholomew uneasily, watching her rummage in her purse for it.

'Borrowed,' she corrected. She shrugged when she saw his expression. 'He rarely treats pregnant women, whereas I encounter them all the time. Who do you think will get more use out of it?'

The stone she showed him was similar to the ones Bartholomew had inadvertently knocked out of Paxtone's cupboard, and he wondered why the King's Hall physician should have felt the need to lie when asked whether he had ever met the man Shropham was accused of killing.

He walked home in a thoughtful frame of mind. Carbo's real name was Neubold, the letter in his habit said he was from Withersfield, and he was Elyan's priest and possibly Gosse's lawyer. He had coal secreted in his robes, and Wynewyk had bought coal from Elyan. He had been seen talking to Shropham, who had later killed him. Connections were beginning to form thick and fast, and Bartholomew only hoped Michael would be able to make sense of them all, because he could not.

The next day saw an improvement in the weather. The heaviest clouds lifted, and a frail, silvery light trickled through the few that remained. Bartholomew was heartened by the watery rays that illuminated the east window of St Michael's Church, and began to hope that the rain and wind of the last few weeks were coming to an end.

'I do not want to go to Suffolk,' grumbled Michael, as Langelee led the procession back to the College for breakfast.

'I do,' said Bartholomew. He found he was looking forward to a respite from demanding students and too many patients. And there was the added bonus that he would be able to ask questions about Joan for Edith, which might make her less inclined to launch an investigation of her own.

'But Suffolk is such a long way,' moaned the monk.

'Seventeen miles – half a day's ride.'

'Only if the roads are good, and they are probably knee deep in mud after all this rain. I know thirty marks is a lot of money, but is it worth our lives? Langelee wants us to leave today, you know.'

'Tomorrow,' corrected Clippesby, coming to walk next to them. He had the College cat in his arms, which looked none too pleased to have been plucked from its domain and forced to spend part of its morning in church. 'He has hired you horses from the Brazen George – stronger and younger than the College nags – but they are not available today.'

'I suppose it gives us time to organise our teaching,' said Michael. He glanced at Bartholomew. 'And for you to warn your more grubby patients not to inflict themselves on Paxton or Rougham in your absence. It would be a kindness – and not just to your colleagues.'

'The Brazen George horses are experts on financial matters,' said Clippesby. His hair was on end that morning, and his habit was not very clean. Wynewyk's death had upset him badly, and Bartholomew suspected he was likely to be odder than usual until the shock had worn off. 'They will advise you on the best way to reclaim the lost money. They told me.'

'Lord!' breathed Michael, as the Dominican stopped to exchange pleasantries with a dog. The cat decided this was too much, and freed itself with a hiss. 'Should we really

186

let him loose on students? God knows what he might teach them – he told me the other day that there is a good chance that St Paul was a donkey, and that he wrote his Letters in a stable. That is verging on heresy.'

'He was amusing himself at your expense,' said Bartholomew, hoping it was true and that the unpleasantness of the last few days was not going to precipitate a more serious 'episode'.

'If you say so,' said Michael, unconvinced.

'I am taking Risleye, Valence and Tesdale to Suffolk, by the way,' the physician went on. 'Risleye is too quarrelsome to leave unsupervised, while Tesdale is too lazy – at least if he is with me, I can make sure he learns *something* to help him through his disputations.'

'And Valence?'

'I need him to keep the peace between the other two. Besides, he has worked hard since that exploding-book incident, and it would be unfair to take Risleye and Tesdale, but leave him behind.'

'But they are your most senior students.' said Michael. 'Who will mind the others?'

'Deynman. He is quite capable of keeping a class in order, and Clippesby has offered to do the reading. It will do them good to spend a few days re-hearing some basic texts.'

'It is a bad time for me to leave,' said Michael, more interested in his own concerns. 'I still do not know who attacked Langelee. I have failed to discover who took your pennyroyal, although Risleye assures me it was a servant. The Stanton Cups remain missing. And Bene't College was burgled last night – Gosse, most likely, although I cannot prove it. Again.'

'We will not be gone long, Brother. Three days at the most.'

'Moreover, King's Hall is not happy about me keeping Shropham in gaol,' Michael went on, declining to be appeased. 'But what else can I do? I can hardly release him, when he will not speak to defend himself. What message would that send to criminals?'

'Yolande said she saw Carbo talking to three King's Hall men on the High Street.' Bartholomew hesitated before adding, 'She said Wynewyk was with them.'

Michael gazed at him. 'What do you think that means?'

'That King's Hall is keeping something from you – something relating to why Shropham killed Carbo. However, Wynewyk had taken to socialising with Paxtone and Warden Powys in the last few weeks, so I do not think his presence at this gathering was significant.'

'He cheated his College in the last few weeks, too,' Michael pointed out. 'Do not be too ready to dismiss the facts, Matt. But this means I should visit King's Hall today. I understand Shropham lying – felons do that when they are in a tight corner – but it is unacceptable for his colleagues to indulge their penchant for fabrication at such a time.'

'Perhaps you should wait. Your various investigations – Carbo's murder, Wynewyk's business, and even Joan's death – have links to Suffolk. Our journey there may provide answers, and it would be a pity to have made accusatory remarks to members of a rival foundation if it transpires to be unnecessary: King's Hall's association with Carbo may be innocent.'

Michael did not look as though he thought it would, but he accepted the physician's point about acquiring ammunition. 'Carbo is puzzling. I find it strange that he should know two people – Joan and Wynewyk – who are both suddenly dead. *And* that he is Gosse's lawman.'

'Coal,' mused Bartholomew. 'Wynewyk bought some we

never saw; Carbo had a piece sewn in his habit; Joan's husband sells it; and it was discussed by Carbo, the King's Hall men and Wynewyk before any of them were dead. Coal is a clue, I am sure of it. And this coal is supposed to come from Haverhill. It is something else we must investigate while we are there.'

When they reached the College, Michael waited like a vulture for Cynric to ring the breakfast bell, and Bartholomew went to talk to his students. They had gathered outside the hall, jostling Deynman and some theologians and clearly intent on being the first in. He wondered why they always felt compelled to race, when meals never started until everyone was standing at his place anyway.

His announcement that he would be away for a few days was met with a variety of reactions. The more studious lads were disappointed, the lazy ones looked relieved, Risleye was angry that he had paid for teaching that would now not be given, and Tesdale was concerned.

'It is a long and dangerous journey,' he said. 'You may not come back, and then what will happen to us? Paxtone will not accept us, because he might think we are all like Risleye, while Rougham is too sharp and impatient a master for my taste.'

'You are coming with me,' said Bartholomew, a little dismayed that Tesdale should see his demise only in terms of the inconvenience to himself; he had thought his students liked him. 'So is Risleye—'

'Me?' cried Tesdale in dismay. 'I cannot go! I do not want to!'

'More importantly, neither can I,' declared Risleye self-importantly. '*I* do not like travelling.'

Bartholomew was taken aback by their responses, recalling that *his* master had dragged him as far as Greece

189

and Africa when he had been a student. Suffolk was hardly in the same league.

'You are coming,' he said in the tone of voice that made it clear it was not a matter for debate. 'So is Valence. And the rest of you will learn—'

'Really?' interrupted Valence, his face alight with pleasure. 'When do we leave? Is there time for me to say goodbye to my grandfather? Shall I pack a medicine bag, like the one you carry? You never know when additional supplies might come in useful. Can I borrow your spare cloak, Risleye?'

'I suppose,' replied Risleye unenthusiastically. 'But what about your classes, sir? Who will teach the others, if we three senior students are kicking our heels in some Godforsaken village?'

'I will,' offered Deynman eagerly. 'I was a physician-in-training before I abandoned medicine in favour of librarianship, so I know what needs to be done. I shall ensure they stay at their studies.'

Bartholomew grabbed his arm and pulled him to one side, so the others would not hear. 'I understand you still demand access to my storeroom. Why?'

Deynman looked annoyed. 'Did Tesdale tell you that? The little rat! He said he would keep it to himself if I gave him a shilling. I shall demand the money back, since he reneged.'

'Never mind that. Tell me what you wanted in there.'

'Pennyroyal,' confessed Deynman reluctantly. 'Cynric told me it puts a lovely shine on metal, and I wanted to polish the hasps on my books. Of course, he was wrong.'

Bartholomew frowned. 'What do you mean?'

'Your useless pennyroyal did nothing for my hasps. However, I did not take much, because there was not much left, and I did not think you would mind, as you know I

190

will replace it. I would have bought my own, but the apothecary said there was a sudden demand for it, and he ran out. But I am to return there on Monday, when your supply will be replenished in full.'

'Why did you not tell me all this when I first asked?' Bartholomew distinctly recalled Deynman being with his students the morning he had noticed its disappearance.

Deynman's expression was sheepish. 'I was going to, but you looked so irked that I decided to wait for a better moment. You were furious when Valence borrowed ingredients to make that book explode, and I did not want you to rail at me like you hollered at him.'

He grinned happily, clearly thinking the explanation was enough to see him forgiven. And he was right: the physician was too relieved to be angry. He ordered him not to do it again, although the Librarian was not very good at remembering instructions and was sure to forget. It made Bartholomew all the more determined to improve security in the future. He turned his mind back to his students and teaching.

'Here are the texts I want my students to have heard by the time I return,' he said, handing Deynman an unreasonably ambitious schedule. 'Clippesby has volunteered to read them aloud.'

Deynman scanned the list. 'I have most of these in my library, and the rest I can borrow from King's Hall. Do not worry: your pupils will be safe with me – and with Clippesby.'

Bartholomew hoped so, and decided to ask Wynewyk to keep an eye on them as well. He experienced a sharp pang of grief when he realised that would not be possible.

He saw Valence standing alone and went to speak to him, keen to think about something else. 'I understand you saw Gosse lob a stone at my sister,' he said.

'Mud, not a stone,' corrected Valence. 'And she ordered

me not to tell you, because she said you would be upset. I went with her to see Constable Muschett afterwards, but he said my testimony was inadmissible – that I would lie to get Gosse into trouble because he stole our Stanton Cups.'

'He said that to you?' asked Bartholomew.

Valence grinned. 'He did – but he is right: I *would* do anything to get the chalices back. Gosse is a terrifying man, but it would not stop me from fabricating stories to convict him.'

'The Sheriff will be home soon, and he will put an end to such antics,' said Bartholomew, declining to comment on the lad's ethics. 'Do you know why Gosse threw mud at Edith?'

'Well, he was in the Market Square, and Joan started to chat to him. Your sister asked how she knew him, and Joan said Gosse hailed from Clare, which is near her home village of Haverhill.'

'Then what?'

'Then he started to hint that he would like some ribbon, and your sister thought he should buy his own. When she pulled Joan away, he grabbed a handful of mud from the ground and threw it. I wanted to punch him, but she said you would not approve. Personally, I thought you would not have minded.'

'I *would* have minded,' said Bartholomew. He softened. 'Although I appreciate you looking out for her.'

'Who will do it while we are away?' asked Valence, worriedly. 'Her husband has gone to Lincolnshire, and I dislike the notion of her being unprotected. Perhaps I should forgo this exciting journey, and make sure Gosse does not hurl anything else in her direction.'

'Cynric will stay with her.'

'Then who will look after us?' Valence's expression was

deeply anxious, but then it cleared. 'You will! I had forgotten that you are a seasoned warrior who fought at Poitiers. Cynric is always talking about it. Of course we will be safe with you!'

CHAPTER 6

Bartholomew and Michael made the most of their last day in Cambridge. The monk engaged in a concerted effort to identify the man who had attacked Langelee, and questioned Shropham about Carbo, but his efforts came to nothing. A lead relating to the ambush transpired to be the drunken imaginings of someone who had not been there, while Shropham merely turned his face to the wall and refused to speak. Short of punching the truth out of him – and Michael was not a violent man – he was stumped as how to proceed. He returned to the College late that night in a dark mood, worried about the journey he was being forced to make, and reluctant to leave Cambridge when there were so many matters there that clamoured for his attention.

Meanwhile, Bartholomew passed the morning explaining why his students needed to learn the texts he had selected, making it clear that those not familiar with them by the time he returned could expect to be set exercises that would keep them indoors for a month. He did not really expect trouble. His lads were full of high spirits, but most were keen to learn and took their studies seriously. They were also acutely aware that a lot of men wanted the chance to study at Michaelhouse, and that Langelee would have no compunction in replacing anyone who misbehaved.

The afternoon was spent seeing patients. Some had summoned him, while others suffered from long-term maladies that required regular visits. He ensured all had enough medicine to last for the next week, then issued Paxtone with detailed instructions on what to do if there was a problem.

Sincerely hoping his colleague's expertise would not be required – he liked Paxtone, but did not want him near his patients unless there was absolutely no alternative – he walked to the Dominican Friary, where one of the novices had been injured. Risleye, Valence and Tesdale accompanied him, because the other students were all at a lecture in King's Hall, and were delighted when the case transpired to be a possible cracked skull.

'How do we test for a cranial fracture?' he asked, taking the patient's head gently in his hands.

'We look it up in Frugard's *Chirurgia*,' replied Risleye promptly.

'And what happens if we do not have a copy to hand?'

'We squeeze the bones together, to see whether they grate,' said Tesdale, with rather ghoulish glee.

Bartholomew winced. 'Not unless we want to kill him.'

'Osa Gosse did this,' said Prior Morden, holding the novice's hand comfortingly, but staring fixedly in the opposite direction so that he would not see anything the physician might do. 'He and James had words yesterday, and threats were made. Well, it seems Gosse acted on his violent words.'

'Are you sure it was Gosse?' Bartholomew asked of James. A serious assault would give Michael the excuse he needed to arrest the fellow, and the monk would be much happier leaving his town if the felon was under lock and key.

'Who else could it have been?' asked James miserably. 'The fight I had with the Franciscans was days ago now, and they will have forgotten that I called them villainous knaves whose mothers—'

'James!' exclaimed Morden, shocked. 'You promised to leave the Grey Friars alone.'

'They provoked *me*,' objected James. 'They said I was a dim-witted lout with no manners.'

'Gosse,' prompted Bartholomew, suspecting the Franciscans might have a point. 'Can you be sure he was the one who attacked you today?'

'No,' admitted James reluctantly. 'The villain wore a hood, and I could not see his face. I suppose it *might* have been a Grey Friar. They are certainly the kind of men to attack innocent Dominicans.'

Bartholomew was disappointed, but his duty was to treat the wound, not investigate the crime. He was just assessing James's eyes when Morden suddenly jumped to his feet and shot towards the door.

'I do not have the stomach to watch you crack open his skull and prod whatever you find inside,' the Prior explained. 'Do not look frightened, James. *You* will not be able to see it.'

'Really, Father,' said Bartholomew reproachfully. 'I intend nothing so dramatic. Watch—'

But Morden had gone, leaving a terrified novice behind him, and it took the physician some time to convince James that cracking and prodding had no part in his plans.

When James was calm, he resumed his examination. There was no obvious depression or swelling, but there was a worrying pain caused by a boot stamping on an ear. He did not think the skull was fractured, but decided to apply Roger of Parma's test to make sure. James was instructed to stop up his mouth, nose and ears, and to blow as hard as he could. The escape of air or tissue would imply a fissure.

'But my brains will fly out if I do that,' James wept, distraught. 'And Prior Morden says I am short of them, so I cannot afford to lose any.'

'You will not,' said Valence kindly. 'Doctor Bartholomew knows what he is doing.'

'Besides,' added Tesdale practically, 'brains are too glutinous to fly – they are more prone to ooze. And I shall catch any that dribble out and shove them back in for you.'

'Do not be a baby,' ordered Risleye, regarding the novice disdainfully. 'And if you do not trust your physicians – us – then you deserve to die. But you will not, because *I* will not let you.'

Strangely, it was Risleye's cold arrogance that convinced James to do as he was told. Afterwards, satisfied the pain was caused by simple bruising, Bartholomew showed his pupils how to make a poultice to ease the ache, and when James said he was hungry – a good sign – he sent Risleye and Valence to the kitchen for broth.

While they were gone, Bartholomew found himself recalling how eagerly Yolande had devoured Isnard's stew the previous evening. He suspected her children were also hungry, and did not want to return from Suffolk to find them half-dead from starvation. He handed Tesdale the money Morden had paid him to tend James, and told him what he wanted bought. The student was bemused.

'And I am to leave all this outside their house without them seeing? Why?'

'Pride,' explained Bartholomew. 'No one likes accepting charity.'

'*I* do not mind,' said Tesdale ruefully. 'I am grateful for anything I can get.'

'Please be discreet,' said Bartholomew, hoping Tesdale's innate laziness would not encourage him to be careless. He half wished he had recruited Valence instead.

'You can trust me,' said Tesdale solemnly. 'I used to do similar things for Master Wynewyk – mostly making anonymous donations of food and ale for the Michaelhouse Choir.'

'That was Wynewyk?' Bartholomew recalled Michael often remarking on the miraculous appearance of victuals when his own funds were low. 'I never knew.'

Tears welled in Tesdale's eyes. 'I probably should not have mentioned it, but I thought you should know I have experience with this kind of thing, so you can depend on me to—' He stopped speaking abruptly when Risleye and Valence entered the sickroom with the soup.

'Depend on you to what?' asked Risleye.

'To . . . to return my library books before we leave on our journey tomorrow,' replied Tesdale in a guilty stammer. Risleye narrowed his eyes.

'I do not believe you,' he said accusingly. 'You were probably ingratiating yourself so Doctor Bartholomew will save you first if we are attacked. We all know it is perilous and stupid to travel in winter.'

'It is not perilous,' said Bartholomew, deliberately turning his mind from the very real dangers of robbers, floods, getting lost and being thrown from panicky horses.

'Master Wynewyk did not agree,' said Risleye resentfully. 'He *hated* leaving Cambridge at any time of the year.'

'He left it to visit his father last term,' Tesdale pointed out. 'In Winwick, which is a long way west of Huntingdon. Personally, I cannot imagine why anyone would want to leave home. It is hard work, and I would much rather stay in by the fire.'

'Actually, he did not go to Winwick,' said Risleye. His expression was smug. 'He made me swear not to tell anyone, but I am released from that promise now he is dead. Am I not?'

Bartholomew stared at him. 'He *did* go. He brought back a lot of earthenware jugs – enough to replace all the ones that were cracked. Their design is alien to Cambridge, and—'

'I did not say he did not leave Cambridge, I said he did not go to Winwick,' corrected Risleye pedantically. 'I was visiting friends in Babraham, you see, and there was a hailstorm. I ducked inside a tavern, and there was Wynewyk, also sheltering from the weather. Babraham is south-east of Cambridge, but Winwick is a long way west, as Tesdale pointed out.'

'So?' demanded Tesdale. 'Perhaps he decided to take the scenic route.'

'In completely the opposite direction?' demanded Risleye archly. 'He winked at me, and said his father had been dead for years – it was actually an old flame who needed the visit. He gave me a shilling, and we agreed not to mention the matter again. A pact between gentlemen.'

'But only until death,' said Valence, eyeing him in disgust. 'At which point, you reveal his private business to the first people who ask. There is nothing of the gentleman about you, Risleye.'

'Give your patient the soup,' ordered Bartholomew, seeing Risleye gird himself up for a spat. 'Slowly – a little at a time. And check the size of his pupils again.'

While the students did as he ordered, Bartholomew recalled that Michael had given Wynewyk money for his journey, sorry for a colleague rushing to a father's sickbed. Was Risleye telling the truth about what had transpired in Babraham? Bartholomew thought he was – the lad had no reason to lie – and wondered what his colleague could have been doing. He did not believe Wynewyk would have accepted Michael's charity to frolic with a lover; Wynewyk, he decided, had spun Risleye a yarn he thought the lad would believe in order to secure his silence. So what was the truth? He had no idea, and could only hope that all would become clear when they made their enquiries in Suffolk.

It was early evening by the time Bartholomew and his students left the Dominican Friary, and lamps were lit in the wealthiest homes. In most, though, doors and windows were open to catch the last of the daylight. It let in the cold, but candles were expensive, and most folk could not afford to use them as long as it was light outside. Rich smells wafted out as meals were prepared over hearths, mostly root vegetables that had been stewing over the embers all day, perhaps with a few bones for flavour. In the Market Square, many of the bakers' ovens were cold, suggesting grain was already scarce and only the affluent were going to have bread to dip in their pottage that night.

Supper had finished when they reached Michaelhouse, and the Fellows were gathering in the conclave. Bartholomew was loath to join them, knowing the topic of conversation would be Wynewyk and the wrongs he had perpetrated on his trusting colleagues. He decided to visit his sister instead, to tell her he was going to Suffolk and would ask questions about Joan on her behalf.

Edith nodded her satisfaction that he was finally taking her concerns seriously. She mulled some wine, and they sat next to the roaring fire, listening to the wind rattle the window shutters. The wood released the scent of pine as it burned, combining pleasantly with the aroma of the cloves and ginger that were tied in small bags around the house – a common precaution against winter fevers. He was warm and content, and might have been happy, were it not for Wynewyk and the nagging fear that Edith might do something reckless in her quest to understand why her friend had died. And he missed Matilde, of course, but he had come to accept that as a hurt that would never go away.

'There is a condition,' he said, sipping the wine and thinking Matilde would have liked it, because it was heavily laced with cinnamon: 'That Cynric stays with you.'

'There is no need – Oswald's apprentices are here, not to mention the burgesses he charged to watch me. Indeed, I think he ordered half the town to keep me from danger.'

'It is the other half I am worried about,' said Bartholomew.

'Then perhaps I shall come with you to Haverhill,' said Edith slyly. 'You can look after me, and I can ask my own questions about Joan.'

'Absolutely not! Oswald would never forgive me if he came home to find you gone.'

'But I must do something! The more I think about it, the more I am certain Joan was murdered.'

'There is no evidence to suggest—'

'There *is* evidence – *my* testimony. Joan was delighted about the child, and would *not* have tried to rid herself of it. And nor would she have merrily downed a tonic without first assessing what was in it, so her death was not an accident, either. Therefore, the only option left is murder: someone gave her the pennyroyal, intending to cause her harm.'

'It is possible,' said Bartholomew, more to calm her than because he believed it. 'Of course, if she was selective about what she drank, we must assume she accepted the potion from someone she knew and trusted. Yet she was a virtual stranger here.'

'And *that* is why I must visit Suffolk. The killer followed her here, gave her the potion and left when it killed her. He is at home now, smug in the belief that no one will ever catch him.'

201

'How odd it is that everything seems to lead to Suffolk,' said Bartholomew, more to himself than Edith. 'Wynewyk did business there, it was Joan's home, and Shropham killed one of its priests – who also happens to be the lawyer for another Suffolk man, namely Osa Gosse.'

'You think all these things are connected?' Edith was bemused.

'Perhaps, although I cannot see how. The other common element is coal. Carbo had some sewn in his habit, Wynewyk bought some from Elyan . . .'

Edith nodded vigorously. 'And Joan told me that Elyan's priest – Neubold – came here to sell coal to King's Hall, which was what afforded her the opportunity to travel in the first place.'

'Did you ever meet Neubold?' asked Bartholomew, supposing that if Edith was right and Joan had been murdered, then Carbo was the obvious suspect – he had been in Cambridge when she had swallowed the pennyroyal, and had failed to respond when he had been summoned.

'Briefly, before Joan died. Afterwards, I asked for him at the Brazen George, but the landlord said he had gone – disappeared.' Her eyes narrowed when she saw what he was thinking. 'You suspect he is her killer? But when *I* suggested him as a culprit on Sunday, you dismissed the notion.'

Bartholomew rubbed his eyes. 'I will ask questions about him in Suffolk,' he replied vaguely.

Edith was thoughtful. 'I went to King's Hall after my enquiries in the tavern. Warden Powys told me Neubold had finished his business there sooner than anticipated and has not been seen since.'

Bartholomew rubbed his chin. It was common knowledge that Elyan had sent his priest to negotiate with King's

Hall, so why had the Warden, Paxtone and Shropham denied knowing Carbo? Had Shropham killed him over a contract for coal? He had negotiated too hard a bargain, and the scholars had decided that King's Hall's interests would better be served if he was dead? And had they then agreed to a conspiracy of silence about it?

'Neubold is dead,' he said. 'Shropham killed him.'

Edith looked doubtful. 'I thought Shropham had stabbed a fellow called Carbo.'

'They are one and the same. Yolande told me.'

Edith looked startled. 'Then Yolande told you wrong! There is a similarity in their build, hair and facial features – and both are Dominicans – but Neubold is elegant and well-groomed, while Carbo was a beggar. And how could you think that Elyan would send a scruffy, half-mad hedge-priest to represent him to the scholars of King's Hall? Or that Joan would travel in such company?'

'But Yolande saw Carbo talking to the King's Hall men, and—'

'Yolande would have seen *Neubold*. I imagine what happened is this: she heard Shropham had stabbed a visiting Dominican, and made an erroneous assumption – that he killed the priest she saw him chatting to. But she is mistaken, and you have let her lead you astray.'

'I . . .'

But she was right: of course Carbo and Neubold could not be the same person, and her scornful words made Bartholomew feel a fool for ever having thought so. He had set too much store by a letter from Withersfield and the coal in Carbo's habit, and they had led him to conclusions that were, as Edith pointed out, preposterous. Moreover, it meant the King's Hall men had not been lying when they had denied knowing Carbo. He closed his eyes wearily when he saw that he and Michael would have to revise all their reasoning regarding the murdered friar.

Edith was reviewing her theories, too. 'I know I suggested on Sunday that Neubold might have harmed Joan, but I have reconsidered – I do not believe a trusted clerk would have poisoned his master's wife. So perhaps Neubold *witnessed* Joan being plied with pennyroyal, and was killed to ensure his silence. And *that* is why he has disappeared so mysteriously.'

'You said you had not seen Joan in years. People change, Edith.'

Her eyes narrowed suspiciously. 'What are you saying? I do not understand.'

'Everyone knows first pregnancies can be difficult, and that the mother – especially an older one – must take precautions. She is advised to eat certain foods, avoid others. She needs rest, so that exertion does not prematurely expel the child from her body. Joan was rich, well placed to do all this.'

'So?' asked Edith, when he paused.

'So why did she risk a long journey for a few bits of cloth? Why not send a servant for the ribbons? And why go with only a priest for protection? Do you not think it a little strange?'

Edith stared at him for a long time. 'You think the journey was an attempt to rid herself of the baby – and she swallowed pennyroyal when it did not work?'

'It is possible. You should be aware that Joan may not have been entirely honest with you.'

Edith continued to stare. 'She seemed the same. I confided in her – told her about you and Matilde. Do not look dismayed! I felt like sharing something personal, and I do not have any interesting secrets of my own. Oswald and I lead very staid lives.'

'You could have told her about Richard,' he said tartly, referring to her wayward son. 'Did you persuade him to abandon his tryst with the Earl of Suffolk's daughter, by the way?'

'No,' she replied stiffly. 'And he says the baby is not his, although the Earl does not believe him.'

'Christ!' muttered Bartholomew. 'I am sure Joan would have found *that* a lot more interesting.'

'Will you ask after Matilde when you visit Haverhill?' asked Edith, deftly changing the subject. 'You searched for her in distant places, but perhaps she did not go far. She might be in Suffolk.'

Bartholomew thought it unlikely, but part of him hoped Edith was right: that one day he would find Matilde, and she would agree to become his wife. But it was a hope that was too deeply personal to talk about, so he mumbled a vague reply about the trail being cold after so long.

'You should go,' said Edith, seeing she was going to be told no more. 'It is late and you have a long journey tomorrow. And I have heard the rumours that say you are a formidable warrior these days, but we both know they are untrue. Take Cynric with you – you need him, I do not.'

The following day, Bartholomew awoke to find his book-bearer packing a bag with items he thought might be needed for the foray into Suffolk; his dark face was alight with excitement, and he was clearly looking forward to the adventure. Meanwhile, the physician's room-mates were groaning and pulling blankets over their heads, because dawn was still some way off, but Cynric was creating enough racket to raise the dead. Bartholomew was a heavy sleeper, and the fact that *he* had been disturbed was testament to the rumpus Cynric was making.

'That should do,' declared the book-bearer eventually, sitting back to inspect his handiwork. 'We will not be gone long, anyway. My wife wants me home in four days, because her mother is coming to stay.' He reflected for a moment. 'But we can take longer, if you like.'

Bartholomew prised himself out of bed, and looked in the bag. There was not much in it, because Cynric was of the opinion that clean clothes were a waste of time when travelling on muddy roads. He had, however, packed a variety of items that could be used as weapons, including a selection of knives, a length of rope and a piece of lead piping. Yawning, Bartholomew dressed and went to wait for Michael in the yard. It was drizzling and still pitch dark. After a moment, Langelee appeared.

'I did a stupid thing yesterday,' he said, rubbing his hands to warm them. 'I asked Clippesby to sort through Wynewyk's belongings, because everyone else was busy. Do you know what he claims to have found? Copies of letters to noblemen, asking if they would like to buy some diamonds.'

Bartholomew regarded him in surprise. 'Wynewyk had no diamonds!'

Langelee grimaced. 'Clippesby was in the process of burning these so-called missives when I happened across him. He said the College cat had told him to do it, to protect Wynewyk's reputation. God only knows what he really destroyed.'

'Perhaps I should talk to him before we go,' said Bartholomew anxiously.

'Please do,' said Langelee. 'He has been up all night, doing something in the library.'

He made it sound sinister, and Bartholomew hurried to the hall in alarm. Clippesby had lit a lamp and was sitting at a table. The physician faltered. The last time he had seen the Dominican at that desk he had been talking to a jar of moths, berating them for eating Michaelhouse's linen.

Clippesby jumped when he realised someone was behind him. 'You startled me,' he said with a smile. 'What is the matter? Can you not sleep?'

'What are you doing?'

Clippesby gestured to the book that lay in front of him. 'Reading. What else would I be doing in here?'

Bartholomew did not like to imagine. He peered over the Dominican's shoulder and saw Aquinas's *Cathena aurea*, a standard biblical commentary. Clippesby was halfway through it.

'I often read at night,' Clippesby went on. 'It is the only time I can be guaranteed peace and quiet. I begin Aquinas with my third-years next week, and I wanted to refresh my memory. But I suspect you are not here to discuss teaching. I imagine Langelee told you what I found in Wynewyk's room.'

Bartholomew nodded, thinking Clippesby was often perfectly sane when they were alone together, and it was only the presence of others that seemed to bring out the mischief in him. That morning, there was not an animal in sight and the notes he had jotted on a scrap of parchment pertained to serious theological issues.

'Langelee promised not to say anything,' Clippesby went on. His voice was uncharacteristically bitter. 'But I suppose he thinks a vow to a madman does not count.'

Bartholomew was not sure what to say, because Clippesby was right: his eccentric behaviour did mean his colleagues often declined to afford him the courtesies they extended to others. He settled for a shrug, thinking the Dominican had only himself to blame.

'I should have kept quiet,' Clippesby continued. 'But

he caught me feeding parchments to the flames, and demanded an explanation. He was furious.'

'He had every right to be. You have no business burning documents that might explain what Wynewyk had been doing.'

'The cat suggested I light the fire—'

'Stop,' ordered Bartholomew. 'Do not play this game with me, John. We both know you are only pretending to be fey in order to avoid difficult questions. What did the letters say?'

Clippesby grimaced. 'They asked whether certain people would be interested in buying diamonds. But *you* know Wynewyk is innocent, so you understand why I destroyed them. I was trying to protect his good name – to prevent the others from obtaining more ammunition to use against him.'

'What "certain people"?' demanded Bartholomew, more interested in the letters than Clippesby's concerns about their colleagues.

'The Earl of Suffolk, the Bishop of Lincoln. Important men, rich men.'

'You told Langelee these letters were copies. Does that mean the originals have been sent?'

Clippesby nodded unhappily. 'I believe so. The abbreviations and contractions in the documents I found suggest they were being kept as a record, to remind the author of what had been said.'

Bartholomew was bemused. 'Did he say where these diamonds were supposed to come from?'

'No. Langelee's first thought was that he was selling them for Gosse, who is almost certainly responsible for the theft of precious stones from around the University. But he must be wrong.'

'So you do not think Wynewyk had diamonds to sell?'

'If he did, then they are not in his room.' Clippesby hesitated, and Bartholomew saw no trace of madness now, only sorrow. 'After I had burned the letters and had my set-to with Langelee, I returned to Wynewyk's room and resumed packing up his belongings. And it was then that I found something else – something even more disturbing.'

'What?' prompted Bartholomew, when the Dominican paused again.

'A purse with the strings cut. It contained a few coins, and a schedule of camp-ball games.'

Bartholomew gazed at him, not liking the implications of that discovery. 'Wynewyk watched camp-ball if one of his lovers was playing.'

Clippesby reached into the scrip at his side, and pulled something out. The purse was grubby, manly and large, and certainly not something the fastidious Wynewyk would have owned.

'He must have come by it *after* Langelee was attacked,' said Bartholomew, refusing to believe what the evidence was telling him.

Clippesby would not meet his eyes. 'The word is that Langelee was ambushed by someone slight, who wore a scholar's tabard. It was also someone who was very specific about selecting his victim – he let others pass unmolested before launching his assault.'

'No,' said Bartholomew, shaking his head. 'Wynewyk did *not* stab Langelee.'

'Langelee was attacked two nights before he told you what he had discovered in the accounts,' Clippesby pressed on. 'And Wynewyk *was* out that particular evening, because the owls . . . because *I* saw him. It pains me to say it, but I think Wynewyk knew he was on the verge of being exposed, and tried to prevent it.'

209

'No,' said Bartholomew again, aware that his voice shook.

Clippesby touched his arm sympathetically. 'I still feel he would not cheat us, but he must really have wanted to keep his secrets, because to tackle Langelee . . .'

Bartholomew stared at the purse, thoughts churning wildly, and for some moments they stood in silence. Then Clippesby sketched a benediction at him, and returned to his reading. Bartholomew left the hall and walked slowly across the yard to where Langelee was inspecting the horses that had just been delivered from the Brazen George. The physician, who was not a skilled rider, regarded the snorting, stamping beasts with trepidation, and wondered whether it might be safer for him to walk.

'Have you remembered anything else about the night you were attacked?' he asked the Master.

Langelee patted the neck of a large, black creature that had a distinctly malevolent look in its eyes. 'I keep recalling flashes, but it was very dark. I saw an academic tabard, though. Black, like ours.'

Bartholomew swallowed hard. 'You think it was Wynewyk. That is why you ordered Michael to forget about it – pretend it did not happen.'

Langelee turned towards him, and his expression was haggard. 'I would like to believe I am mistaken – that I was too drunk to remember clearly – but I am deluding myself. Wynewyk *did* try to kill me, and he damn near succeeded.'

'There must be an explanation—'

'So you keep saying,' interrupted Langelee bitterly. 'But I think he knew what I had found in the accounts, and wanted to prevent me from telling anyone else. Moreover, I believe he stole my purse to make the assault look like a common robbery.'

210

'Perhaps he just meant to frighten you,' began Bartholomew tentatively. 'He would not have—'

'He *did* frighten me,' snarled Langelee. 'He frightened me into telling you what I had discovered as soon as I could get you alone for a few hours. And then what did he do? He laughed himself to death!'

It was fully light by the time Bartholomew, Michael, the three students and Cynric finally set out, mostly because Tesdale, never a morning person, proved difficult to prise out of bed.

'We cannot be gone long,' said Michael, more to himself than anyone else. 'The Blood Relic debate is on Monday, and I would not miss that for the world. Not only am I one of the primary disputants, but I am worried that Gosse might use the opportunity to burgle empty Colleges and hostels. I need to be here to ensure he does not succeed.'

'I do not think it will take five days to demand thirty marks from three Suffolk lords,' said Bartholomew, struggling to mount his horse. 'We should be home long before then.'

'I hope we find answers there,' said Michael unhappily. 'When I first saw Carbo dead with Shropham's knife in him, I thought the case was cut and dried. But now I am uncertain. I cannot put my finger on it, but there is something badly amiss.'

'I do not understand your reservations,' said Bartholomew, becoming frustrated by the nag's refusal to stand still. It was the fierce black one, and he was not sure he agreed with Michael's assessment that it was the most docile of the bunch. 'Your Junior Proctor arrived very quickly, and he says no one else was in sight. Moreover, Shropham was injured, which suggests he was involved in some sort of spat.'

'That is what the application of cold logic would dictate. But we both know things are seldom what they seem, and I am beginning to think there may be a good reason for Shropham's bewildering silence. The problem is that unless he confides in me, I may never know what it is.'

'Shropham is so quiet and unassuming that it is difficult to gain his true measure. Who knows what he is really like? I do not. Perhaps he *is* a killer, but has managed to conceal it – until now.'

'There is also the issue of motive,' continued Michael, lost in his reverie. '*Why* should Shropham stab Carbo? Edith says Carbo is not Neubold, so we must abandon the theory that it was something to do with King's Hall's negotiations for coal.'

'Perhaps he did it because he could.' Bartholomew managed to climb into the saddle at last, then hung on grimly while the horse pranced about. 'I have just said he might be a natural killer.'

'Or perhaps Carbo tried to blackmail Shropham,' suggested Michael, seeing the physician was going to be thrown, and leaning forward to grab the reins. He glanced at the students, who were watching their master's antics in open-mouthed disbelief; politely, Cynric was pretending not to notice. 'That would explain why Shropham is now reluctant to explain why he stabbed the man.'

'Then he will not thank you for trying to discover the secret he committed murder to hide,' said Bartholomew, breathing a sigh of relief when Michael brought the animal under control. 'He does not value his life, or he would have pleaded self-defence. But perhaps he will feel differently by the time we return – or we will have answers that make his silence irrelevant.'

'Perhaps Paxtone is the killer,' suggested Michael.

Bartholomew looked sharply at him, and the monk shrugged as he handed back the reins. 'It is just a suggestion.'

'Based on what evidence?' Bartholomew was shocked.

'On the fact that Shropham has developed a rather unhealthy admiration for him, so might be prepared to take the blame for a crime his hero committed. Did you know he rinses Paxtone's urine jars? I would not do that for you, and we are genuine friends.'

'He debases himself by waiting on *all* the King's Hall Fellows, not just Paxtone.'

'I am just playing with ideas here, Matt. In the past one of us has proposed a wild theory, and the subsequent discussion has allowed us to deduce sensible answers. I hoped that would happen now.'

'In other words, you are desperate.' Bartholomew grabbed the horse's mane when it began to buck again, and wished he had paid closer attention to the riding lessons he had been given as a child.

'I cannot rid myself of the notion that Shropham is innocent. Do not ask why, when common sense, logic *and* the testimony of my Junior Proctor tell me otherwise. But it is a strong feeling, and I have learned not to ignore my instincts.'

'We should go,' said Valence, uneasy about the amount of time that was passing. 'Or we run the risk of being out on unfamiliar roads after dark.'

'I do not want to be out at all,' said Tesdale fervently. 'I will be useless in a skirmish. Kelyng was a veritable Ajax – almost as skilled as Doctor Bartholomew or Cynric with weapons – but I am not.'

'You are good with a knife, though,' said Risleye. He did not often compliment people, so Bartholomew assumed Tesdale must be outstanding. 'Did you hear

213

Kelyng's parents have written to Master Langelee, by the way? They want to know why they have not heard from him since August.'

Michael raised his eyebrows. 'To what extents a man will go to avoid his debts!'

'I do not think he fled for debts,' whispered Cynric to Bartholomew. 'I think Wynewyk hired him as personal protection. But he found the work too dangerous, so he took to his heels while he was still able.'

'Christ, Cynric!' exclaimed Bartholomew, amazed, as always, by the Welshman's capacity for devising wild theories. 'How in God's name did you come up with that?'

'Because Kelyng was Wynewyk's student,' explained Cynric, unperturbed by his master's less than positive reaction to his thesis. 'And he is poor, so will do anything for money. Meanwhile, Wynewyk was busily cheating his colleagues, which means he would have felt vulnerable—'

'No,' said Bartholomew. He realised he should not be surprised that Cynric knew of Wynewyk's alleged crimes, when only the Fellows were supposed to be party to the secret – the Welshman was an inveterate eavesdropper. 'Kelyng did *not* leave Cambridge because of Wynewyk.'

'We shall see, boy,' said Cynric comfortably.

Six riders represented quite a cavalcade in Cambridge's narrow streets, and people stopped to look at them or call greetings as they rode past. Edith was waiting with a bag of food for their journey. She started to give it to Bartholomew, but changed her mind when she saw he was not in sufficient control of his horse to allow her to approach safely. Michael thrust out an eager paw, but she handed it to Cynric instead.

Then Paxtone hurried forward to assure Bartholomew – again – that he should not worry about his patients, that he was ready to step into the breach in the event of an emergency. Bartholomew smiled, but sincerely hoped the King's Hall physician would not attempt to inflict his rigid, uninspired medicine on Cambridge's hapless poor.

'There is Gosse,' muttered Michael, as they rode past the leafy churchyard of St Mary the Great. 'And Idoma is with him. What are they doing?'

'She is angry,' said Bartholomew, watching the furious way she shoved her brother away from her. He declined to be repelled, and moved forward again each time he was pushed, all the while speaking in a low, calm voice. Idoma said nothing, but even from a distance Bartholomew could see the expression on her face was dark and dangerous. 'And he is trying to soothe her.'

Michael grinned slyly. 'I wonder if her ire stems from the fact that I thwarted an attempt to burgle Bene't College last night.'

'Did you?' asked Bartholomew. Gosse seemed to be winning the battle; Idoma's jostles were becoming less forceful. She still looked incensed, though, and the physician was glad their paths would not cross. 'How?'

'Beadle Meadowman reported two cunningly broken windows there – clearly, a villain had damaged them with a view to gaining easy access at some point in the future. I had them mended, and arranged for a couple of fierce dogs to be stationed nearby. There was a commotion at midnight, and a would-be burglar was seen running for his life.'

'Was it Gosse? Or Idoma?'

'Not Idoma – she is too large for scaling walls and squeezing through windows. But witnesses say the culprit was the right size for her brother. Of course, the sly devil was heavily disguised, and no one can identify him with certainty. Still, at least he did not manage to steal anything, and the fright he had may make him think twice before targeting other University buildings.'

'Has he turned his attention to the town yet, or is he still only interested in what scholars own?'

'The latter. Unfortunately, this has made him rather popular with the townsfolk: they applaud anyone who has the audacity to strike at us. It means that even if there are witnesses to his crimes, they are unlikely to come forward. And Gosse knows it. Indeed, it is probably why he picks on us.'

'You do not think it is anything to do with the message he gave me – that we have something he believes belongs to him?'

Michael rubbed his chin. 'Not really, Matt. He has cornered other scholars and made similar demands of them, too. But I believe it is a ruse to baffle the Senior Proctor. He is a clever man – unlike most criminals – and hopes to confound me with these curious claims.'

Bartholomew glanced to where Gosse was muttering in Idoma's ear, having calmed her to the point where she no longer felt the need to shove him. She listened, nodding occasionally, but when she happened to glance towards the road her face became suffused with rage again. For one alarming moment, Bartholomew thought she was going to make a run at them, but she contented herself with a glare. Even so, the malice that blazed from her shark-fish eyes was disconcerting, and he felt a shiver run down his spine. Gosse turned to see what had attracted her attention, but the expression on his face was unreadable. Somehow, this was worse.

'My beadles have laid traps in one or two other Colleges,' said Michael, glancing in their direction, then contemptuously looking away, as if it was beneath him to acknowledge what he saw. 'I doubt they will catch Gosse, but it will make

216

life a little more difficult for him. And who knows? By the time we return, he may have decided that Cambridge is not worth his time.'

Bartholomew doubted it, and was not sure Michael was right to dismiss Gosse's claim that the University had something that belonged to him. He regarded the pair unhappily, and wished Edith had not rejected his offer of Cynric's protection. Or was he just unsettled by their unsavoury reputation? Gosse and Idoma certainly exuded a malevolent aura, but there were no reports of actual violence. James the Dominican was more likely to have been attacked by offended Franciscans, while Bartholomew's own encounter had involved a lot of menace but no real attempt to do harm; even their threats had been ambiguous.

'I do not want to go.' Tesdale's words dragged the physician's attention away from his own concerns. 'I am already tired, and we have a long way to travel yet. I was not built for hard riding.'

'It will be fun,' countered Valence, clearly relishing the prospect of an adventure. 'And you cannot be tired. You slept almost all of yesterday.'

Tesdale ignored him and addressed Bartholomew. 'Are you sure you need me, sir? Master Langelee said the purpose of the journey is to retrieve some College money, but I am not very good at demanding cash from people.'

'That is why he wants you to go, stupid,' said Risleye scornfully. 'To learn how to demand payment from debtors. It is a vital lesson for any would-be physician.'

Michael glanced at Bartholomew. 'Perhaps it *was* wise to bring these lads along. They may have a corrupting influence on the others, and I would not like to return home to find *my* students have become lazy, selfish and grasping. I do not know how you put up with them.'

* * *

The scholars rode through the Barnwell Gate, then turned right along the Hadstock Way, passing the Dominican Friary and the boggy expanse of the Barnwell Field. Houses became fewer and more scattered as they travelled farther from the town, and were soon reduced to the occasional squatters' hut. Smoke issued through some roofs, but most were silent and still, their inhabitants either begging for bread on the streets of Cambridge or poaching wildfowl and fish in the marshes.

The road led as straight as the path of an arrow through the fertile meadows at the foot of the Gog Magog hills, then headed upwards, passing a series of banks and ditches at the summit, where legend had it that an ancient queen had once defied a Roman army. Behind them, Cambridge was a cluster of red tiles and yellow thatches set amid a sea of winter-brown fields. The towers of St Mary the Great, St Botolph and St Bene't could just be made out, although they were mostly obscured by the pall of smoke created by hundreds of household fires.

It was not long before the drizzle turned into something more persistent. The horses stumbled constantly, and some of the deeper puddles in the rutted track were well past their knees. The little party passed no other travellers once it had crossed the Gog Magogs, indicating they were the only ones foolish enough to embark on a journey in such foul weather.

Gradually, the flat lands of Cambridge gave way to the more rolling country of the west. Copses became more frequent, swathes of mixed woodland in which could be heard the trill of birds and the occasional bark of deer. Trees hissed and waved above them, and wet leaves fell in sodden showers.

They stopped when Michael declared himself hungry, and ate Edith's pies and honey cakes under an ancient oak. The tree did not afford much shelter, but water had seeped through Bartholomew's cloak hours before, and he could not have been wetter had he jumped in the river. It was eerily quiet, and no one objected when the physician brought an early end to the meal and began the hazardous process of remounting his horse.

The farther they travelled, the worse the road became. Ruts were larger, filled to the brim with filthy water. Fallen trees and branches littered the track, and with each one, Bartholomew half expected robbers to emerge – that the blockages were a deliberate ploy to slow travellers down and allow them to be ambushed. The afternoon grew gradually darker and colder, and just when he was thinking they might have to spend the night under a hedge, the highway stopped altogether, as if its builders had run out of materials and had decided to abandon the project.

'Where has it gone?' demanded Michael. 'Langelee said it went all the way to Colchester.'

'My grandfather came this way once,' said Valence helpfully. 'And he told me it goes nowhere near Colchester, although he thinks it was originally meant to.'

'So what are we supposed to do?' snapped Michael. 'Stay here until they decide to finish it?'

'Actually, it does not stop – it splits into three separate tracks,' said Cynric, dismounting to peer into the undergrowth. 'Obviously, they are not wide and straight, like the highway itself, but they all look as if they go somewhere.'

Bartholomew saw the book-bearer was right. One path wound through a dense coppice towards a hill on the left; a much narrower one disappeared into some long grass directly ahead; and the last went downhill, off to the right.

'I vote we go left,' said Michael. 'The track is in marginally better repair than the other two.'

219

'But I suspect Haverhill lies straight ahead,' countered Bartholomew. 'The directions Langelee gave us did not include any left-hand turns.'

'We should go right, because it is downhill,' argued Cynric. 'There is more chance of a settlement in a valley than on a rise.'

'No, we should turn around and go back the way we have come,' said Valence, casting an anxious glance at the darkening countryside. 'There was a village several miles back, with an inn.'

'Nonsense,' declared Risleye. 'We should make camp here, and decide in the morning. Only fools plunge into unknown territory when nightfall cannot be more than an hour away.'

'Or we could make a big fire, so someone sees it and comes to rescue us,' suggested Tesdale with a yawn. 'You five can collect the wood, while I see about drying out my tinderbox.'

'Six possible options, and six views as to which one we should take.' Bartholomew was amused, despite his tiredness and discomfort. Such dissent was typical among scholars.

'I should not have stopped in the first place,' muttered Michael. 'I should have just ridden in the right direction and you would all have followed. This is the problem with democracy: nothing is ever decided. But I am Senior Proctor, and I outrank you all. We shall go left.'

He jabbed his heels into his horse's flanks and rode off before objections could be raised. Bartholomew exchanged a shrug with Cynric, and supposed all three paths must lead somewhere, or they would not be there.

The track Michael had chosen narrowed after a few yards, forcing them to ride single file. Soon, the trees had closed in so tightly that they met overhead to form a gloomy tunnel. Leaves slapped at them as they passed, drenching them in droplets. Then the path jigged to the right, where the wood suddenly gave way to open meadows. Beyond, a few houses could be seen on the brow of a hill.

'Haverhill!' exclaimed Michael victoriously. 'I told you so!'

He was about to move ahead again, when there was a shout. Someone emerged from the woods on the left and began running towards them. There was a mob at his heels, armed with pitchforks. With a gasp of relief, the man reached Michael's horse and seized the reins. For a moment, Bartholomew thought he was going to haul the monk from the saddle and effect an escape, but he evidently took stock of Michael's size and thought better of it.

'Thank God you are here!' he cried. 'You must save me from this vicious, heathen crowd.'

'Sweet Jesus and all the saints preserve us!' breathed Cynric, staring at him in alarm. 'It is Carbo – the priest Shropham murdered. He has risen from the dead, and is here to snatch our souls!'

'That is not Carbo,' said Bartholomew, although the fellow who ducked and bobbed behind Michael's horse was more concerned with the crowd that was pursuing him than with the fact that the book-bearer was accusing him of being a corpse. 'It is someone else.'

'There is an unsettling similarity, though,' acknowledged Michael. 'This fellow is heavier and his hair is longer, but I can see why Cynric confused them.'

'Are you sure?' demanded the book-bearer uneasily. 'You are not mistaking these small differences for what happens to a man once he is in his coffin?'

'They are two different people,' said Bartholomew

221

firmly. The last thing they needed was for Cynric to indulge in a frenzy of superstitious terror when upwards of forty people were converging on them, all brandishing agricultural implements with razor-sharp points. 'Carbo hailed from near here, so it is not surprising to encounter folk who look like him – they will be his kin.'

Once Cynric was settled, Bartholomew turned his attention to the crowd. The men were tall and strong, while their womenfolk gave the impression that they could wrestle with cows, toss haystacks over their shoulders, and tear down trees with their bare hands. Even the children seemed powerful, and were armed with the same ruthlessly honed tools as their elders.

By contrast, the man who cowered behind Michael was a puny specimen. Like Carbo, his complexion was pallid and unhealthy, and his hair fell in oily tendrils around his shoulders. Unlike Carbo, his clothes were well-made and expensive. He was clad in a handsome blue gipon with silver buttons on the sleeves, a gold brooch held his cloak in an elegant fold over his shoulder, and his leggings were bright orange and appeared to be made of silk.

'We have no grievance with you, Brother,' called one of the mob when he drew close enough to be heard, evidently assuming the monk would be in charge. 'Our business is with Adam Neubold. So we shall take him from you, and go our separate ways.'

'Neubold,' mused Michael. 'Well, well, well!'

'You will let them do no such thing,' countered Neubold vehemently. '*I* am a Dominican friar and I demand your help.'

'Is that so,' said Michael archly. 'Then where is your religious habit?'

'In the wash,' replied Neubold, more curtly than was wise when addressing the man he was expecting to save

222

him. 'But my choice of apparel is none of your affair. My grievous treatment at the hands of these savages *is*, however, and I order you to intervene.'

There was an angry murmur from the crowd at the insult, and metallic clangs sounded as implements were brandished. Neubold became alarmed again, ducking behind Bartholomew and eyeing him speculatively, as though wondering whether *he* might be unhorsed, given that the portly monk was clearly out of the question.

'Helping this man is not a good idea,' murmured Cynric, glancing around to assess potential avenues of escape. 'We cannot best forty angry peasants.'

'We should leave,' agreed Risleye. 'This is not our quarrel, and we have no right to interfere.'

'You cannot abandon me,' cried Neubold in horror. 'It would be tantamount to murder!'

Michael addressed the villagers, drawing on all the tact he had learned during his years of dealing with prickly scholars. 'I am sure this can be resolved without a spillage of blood. Perhaps we can adjourn to the nearest church, and discuss the matter like civilised—'

'If you want to be useful, you can lend us a piece of rope, so we can hang this scoundrel,' interrupted the largest and burliest of the villagers. He looked to be in his late thirties, and boasted an unlikely thatch of corn-yellow hair. 'And *then* you can go on your way.'

'No!' screeched Neubold. He grabbed the hem of Michael's habit, while the rabble showed their appreciation of their comrade's remark by hammering their tools on the ground. It sounded like galloping horses, and Bartholomew's nag began to rear in alarm.

'Executing a priest is no way to solve problems,' said Michael, glancing uneasily at the physician's inept attempts to control his mount. The animal was on the verge of bolting – and to do so it would have to go through the press of villagers who now clustered around them. Injuries would be inevitable, and then it might not only be Neubold who was in danger from a furious horde.

'Actually, it would solve a good many problems,' countered Yellow Hair, stepping forward to soothe the beast with large, competent hands. 'But we are not really going to lynch him, tempting though it is. He was trespassing, and all we intend to do is make him apologise for his audacity.'

'Never!' declared Neubold. 'And we shall see what Elyan has to say about this outrage.'

'Elyan?' asked Michael. 'Henry Elyan? What does he have to do with the situation?'

'Neubold is his clerk, as well as his parish priest,' explained Yellow Hair. He regarded Neubold coldly. 'We shall make *him* apologise, too, for sending you in the first place.'

Neubold glowered back at him and made no reply. Michael regarded the Dominican thoughtfully. 'Were you in Cambridge recently, dealing with King's Hall on Elyan's behalf?'

Yellow Hair sneered. 'He sold coal at a greatly inflated price, and was so excited by his success that he came racing home forthwith. Unfortunately, he forgot to collect Elyan's wife on the way, and she promptly fell ill and died. No doubt, that is why he is here now – trying to worm his way back into his master's favour by offering to spy on us.'

'You can go to Hell, William!' spat Neubold. 'You have no right to accuse me of spying, and if you do it again, I shall take legal action and have you fined. And you know I will succeed, because I won Osa and Idoma Gosse a fortune in compensation when they were slanderously maligned.'

There was a growl of disapproval from the throng.

'Aiding those evil villains is not one of your finest achievements,' said William, regarding the priest with disdain. 'And you would do well not to brag, because we despise you for it.'

'They are better than you,' declared Neubold, nettled. 'At least they do not molest priests.'

'They have not been seen for several weeks now,' said William with some satisfaction. 'And word is that they have abandoned their home in Clare. We must have frightened them off when we threatened to hang first and consider the law later.'

'If you had touched them, I would have sued the lot of you,' snarled Neubold. 'You cannot go around stringing up whoever you feel like.'

'No?' asked one villager, fingering his belt meaningfully. 'And who is to stop us?'

'Good people of Haverhill,' said Michael soothingly. 'Do not be hasty in your—'

'Haverhill?' interrupted William, dropping Bartholomew's reins and spinning around to face the monk. Finding itself free, the animal bucked violently. 'Haverhill? How dare you insult us!'

'I assure you, I—' began Michael, bewildered.

'We are the good people of *Withersfield*. We are *not* from Haverhill.' William spoke the name of the neighbouring village as though it was another word for Hell.

'If you wanted Haverhill, you should have continued straight when the old road ended,' called one of the women, evidently trying to be helpful. 'You must have turned left.'

Michael did not look at Bartholomew. 'Well, perhaps we should go back the way we came, then, and set ourselves aright before the daylight fades completely. Assuming my colleague can ever regain control of his horse, that is,' he added, shooting the physician an exasperated glance.

'You do not have time,' said William, coming to the rescue a second time. 'It is not a good idea to enter Haverhill after dark, because you never know who you might meet. So, you had better come with us, and resume your journey in the morning. We shall take you to Roger Luneday of Withersfield Manor. His house has a chimney.'

A ripple of pride ran through the assembled villagers. Chimneys were apparently architectural extras that were highly prized in west Suffolk.

'Well, in that case, we accept,' said Michael, exchanging a brief glance with Bartholomew: it was an excellent opportunity to see whether Luneday would admit to receiving five marks from Wynewyk for pigs. 'We are not men to decline shelter in a house with a chimney.'

'What about me?' demanded Neubold, full of angry indignation. 'Am I to be abandoned to these ruffians, while you flounce off to enjoy Luneday's flue?'

'You will accompany us, and your fate will be decided tomorrow, when tempers have cooled,' decreed Michael. 'It is too late to resolve what promises to be a lengthy business this evening.'

'But I—' objected Neubold.

Michael raised an imperious hand to silence him. 'Who will lead the way to this chimney?'

It was not far to Withersfield. They followed a winding path down to a hollow, where a pretty church nestled in a fold in the hills next to a bubbling brook; several cottages huddled around it. The manor house was set across an undulating sward of common land. It was a handsome building with a thatched roof, and its elegant chimney boasted an ornately carved top. Its orchard was full of

226

apple, pear and cherry trees, and its vegetable plots were home to leeks, onions and cabbages. The scent of herbs and recently scythed grass was rich in the chill evening air.

William led the way towards it, followed by the Michaelhouse men, while the remaining villagers brought up the rear. A reluctant Neubold was among them, protesting vociferously about the way he was being manhandled.

'Be quiet,' snapped William, becoming tired of it. 'If you persist in whining, one of us might give you some real cause for complaint.'

'I have every reason to be indignant,' shouted Neubold. 'I have been shamefully wronged.'

'What exactly did he do?' While Bartholomew's better judgement told him it might be wiser not to ask, it was unusual for a priest to be pursued quite so hotly by a mob. It was also unusual for one to dispense with his habit and sport elegant secular clothing, and the physician's curiosity was piqued.

'Spying,' replied William shortly. 'But he has no excuse this time – he was caught red-handed.'

'Spying on what?' Withersfield was an attractive place, and its villagers were well-fed and healthy, but Bartholomew could not imagine it owned anything to warrant espionage.

'Neubold is parish priest of Haverhill's Upper Church,' William started to explain. He saw the physician's blank look and sighed impatiently. 'The older of its churches.'

'There are two?'

'Actually, there are three. Well, two and a chapel, to be precise. Besides the Upper Church, there is St Mary the Virgin, which is bigger and newer, and there is the chantry chapel.'

'You said Neubold was spying,' prompted Bartholomew. 'On what?'

'I am getting there,' said William testily. 'As I was saying, Neubold is one of Haverhill's priests, so he has no right to set foot on Withersfield soil. The fact that he is here means he is spying – there is no other reason for him to foul our land with his presence. And what do you *think* he wants? Pigs!'

'Pigs?' echoed Bartholomew, mystified.

'Pigs,' repeated William, adding darkly, 'We have them, and Haverhill wants them.'

'Oh,' said Bartholomew, not sure how else to respond.

William's expression was grim. 'But we had better not talk about it any more, because it might induce me to wring Neubold's miserable neck. Tell me about your business instead. Have you come to purchase pottery? I hate to say something good about Haverhill, but they do produce lovely jugs.'

'We might look at them,' hedged Bartholomew, reluctant to admit that they had come to investigate the loss of thirty marks. He was bemused by the antipathy of the Withersfield folk to their Haverhill neighbours, and decided it was safer to keep the real purpose of the visit secret until he and Michael had a fuller understanding of the situation.

William started to press him further, but the physician was spared from answering, because they had reached the manor house. One of the children had evidently run ahead to warn its residents that there were to be guests, for its lord and lady emerged from the house as the party approached.

Luneday was a sturdy fellow in middle years, whose black beard was tinged with grey. He wore a laced gipon of emerald green, and his shoulder cloak was brown and held in place by a gold pin. His boots were thick and practical, and bore stains that suggested he had been out on the land that day. The woman next to him was clad in a close-fitting kirtle, an unflattering garment for someone on the plump side. Her fair hair was coiled and held in place by a fine net of silver thread, called a fret.

'I hear we are to have the pleasure of company tonight,' said Luneday, smiling a welcome. 'A monk from St Edmundsbury Abbey and his companions.'

'Actually, they are only scholars from Cambridge,' said William apologetically. 'They do not have the good fortune to hail from Suffolk.'

Tesdale bristled with resentment at the remark. He was proud of the fact that he was Cambridge born and bred, and Bartholomew was obliged to nudge him, to prevent him from making an acid retort. Risleye merely regarded the lord of the manor with an aloof expression, as if he considered a mere landowner beneath him, although Valence smiled engagingly.

'It does not matter,' said Luneday. He tried to conceal his disappointment, but did not succeed – scholars were evidently a very poor second to visitors from St Edmundsbury. He cleared his throat, and gestured to the lady at his side. 'This is my woman, Margery Folyat.'

'Your wife?' asked Bartholomew, a little bemused by the odd introduction.

'Oh, no,' replied Luneday airily. 'My wife has been on business in Thetford since the plague, so Margery moved in three years ago, to keep me from being lonely.'

'And to keep his purse empty,' muttered William, not quite loud enough for Luneday to hear. Bartholomew glanced at him, and saw him regarding Margery with considerable dislike. But when he turned back to Margery, he supposed she did look like a woman out for her own ends. The hand on Luneday's arm was more possessive than affectionate, and it was clear from her fine clothes that she liked spending money.

With unexpected grace for a man so large, Michael slid from his saddle and effected an elegant bow. Impressed by his gracious manners, Margery stepped forward to return the greeting.

'I do like your cloak, Brother,' she said, with a predatory smile that made Bartholomew wonder whether she intended to have it off him. 'I do not think I have ever seen such fine wool – nor such generous folds. It must have cost a fortune.'

'Her husband lives in Haverhill,' Luneday went on, hastily stepping between them, 'where he works as a gate-keeper. But we rarely visit the place, so we do not run into him very often. It is just as well, as he does not like her being up here and complains about it every time we do meet.'

'You caught him, then,' said Margery, indicating Neubold with a nod of her head. Then it was the priest's turn to shoot her a look of dislike; she returned it in full. 'I thought he was going to escape, because I have never seen anyone run so fast. He was like a rat, scuttling away.'

'Lock him in the barn, William,' ordered Luneday, also treating Neubold to a contemptuous glare. 'We shall have his apology in the morning. I do not like men who steal pigs, especially Lizzie.'

'He was trying to *steal* Lizzie?' William was appalled. 'I thought he was just inspecting her litter.'

'He had a halter around her neck,' said Luneday. He presented a harness, fashioned from rope, which William snatched from him in shocked anger.

Neubold became flustered when confronted with the evidence of his crime. 'That is not a halter,' he declared.

His eyes were everywhere, like a frightened ferret. 'It is a charm.'

'A charm?' echoed Margery, her voice dripping contempt. 'Do not insult us with lies!'

'What kind of charm?' asked Luneday.

'One that will ensure Lizzie wins the Haverhill and Withersfield Livestock Competition again next year,' babbled Neubold. 'It is for luck.'

Margery released a sharp bark of laughter, which was echoed by the listening villagers. 'You should stick to the law,' she said. 'You may impress the likes of Osa Gosse by manipulating obscure statutes, but you are a pathetic thief. Even your brother is better than you, and he is mad.'

'Carbo is not a thief,' objected Neubold stiffly. 'And neither am I.'

'There,' murmured Michael in Bartholomew's ear. 'Cynric was right to notice the similarity between this man and Carbo. They are siblings.'

'No?' Margery was demanding. 'Then who stole Hilton's spare habit?'

'You bought him a lovely new one,' snapped Neubold. 'So Carbo actually did Hilton a favour.'

'Is your brother a Dominican?' asked Bartholomew, trying to sound casual.

Margery's laughter was spiteful. 'Carbo wanted to become a priest when he finished working here, but the Dominicans would not have him. Nor would any Order.'

'That does not say much for his character,' Michael muttered, while William and Luneday exchanged an uncomfortable glance: evidently, Margery's tongue was too sharp for their liking. 'The Black Friars accept virtually anyone, and the fact that they drew the line at Carbo tells us a lot.'

'Where is Carbo these days?' asked Luneday with a sudden frown. 'I have not seen him in ages.'

'Neither have I,' replied Neubold shortly. 'But I have been away on important business in Cambridge. However, I am sure he will reappear when he hears I am home again.'

'Actually,' began Tesdale helpfully. 'Carbo is the man who Shropham—'

'Does your mother live in Withersfield, Neubold?' interrupted Bartholomew, saying the first thing that came into his head. He did not want the priest to learn about his brother's death in such circumstances – it would be kinder to break the news when they were alone.

Neubold regarded him askance. 'What a curious question! She died almost two years ago. Carbo took it badly – it was what caused him to lose his post as steward here. He loved her very much.'

'Yes, but I could only be expected to tolerate his negligence for so long,' said Luneday. He sounded defensive, as if dismissing Carbo had been a difficult decision. 'He did no work for months, and had plenty of warnings. I had no choice but to give William his job.'

'I will sue you for it,' declared Neubold. 'There is bound to be some statute forbidding shabby treatment of stewards, and I shall find it. I will have your fine pig in compensation for—'

'Get him out of my sight,' said Luneday to William. 'I am tired of his bleating. Lock him in the barn, where we will not be able to hear him.'

Not surprisingly, Neubold did not go quietly. 'You cannot lock me up,' he yelled. 'I am a priest!'

'Then where is your habit?' demanded William. He smirked. 'But we know the answer to that: you cannot steal a pig wearing priestly robes, so you dispensed with them, and donned a disguise.'

Neubold's face was black with anger, suggesting there

232

was at least some truth in the accusation. He was still objecting as he was dragged around to the back of the house, and his enraged howls remained quite audible for some time after.

CHAPTER 7

The inside of Withersfield Manor was as neat and pleasant as its outside. There was a huge hall on the ground floor, with two chambers for sleeping above it – one for Luneday and his woman, and one for their servants. The stone floor was strewn with rushes, and the walls had been painted with hunting scenes. A fire blazed merrily in the hearth, large enough for all to enjoy its warmth. Cynric and the students retreated to the far side, where the book-bearer honed his sword and entertained Valence, Risleye and Tesdale with yet another account of Poitiers.

'Withersfield is a jewel in the Suffolk countryside,' boasted Luneday, as he handed goblets of mulled wine to Bartholomew and Michael. The brew was rough, but the scholars were cold and thirsty, so did not mind. 'Of course, you do not need me to tell you that, since you have ridden through it. You will already have seen that it is a foretaste of Heaven.'

'You have not told us your business in the area, Brother,' said Margery, more inclined to fish for information than to dispense it. 'Why have you come all this way?'

Bartholomew glanced at Michael, and saw him consider his options: launch into an enquiry about the five marks Wynewyk was supposed to have given Luneday, or wait until morning. The wrong questions might cause Luneday to take umbrage and order them to leave

– and the weather was worsening. But postponing the matter might mean an opportunity lost and never regained.

'My College has done business with Haverhill for years,' began Michael, evidently deciding to put duty before comfort. 'Coal, timber, pigs—'

'Pigs?' echoed Luneday, raising his eyebrows. 'Haverhill cannot have sold you pigs, for they do not own any worth mentioning. Are you sure about this?'

'No,' said Michael. 'A colleague named Wynewyk made the arrangements, but he is dead.'

Bartholomew was watching Luneday closely, but the lord of Withersfield Manor showed no spark of recognition at Wynewyk's name. A fleeting frown crossed Margery's face, but the physician could not tell whether it was significant, or whether she was merely searching her memory.

'I am sorry to hear that,' said Luneday. His tone was bland, impossible to interpret. 'However, if he bought pigs from Haverhill, then perhaps it is just as well – he cannot have been a sensible man.'

'How about if he had done business with Withersfield?' asked Michael innocently.

Luneday smiled again. 'Then he would have been very wise.'

'Our Master, Ralph de Langelee, is always telling us that Withersfield is the only place to come for pigs,' Michael went on, pushing the matter further. 'It is a pity Wynewyk did not listen to him.'

'It is indeed,' agreed Luneday. He smiled again. 'But I like the sound of this Langelee.'

'He is a great philosopher and a man of outstanding wisdom.' Michael faltered when Bartholomew choked into his wine. The physician was glad the students were not within earshot; they would have laughed openly, thinking the monk was making a joke.

'Then he should have come to trade in person,' said Luneday, standing to pound on the physician's back. He banged rather harder than was necessary, and Bartholomew was not sure whether Luneday was just a naturally vigorous person, or whether it was revenge for Michael's sly probing. 'Your Wynewyk does not seem to have been capable – not if he went to Haverhill.'

Michael pretended to look thoughtful. 'Do you know, I think Wynewyk *did* tell me came here. I distinctly recall him mentioning a chimney. And I am sure he said he spent five marks on pigs.'

'Five marks is a lot of hog,' said Luneday, sitting again when Bartholomew had recovered his breath. 'I do not recall Wynewyk, though. Are there documents to substantiate his claim?'

'Not that we have found. It must have been a gentleman's agreement – five marks given on the understanding that the contract would be honoured by men of decency and principle.'

'It is getting late,' said Margery with a yawn. 'And we retire early here, because there is so much to be done in the fields – not that *I* labour, of course. I prefer to stay inside and have my hair dyed.'

Luneday jumped to his feet again. 'My woman is right. We all need our sleep, and you look tired, Brother. The maid will bring you bedding, and we shall bid you goodnight.'

Michael's smile was pained, but there was no way he could force Luneday to stay and answer questions. He nodded his thanks, and watched the lord of the manor and his woman disappear up the stairs. There was a short delay as a maid hunted for spare blankets and straw-filled mattresses, then she followed her master's example and went to bed, too. It was not long before the house was silent.

'I am not sure what to think,' said Bartholomew, removing some of his clothes and setting them to dry by the fire. Cynric and the students were examining the bedding, paying no attention to the discussion between physician and monk. Risleye was agreeing with Cynric that everything was damp and smelled of mould; Tesdale was declaring that he did not care and just wanted to lie down; and Valence said he was grateful just to have a roof over his head. 'Was Luneday lying about not knowing Wynewyk?'

'I could not tell,' said Michael. He frowned. 'But do you remember what Risleye said about meeting Wynewyk in Babraham when he should have been visiting his father?'

Bartholomew nodded. 'Are you thinking that Risleye caught Wynewyk returning from Suffolk – that he *did* come here to buy pigs from Luneday?'

'Yes. He paid Risleye to keep the encounter quiet, which is suspicious in itself. *Ergo*, I suspect he came in person to facilitate these arrangements – he would not have done it in writing, as the transactions were illegal. He was a lawyer, and knew better than to leave a document trail.'

'The transactions were not illegal,' argued Bartholomew. 'They are inexplicable, which is not the same thing. However, you may be right about his travels – perhaps he did come here. If so, then maybe he used another name. That would explain why Luneday did not recognise "Wynewyk".'

'It is possible, although you should bear in mind that

men engaged in legitimate business do not feel the need for such subterfuge. Of course, we must also remember that Wynewyk may have chosen these names randomly – that Luneday, Elyan and d'Audley are innocent of any wrongdoing.'

'*Wynewyk* is innocent of wrongdoing,' persisted Bartholomew doggedly.

'How can you still think that?' asked Michael wonderingly. 'He tried to kill Langelee, he sent letters to noblemen offering to sell them diamonds, and he cheated your College. It is not as if it is just one dubious incident here, Matt – it is several, and they do not add up to anything pleasant.'

'That is because we still do not have the whole picture, and it is leading you to premature conclusions. However, there are a lot of connections between these Suffolk men and Cambridge. Something is going on – and it is bigger than Wynewyk.'

Michael regarded him soberly. 'I hope you will not be too devastated when you learn your faith in him is misplaced. But we should not discuss this tonight, when neither of us has new evidence with which to sway the other. We will only quarrel, and I am too weary for a spat.'

Bartholomew was only too happy to oblige. 'Perhaps we should talk about Carbo instead.'

Michael winced. 'Perhaps we should not – it is too depressing. We still know nothing about him.'

'Nonsense, Brother! We have learned that the death of a much-loved parent lost him his post as Luneday's steward. And we know he was no priest – his Dominican habit was stolen property. Tomorrow, I shall ask Neubold how his brother came by the injury to his head – the one I think was responsible for his odd demeanour.

I said the scarring looked as if the wound had been inflicted in the last two years or so, and—'

'And his mother died a little less than two years ago,' finished Michael. 'How do you think he came to be hurt? An accident? He was a steward, and we all know agriculture is a dangerous business.'

Bartholomew shrugged. 'Who knows? The possibilities are endless – a fall, a kick from a horse, being struck with something heavy, either accidentally or deliberately. That is why we need to ask Neubold. Are you going to tell him his brother is dead?'

'We must, so he can go to Cambridge and retrieve the body, otherwise it will end up in the Dominican cemetery. Of course, Carbo might not have minded that, given that he wanted to enrol.'

'What was he doing in Cambridge, do you think? What drew him there?'

'I have no idea. It is yet another of these curious coincidences that keep cropping up in this case. They are beginning to be aggravating, so let us hope tomorrow brings some solutions.'

'Be careful how you go about getting them, Brother,' said Bartholomew uneasily. 'I cannot say why exactly, but I do not feel safe here.'

Because the inhabitants of Withersfield Manor retired so early – far earlier than Bartholomew went to bed in Cambridge, even during winter – he had no idea what time it was when he woke later. It was still pitch black, and not even the merest glimmer of light came from under the window shutters. The fire had burned out, so he supposed several hours had passed. He lay in the darkness trying to determine whether the vague patterns he could see on the ceiling were the rafters or his imagination.

'Did that noise wake you?' Cynric's low voice so close to his ear made him jump. There was a faint hiss of steel as the book-bearer drew his sword. 'Someone is prowling, edging ever closer to us.'

Bartholomew lay still, straining his ears for anything out of the ordinary. All he could hear was Michael's wet breathing and a strangled moan that told him Tesdale was in the grip of one of his dreams. Then there was a slight rustle to his left, as if a mouse or a rat was scavenging in the rushes. Outside, an owl hooted, and another answered from a distance. He raised himself on one elbow and peered around the hall, although it was far too dark to see anything.

'You must have imagined it,' he whispered. 'Or perhaps someone is moving about upstairs.'

He reached out to the place where Cynric's voice had been, but the Welshman had moved, and the physician's groping hand met nothing but empty air. He sat up and widened his search. He encountered an arm.

'I have a candle in my saddlebag,' called Cynric softly from across the hall. 'I shall light it.'

Bartholomew froze as the arm was wrenched away. The limb had been too small for Michael, and too well-muscled to have been Risleye or Valence. Meanwhile, he could still hear Tesdale dreaming.

'Who are you?' he demanded, clambering hastily to his feet. His voice was loud, and he was aware of Michael and the students snapping into wakefulness. 'Who is there?'

He sensed, rather than saw, someone lunge at him, using his voice as a beacon. He jerked away, and tripped over the mattress he had been using. The other person stumbled, too, and Bartholomew heard a faint thud as something was dropped on the floor. The physician staggered upright

240

again, waving his arms in front of him like a blind man. His flailing hands encountered a cloak.

'Cynric!' he yelled urgently, fingers tightening around it. 'I have him.'

He did not have him for long, however. A fist caught him on the side of the head, and for a few moments he could not decide whether the lights he saw dancing in front of his eyes were real or imagined. The breath went out of him as he hit the floor. Michael started to shout, and Cynric began crashing about furiously on the other side of the room. Bartholomew struggled into a sitting position, and thought he could see a dim rectangle of light in the distance. Then Valence managed to light a candle, and its little flame filled the hall with eerily dancing shadows.

Michael and Risleye had apparently encountered each other in the darkness, and the monk had the student in a throttling grip. Cynric was near the hearth, while Tesdale was still in bed. Valence was kneeling on the floor, holding the candle aloft with a fearful expression on his face. The main door to the manor stood open, and a cold wind snaked through the rushes on the floor. Whoever it was that Cynric had heard, and that Bartholomew had come so close to catching, had fled.

The commotion had roused their hosts, and it was not many moments before Luneday and Margery came clattering down the stairs. Their servants appeared, too, bringing lanterns. The light illuminated a dagger that lay on the floor near Bartholomew's feet, and the physician supposed the intruder had lost it during the scuffle – he had certainly heard something fall. It was a long, wicked-looking thing, with a blade honed to a murderous sharpness.

241

Cynric was suddenly nowhere to be seen, and Bartholomew realised he had gone outside to hunt for their would-be assailant. He started to follow, but his legs were unsteady, and he had not taken many steps before he was obliged to seek the support of a wall.

'What is the matter?' demanded Luneday. He wore a long nightgown and hefty boots. 'Are all Cambridge men in the habit of waking their hosts by screeching in the depths of the night?'

'Someone attacked us,' shouted Michael furiously, pointing to the knife. 'We are lucky Cynric was alert, or we would have been murdered where we lay.'

'No one tried to kill you!' exclaimed Luneday in disbelief. 'This is Suffolk – we do not go around slaughtering people here.'

Cynric appeared, shaking his head in disgust. 'There is no moon, and the clouds are thick. I could not see well enough to track him.'

'Track whom?' demanded Margery. 'There is no one here, other than us.'

'Someone came while we were asleep,' said Cynric with quiet conviction. 'He fled when he saw we were going to be more of a challenge than he anticipated.'

'You imagined it,' said William, who had arrived with the servants, yellow hair awry. 'Being in a strange place made you restless, and you dreamt someone was in here.'

'One of you was certainly whimpering and moaning,' said Margery. 'I could hear him from upstairs, and I am not surprised he disturbed the rest of you.'

'Then how do you explain the knife?' asked Michael coldly. 'We are not imagining that.'

'We do not change the rushes very often,' admitted Luneday. 'It could have been there for ages.'

'Someone came in from outside,' insisted Cynric. 'It caused a draught, which woke me. In fact, the door has been opening and shutting all night, and it has been difficult to get any rest at all.'

'Not so!' cried Luneday indignantly. 'We keep the door closed after dark, and no one wanders anywhere. Why would they, when it is cold and wet outside, but warm and cosy in here?'

'And more to the point, why would anyone attack you?' asked Margery. 'Apart from the good Brother's handsome cloak, you have nothing a thief could possibly want.'

'There are motives for attack besides robbery, madam,' said Michael stiffly.

'Such as what?' demanded Luneday. 'I was under the impression that you are strangers here. If that is the case, then how can you have acquired enemies?'

'There is Neubold,' Michael pointed out. 'He was not pleased when we let William put him under arrest, and he almost certainly hates us for it.'

'No doubt,' agreed Luneday. 'But he is locked in the barn, so cannot have come to stab you, even if he had been so inclined.'

'You are right,' said Michael. Bartholomew glanced sharply at him, bemused by the abrupt capitulation. 'We are all tired. It must have been each other we encountered in the dark.'

Luneday smiled thinly, then turned to William. 'Relight the fire. Perhaps that will ease our guests' minds. But it is late, and we all need to sleep if we are to do business in a rational manner tomorrow.'

He left, taking his people with him, while William busied himself in the hearth. The steward made several snide remarks about leaving a lamp burning as well, lest the scholars were afraid of the dark, but eventually he went, too, and the Michaelhouse men were alone again.

'We did not fight each other,' said Cynric, eyeing the monk resentfully. 'Someone *was* in here – I saw him haul open the door and hare off into the night. It was someone local, because he knew his way around, even though it is pitch black, both inside and out.'

'I believe you,' said Michael. 'Which is why you five will sleep, while I stand the first watch. I shall wake Cynric in an hour. It should be easier now the fire is lit – we will be able to see.'

'If you believe me, then why did you let Luneday think we imagined it?' demanded Cynric, aggrieved. 'Now he thinks we are cowards, frightened of our own shadows.'

'I was being practical,' replied Michael. 'If we had pressed our point, he might have asked us to leave, and I do not want to be out in the dark while assassins lurk.'

'I do not like Suffolk,' declared Cynric sullenly. 'It is a dangerous place.'

The rest of the night passed uneventfully. Michael woke Cynric when he felt himself begin to drowse; then Cynric woke Valence and Risleye, they woke Tesdale, and Tesdale woke Bartholomew within moments on the grounds that no one would know how long he had been awake anyway.

The physician opened a window shutter, and watched dawn steal across the fields. First, the sky turned from black to dark blue, then to violet. The landscape became full of grey shadows, which gradually resolved into trees, hedges, fences and buildings. There was no sign of the sun, hidden as it was behind a layer of cloud, but Bartholomew felt better once the night was over at last.

244

He roused the others when he heard Luneday and Margery stirring above, and walked outside. The air was fresh, full of the scent of wet grass and damp earth. A sheep bleated in the distance, and he could hear the gurgle of the nearby brook. It was a pleasant, almost idyllic scene, and he began to wonder whether he had imagined the botched attack of the night before. Then he touched his hand to his head, where a fist had landed, and felt a tenderness that told him it had been all too real.

He returned to the house, where he and his companions were given slices of cold oatmeal to dip in beakers of cream, and goblets of sweet ale to wash it down. Once they had broken their fast, Michael apologised to Luneday for the disturbance they had caused. Luneday was all smiles, and seemed more than happy to forget the incident. He rubbed his hands together energetically.

'Now,' he said. 'Perhaps I can interest you in a tour of my piggeries?'

Michael hesitated, not enthusiastic about a venture that would consume valuable time, yet realising it was an opportunity to resume his questions about the five marks. But before he could reply, there was a commotion in the yard outside. The racket grew louder, until the door was thrown open and William burst in, a horde of villagers at his heels.

'Did you release Neubold this morning?' he demanded. 'He is not where we left him.'

Luneday was unconcerned. 'He has probably hidden in the hay, to give you the impression he has escaped. It will delight him to think he has deceived you, so do not bray too loudly about—'

'We searched the barn from top to bottom,' interrupted William. 'With dogs. He is not there. However, Margery visited Haverhill last night, after we were all abed. I do not suppose *she* mentioned the fact that we had him here, did she? Let folk know he was in need of rescue?'

Luneday's eyes narrowed. 'How do you know my woman went to Haverhill?'

'Horses make a noise, even when their riders keep to the verges.' William glared at Margery. 'When I heard hoofs, I looked out of my window and I saw her.'

Luneday sighed as he turned to Margery. 'I thought we had agreed that these nocturnal forays would stop. Either you stay in Withersfield with me, or you go back to your old life in Haverhill with your husband the gatekeeper. You cannot have both.'

Margery scowled, and gave the impression she would have both if she wanted to. 'I may have left Withersfield for a while.' She shot William a black look. 'I like to ride at night. It is invigorating.'

'Did you take this invigorating ride to Haverhill?' demanded William coldly. 'And while you were there, did you happen to mention that we had one of their parish priests under lock and key?'

'It may have slipped into a conversation,' replied Margery defensively. 'I do not recall.'

'What could take her to Haverhill in the depths of the night?' asked Michael, more of himself than of the community at large. His comment was heard, however, and William answered.

'She likes to visit her grandchildren – her son's brats. But her husband is gatekeeper, so getting into Haverhill without him seeing her is virtually impossible. However, he is less vigilant after dark.'

Margery sidled towards Luneday, pointedly ignoring the steward. 'I only do it to avoid unpleasant confrontations,'

246

she whined ingratiatingly, taking his arm. 'And I was lonely for the children.'

'Who did you talk to?' demanded Luneday, freeing his hand impatiently. 'Who might have come to set Neubold free?'

'Well, I met d'Audley and Hilton,' admitted Margery reluctantly. 'They had been working on the deeds to the chantry chapel. But I do not think the news of Neubold's detention excited their interest.'

'Yes, but d'Audley would not have kept such a fact to himself,' said Luneday bitterly. 'By dawn, everyone in Haverhill would have known one of their priests had been incarcerated by us. Haverhill must have mounted a rescue mission, and come to take him back.'

'Almost certainly – but I do not think he was grateful for their trouble,' said William grimly. 'There is hay everywhere, as though there was a fight.'

'He made a mess to spite you,' said Margery, shooting William a look to indicate she thought him stupid. 'Why should he sit quietly all night when he could avenge himself with mischief?'

Bartholomew listened to their quarrel, and thought visiting children in the middle of the night was a peculiar thing to do. But it did not seem a good time to say so.

'Did you pass through the hall in order to leave?' he asked instead, recalling Cynric's contention that the door had been opened and shut constantly before the attack.

'Of course,' Margery replied. 'It is the only way out. But if you are wondering why you did not hear me, it is because I know where to step so the floorboards do not creak. I tried not to disturb you.'

'She is probably telling the truth,' whispered Cynric in

Bartholomew's ear. 'I assumed people needed the latrines, and thought nothing of all these comings and goings – until someone crept towards the spot where we were sleeping.'

'Will you tell Master Langelee about me?' asked Luneday, when Michael, who had had enough of Withersfield, stood to leave. 'I like the sound of this fine philosopher who knows his pigs.'

'I certainly shall,' promised the monk. It sounded like a threat. 'We hope to finish our business today and be home by this evening, so he will know all about you by tonight.'

'Ah, yes, your business,' said Margery. 'You did not explain it last night. Will you tell us now?'

'Willingly,' replied Michael. Bartholomew wondered why she was so keen to know – she had asked several times for details. 'We are here to reassess agreements made between our College and three Suffolk traders. Wynewyk negotiated them, but he is dead, so they are invalid.'

Bartholomew watched Luneday intently, to see what he would make of this claim, but the lord of the manor gave nothing away.

'How curious,' Luneday said. 'I assumed you were here about the chantry.'

'Alneston Chantry,' elaborated William, when the monk regarded Luneday blankly. He sighed when his 'explanation' failed to illuminate the matter. 'You must know what we are talking about.'

'Well, I do not,' said Michael irritably.

'Really?' asked Luneday. 'You are not here to challenge d'Audley's hold on it? We heard a Cambridge College was contesting his tenure – allegedly one called King's Hall, but who trusts rumours? – and I assumed *that* was why you made this long and arduous journey.'

'We know nothing of any chantry,' said Michael. He started to leave, but then turned when he reached the door. 'And you are sure Wynewyk never came to do business with you, Master Luneday? I am sure he described your magnificent chimney when he returned home.'

'If he mentioned my chimney, then he admired it from afar, because I have never met him.'

Michael persisted. 'He was a small fellow, neat and clean. And he may have used one of his other names when he introduced himself. It sounds odd, I know, but it was a habit of his.'

'I have never met anyone from Cambridge,' said Luneday. He started to gather his belongings – cloak, hat, dagger and a heavy belt to carry it on – in readiness for an expedition outdoors. 'Visit me again, if you are interested in pigs. They are all for sale with the exception of Lizzie.'

Having been dismissed, Bartholomew and Michael followed Luneday outside. A number of folk milled around the barn, and Bartholomew paused to peer inside it. William was right: it looked as though a skirmish had taken place. Hay had been scattered, and several farming implements lay on the ground. There was, however, no sign that blood had been spilled. Perhaps Margery was right, and Neubold had made a mess for spite. It was not the sort of behaviour usually associated with priests, but Neubold had not seemed like a man particularly devoted to his vocation.

'This is a dismal start,' said Michael, as they rode away. 'I was not expecting Luneday to hand us five marks with a smile and a blessing, but I hoped our questions would elicit *some* answers. We learned nothing from our night in Withersfield, except for the fact that we need to be on our guard.'

'Perhaps that is your answer,' suggested Bartholomew. 'We were attacked because Luneday *does* have our money and he is not keen on giving it back.'

Michael nodded slowly. 'I cannot escape the feeling that there is something very odd and very dangerous going on here. And that it most definitely involves Michaelhouse's thirty marks.'

Blue patches were showing through the clouds by the time the deputation from Cambridge left Withersfield. They rode along a pleasant track that eventually descended into a wide, shallow valley. A stream meandered across water meadows that were fringed by ancient oaks. Tesdale was unusually quiet, and tearfully admitted to dreaming about Wynewyk the previous night – that he was still alive, and had asked him to mind his classes while he went to the castle.

'Wynewyk would not have asked *you* to help,' scoffed Risleye, before Bartholomew could say it was normal to dream about the recently dead. 'He would have hired his own students.'

'You are wrong,' declared Valence. 'He knew Tesdale and I were short of money, so he often passed small tasks our way. He was a good man, and I wish he had not died. He was too young.'

'It is something you will have to get used to, if you are going to be a physician,' said Risleye unfeelingly. 'Death will be our constant companion once we are qualified.'

Bartholomew was unsettled by the bleak remark. 'It becomes easier with time,' he said kindly to the other two, although he did not add that it was not by much. 'The secret is to concentrate on helping the patient, rather than railing against matters over which you have no control.'

250

'I should have stopped him from laughing so heartily,' said Tesdale miserably. 'Or warned him that eating four slices of almond cake was too much.'

Bartholomew regarded him uneasily. 'He had four pieces? That *is* a lot.'

'Especially for a man who tended to cough and gasp when he swallowed nuts,' said Valence. 'He must have been so amused by the debate that he did not realise what he was doing. He had his own piece, then he devoured the three that Thelnetham set aside for himself, Clippesby and Michael.'

'Thelnetham put them close to Wynewyk deliberately,' asserted Risleye. 'I saw him. He knew Wynewyk had wolfed his own, and it was a taunt – that others still had theirs to enjoy.'

'Thelnetham is not like that,' cried Valence. 'What is wrong with you?'

'Actually, Thelnetham *is* like that,' countered Tesdale. 'He can be very cruel. Well, he is a lawyer, so what do you expect?'

While he and Risleye continued to attack the Gilbertine, and Valence struggled to defend him, Bartholomew considered what had been said about Wynewyk. His colleague had always been careful about avoiding nuts. Was it significant that he had thrown caution to the wind at the exact same time that Langelee had revealed the inconsistencies in the accounts? Could Wynewyk really have forced himself to eat four slices of cake, in the full knowledge of what would happen to him? Bartholomew rubbed his eyes. Why had Wynewyk not come to him for help? He was sure they could have worked together to devise a solution to whatever predicament he had embroiled himself in.

He realised with a guilty start that he was allowing

Michael's convictions to influence him – that he was starting to believe Wynewyk *had* done something wrong. Of course, it was not unreasonable, because the evidence was certainly mounting up. But then an image of Wynewyk's face swam into his mind, and he felt ashamed for doubting the man who had been his friend.

'Ignore them, Matt,' said Michael, assuming the physician's unhappy expression was a result of the increasingly acrimonious squabble that was taking place between the students. 'One will kill the others soon, and then you will not have to intervene in their childish spats.'

'Do not say such things,' snapped Bartholomew. He saw Michael's startled look, and relented. 'I am sorry, Brother, but death in Michaelhouse is not a joke. Wynewyk's is hard enough to cope with.'

'Then we shall talk about something else. Who do you think attacked us last night?'

Bartholomew was not sure this was a topic *he* would have chosen to cheer a despondent colleague, but it was better than thinking about Wynewyk.

'Neubold?' he suggested. 'He escaped, then decided to avenge himself on the men who saw him incarcerated in the first place?'

'I doubt it,' said Michael. 'He was annoyed with us, but not murderously so. Besides, I doubt he is man enough to invade the home of his enemy and spit six men in their beds.'

Bartholomew listed his other suspects. 'Luneday was wearing a strange combination of nightshift and boots when he came to see what was wrong, while Margery's midnight jaunt to visit children was odd, to say the least. *And* she was suspiciously determined to discover the purpose of our visit.'

'But she said the only way out of the manor house was through the hall. And she and Luneday came from upstairs when we raised the alarm. Our would-be killer had fled outside at that point.'

'She *said* it was the only exit,' replied Bartholomew with a shrug. 'Why should we believe her? And I am not sure what to make of William the steward, either, or those vengeful villagers. As far as I am concerned, any of them could have come after us with a sharp knife.'

Michael rubbed his chin. 'Meanwhile, Luneday denies knowing Wynewyk, but I am not sure he is telling the truth. And five marks is a lot of money.'

'It is,' agreed Cynric. Neither scholar had known he was listening, and his voice made them jump. 'There are those who would kill an entire village for less.'

'Then let us hope none of them live in Haverhill,' said Michael feelingly.

'What shall we do first?' asked Michael, when they had ridden in silence for a while. 'Go to see Elyan, who was paid eighteen marks for coal? Visit d'Audley, who was paid seven marks for timber? Or simply stroll into Haverhill and see what might be learned by chatting to the locals?'

'The latter,' advised Bartholomew. 'You had no success dangling Wynewyk's name in front of Luneday, so there is no reason to think these other two lordlings will be any different.'

'What are those?' asked Michael suddenly, pointing to several mounds of soil in the distance. 'They look like earthworks – the kind thrown up around a castle to act as additional defences.'

'It must be the colliery,' replied Cynric. 'Elyan sells coal in Cambridge, do not forget.'

253

'I cannot imagine there is coal here,' said Bartholomew doubtfully. 'It is not the right kind of landscape, for a start, and there is no sign of black dust in the ground.'

'But he must get it from somewhere,' Michael pointed out. 'And I am sure I can see a dark streak in the exposed rock – it is next to that little hut.'

'You are right,' said Cynric, standing in his stirrups for a better view. 'I can see two men with pickaxes, and about six others lounging around talking to each other. It must be the mine.'

Bartholomew did not argue, but he remained sceptical: he had been in coal country, and it was different from west Suffolk. But they had reached the outskirts of Haverhill, and he soon forgot minerals as he looked with interest at the houses they passed. Most were large, well-built and handsome, and it seemed there was money in the area. The main road led to a vast triangle of open land in the village's centre, which appeared to be a market. It was overlooked by a large church. Nearby was a ramshackle little building with a bell-cote. A second street wound up a hill, on which stood a smaller church and another cluster of cottages.

'The place on the rise must be the Upper Church,' said Bartholomew, recalling what William had told them the previous day. 'Neubold's parish. And that half-derelict place below must be the Alneston Chantry – which Luneday thought we were going to try to wrest from d'Audley.'

'Well, it is all very pretty,' said Michael, barely looking to where the physician was pointing. 'But we are not here to admire the scenery: we are here to retrieve our money. What is this?'

His progress was impeded by a fence that stretched across the road. There was a gate in the middle, but it was closed. As his horse skittered about in confusion, a small,

254

well-dressed man emerged from a pleasant little cottage to one side.

'I am Gatekeeper Folyat,' he announced without inflection, as if he recited the words many times a day. 'State your intentions and purpose.'

'Folyat?' asked Michael, raising his eyebrows. 'There is a name I have heard before. Are you the Gatekeeper Folyat who was once wed to Margery of Withersfield?'

Folyat's eyes narrowed. 'No. I am the Gatekeeper Folyat who *is* wed to Margery. And she is not of Withersfield, but of Haverhill. She thinks our union will be annulled one day, so she can marry that adulterous Luneday, but it will be over my dead body. However, my marital status is none of your concern. I asked what *you* wanted in our village.'

'Jugs,' lied Michael. 'We may be interested in purchasing some.'

'Three pennies, then,' said Folyat. 'Or a chicken. I have no strong feelings one way or the other, so do not trouble yourselves on my account.'

'But we intend to spend money here,' objected Michael. 'Why should we pay for the privilege?'

'Because everyone else does,' replied Folyat. 'Roads are expensive to maintain, so why should you ride about on them without donating something towards their upkeep?'

'No wonder this is a wealthy place,' muttered Michael resentfully. He rummaged for the requisite number of pennies. 'You will have to accept coins, I am afraid – I left my poultry at home.'

Folyat counted the money. 'Are you only interested in jugs or do you have other business? If yes, I may be able to point you in the right direction, especially if you have come to arrange a slaughter.'

'A slaughter?' echoed Michael warily, eyes narrowed.

'By our butchers,' explained Folyat. 'They are famous for taking a herd of cattle and rendering it down into easily portable lumps.'

'Lord!' breathed Michael. 'We had better remember that.' He cleared his throat and spoke a little more loudly. 'We may also buy some fuel – coal or wood.'

'You are interested in Elyan's mine, are you? Did you see it as you rode in? The seam was only discovered in the summer, but Elyan believes it will make him very wealthy, even though it is small. Still, a commodity is a commodity, as my wife always likes to say.'

Without conscious thought, Bartholomew and Michael headed for the nearer of the two churches – the large one in the marketplace that Folyat told them was dedicated to St Mary the Virgin. Travellers were expected to give thanks when they arrived safely at their destination, so it was not an unusual thing to be doing. But more pertinent to Michaelhouse's thirty marks was the possibility that a garrulous priest might be there, or the kind of parishioner who liked to gossip. It would not be the first time the scholars had gleaned important information from places of worship.

As they drew closer, they saw St Mary's was being treated to some building work. A new three-storey tower had been raised, while the nave and chancel were in the process of being beautified. The end result promised to be magnificent – imposing as well as elegant. Bartholomew glanced at the Upper Church in the distance, and wondered how long it would survive once St Mary's had been completed. The upkeep of such edifices was costly, and looking after two in one village – plus a chantry chapel – would be financially demanding.

Michael pushed open the door and stepped inside, leaving the students to mind the horses. Cynric stayed with them, glancing around uneasily, as if he expected their nocturnal attacker to try his hand a second time. Bartholomew followed the monk, admiring the fine stained glass in the windows and the ornate altar rail. He started to remark on them, but Michael was never very interested in such matters, and began to stride purposefully towards the high altar, where a friar could be seen kneeling.

'A Benedictine,' said the priest, standing as the visitors approached. 'We do not see those very often, despite the fact that one of their greatest abbeys lies not twenty miles away, in St Edmundsbury.'

The speaker was a Dominican, dressed in a spotless habit. He was more closely shaven than most, with curly grey hair and a perfectly clipped tonsure. He exuded a sense of quiet competence.

'Actually, we are from Cambridge,' said Michael. 'The place with the University.'

'I have heard of it,' replied the Dominican dryly. 'It has a reputation for brawls, smelly streets and producing exceptionally cunning lawyers. I am John de Hilton, by the way. May I ask what brings scholars to my humble parish?'

'It is not humble,' countered Michael. 'It is wealthy – large houses, money poured into rebuilding its church, a vast market, efficient slaughterhouses . . . Haverhill has it all.'

'It suits my modest needs.' Hilton smiled, revealing long brown teeth. 'And when my church is finished, it will be one of the finest in Suffolk. What more could a priest want?'

'A princely living?' suggested Michael, making it clear

he would not be satisfied with what the village had to offer. 'Rich parishioners who pay to have documents written? Intriguing confessions?'

Hilton laughed. 'I hear my share of intriguing confessions, I assure you. Haverhill is at loggerheads with its Withersfield neighbours, you see, and I am always being told of some plot to best the enemy. Some are extremely inventive.'

'Why do they dislike each other?' asked Bartholomew curiously.

Hilton shrugged. 'No one remembers exactly how it all started. But these days, we are jealous of Withersfield's pigs, while they covet our jugs and slaughterhouses.'

'It sounds petty,' said Bartholomew, thinking it a shame that two such prosperous communities should waste their energies so.

'It *is* petty,' agreed Hilton. 'I encourage the lords of the manor – Luneday in Withersfield, and Elyan and d'Audley here – to lead by example and resolve their differences, but they are worse than their people. Elyan flaunts his new mine, d'Audley likes to spread sly rumours about Withersfield, while Luneday parades Lizzie in a way that is sure to antagonise.'

'I have only been here a few hours, but I have already witnessed some shocking behaviour,' said Michael, aiming to encourage more confidences. 'Withersfield's master has purloined the wife of Haverhill's gatekeeper, while the Upper Church's priest was caught trying to steal Luneday's sow.'

Hilton's expression was unreadable, and Bartholomew wondered whether everyone in west Suffolk aimed to be inscrutable. 'Neubold has a talent for secular business, although I had thought he confined himself to the law. I did not realise he had graduated to pig rustling.'

258

'Can I assume that while Neubold clerks for Elyan, you clerk for d'Audley?' asked Michael. 'Margery told us you were working on some deeds together when she saw the pair of you last night.'

'I clerk for anyone who needs a scribe or basic legal advice,' replied Hilton. His tone was a little chilly. 'I do not have the same relationship with d'Audley that Neubold enjoys with Elyan.'

'And what relationship is that?'

'Neubold and I are priests,' said Hilton stiffly. 'We are not supposed to neglect our sacred duties for secular ones that pay. Elyan should not make so many demands on Neubold's time – sending him on missions to distant towns, giving him piles of documents to interpret. It is not right.'

'I quite agree. Incidentally, Margery also told us that Neubold's brother stole your spare habit.'

Hilton raised his eyebrows. 'Did she? What a curious tale to relate to strangers! But I did not begrudge it to him – Carbo is a troubled soul, and I only hope it brings him some peace.'

'Unfortunately, it did not,' said Michael quietly. 'He is dead.'

Hilton gaped at him, then crossed himself. 'Poor Carbo! The news is a shock, but not a surprise. He was barely rational most days. He used to be decent and staid, quite unlike his rakish brother, and we were all saddened by his sudden decline.'

'What happened to him?' asked Bartholomew, with the interest of a professional.

Hilton shook his head. 'We are not sure. He was just like you and me two years ago, but then he went missing for several months. When he returned, he was a changed man. It was rather horrible, actually. People believe grief for his mother turned his mind.'

'Was there an accident?' asked Bartholomew. 'Or was he attacked?'

Hilton frowned. 'Not that I have heard. Why?'

'There is a scar on his head, suggesting a serious injury. Perhaps that accounts for the time he was missing – and why he was different when he returned.'

Hilton regarded him uneasily. 'He never mentioned anything about being wounded. But then he never said *anything* about the time he was away. Perhaps you are right, although I am appalled to hear it – appalled that whoever cared for him did not think to come and offer us an explanation. And appalled that he did not come to me for help.'

'Was he ever violent?' asked Michael hopefully. 'Inclined to attack people for no reason?'

'Not to my knowledge. How did he die?'

'In a brawl,' replied Michael. 'Someone stands charged with his murder, but I do not think justice will be served if this man is hanged for the crime.'

'I disagree. Carbo needed kindness and understanding, not people fighting him. His killer should be ashamed of himself for picking such a vulnerable victim.'

'Can you tell us anything else about Carbo?' asked Bartholomew, before Michael could argue.

Hilton shook his head slowly. 'Not really. He was Luneday's steward, but he became incapable of performing his duties, and Luneday was forced to dismiss him. Afterwards, he took to wandering aimlessly about the parish. He found coal on Elyan Manor in August, but the discovery did nothing to improve his health; on the contrary, it seemed to make him more lunatic than ever.'

'He was obsessed with coal when we met him,' said Bartholomew.

Hilton nodded. 'He *was* obsessed – he even changed his

name for it. Unfortunately – but inevitably, I suppose – he became a scapegoat for everything that went wrong in the area. Even a Clare villain – a fellow named Osa Gosse – claimed Carbo stole from him, which is a joke, because not even Carbo was *that* deranged.'

'We know Gosse,' said Michael. 'What did he say Carbo took?'

'A sack, although Gosse refused to say what was in it. Then there was a rumour that Carbo had stabbed a man at Elyan's mine, but I did not believe that, either.'

'Why not?' asked Michael, exchanging a glance with Bartholomew. If Carbo had killed before, then Shropham was more likely to be pardoned.

'Because I felt it was a lie invented by those who are unsettled by ailments of the mind – an excuse to ostracise him, in other words. Once the tale was out, no one was willing to give him kitchen scraps or let him sleep in their barn. The poor man was half starved when I last saw him.'

'He died on Saturday, and it is now Thursday,' said Michael. 'And he had been in Cambridge for several more days before he was knifed. Has no one been concerned by his absence?'

'Not really – he often disappeared. So he went to Cambridge, did he? Perhaps he followed Neubold there, in the misguided belief that his brother would help him. Poor Carbo! But now you must excuse me, because I am needed.'

Bartholomew and Michael watched him walk to where one of his parishioners was jumping from foot to foot in obvious agitation. He led the man to a quiet corner, where the penitent knelt and began a confession that had Hilton's jaw dropping in astonishment. Bartholomew supposed it was one of the 'intriguing' ones the priest had said he heard from time to time.

'At least we can safely say Shropham killed no priest,' said Michael, turning away. 'That will help his case. Carbo must have come at him in a fit of madness, and he did no more than defend himself.'

'Then why does he not say so? He has been given every opportunity.'

'Perhaps he felt guilty at the notion of dispatching a friar,' suggested Michael. 'And he sees his fate as punishment for having struck down one of God's own.'

'If Carbo came at him in a spate of madness, then he is unlikely to have seen him as one of "God's own". He is not stupid, Brother.'

'No,' said Michael with a sigh. 'But let us go and talk to Elyan and d'Audley before any more of the day is lost. I want to be in my own bed tonight, where no one will try to spear me while I sleep.'

As Bartholomew and Michael left St Mary's, Hilton interrupted his parishioner's litany of sins just long enough to inform them that Elyan and d'Audley could usually be found in the marketplace of a morning. Once outside, the physician looked for his book-bearer, but Cynric had used the time to identify the village's best tavern, and had taken the students there to listen to more of his war stories; the horses had been stabled. Satisfied that his companions were warm and safe, he turned to Michael.

'I would not mind sitting in a cosy alehouse,' grumbled Michael, before the physician could ask which lord they should tackle first. 'It is cold out here, and I am daunted by the task Langelee has set us. Short of demanding the money outright, I cannot see how we will reclaim our thirty marks.'

'The Senior Proctor will think of a way,' said Bartholomew encouragingly.

Michael did not look convinced, but turned his attention to the marketplace. It was busy, and apparently attracted people from a large hinterland, as well as the residents of Haverhill. It had a sizeable section dedicated to meat, and the stink of blood and hot entrails was thick in the air. Nearby were rows of glistening river fish, while other stalls hawked jugs, thread, cloth, pots, candles, poultry, furniture and sacks of flour. It was noisy, colourful and lively, and people were exchanging cheerful greetings at the top of their voices, competing with the lowing of cattle and the honks of geese.

'I did not take to Hilton,' said Michael, after a search told them that neither Suffolk lordling was there. 'He said he did not care about Carbo stealing his habit, but I would have been livid. And he was a little too nice for my liking. There he is, standing by the cheese shop. Shall we demand to know why he told us to waste time here, when Elyan and d'Audley are nowhere in sight?'

'I said they can *usually* be found in the marketplace of a morning,' corrected Hilton pedantically, when Michael put his question. 'However, Elyan spends hours up at his mine these days, while d'Audley needs to supervise the cutting of timber from his woods. They may come today, but they may not.'

'I see,' said Michael irritably. 'It is a pity you could not have been more specific sooner. Then we would not have squandered half the day dawdling around slaughterhouses and pottery emporiums.'

'Come, Brother,' said Hilton reproachfully. 'It was hardly "half the day", and visiting their homes would have done you no good, either – they are almost certain to be out. But why do you want to see Elyan? I imagine you are here to discuss the Alneston Chantry with d'Audley – he said a deputation might arrive from

Cambridge soon – but what does Elyan have to do with it?'

'Actually, it is King's Hall that is interested in the chantry,' explained Bartholomew. 'We are from Michaelhouse, which is a totally separate foundation.'

Hilton frowned in puzzlement. 'Then why *are* you here? We do sell pottery and meat to the University, but they always send servants to negotiate. Scholars do not deign to come themselves.'

'No?' pounced Michael. 'One of our colleagues did. His name was Wynewyk, and he did business with d'Audley for wood, with Elyan for coal, and with Luneday for pigs.'

'He bought coal?' asked Hilton, startled. 'But Elyan's mine is not producing yet. He does import a small amount from Ipswich, but it is barely enough to satisfy local demands, and I am amazed that he should have hawked some to your colleague. What did you say his name was again?'

'Wynewyk,' replied Michael. 'Pleasant face, slight build, gentle manners.'

'He does not sound familiar,' said Hilton, after appearing to give the matter some careful reflection. 'But he may have gone directly to Elyan Manor, in order to avoid paying Folyat's toll.'

'What about the timber?' asked Michael. 'Are you surprised he did business with d'Audley, too?'

'A little,' admitted Hilton. 'I thought he restricted himself to customers from Suffolk.'

'And pigs from Withersfield?' asked Bartholomew.

Hilton smiled. 'That does *not* surprise me. Folk travel miles for Luneday's pork, and your Wynewyk is a discerning fellow if he stocked his larders with Withersfield fare. But your ire with me was wholly unnecessary, Brother, because

264

here come Elyan and d'Audley now. They must have been out hunting.'

The two scholars turned at the sudden rattle of hoofs. Elyan was at the head of the cavalcade, a dead deer slung over his saddle. He had apparently decided that black suited him, because every item of his elegant finery was that colour. It was a different outfit to the one he had worn in Cambridge, suggesting he had already invested in a considerable wardrobe of mourning apparel. He dismounted and headed straight for a stall that sold cloth, fingering the more expensive wares appreciatively. The owner hurried to join him, and they were soon deep in discussion.

'He likes clothes,' explained Hilton, rather unnecessarily. 'Barely a week goes by without him ordering some new garment.'

As if to prove him right, Elyan held a length of worsted to his chest, admiring the way it fell towards his feet.

Lady Agnys had also ridden in with the horsemen. Her equestrian skills were even worse than Bartholomew's, and she had been jostled about so much that her veil had come loose and strands of white hair flapped around her face. As her grandson's attention was on the cloth, she was obliged to wait for someone else to help her dismount. With a sigh of surly resignation, d'Audley stepped forward, all scrawny neck and ridiculously thin legs. He staggered when she launched herself into his arms, and the manoeuvre deprived her of a veil and him of a hat.

'I am surprised d'Audley rides in company with Lady Agnys,' said Bartholomew to Hilton. 'When I saw them together in Cambridge, she was not very polite to him.'

Hilton grimaced. 'She has a blunt tongue, and makes no bones about the fact that she cannot abide d'Audley.

Did you see them when they went to collect poor Joan? That was a bad business, especially given that Joan was carrying Elyan's heir. We had all but given up hope in that quarter, and were surprised when she became pregnant. Elyan was delighted, of course.'

'Of course,' said Bartholomew. But the physician in him was curious. 'It is unusual for a woman of Joan's mature years to conceive for the first time. Did she—'

'She prayed to God,' interrupted Hilton, rather sharply, as if he imagined Bartholomew was going to suggest something untoward. 'The Almighty can make a twenty-year union fertile, and Joan was a good and virtuous lady. God rewarded her by granting her a child.'

'I see,' said Bartholomew, thoughts whirling. It had not occurred to him that the reason for Joan's unexpected pregnancy was that she had gone outside her barren marriage, but the priest's defensive answer made him wonder. And if that were true, then perhaps Edith was right to be suspicious of Joan's death. After all, no husband wanted another man's brat to inherit his estates.

Bartholomew was unsure what reception he would receive from Elyan, since their first encounter had been over the body of his wife, but his concerns were unfounded. Neither Elyan nor d'Audley recognised him, partly because it had been dim inside St Mary the Great, partly because they had not paid much attention to him, and partly because he was no longer wearing academic garb. Agnys was more observant, though, and smiled warily when Hilton brought the scholars to be introduced.

'Michaelhouse,' mused Elyan, rather more interested in the worsted. 'Is that the big place overlooking the river? The only time I ever visited Cambridge was to collect the corpse of my poor wife, and I was so upset then that I paid scant heed to my surroundings.'

'We heard about Joan,' said Michael sympathetically. 'Please accept our condolences.'

'Someone gave her pennyroyal,' Elyan went on bitterly, looking at him for the first time. 'And as she was with child, it killed her. In other words, she was murdered.'

'She was *not* murdered, Henry,' countered Agnys firmly. 'She was a dear, kind soul, loved by all.'

'True,' agreed Elyan unhappily. 'She did not have an enemy in the world. However, *I* do, and it is my contention that they attacked me through her.'

'What enemies?' asked Michael.

'He is lord of a profitable manor,' said d'Audley, before Elyan could reply for himself. 'So naturally his less wealthy neighbours are jealous of him. Luneday will do anything—'

'Luneday did *not* kill Joan,' interrupted Agnys, shooting him a long-suffering glare that indicated it was not the first time he had aired his suspicions. 'I know we have had our differences with him, but he is not that sort of man. Besides, he was at home in Withersfield when Joan died.'

'Then he hired someone,' d'Audley flashed back. 'Carbo, for example. Did you know Carbo was wandering around Cambridge when Joan was there?'

'So you have said before,' said Agnys. 'But Luneday would not have hired Carbo for such a task, because the poor man cannot be trusted to carry it out. And she was not murdered, anyway. It was an accident, as I keep telling you.'

'I do not want to talk about it,' said Elyan, handing the cloth to the stall-owner, as if it no longer gave him pleasure. 'Let us discuss something else instead. If you are from

267

Cambridge, then you must be acquainted with Warden Powys and his colleague Paxtone. I have never met them, but my priest Neubold tells me they are fine, upstanding gentlemen.'

'Then he is wrong,' muttered d'Audley. 'They are sly and dishonest, and I hate the lot of them.'

'King's Hall is trying to deprive him of his chantry,' explained Agnys, when Bartholomew and Michael exchanged puzzled glances. 'But they have always dealt decently with us.'

'D'Audley's bad experiences derive from the fact that he uses Hilton to negotiate,' added Elyan. 'He should employ Neubold instead, because he is slippery. Hilton is far too honest.'

Agnys's glower moved from d'Audley to her grandson. 'I cannot believe you still deal with that vile man – not after he abandoned Joan, just to hare home and gloat over some transaction he had brought about. I want nothing more to do with him.'

'I buy his legal skills,' said Elyan. 'That does not mean I like him. Indeed, I find him loathsome, but he is good at his job – unlike Hilton, whose integrity will see d'Audley lose his chantry.'

'Neubold will *not* be more cunning than the University's clerks,' declared Agnys. 'They will see through his amateur tricks in an instant. Hilton has a far better legal mind.'

'I hope you are right,' said d'Audley uneasily. 'Because I would hate to lose the place.'

Bartholomew studied the chantry chapel. It was small and mean, and did not look like an asset worth fighting over. 'Does it belong to an ancestor?' he asked politely.

'It was built by a fellow named Alneston,' replied d'Audley, 'which is why it is called the Alneston Chantry, I suppose. However, I can tell you nothing else about him, other than that he died years ago and bequeathed seven fields – the rent earned from them pays for the services of a priest to pray for his soul.'

'A shilling,' murmured Hilton. 'I am paid a shilling for fifty masses a year. The rest goes—'

'The rest goes towards the upkeep of the building,' interrupted d'Audley, although it was obvious to anyone looking at it that the funds had been diverted – and for a considerable period of time. 'It has been under the stewardship of my family for generations, and I refuse to let some grasping College reap the benefits . . . I mean, assume the responsibility.'

'I have been looking through old deeds, to see whether King's Hall has any right to challenge his possession,' said Hilton to Bartholomew and Michael. 'Unfortunately, many are missing, and it is difficult to tell who holds legal title to what.'

'*I* hold legal title,' stated d'Audley firmly. 'And I have the documents to prove it.'

'Unfortunately, you do not,' said Hilton. 'But the chantry ownership is of no interest to our visitors, and we are wrong to bore them with it.'

'On the contrary,' said Michael smoothly. 'We find it fascinating. Our colleague Wynewyk mentioned none of this when he told us of his visits here.'

For the first time since arriving in Suffolk, Wynewyk's name provoked a reaction other than a blank stare. D'Audley's eyes widened, and he shut an uneasy glance towards Elyan, but his neighbour's expression was bland, and Bartholomew could not tell if he was party to whatever had startled d'Audley.

'Who is Wynewyk?' asked Agnys.

'No one,' replied d'Audley with a brittle smile. 'I have never heard of him.'

'The day is wearing on,' said Elyan, glancing up at the sky. He gave the impression that he was bored with the scholars from Cambridge, and their questions and remarks. 'It is time I inspected my mine.'

Agnys sighed disapprovingly. 'You visit that place far too often, Henry, and it is beginning to impinge on more important estate business. It is not—'

'There *is* nothing more important,' declared Elyan, springing lithely into his saddle. He patted his clothes into place. 'Are you coming, grandmother? Or shall I allow d'Audley to escort you home?'

Neither Agnys nor their neighbour seemed very keen on that proposition. The old lady headed for her horse, while d'Audley suddenly developed an intense interest in worsted.

Gallantly, Hilton stepped forward to help Agnys mount, and, seeing the priest might be struggling for some time unless someone else lent a hand, Bartholomew went to join him. Sensing the presence of two men who were uneasy in its company, the horse began to misbehave. It snickered and pranced, and they might have been there all day, if Michael had not taken charge.

'Hurry up, Hilton,' ordered Elyan irritably. 'I have need of your services today, because Neubold is nowhere to be found. Come with me to the mine, and we shall talk on the way.'

He spurred his horse forward, flicking his fingers as he did so, to indicate Hilton was to trot along at his side. Agnys followed more sedately. D'Audley abandoned the worsted and started to walk in the opposite direction, but found his path blocked by Michael.

'Tell me about Wynewyk,' said the monk pleasantly. 'Your reaction to his name made it obvious you *do* know him, so please do not claim otherwise. Could it be connected to timber, at all?'

'Timber?' echoed d'Audley in a squeak. 'Why should I know him in connection with timber?'

'Because he bought some from you. It cost him seven marks, although our woodsheds remain curiously empty.'

'Do they?' D'Audley swallowed uneasily. 'I cannot imagine why you should think—'

'My colleague and I have come to reclaim the money, so how will you pay? Cash or jewels?'

'I am not paying anything,' declared d'Audley, alarmed. 'I cannot imagine why Wynewyk said he gave me seven marks, for he did no such thing. You cannot prove otherwise, so leave me be.'

He spun on his heel and attempted to stalk away, but found his path blocked by Bartholomew.

'How long have you known Wynewyk?' the physician asked quietly.

D'Audley sighed angrily when he saw there was no escape – and that the scholars were not going to be fobbed off with lies. 'Since the summer. He visited Withersfield, too, although why he sullied his feet by going there is beyond my understanding.'

'Why did Luneday deny knowing him, then?' demanded Michael.

'Probably because the man cannot open his mouth without lying,' spat d'Audley. 'He is a murderous villain, who should be hanged for what he did to poor Joan.'

'And what about Elyan?' asked Michael, more interested in Michaelhouse's money than d'Audley's wild theories. 'Why did he leave so suddenly when we mentioned Wynewyk's name?'

'He did not leave suddenly – he is just a busy man,' replied d'Audley. 'But Wynewyk did not give us money for timber, coal or anything else. And *I* am a busy man, too, so you must excuse—'

271

'How do you know coal is one of the commodities Wynewyk purchased?' pounced Michael.

D'Audley swallowed uneasily, and he looked furtive. 'It was a guess. Coal is one of Haverhill's most lucrative exports.'

'It is not,' retorted Michael. 'Elyan sells a small amount locally, but his mine has not yet started producing. So you are not being entirely truthful with us, and—'

He turned quickly at a sudden commotion at the far end of the market. Hilton was running towards the Alneston Chantry, where a crowd had gathered. Gatekeeper Folyat was busily darting here and there, whispering in people's ears. When he saw d'Audley with Bartholomew and Michael, Folyat raced towards them.

'It is Neubold,' he gasped, breathless from his exertions. 'He has hanged himself in the chapel.'

CHAPTER 8

Bartholomew and Michael joined the throng that hurried towards the Alneston Chantry. The chapel was tiny, and looked even shabbier up close than it had at a distance. The scholars entered to find themselves in a plain, single-celled building with a small altar at its eastern end. Above the altar was a window that had probably once contained glass, but that was now open to the elements. The floor was beaten earth, and was soft with bird droppings. It reeked of old feathers, damp and neglect.

'I would not want to pray long in here,' muttered Michael, wrinkling his nose in distaste. 'No wonder Alneston's soul only gets one mass a week.'

Neubold was indeed hanging from the rafters. He was in the same clothes he had worn the night before – blue gipon and orange leggings. Hilton and d'Audley were cutting him down, clearly in the hope of reviving him, but Bartholomew could see it was too late.

'Neubold's hands are tied,' he whispered to Michael, watching Hilton push on the dead man's chest in an effort to make him breathe. 'And there is blood on his head. He was murdered.'

'Then I hope no one will think *we* killed him,' Michael murmured back. 'Strangers are often blamed in situations like this, and we were in Withersfield last night. Perhaps we should leave.'

'That will definitely look suspicious. And we cannot get out anyway – the place is too tightly packed, and more

273

people are prising their way inside by the moment. We are effectively trapped.'

'Can you save Neubold? That might make folk more kindly disposed towards us.'

'Unfortunately not – he looks to be as stiff as a board, which suggests he has been dead for hours.'

'Then we had better stand in the shadows,' said Michael. 'And hope no one notices us. What did you make of d'Audley's testimony, by the way?'

'It confirms what we had already guessed – that Wynewyk travelled to Suffolk in the summer, instead of going to see his ailing father. Of course, we would have known that without d'Audley – Wynewyk brought home a lot of jugs . . .'

'And they are of the same distinctive design as the ones for sale in Haverhill market,' finished Michael, nodding. 'Moreover, d'Audley's furtive manner leads me to surmise that Wynewyk almost certainly brokered some sort of deal with him. And probably with Elyan and Luneday, too.'

'But it does not prove any wrongdoing on Wynewyk's part,' Bartholomew warned, predicting the monk's next conclusion. 'He may have organised the contracts in good faith, and it is these lordlings who are cheating Michaelhouse.'

'Then why the secrecy?' demanded the monk. 'And why did he accept the money I gave him when I thought he was visiting sick kin? Such behaviour is not the act of a decent man.'

That was true, but Bartholomew was unwilling to admit it. He indicated that they should listen to what was happening by the altar; he seriously doubted any exchange between villagers would help them discover what Wynewyk had been doing in Suffolk, but it was a convenient way to bring an end to a conversation that was becoming uncomfortable.

'Did anyone see Neubold this morning?' Elyan was asking. 'He was not at dawn mass, and he was unavailable when I asked for him last night. Does anyone know where he was?'

'In Withersfield,' replied Folyat. Bartholomew wondered who was collecting the tolls, or whether they were only levied when the gatekeeper felt like it. 'He was caught trying to steal Lizzie, and Luneday locked him in his barn. I heard he escaped during the night.'

Elyan's expression became suspiciously bland when Lizzie was mentioned, and Bartholomew was seized with the absolute conviction that he had known exactly what Neubold had been doing – that the priest had either been acting on his orders or with his complicit approval.

'Luneday *said* he escaped,' sneered d'Audley. 'But it is obvious what really happened: the villains at Withersfield killed him, and invented the tale of Neubold's escape, to confuse us.'

'No,' contradicted Lady Agnys sharply. She glared at d'Audley. 'There is no evidence to suggest such a thing, and making such statements is both dangerous and offensive.'

'I speak as I find,' d'Audley snapped back.

They argued until Hilton stood, indicating that his efforts to save Neubold were over. He bowed his head and began to pray, which immediately stilled the clamour of accusations. But they started again the moment he had finished.

'Neubold killed himself,' said Elyan with considerable authority. 'His brother Carbo went insane, so lunacy must run in the family.'

'Then why are his hands tied?' asked Agnys. 'And how did he come by that cut on his head?'

'He tied his hands to make sure he did not change his mind,' replied Elyan, with the kind of shrug that said he

275

thought his grandmother's points were irrelevant. He smoothed down his immaculate gipon. 'And of course there will be cuts when a man dies a violent death.'

'Remember the mess in Luneday's barn?' murmured Bartholomew to Michael. 'Perhaps Neubold was not rescued by whoever unbarred the door, but was dragged to his death instead. Do you think his murderer and the man who attacked us last night are one and the same?'

'But why would anyone target us *and* Neubold? We have no connection to each other.'

'He killed *himself*!' Elyan was shouting, dragging the scholars' attention back to the altar. 'No one at Withersfield would risk his immortal soul by murdering a priest. You speak rubbish, d'Audley!'

'Neubold is not wearing his habit,' countered d'Audley. 'And it was dark out last night – no moon, and thick clouds. Perhaps Luneday could not see, and hanged him without realising who he was.'

People were looking back and forth between the two men, as if watching a ball batted between two combatants. Hilton attempted to intervene, but the lords of the manor overrode him.

'Then why is Neubold not dangling from the gibbet in Withersfield?' demanded Elyan. He turned to the gatekeeper. 'Folyat? Carry the body to the Upper Church. It can stay there until we decide where it can be buried. Suicides are banned from holy ground, but he will have to go somewhere.'

'Elyan seems very keen for a verdict of self-murder,' mused Michael. 'Suspiciously so.'

'And d'Audley seems equally keen to have Luneday blamed,' Bartholomew whispered back. 'Just as he is eager to have Luneday charged with harming Joan in Cambridge.'

'Wait,' said Hilton, putting out his hand to stop Folyat

276

from doing as he was ordered. 'Let us take a few moments to consider what *really* happened – not suppositions and theories, but proper facts.'

'That is a very good idea, Hilton,' said Agnys approvingly. 'But none of us are qualified to do that sort of thing, so you had better oblige. *You* can find the truth.'

Elyan was furious. 'No! I have a lot of clerking for him to do. Now Neubold is gone, he is the only one who can read and write for miles around.'

'And I need him, too,' declared d'Audley, equally peeved. 'I do not want to lose this lovely chapel to King's Hall. Besides, there is no need for an enquiry when the culprit is obvious.'

'I am a priest, not a coroner,' objected Hilton, also unhappy with Agnys's decree. 'I am not qualified to meddle in such matters, madam. You must send word to the Sheriff—'

'You will do as I say,' commanded Agnys firmly. 'And we *shall* send for the Sheriff – but you will have answers for him when he arrives. The last time he came, he liked it so much that he declined to leave, and I do not want to give him an excuse to outstay his welcome again.'

'Get a witness to say Neubold was despondent, and there will be an end of the matter,' advised Elyan, seeing Hilton was to be given no choice. 'In fact I can tell you right now that he would have been mortified at having to pass a night in a barn.'

'That is not a reason for suicide,' said Hilton wearily. 'Even for a vain man like Neubold.'

'Luneday probably had help when he committed his crime,' said d'Audley, looking around suddenly. He spotted Bartholomew and Michael, and jabbed a finger at them. 'There are strangers in our midst, and it is odd that they should appear just as a man dies in peculiar circumstances.'

'It is, indeed,' agreed Folyat. 'And they were vague about the nature of their business here when I asked. They said they were going to buy jugs, but they have not yet made a single purchase!'

'Damn!' murmured Michael, as everyone turned to look at them. 'This is going to be awkward.'

There was little Bartholomew and Michael could do as they were shoved unceremoniously towards the altar. D'Audley was delighted by their discomfiture, while Elyan stood with his hands on his hips and nodded, as if he had known the scholars would be trouble.

'They are from Cambridge,' said Hilton, reaching out to steady Bartholomew after a particularly vigorous push propelled him forward faster than was pleasant. 'They are not—'

'From King's Hall?' cried Folyat in dismay. 'The ones who are trying to wrest Alneston Chantry from us, and who have set their sights on Elyan Manor, too?'

Michael frowned in puzzlement. 'King's Hall wants Elyan Manor?'

'Silence!' snapped d'Audley, rounding on him. 'You have no right to ask us questions – you, who are the accomplices of a murderer!'

'They are no such thing,' countered Agnys, poking her neighbour in the chest with a gnarled forefinger. 'And you are a troublemaker, bandying accusations like some common fishwife.'

The blood drained from d'Audley's face as a titter of amusement rippled through the onlookers, and for a moment, Bartholomew thought he might reach for his dagger. But he settled for treating the old lady to a venomous scowl. Then he turned on his heel and shouldered his way outside.

The moment he had gone, Agnys started to make pointed remarks about villagers with too much time on their hands, and the chores she could devise to remedy the matter. Her words precipitated a concerted dash for the door, and it was not long before the chapel was virtually empty. Only Elyan, Hilton and Folyat remained, struggling to tie Neubold into his cloak.

Michael heaved a sigh of relief. 'Thank you, madam. But I am confused. Did Gatekeeper Folyat say King's Hall intends to claim Elyan Manor, as well as this chantry?'

It was Hilton who replied, looking up from his knotting. 'They can only press their claim if Elyan dies childless. We thought our worries were over when Joan conceived, but—'

'But Joan died, and the vultures circle,' finished Agnys. 'And if my grandson does not produce an heir, there are several parties who think they have a right to our estates. King's Hall is one of them.'

'How did that come about?' asked Michael, astonished.

'From ancient wills and records,' replied Folyat disapprovingly. 'Lawyers' tricks. If they win, King's Hall will rule from afar by appointing some non-local steward. And we all know what happens to manors with distant landlords – they are run for profit and nothing else. No kindness.'

'All that is true, Folyat,' said Hilton. 'But these scholars are from Michaelhouse, not King's Hall. It is a totally separate foundation, so do not blame them for their colleagues' greed.'

'A scholar is a scholar,' muttered Folyat, turning back to his work. 'Just as a chicken is a chicken.'

Imperiously, Agnys indicated Bartholomew and Michael were to follow her to an alcove, where she could speak without being overheard by Elyan, Hilton and Folyat. The priest and the gatekeeper did not seem to care, but

Elyan watched resentfully, although he made no move to intervene.

'Henry and d'Audley do not recognise you,' Agnys said to Bartholomew in a low voice. 'But I know you are the physician who tended Joan in Cambridge. However, if you have come to inform us that you have uncovered evidence to prove suicide, then I do not want to hear it. You can go home.'

'What makes you think it was suicide?' asked Bartholomew.

'It was *not*,' said Agnys firmly. 'There are folk who say she was unhappy in the few weeks before she died, but her troubles did not run deep enough to warrant self-murder.'

'You loved her,' said Bartholomew gently. 'That much was obvious in St Mary the Great. And you do not want her dragged from her grave and reburied in unhallowed ground, even though you suspect – as do I – that she probably did take her own life.'

Agnys looked as though she would argue, but then inclined her head stiffly. 'I taught her about pennyroyal, so she would not have swallowed it by accident. However, I will not have it said that she murdered her unborn child. She is dead, and that is bad enough. Please, leave her in peace.'

'I doubt she took her own life,' said Michael. Bartholomew and Agnys looked sharply at him, and he shrugged. 'We have just been told a lot depended on this heir – that the inheritance of Elyan Manor is contested without one. That is a powerful motive for wanting Joan dead before it was born.'

'But this is Suffolk,' said Agnys indignantly. 'We do not murder pregnant women here.'

'She did not die here, she died in Cambridge,' Michael pointed out. 'And Matt's sister is convinced there is something odd about her demise – so much that she has ordered him to ask questions about it.'

'Because it was distressing to see an old friend die,' argued Bartholomew, alarmed that the monk should be voicing such opinions. It would bring nothing but trouble, and there was good evidence for suicide, especially now Agnys said Joan had been unhappy. 'Edith is racked by grief, and—'

Michael ignored him and addressed Agnys. 'Tell us about Joan – about her child.'

Agnys's fierce expression softened. 'She had longed for a baby for many years, but failed to make one. Then, when we had all but given up, her prayers were answered. She was delighted.'

'Yet you said she was troubled,' said Michael. 'Despondent.'

'That came later – a few weeks ago. Unfortunately, she would not tell me the reason, no matter how much I begged her. Then one day, out of the blue, she insisted on travelling to Cambridge to buy ribbons. Henry should never have let her go.'

'Then why did he?' asked Michael. He shrugged when Agnys regarded him stonily. 'I am sorry if I cause offence, but Joan's child was important. I cannot imagine why he agreed to such a journey.'

Agnys grimaced. '*He* trusted Neubold, even if I despised the man. Unfortunately, she left when I was visiting Clare Priory – probably because she knew I would have talked her out of going, had I been here. I assumed she had decided an excursion might lift her spirits.'

'Was it a happy marriage?' asked Michael.

'Yes. It was not a very physical relationship, but they cared deeply for each other even so.'

Bartholomew saw Michael's thoughts reflected his

own: that Joan might have secured the services of a more fertile fellow, given that Elyan had not been up to the task. The medical profession usually maintained that the fault lay with the woman in such cases, but Bartholomew knew plenty of ladies who refused to accept this 'traditional wisdom'. Joan, who had sounded a strong-minded, independent sort of person, might well have been one of them. Bartholomew half expected the monk to pursue the matter, and braced himself for trouble, but Michael turned to another question instead.

'Will you tell us why King's Hall think they have a right to your grandson's manor?'

'We have known for years that there will be two claimants, should Henry die without issue: d'Audley, who is a snake but a Haverhill man; and Luneday, who is nicer but from Withersfield. We asked the priests – Neubold and Hilton – to determine who has the stronger claim. Unfortunately, not only did they discover that certain ancient marriages had not been legitimate, but they learned that a will made by Alneston – who founded this chapel – brought another contestant into play.'

'King's Hall?'

'King's Hall,' agreed Agnys. 'The whole situation is rendered even more confusing by the fact that certain documents are missing. Or are owned by Luneday, who cannot read and who will not let anyone else see them. He is afraid of being cheated, which is understandable enough – d'Audley is vicious and will do anything to harm him, while King's Hall seem somewhat unscrupulous, too.'

'Is this why King's Hall want Alneston Chantry?' asked Bartholomew. 'To strengthen their claim on Elyan Manor – saying they already own property here, so they should have more?'

'I cannot imagine why else they should want it,' said

Agnys, looking around in distaste. 'It is a paltry place, and reeks of chickens for some inexplicable reason.'

'But all this would be irrelevant if Henry had a child,' mused Michael, regarding her thoughtfully. 'Do you think d'Audley or Luneday went to Cambridge and gave Joan pennyroyal? You said she would not have swallowed it by accident, which only leaves two possibilities: she did it deliberately, or someone gave it to her.'

Agnys was unhappy. 'I would hate to think so. However, when he heard Joan was in Cambridge, d'Audley left Haverhill, saying he was going to visit kin. Luneday's woman was also mysteriously absent at the pertinent time. And the men of King's Hall were there already.'

'King's Hall will not have harmed Joan,' said Bartholomew, thinking of Paxtone, Warden Powys, and other scholars he knew and liked there. Then a picture of Shropham sprang unbidden into his mind, a man who was in prison for murder.

'I would have said the same about d'Audley and Luneday,' said Agnys grimly. She shook her head slowly. 'I admit my initial assumption was that Joan had killed herself – yet she *was* happy about the child, even in the last few weeks when she became unaccountably troubled. Meanwhile, the notion of her swallowing pennyroyal by accident is preposterous. So that leaves murder. And I have just decided that you two are going to help me find the culprit.'

There was a silence after Lady Agnys made her announcement. Bartholomew's heart sank, and he wished Michael had held his tongue over something that was – after all – none of their business.

'And how do you propose we do that?' asked Michael eventually.

283

Agnys smiled. 'Oh, I expect a cunning fellow like you will think of a way, especially if I offer you information in return. You mentioned a man called Wynewyk earlier. My ageing memory needed a while to work, but I do recall a fellow of that name visiting my grandson in August.'

'Do you know why?' asked Michael. 'Or what was discussed?'

'No, but I can find out.'

Michael regarded her suspiciously. 'You would pry into your kinsman's affairs on our behalf?'

Agnys's grin became slightly malevolent. 'Henry will not have done anything untoward. However, d'Audley had a *very* curious reaction to the name, and I would enjoy discovering something to discomfit him. You may think me unneighbourly, but I cannot abide the fellow.'

'We think your grandson sold Wynewyk some coal in August,' said Michael. His tone was cautious. 'But Hilton maintains he does not have enough of it.'

Agnys shrugged. 'Henry imports it from Ipswich for local needs, but the discovery of a seam on our land means he hopes to hawk more in the coming years. Perhaps Wynewyk's purchase was for coal to be delivered in the future.'

Michael was about to ask more, but the door banged open and Cynric hurried towards them. The Welshman's face was grim as he pulled Bartholomew to one side.

'I have been making friends in taverns,' he said in a low voice. 'And two have just told me that they were paid to dig a secret grave, up by the mine. In the summer.'

Bartholomew winced. 'That is unpleasant, but not our affair.'

'They said the body belonged to a stranger.' Cynric's expression was deeply troubled. 'A young man. And they described an unusual black garment over his tunic and hose.'

284

Bartholomew stared at him. 'You mean like an academic tabard?'

Cynric nodded soberly. 'That is what it sounded like to me. Kelyng *always* wore his tabard, because he was proud of it – and you know I think Wynewyk hired him for protection.'

'You think it is our missing Bible Scholar in this grave? That is not very likely, Cynric.'

'It is if you think about it,' pressed Cynric urgently. 'Kelyng went missing in August, after Wynewyk had made that suspicious journey to see his sick father. And while the rest of you assumed Kelyng had fled his debts, Wynewyk never did.'

'But if this is true, and they were attacked, Wynewyk would have told us—'

'Would he?' interrupted Cynric. 'Even though it would have meant admitting that he did not travel to Winwick, but went to Suffolk instead? And would have to tell you why?'

Bartholomew shrugged. 'Perhaps you are right, but I do not see how we will ever find out.'

'I do. I got precise directions to this tomb, and I know where I can borrow a spade.'

'No!' Bartholomew was horrified.

But Cynric was adamant. 'I liked Kelyng, and his parents have a right to know what happened to him. I will do it alone, if need be. But it will be easier with two of us.'

'When?' asked Bartholomew heavily.

Pleased, Cynric gripped his shoulder, warrior fashion. 'At midnight. When else?'

Lady Agnys declared she was thirsty when Bartholomew returned, and asked him and Michael to join her for an ale at the Queen's Head. It was an unusual invitation, because taverns were rarely frequented by ladies. First, they were the domain of men, and second, those women who did venture inside tended to be prostitutes.

Michael was grinning as they followed her out of the chapel. He admired doughty old ladies, and liked the fact that Agnys was prepared to ignore convention and do as she pleased. Bartholomew would have preferred to sit by himself and consider Cynric's theory about Kelyng, but Agnys was astute, and he did not want to arouse her suspicions by asking to be excused.

The Queen's Head was neat, clean and smelled of the new rushes on the floor. The landlord did not seem surprised when Agnys sailed into his establishment; he only doffed his cap and ousted three patrons so she could sit by the fire. When Michael started to ask for claret, Agnys stopped him.

'The Queen's Head is noted for its ale, so you will have ale. And it is famous for its roasted pork, too, so we shall have a plate of that, as well. You look like a man who appreciates his food, Brother.'

'I am not fat,' said Michael immediately. 'Matt tells me I have unusually heavy bones.'

'Actually, that is something you invented of your own—' began Bartholomew.

'I have heavy bones, too,' said Agnys, with a conspiratorial wink as she patted her own ample girth. 'God made the ones in my hips out of lead.'

Michael rubbed his hands approvingly as the landlord brought the victuals. The ale was sweet and clear, and the pork succulent. It made Bartholomew realise yet again how much he had missed decent food since Wynewyk's tampering with the accounts had forced them to tighten their belts.

When they were settled, and were working their way

286

through a platter of meat that would have fed half the King's army, Michael regaled Agnys with a truncated and not very accurate account of why they had travelled to Suffolk. Bartholomew tried to listen, but most of his mind was on what Cynric had told him. What if the body in the grave did transpire to be Kelyng's? How could there be an innocent explanation for Wynewyk taking a student on a journey from which he never returned?

'. . . Neubold,' Michael was saying. 'What do you think happened to him?'

'I do not believe he took his own life,' replied Agnys. Bartholomew forced himself to pay closer attention. The sooner he and Michael had answers to their questions, the sooner they could leave – and he was unsettled and wary in Suffolk, and desperately wanted to go home. 'First, he had no reason to do so – my grandson admits to paying him handsomely to steal Luneday's pig, and no man kills himself while he has a fortune to enjoy. And second, he was happy with his lot.'

'The Withersfield villagers chased him for miles when he was caught thieving,' said Michael. 'I think he was genuinely afraid of them.'

'He had a slippery tongue and an inflated sense of his own cleverness,' argued Agnys. 'He may have been given a fright at first, but he would have assumed he could talk himself out of any trouble.'

'I wonder if he was dispatched in Withersfield,' mused Michael. 'There was evidence of a struggle in the barn, although no blood that I could see.'

'There was a cut on his head, though,' said Agnys. 'So perhaps we must conclude that he was killed elsewhere. The chapel, for example.'

Bartholomew started to say that the barn was a big building, and the wound on Neubold's head had not been serious – it would need more than a passing glance to detect any drops of blood that might have been shed there. But he stopped, although he could not have said why. Were his feelings of unease leading him to question the probity of everyone in Suffolk, even those who seemed to be on their side? He rubbed a hand through his hair, troubled and tense.

'We were attacked last night,' said Michael, sopping the grease from the platter with a piece of bread. He tore the fat-drenched morsel in two and offered half to Agnys, who accepted it appreciatively. 'Perhaps Neubold was murdered, then the culprit decided to kill us, too, lest we had witnessed anything. After all, the barn and the hall are not very far apart.'

'Or perhaps *your* assailant heard only that you are scholars from Cambridge, and jumped to the not unreasonable conclusion that you hail from King's Hall,' suggested Agnys. 'And King's Hall is not popular around here. Alternatively, it is possible that your attacker wanted Luneday dead, because he had dared to incarcerate a Haverhill man in his barn – you were not the intended victims at all.'

Both theories had one obvious suspect: d'Audley. Bartholomew studied Agnys as he thought about it. D'Audley certainly had a motive for harming representatives from King's Hall, given that they intended to claim property he considered to be his own, while his obvious hatred for Withersfield might well lead him to mount an attack on Luneday. But was he a murderer? Or did it just suit Agnys to have him considered as one?

'Who do *you* think killed Neubold, My Lady?' asked Michael, sitting back and folding his hands across his paunch, finally replete. 'It must be someone from this area, because strangers would have been noticed – as we were.'

Agnys raised her hands in a shrug. 'I barely know where to start. Luneday and his people despised Neubold for a whole host of reasons. D'Audley claims to have admired Neubold's talent, but he is a devious fellow, and who knows what he really thinks? Gatekeeper Folyat was always quarrelling with Neubold over petty matters. And do not forget that Neubold was recently in Cambridge.'

'What does that have to do with anything?' asked Michael.

'It is where Joan died. Perhaps he knew something about her passing, and was killed to ensure his silence. He claimed he left Cambridge before she became ill, which is why he failed to tend her on her deathbed, but he may have been lying. He was not an honest man.'

'Did he say why he abandoned his master's heavily pregnant wife in a strange town?' asked Michael. 'It is hardly a responsible thing to have done.'

'He told me he wanted to inform Henry about his successful negotiations with King's Hall as soon as possible,' replied Agnys. 'He thought Joan would be safe with Edith, and planned to collect her later, when she had finished shopping. Or so he said. Perhaps he was telling the truth, perhaps he was not.'

'Are you sure he went to discuss coal?' asked Michael. 'His real intention was not to tell King's Hall how they might strengthen their claim on Elyan Manor?'

Agnys blew out her cheeks in a sigh. 'With Neubold, anything was possible. It would not surprise me to learn that he offered to destroy documents or change others – for a price. He was not loyal to us.'

'It is a pity we did not know all this sooner,' said Michael. 'He has taken his secrets to the grave so we can no longer ask him about them.'

'I questioned him at length about Joan, but my efforts

to catch him out were wasted. Perhaps he *was* telling the truth – I tended to disbelieve anything he said, but maybe I do him an injustice.'

'You say Joan became troubled about something in the last few weeks,' said Bartholomew, changing the subject back to his sister's hapless friend. 'But you do not know what.'

A cloud passed over Agnys's face. 'I wish now that I had made more of an effort to find out – there is a fine line between anxious concern and the interference of a husband's grandmother, and I thought I was doing the right thing by recognising her right to privacy. But . . .'

'Your grandson can always remarry,' Michael pointed out. 'Joan's death does not necessarily mean Elyan Manor will go to one of these claimants.'

Agnys winced. 'It took him twenty years to impregnate Joan, by which time we had all but given up hope. And to be honest, I suspect she reverted to other measures in the end.'

'Other measures,' queried Michael innocently. 'You mean the child was not his?'

'I doubt it, although I shall deny ever saying so, should anyone ask.'

Bartholomew regarded Agnys thoughtfully, wondering why she had confided such a suspicion to strangers. She professed to be fond of Joan, so why tell tales that implied she was wanton?

'Is your grandson the kind of man to avenge himself on an unfaithful wife?' he asked.

Agnys was silent for a long time before she replied. 'No, I do not think so.'

But she did not sound convinced by her answer, and neither was Bartholomew.

* * *

'Lord, Matt,' breathed Michael, as they took their leave to walk through the marketplace. They were going to visit the Upper Church, where Bartholomew hoped to examine Neubold's body, preferably without an audience. 'I wonder whether we are wise to become embroiled in all this.'

'In all what, specifically?' asked Bartholomew. 'Neubold's murder?'

'The various deaths that have occurred since Wynewyk decided to cheat Michaelhouse – his own curious demise, Joan's poisoning, Carbo's stabbing and now Neubold's hanging. I am sure they are all connected somehow.'

'And Kelyng,' said Bartholomew unhappily, and told him what his book-bearer had learned.

'Cynric is right,' said Michael, when he had finished. 'We do need to excavate this grave. If it is not Kelyng's, then it can be refilled, and that will be the end of the matter. But if it is him . . .'

'Then we shall have yet another mystery to solve.'

Michael nodded soberly. 'Kelyng was Wynewyk's student, and Cynric is correct in saying that he was handy with a weapon. Wynewyk was not, and it makes sense that he should have hired himself a bodyguard. Kelyng would have been the obvious choice.'

Bartholomew was sceptical. 'Then why was Wynewyk so concerned when Kelyng failed to arrive at the beginning of term? We all assumed Kelyng had fled his debts, so why did Wynewyk keep worrying after him – if you are right, and he did drag the lad to an early death here, then surely it would have been better never to mention him again? Your theory makes no sense!'

'It does, if he "worried" as a sort of smokescreen. It means we would not look to him should Kelyng's body ever be found – he could say *he* was the one who was anxious, while the rest of us dismissed the lad as a debtor.

It is callous, but we are talking about a man who cheats his friends here.'

'Wynewyk had nothing to do with Kelyng's death because—'

'I applaud your loyalty, Matt,' interrupted Michael harshly. 'I really do. But it is beginning to fly in the face of reason.'

'Actually, Brother, I was going to say that Wynewyk had nothing to do with Kelyng's death, because of something Hilton told us earlier. He said there is a rumour that Carbo had killed a man by the mine, although he did not believe it. Well, perhaps the tale is true, and the victim was Kelyng.'

Michael raised his hands in the air. 'We are getting ahead of ourselves here – it is foolish to speculate who knew what about Kelyng's demise when we cannot even be sure if he is dead. Let us review what we *do* know, and see what headway we have made.'

Bartholomew took a deep breath and tipped back his head, looking up at the sky. It was iron grey, and he wondered whether it would rain again. He hoped not, because it would make digging unpleasant, especially as Cynric had neglected to bring him a change of clothes.

'Neubold went to Cambridge to do business with King's Hall,' he said, trying to do as Michael suggested. 'He took Joan with him, and Carbo must have followed on their heels – we do not know why, but he was ill, so perhaps he simply chased after two familiar faces.'

'That sounds plausible,' said Michael. 'Then what?'

'Then the three of them died – Joan of pennyroyal, Carbo of being stabbed by Shropham, and Neubold of hanging. And Wynewyk . . . I am still not sure what caused his demise. However, all four deaths are associated with coal: Joan's husband has a mine, Neubold was selling the stuff to King's Hall, Carbo was obsessed by it, and Wynewyk bought some for Michaelhouse.'

Michael began to list other points on his fat fingers. 'Meanwhile, we have two lords of the manor with ample reasons for wanting a third one dead; we have a wife under pressure to produce an heir; we have King's Hall determined to inherit a distant manor; and we are nowhere near the truth regarding Michaelhouse's missing money.'

Bartholomew glanced at his friend, and saw that despite his discouraging words, the monk's eyes gleamed in the way they always did when faced with an intricate mystery. The physician did not feel the same way at all, and was beginning to dread where their enquiries might lead them.

'I hope we do not learn that King's Hall has done something untoward to get this manor,' he said uneasily. 'I like Warden Powys, and would hate to see him fall from grace.'

Michael made a disgusted sound. 'Powys was hand-picked by the King himself, and such men do not "fall from grace". They might have mysterious accidents or take early retirement, but they certainly do not do anything that might suggest His Majesty made an unwise choice.'

Bartholomew regarded him in horror. 'If unravelling this mess might result in another murder, then I am stopping right now. Powys is a—'

'Powys is unlikely to be doing anything without royal approval,' interrupted Michael. 'So I very much doubt he will come to any harm. However, the same cannot be said for us – we have been attacked once already, and I want to finish our enquiries and go home as soon as possible. It is too late today, and you have a grave to despoil anyway, but we will be gone at first light tomorrow. I am not missing Monday's Blood Relic debate for anyone.'

'I had forgotten about that,' said Bartholomew. 'Somehow, an academic gathering pales into insignificance when compared to Wynewyk, Kelyng and whether we can leave Suffolk alive.'

Michael grinned. 'We shall outwit these clumsy assassins, never fear. Better yet, we may uncover evidence to strengthen King's Hall's claim, which will put Powys – and the King – in our debt.'

'Christ,' muttered Bartholomew, not liking the fact that the stakes had risen so high. 'But here come Cynric and the students. They can visit Elyan's mine while we inspect Neubold; as I said, coal features large in our investigation, so we should try to learn more about Elyan's lode.'

Cynric and Valence did not mind being asked to explore, but Risleye and Tesdale were much less enthusiastic. Risleye said he did not like the look of the weather, while Tesdale was appalled by the notion of doing anything as strenuous as a walk followed by a loiter in the woods.

'It is a long way,' he complained pitifully. 'And I am very tired.'

Valence punched him playfully. 'It will be fun to visit a mine – I have never seen one before.'

'I have,' said Risleye sullenly. 'They are nasty, dirty, dangerous places, especially in the rain.'

Valence raised arch eyebrows. 'Will you let a bit of drizzle prevent you from seeing patients when you are qualified? You will ignore their summons, lest you get wet?'

'That will depend on what they agree to pay me,' replied Risleye, quite seriously. He smiled at Bartholomew. 'Are you offering to recompense me for this jaunt? That will put a different complexion on matters. I will go anywhere for silver!'

'Well, I will not,' said Tesdale miserably. 'I had a bad dream about a mine last night.'

'In that case, you can find out whether there is an apothecary in Haverhill,' said Bartholomew, reluctant to exacerbate the lad's nightmares. 'If there is, ask who has bought pennyroyal oil recently.'

'Pennyroyal oil?' asked Tesdale, startled. 'Do you think Joan was killed with supplies purchased in Suffolk, then? I assumed she came by hers in Cambridge.'

'Well, if she did, then it was not from Doctor Bartholomew's storeroom,' said Valence. 'Because Deynman has already confessed to borrowing that.'

'This is grossly unfair!' cried Risleye, when Cynric indicated he was ready to go. 'Tesdale does not have to traipse up to this wretched colliery, so why do I?'

'Because Doctor Bartholomew has asked you to,' said Valence virtuously. 'Do not glower so! We shall be back long before it rains.'

The Upper Church comprised a nave with an apsidal end and two flanking aisles. It was ancient, built in the sturdy manner of the Normans, and reminded Bartholomew of the abbey at Peterborough, where he had gone to school. There was a low tower, decorated with blind arcading, and its thick walls were pierced at regular intervals by round-headed windows. Inside the church, every available surface had been daubed with energetic murals. The result was disquieting, especially when the statues were taken into account: they had been provided with the most vivid colours imaginable for their robes, and Bartholomew had never seen so many intense blue eyes.

As he and Michael walked towards the north aisle, where Neubold had been deposited, they found Hilton ushering the last of his inquisitive parishioners away, leaning forward to rest a hand on their heads in blessing as they went. When he thought he was alone, he crossed himself, muttered a very brief prayer and headed for the door.

'Is that it?' asked Michael, stepping out from behind

one of the pillars. Hilton jumped violently, and clutched his chest, to indicate he had been given a serious shock. Michael ignored his reaction. 'Are you in such a hurry that you cannot do more for your colleague's soul?'

'I will return later, and perhaps keep vigil tonight. But I *am* in a hurry to leave. Lady Agnys ordered me to look into Neubold's death, and I must do as she says, because she is inclined to be testy when people ignore her instructions. And I *do* think Neubold was unlawfully killed, because of his tied hands – Elyan is wrong to say he committed suicide.'

'How do you plan to proceed?' asked Michael.

Hilton did not look happy. 'By visiting the barn at Withersfield – the last place he was seen alive.'

'Someone must have let him out,' mused Bartholomew. 'The door was barred from the outside, so he cannot have left without help. However, the question is, was he killed by his so-called rescuer, or did he return to Haverhill and meet his murderer here?'

Hilton nodded slowly. 'You have put your finger on the crux of the matter. Unfortunately, it does not help me – I still have two villages full of suspects, because a lot of people disliked Neubold.'

'Why was he so unpopular?' asked Bartholomew.

Hilton raised his hands. 'Where do I start? He neglected his religious duties – bodies left unburied and weddings postponed, which is inconvenient if you are about to have a child. He manipulated the law to secure favourable verdicts for anyone who could pay. He undertook spying missions for Elyan. He dabbled in market business, by brokering deals and negotiating contracts. Indeed, there was little he would not do if the money was right.'

'I understand you and he were looking into the matter

of who will inherit Elyan Manor,' said Michael. 'Do you think that earned him enemies?'

'I hope not!' exclaimed Hilton, horrified. 'Because that means *I* might be in danger, too.'

'Can you name any *good* suspects for Neubold's death?' asked Bartholomew, feeling they were beginning to go around in circles. 'There must be a few who stand out from the masses.'

'Not really. I do not think you understand the extent to which he was held in contempt.'

Michael sighed. 'Then let us eliminate a few. I think we can discount Elyan: first, he admired Neubold's cunning ways with the law, and second, there cannot be many men who would agree to act as pig-rustlers on his behalf.'

'But Neubold failed to get Lizzie,' Hilton pointed out. 'Worse, he was caught, bringing embarrassment to his employer. Moreover, ever since Neubold abandoned Joan in Cambridge, Agnys has been telling Elyan to dispense with his services – perhaps this is Elyan's way of obliging her. And finally, I am suspicious of his insistence that Neubold committed suicide. So, you see, we cannot discount Elyan.'

While Michael and Hilton continued to debate potential culprits, Bartholomew edged towards the north aisle. He glanced at Michael, and saw the monk take Hilton's arm and draw him outside, ostensibly for air. Suspecting he would not be left alone for long, so should complete his examination as quickly as possible, Bartholomew removed the pall and stared down at Neubold's body.

The priest did not look any more pleasant in death than he had in life, and his narrow, pinched features had a bluish sheen that made him look dirty; Bartholomew was starkly reminded of Carbo. Another similarity was their stained hands, although the blackness of Neubold's could

297

be attributed to ink, whereas Carbo's had been just plain filthy.

There was a red ring around Neubold's wrists, showing he had struggled against his bonds. A rip in his tunic and the cut on his head were further evidence that he had fought his attacker. The cause of death was strangulation – Bartholomew supposed he had been hauled up by the neck and left to asphyxiate. There were no other injuries, so he replaced all as he had found it, and hurried outside.

'Did you like them, Matt?' asked Michael innocently. Hilton was regarding the physician warily. 'I have just been telling our friend here about your penchant for garishly painted saints. He does not believe me, and is under the impression that you lingered inside for some other purpose.'

'The statues are very colourful,' said Bartholomew sincerely, thinking he had never seen such a gaudy collection, not even in France.

'Now, Father,' the monk said briskly, cutting across a remark Hilton started to make about physicians with peculiar tastes in sculpture, 'you were telling me how Neubold's body was found.'

'Folyat discovered it,' replied Hilton, dragging his wary gaze away from Bartholomew. 'He said he came to tell me first, although I suspect he shared the news with those he passed *en route*. Neubold cannot have been there for long, because I said a mass for Alneston at dawn, and I assure you I would have noticed, had Neubold been present. His feet would have been in my face for a start.'

'Well?' asked Michael of Bartholomew, when Hilton had gone. 'Were my lies in vain, or have you discovered something useful from the corpse?'

'Hilton says Neubold was not in the chantry at dawn, which is strange: estimating a time of death is not an exact science, as you know, but I would guess he died last night. So, if Hilton is telling the truth, it means Neubold was killed elsewhere, then strung up in the chapel this morning.'

'Why would anyone do that?' asked Michael, puzzled.

'I really have no idea.'

Michael did not want to discuss Neubold's murder where they might be overheard, so he led the way to the market-place. Stone benches had been placed around its perimeter, some with straw thatches, so that potential buyers could sit out storms and sun and would not be tempted to leave before they had spent all their money. The monk selected the one that was farthest from the bustling stalls and sat, indicating Bartholomew was to perch next to him. It might have been pleasant, watching the lively hurly-burly of the traders, had their minds not been full of murder.

'If you are right in saying Neubold has been dead for some time,' said Michael, 'then it means he was murdered in Withersfield. And his body transported to Haverhill to be hung like a piece of meat.'

'Not necessarily. For all we know, he was rescued within moments of the barn door being barred. *Ergo*, he could have been wandering around Haverhill for hours before he was killed.'

Michael frowned. 'So he was hanged in Haverhill, then? How do you know?'

'I do *not* know, Brother – I am just trying to note all the possibilities. However, since you ask, I am inclined to say he died in Withersfield. The barn looked as though it had seen a struggle – we saw no blood, but I imagine we *would* find some, were we to look under all the hay.'

'Very well – I accept your reasoning so far. However, do you not think it would be risky to bring a corpse all the way from Withersfield? How would it get past Gatekeeper Folyat, for a start?'

'William told us he relaxes his guard after dark, when the market is closed. And he said Margery came to Haverhill last night – perhaps she carried Neubold on her horse.'

'That cannot be true. First, if William saw enough to be able to identify Margery as the rider, he would have noticed a priest-shaped bundle behind her saddle. And second, Hilton has just informed us that there was no corpse in Alneston Chantry when he arrived at dawn.'

Bartholomew was beginning to be exasperated by the lack of answers. 'We are looking at this the wrong way around – trying to establish a chain of events when we do not understand *why* the villain should act as he did. Perhaps we should determine the identity of the culprit first – then we might grasp why he deemed it necessary to tote a priest's body around in the dark.'

'We might, I suppose,' said the monk dubiously. 'So name your chief suspects.'

'We have several in Withersfield to choose from. Margery despised Neubold – perhaps she hired a servant to bring the body here. Luneday may have decided murder was the best way to protect his pig. William the steward also hated Neubold, and his capture may have presented too tempting an opportunity.'

'It was William who raised the alarm to say Neubold was missing,' Michael pointed out.

'Perhaps that is what he hopes we will think – that his "discovery" will be enough to spare him from suspicion. Of course, it could be Lizzie.'

'Lizzie?' asked Michael, regarding him askance. 'The pig?'

'Sows can be dangerous when they have a litter.'

300

'Do not be flippant,' snapped Michael. 'I believed you for a moment. Personally, my money is on Margery. She loathed Neubold, and has admitted to being abroad and unaccounted for last night.'

Bartholomew thought about it. 'He suffered a blow to the head, which may have been enough to subdue him and allow her to tie a rope around his neck. And his hands.'

'What a mess,' groaned Michael. 'We are still no closer to learning anything new about Wynewyk, but we have a priest murdered and this mysterious grave to explore. But here comes Cynric with the students. I wonder what they have to report.'

'There *is* an apothecary,' announced Tesdale as he approached. He was pleased with himself, and gave Cynric a slight push when the book-bearer started to interrupt. 'He told me that three people bought pennyroyal oil recently. He said he was surprised, because it is cheaper to make your own.'

'Who?' asked Michael.

'Lady Agnys had a jar for flatulence. Hilton wanted a bit to put in some tonic he likes to drink at night. And Neubold purchased a pot, but would not say why.'

'Hilton?' asked Michael in a low voice, looking at Bartholomew. 'Why would he mean Joan harm? He has nothing to gain by her death.'

'We cannot know that, Brother. Perhaps he was paid to ensure Elyan's heir never lived to inherit. The same is true of Neubold.'

'And Agnys?' asked Michael quietly.

Bartholomew shrugged. 'She knows pennyroyal killed Joan, so why did she not mention the fact that she purchased some? I would have done, just to mark it as a curious coincidence.'

'So would I,' said Michael unhappily. 'And we only have

301

her word that she was pleased by Joan's pregnancy. Perhaps she would rather see Elyan Manor go to one of the three claimants than a brat sired by the local stud.'

Risleye edged closer, trying to hear what they were saying. The moment they stopped speaking, he began to hold forth, his voice loud and full of self-importance. Cynric rolled his eyes when it became obvious that the student did not intend to share the credit for what they had done together.

'I visited the mine, but I was not the only one interested in it,' the student began. 'I found clear evidence that others have been watching it, too. It was not possible to tell who, of course, but I could tell from the crushed grass and broken twigs that someone – perhaps more than one person – had lurked in the woods and observed what was happening, just as I was doing.'

'Did you indeed?' asked Michael, an amused smile plucking at the corners of his mouth. He did not look at Cynric. 'And what else did you notice?'

'That not much is happening there,' said Valence, cutting across Risleye. 'There are two men with picks, but they do not seem to be making much progress. I cannot see it making Elyan rich.'

'Valence is right,' said Cynric. 'Welsh mines are full of labourers, but two men are too few. However, while this pair mined, six others were on guard. Elyan clearly thinks there is something worth protecting, and it was hard to get close.'

'But you managed,' predicted Bartholomew.

The book-bearer grinned. 'We did. But I was surprised by what we saw. The seam is just a thin layer of poor-grade coal, which may not even burn – or will smoke so much that it is useless.'

'Then why does Elyan guard it so jealously?' asked Michael.

Cynric shrugged. 'That is yet another mystery for you to solve, Brother.'

It was too late to do much else that day, and dusk was approaching early because of the rain clouds that were gathering. Michael complained bitterly that he was obliged to spend a second night in Suffolk, but Bartholomew felt he had far more cause to gripe – it was not the Benedictine who was obliged to disappear into the darkness with a shovel, to see whether one of their students was buried in an unmarked grave.

They hired beds in the Queen's Head – in two separate rooms, so they would not have to explain their actions to Valence, Risleye and Tesdale – and retired early. Cynric fell asleep at once, but Bartholomew tossed and turned until Michael told him it was time to leave.

'The students are still drinking downstairs,' said the monk. 'You will have to climb out of the window, or they will see you and wonder where you are going.'

'God help me, Brother!' muttered Bartholomew. 'I am getting too old for this sort of caper.'

'There is plenty of life in you yet,' said Michael, opening the shutter and standing back smartly as the wind hurled a cascade of rain inside. 'Are you sure you do not need my help?'

'It is better that you stay here,' replied Cynric, before Bartholomew could say that the monk's strength would be very welcome. 'Then if anything goes wrong, you can give us an alibi.'

'What can go wrong?' asked Bartholomew, alarmed.

'Probably nothing,' said Cynric, clearly looking forward to the escapade. He loved sneaking around in the dark. 'But keep the door locked, Brother. And the windows, too.'

With serious misgivings, Bartholomew clambered on to

the sill and began to climb down the back wall. It was not far to the ground, because the ceilings were low, and there were ample beams to use as foot- and hand-holds. Even so, it was a struggle, and he could feel Cynric's disapproval coming in waves as he scraped and rattled his way to the ground. The book-bearer dropped lightly beside him, then disappeared. When he returned, he was carrying two spades and a lamp.

They set off along the Withersfield road, Bartholomew following Cynric's lead by keeping to the shadows. They passed one or two people, who weaved along in a manner that suggested they would not have noticed other travellers anyway, but most folk were in bed, and the houses along the street were dark. A light shone from one, and they could hear a baby wailing inside, its mother trying wearily to soothe it with lullabies.

It was not long before Cynric left the road and set out across the fields. The going was miserable, because it was pitch black, and the rain made the route treacherously slippery. Wet vegetation slapped at them as they passed, and they were soon drenched through. As they neared the mine, thorns snagged their clothes and Bartholomew heard something rip in his tunic. He grimaced, hoping it could be repaired. After a while, Cynric slowed.

'The mine,' the book-bearer whispered, pointing through the undergrowth. 'The guards are still here, although I cannot imagine why, because the diggers have gone home. Can you see their lamps?'

Bartholomew nodded. 'How are we going to get past them?'

'There is no need. I took the precaution of locating the grave when I was here with Risleye and Valence earlier, and it is not too near the coal, although we must still tread softly.

Fortunately, the wind should carry away most sounds we make. We should be all right.'

Bartholomew's heart was pounding. It was only the need to know about Kelyng that stopped him from turning around and running back to the Queen's Head as fast as his legs would carry him. He followed Cynric to an oak tree with a jumble of brambles growing around its trunk. The book-bearer tugged a few away, and Bartholomew saw a mound of raised earth. He was surprised Cynric had found it, because he certainly would not have done, and could only suppose the directions to it had been very precise. Wordlessly, the Welshman handed him a spade.

It was grim work: the ground was sodden, and the rain seemed to be coming down harder than ever. They lit a lamp, but it had to be shaded so the guards would not notice it, which meant it was difficult to see what they were doing. Every so often, Cynric would disappear, to ensure no one had been alerted to their presence. While he did so, Bartholomew continued to dig, although it was unnerving to be alone and he was always relieved when the book-bearer returned.

'I think I can feel cloth, Cynric,' he whispered eventually. 'And bone.'

'You can do the rest, then,' said the book-bearer promptly. 'This is the bit I do not want to see.'

It was the bit Bartholomew did not want to see, either, and it took considerable willpower to scrape away the remaining soil with his hands; he dared not use a spade, lest the blade damaged the body. Kelyng had been missing for two months, so identification was going to be difficult enough, without having a broken skull to contend with.

At last he encountered an arm, although it was little more than bone and sinew. He worked upwards to where he thought the head might be. After a while, he sat back and moved the lamp over what he had exposed. There was a crooked front tooth that had once formed a distinctive part of Kelyng's impish grin, along with tufts of reddish hair, where the rain was washing it clean of mud. There was also a tin brooch the Bible Scholar had liked, and the tattered remnants of Michaelhouse's uniform black tabard.

'Is it him?' asked Cynric.

Bartholomew found he was unable to speak. He nodded.

It was some time before either man spoke again. Bartholomew sat on his heels and stared at the sorry remains, thinking sadly of the cheerful youth whose voice had accompanied so many College meals. Cynric clutched one of the charms he wore around his neck – a ward against restless spirits – as he stood with his head bowed, muttering prayers to whatever god happened to be listening.

'What shall we do?' the Welshman asked after a while. 'Can you get him out in one piece?'

Bartholomew shook his head, trying to find his voice. 'No, and we cannot arrive at the Queen's Head with a skeleton anyway. All we can do now is rebury him.'

'And reclaim him another time – on another visit to Suffolk?'

Bartholomew felt his resolve begin to strengthen. 'Yes, but when we do, it will be openly and in full daylight. And his killer will be under lock and key.'

'He was murdered, then?' asked Cynric unhappily.

'Stabbed. You can see the mark quite clearly on his ribs.'

'Cover him,' urged Cynric, looking around uneasily. 'This has taken too long, and we need to be back in the tavern before dawn, or we will start meeting labourers as they go out to the fields.'

Bartholomew placed a clean bandage from his medical bag across Kelyng's face, and began to do as Cynric suggested.

But it was even more difficult shovelling dirt on top of the Bible Scholar than it had been unearthing him, and he was obliged to stop when he thought he might be sick. He pretended to check on the guards, hoping Cynric would have finished when he returned.

He need not have worried. Cynric was eager to be gone, and had worked fast and efficiently, so that by the time Bartholomew had made sure the watchmen were still in their makeshift hut by the coal seam, the Welshman was patting the soil into place and tugging the brambles across it.

Suddenly, Cynric stiffened and cocked his head, listening intently. Automatically, Bartholomew did the same, but all he could hear was the wind sighing through the branches above his head and the patter of rain on the saturated ground.

'What—' he began, but Cynric silenced him with a sharp glance. Then the Welshman kicked the lantern so it went out, plunging them into utter blackness.

It took a moment for Bartholomew to attune his ears to what had startled Cynric, but once he did, it seemed as loud as thunder. The sound was footsteps, and they were coming closer. Cynric grabbed the physician's arm and pulled him behind the oak tree. Almost immediately, one of the guards emerged from the undergrowth to stand where they had been. He bent down, and touched a finger to the earth. Then he straightened and looked around him.

'There!' he hissed, stabbing a finger in the direction of the oak. 'I told you I heard someone!'

All at once the other watchmen were thrusting through the bushes. Cynric turned and fled, leaving Bartholomew to follow. The physician was slower and much less sure-footed, and soon began to fall behind. Cynric stopped and urged him on, although Bartholomew needed no such encouragement – he was running as hard as he could, stumbling and staggering as he tripped over roots in the darkness. But it was not fast enough, and he could hear their pursuers coming closer.

His arm was almost wrenched from its socket when Cynric jerked him to a standstill before hauling him into a thicket. The Welshman put his finger to his lips, and an instant later, the guards shot past.

'You must have made more noise than you thought when you went to check on them,' said Cynric a little while later, when they had taken a tortuous route across several fields and were finally in sight of Haverhill. Bartholomew did not think he had ever been so relieved to see a place in his life.

'Sorry,' he said sheepishly. 'I did my best.'

Cynric squeezed his shoulder in a rare gesture of affection. 'It is all right, boy. It is not your fault you have no skill for this kind of thing. Still, we learned one important thing from the chase: the watchmen are not just for decoration – they take their duties seriously.'

'But *why* does the mine warrant such vigilance?' demanded Bartholomew, becoming frustrated by the lack of answers. 'You say it does not even have decent coal.'

'Perhaps it is magic coal,' suggested Cynric matter-of-factly. 'And if Kelyng happened across it, he might have been stabbed to ensure his silence on the matter. It might even explain why Wynewyk gave the mine's owner eighteen marks.'

'It might,' said Bartholomew, too tired and fraught to argue with him.

'Of course, there is another explanation,' Cynric went on, padding at the physician's side with cat-like grace.

'Wynewyk brought Kelyng here. Perhaps *he* was the one who wielded the knife.'

'Not you as well, Cynric,' groaned Bartholomew. 'Is there no one who believes he is innocent?'

'Not at Michaelhouse,' replied Cynric.

CHAPTER 9

Michael was horrified when he saw his friend's clothes were torn, sodden and filthy, and ordered Cynric to clean them as best as he could. Bartholomew agreed, aware that the guards would know exactly who he was if he was seen in such a bedraggled state. While the book-bearer went off in search of water and thread, Bartholomew told Michael what had happened.

'So now we have a second Michaelhouse death to investigate,' he concluded, shivering as he huddled next to the fire. There was a chill inside him that had nothing to do with the cold. 'And this one is certainly murder. I am still not sure why Wynewyk died, but Kelyng did not stab himself.'

The monk's face was pale in the flickering light. 'I do not suppose the grave contained any evidence of who might have done this dreadful thing? An identifiable knife, perhaps?'

Bartholomew shook his head. 'Cynric thinks Wynewyk did it. I suppose poor Wynewyk will be blamed for anything untoward that happens now.'

'Poor Wynewyk has only himself to blame,' Michael said, placing sarcastic emphasis on the first word. 'No one forced him to steal from us – or try to kill our Master.'

'I wish we had not brought Valence, Risleye and Tesdale with us,' said Bartholomew, changing the subject before they quarrelled. 'I am taking them home this morning.'

'Give me one more day.' Michael spread his hands in a

shrug when the physician started to object to the delay. 'I am eager to leave, too – it is already Friday, and I need to prepare for Monday's Blood Relic debate. But we cannot, not until we know what is going on.'

'You think you can resolve all your mysteries in a day?' Bartholomew sincerely doubted it.

'I can try,' said Michael quietly. 'I am going to dawn mass in Hilton's church. Are you coming?'

Bartholomew started to say he had no clothes, but he had reckoned without Cynric, who arrived with a new tunic, mended leggings and a cloak that had been brushed clean. It was still damp, but at least it did not look as if its owner had been grubbing about in graves. And as for the tunic, Bartholomew did not want to know how Cynric had come by it, afraid it might have been on someone's washing line. Fortunately, it was nondescript homespun, indistinguishable from virtually everyone else's, so its hapless owner was unlikely to challenge him over it. He accepted it grudgingly, telling himself he would arrange for its return later, when his own was dry.

Most of Haverhill was present for the morning mass at St Mary the Virgin – parishioners from the Upper Church were obliged to make use of Hilton's services, now Neubold was unavailable. Elyan stood at the front, wearing yet another set of fine black clothes, while his grandmother sat in a great throne next to him; d'Audley hovered behind them like a malevolent bird of prey.

Bartholomew and Michael found a place at the back, keeping to the shadows so no one would notice them. It was just as well, because the students were deeply embroiled in a hissing debate about whether the Stanton Cups were sufficiently heavy to brain someone with.

'Of course they are,' asserted Risleye confidently. 'Especially the base.'

'But you would have to use a *lot* of force,' argued Tesdale. 'Or batter your victim multiple times. It would take a good deal of hard work.' He shuddered, although Bartholomew thought it was the notion of physical labour that repelled him, not the mess such an attack would make of a head.

'Tesdale is right,' said Valence. 'You could not guarantee a clean kill with either of those chalices, so it would be more humane to employ something else. A large stone would—'

'Stop,' ordered Bartholomew, though there was no real censure in his voice. He found himself strangely comforted by their familiar sparring after what he had seen of Kelyng the night before. 'What sort of subject is that to be airing in a church?'

'It is an academic exercise,' said Risleye, stung by the reprimand. 'We are honing our minds.'

'Then do it another time, not during mass,' snapped Michael.

He turned towards the altar and pressed his hands together, indicating the discussion was over. He did not close his eyes, though, and Bartholomew could tell by his distant expression that his thoughts were no more on the divine office than were the students'. He was thinking about the mysteries that confronted them, and how to find answers before they left for Cambridge the following day.

When the service was over, most of the congregation left in a rush, eager to be about their daily business. The students and Cynric went, too, because, for some inexplicable reason, Risleye wanted to show them a forge that produced weapons. Others lingered, though: Hilton was reporting the results of his investigation to Agnys and Elyan, while d'Audley and Gatekeeper Folyat loitered nearby, pretending to talk to each other, but it was clear their intention was to eavesdrop. Michael decided to do likewise. He edged towards the priest, Bartholomew in tow.

'I am not sure how to proceed,' Hilton was saying unhappily. 'Neubold was certainly murdered—'

'I thought I told you to decide it was suicide,' snapped Elyan irritably.

'How can he find it was suicide, when it is a clear case of unlawful killing?' demanded d'Audley, abandoning Folyat and stepping forward to say his piece. 'Luneday *must* be brought to justice.'

'He is right,' agreed Folyat, following him. 'The culprit is that wife-stealing Withersfield villain.'

'But if Luneday dispatched Neubold in Withersfield, then how did the body end up here?' asked Agnys, rounding on him impatiently.

'Lady Agnys has a point,' mused Hilton. He also turned to the gatekeeper. 'Did you see anyone who might have been carrying a corpse that night – from Withersfield or anywhere else?'

Folyat shrugged. 'Margery was the only visitor. She came to sniff around our grandchildren near the Upper Church, but she did not have a body with her. I would have noticed.'

'I wonder . . .' whispered Bartholomew to Michael. He rubbed his chin, collecting his thoughts. 'I wonder if Margery rode to Haverhill to create a diversion. She certainly claimed Folyat's attention, if he knows she visited their grandchildren – the Upper Church is some distance from the gate, which suggests he followed her there.'

'Thus leaving the gate unguarded,' finished Michael, nodding. 'That makes sense. Then, while Folyat was stalking his estranged wife, the killer sneaked the body into Haverhill.'

'So, the question is, did Margery distract Folyat deliberately, or did the killer just seize an opportunity that happened to present itself? But then what? The culprit did not take Neubold straight to the chapel, or Hilton would have seen the body when he came for his morning prayers.'

Michael pondered the possibilities for a moment, then beckoned Hilton towards him. 'How often do you say masses for Alneston?' he asked.

'Once a week, on Thursdays,' replied the priest warily. 'Why?'

'Does anyone else pray in the chapel?' asked Michael, ignoring the query.

Hilton shook his head, bemused. 'You saw for yourself that the place is small and mean. No one spends time there unless he must.'

'Who actually found Neubold? Folyat, who then raced about spreading the news?'

Folyat heard his name, and began to walk towards them. His reaction intrigued the others, who followed, curious to know what the monk was saying.

'Yes, I found him,' said Folyat, when the monk repeated the question. 'But I am not his killer.'

'No,' agreed Michael. 'You unwittingly let the culprit into the village unchallenged, but you did not execute anyone. But tell me, how did you come to find the body in the first place? Hilton has just said the Alneston Chantry is no place to linger.'

'I . . .' Folyat swallowed uneasily. 'I sometimes . . .' He trailed off.

'You use it for chickens,' supplied Bartholomew, recalling the thick layer of droppings that carpeted the floor. 'As gatekeeper, you accept poultry in lieu of coins, and you house them in the chantry until you can dispose of them.'

'What?' demanded Hilton, horrified. 'But it is a chapel,

not a hencoop! No wonder the place is so filthy. I thought it was pigeons, coming in through the broken windows.'

'Well, what else am I supposed to do?' demanded Folyat, going on the offensive. 'It is effectively an empty building, and I have to put them somewhere. It does no harm.'

'I think I am beginning to understand Neubold's post-mortem travels at last,' said Michael, cutting across Hilton's outraged declarations that filling a chapel with bird mess *was* doing harm. 'I still have one or two questions, though. Will you all come to the chapel, to answer them for me?'

'You are doing well, Brother,' said Agnys slyly, as she followed him outside. 'Your clever logic has your audience transfixed, and it is good to see that treacherous d'Audley look so unsettled.'

'You did not tell us you bought pennyroyal shortly before Joan died,' said Michael. He spoke in a low voice, so her grandson would not hear.

Agnys regarded him sharply. 'I did not think it was relevant. It cannot have been my supply that killed her, because she died in Cambridge. Besides, I no longer have it.'

'You mean you have used it all?' asked the monk, regarding her suspiciously.

'I mean I lost it. I suppose it is possible that Joan took the stuff, although it is far more likely that I dropped it on my way home. Regardless, it has gone.'

Michael glanced at Bartholomew, but the physician could only shrug. Was it significant that Agnys had been careless with a potent herb – and was now dismissive about what had then happened to it? And if she had dropped it, who had picked it up? Agnys seemed to consider the matter closed, because she made no effort to convince them further and the party walked in silence towards the Alneston Chantry.

* * *

315

When they reached the chapel, Michael threw open the door and strode inside. Hilton lit a lamp, which cast eerie shadows around the dirty walls. Several hens squawked their alarm at the sudden invasion, and one managed to escape through the open door. Folyat made no attempt to catch it.

'What is kept in there?' Michael asked, pointing to a huge chest that stood near the back.

'Just a couple of altar cloths,' replied Hilton. He shrugged sheepishly. 'I have not looked inside for a while, because it is always full of spiders. I dislike spiders.'

Bartholomew opened the lid, and an inspection revealed a smear of blood and an orange thread. 'Neubold was wearing leggings this colour when he died,' he said, holding the snagged strand aloft.

Michael regarded it in silence for a moment, then began to outline what he had deduced about the priest's death. His audience clustered around him, eager not to miss a word of it. Bartholomew wondered why. Guilty consciences? Or just idle curiosity in a place where not much else happened?

'He was killed in Withersfield, then brought here,' the monk began. 'The murderer slipped through the gate when Folyat left his post to follow his wife. He hid the body in this chest, because he knew Hilton would pray for Alneston the next morning, and he did not want it discovered then.'

'Why not?' demanded Elyan. He looked annoyed that his suicide theory was being demolished.

'Perhaps he thought a week would eliminate any stray evidence that *he* was the killer,' suggested Bartholomew. 'Or that the corpse would look so dreadful that no one would examine it too carefully.'

'You examined it carefully,' said Hilton, proving that Michael's attempts to distract him in the Upper Church had not worked: he had known exactly what the physician had been doing. 'I assume you did not find any evidence, or you would have told me.'

'No,' admitted Bartholomew. 'There was nothing to find.'

Michael took up the tale before awkward questions could be asked – such as why scholars from Michaelhouse should think Neubold's death was any of their business. 'As soon as Hilton finished his prayers, the killer came to hang Neubold from the rafters. I imagine he anticipated the place would remain undisturbed until next Thursday.'

'But he had reckoned without Folyat coming to fill the chapel with chickens,' finished Bartholomew. 'Which meant Neubold was discovered far sooner.'

'Did you see anyone enter or leave this place yesterday, Folyat?' asked Hilton urgently, aware that a solution was at hand and eager to play a role, however small.

'Only you,' replied Folyat unsteadily. He would not meet the priest's eyes. 'I waited to make sure you had really finished your devotions, and then I came to put my hens back inside.'

Hilton blanched as the implications of the gatekeeper's testimony struck home. 'But that means the killer was in here with me all the time I was praying. We have deduced that Neubold was strung up between the time I left and the time Folyat entered, and if Folyat saw no one else coming or going . . .'

'Skulking in one of these alcoves, probably,' agreed Michael, pointing towards the shadows. 'Hoping the dawn light would not be strong enough to give him away.'

'He must have been here when you came with your birds, too,' said Bartholomew to Folyat. 'He probably escaped when you left to raise the alarm, and you are lucky he did not catch you.'

Folyat stared at his feet and made no reply.

* * *

317

'I do not want to stay here until tomorrow,' said Bartholomew to Michael as they left the chapel. Behind them, Agnys was issuing instructions – Hilton was to visit Withersfield, to ascertain whether Margery was a willing accomplice or an unwitting one, while Folyat was to improve Haverhill's security. 'It is not safe, and we should take the students home.'

'They can look after themselves,' said Michael. He glanced towards the forge, where Risleye was performing some fancy manoeuvres with a sword, Tesdale was playing lethargically with a dagger, and Valence was being shown some vicious-looking cudgels by an amiable blacksmith. 'Indeed, Risleye is more skilled than I realised.'

'We need to tell Langelee about Kelyng,' argued Bartholomew. 'As soon as possible.'

'We need to tell him about Michaelhouse's thirty marks, too, but we cannot, because we have no answers. One more day, Matt – we will leave tomorrow, I promise. And we are making some progress with our enquiries – we now know how Neubold's body ended up in Haverhill. Unfortunately, we do not know why. Or who murdered him.'

'He died in a place where we were attacked, and he is associated with coal, King's Hall, Carbo and various other strands in the mysteries that confront us.' Bartholomew's stomach churned, and he felt with every fibre of his being that lingering in Suffolk was a very bad idea. 'I suppose if we solve his murder we *may* find solutions to our other mysteries. But is it worth the risk?'

'I think so, and we shall start with a visit to Elyan Manor,' said Michael, watching Agnys and her grandson mount up and ride off in the direction of their home. 'First, because they have eighteen of Michaelhouse's thirty marks. And second, because I was unconvinced by Agnys's tale of lost pennyroyal. She claims she was ready to overlook the fact

318

that Joan's child was not a Elyan, but I am sceptical. I would like to interview both of them in their lair.'

'Shall I saddle the horses, then?' asked Bartholomew, thinking the monk would want to reach Elyan Manor as soon as possible, thus leaving more time for their other enquiries.

'It pains me to say it, but we had better walk. We do not want the villagers thinking we are fleeing the scene of Neubold's murder, and come after us with bows and arrows. We shall leave Cynric and the students here – that should convince them that we are not running away.'

It was not far to Elyan's home, and it was a pleasant journey, even on an overcast day. The countryside smelled clean and fresh, and the scent of soil mingled with the heavier odour of grass and damp vegetation. The road took them through a wood, and some of its trees seemed to have been there since the days of the Conqueror, they were so gnarled and ancient. A brook accompanied them most of the way, trickling between its muddy banks with a gentle bubbling sound. A blackbird sang from the top branch of the tallest oak, and a dog barked in the distance.

'There is the mine,' said Bartholomew, pointing. The guards prowled, more alert than they had been, presumably because of the trouble the previous night. 'Kelyng is buried over to the right.'

Prudently, Michael did not look in the direction he indicated. 'Do you think Carbo killed him? Hilton told us a tale of Carbo killing someone by the mine, if you recall.'

'He also said he did not believe it. And if Kelyng and Neubold were killed by the same person, then Carbo is innocent – he was dead long before someone hanged his brother.'

Michael glanced around uneasily. 'I wish we had asked

319

Cynric to accompany us to Elyan Manor. You are right: it does not feel safe here.'

Elyan and his grandmother lived in style. Their home was larger and grander than Luneday's, and was supported by well-stocked stables, a sizeable kitchen block, pantries, granaries and a dovecote. Before they could knock at the door, a servant appeared and conducted them to a pleasant solar on the first floor. Both Elyan and Agnys were there, drinking mulled wine. She poured some for the visitors, while Michael quizzed Elyan on why his mine warranted so many guards.

'Coal is valuable,' replied Elyan. 'Why do you think these vultures circle, waiting for me to die so they can inherit my manor? It is not for the sheep and the water meadows, believe me. And someone came a-spying only last night – my watchmen chased two villains intent on mischief.'

'How do you know they were intent on mischief?' asked Michael curiously.

Elyan raised his eyebrows. 'Well, they were not there for a pleasant stroll, not in all that wind and rain. Clearly, the villains waited for a foul night in the hope that the guards would be less vigilant – that they would be hiding inside their hut. But my men take their duties seriously.'

Not that seriously, thought Bartholomew, given that he and Cynric had managed to excavate a grave and refill it before the guards had realised something was amiss.

'I have seen coal mines in Wales,' he said. 'But none of those were protected by armed guards.'

Elyan looked smug. 'But my mine is the only one in Suffolk, which makes it unique. Moreover, its coal is exceptionally hard and pure. Carbo told me so, when he discovered it in the summer.'

'Carbo?' asked Michael, startled. 'Why should you believe anything he said? He was ill.'

'He was not always so, and he claimed his knowledge of minerals came from God. I believed him because . . . well, suffice to say he proved himself to me.'

'Proved himself how?' pressed Michael.

Elyan sighed, resenting the interrogation. 'Because he excavated some very fine specimens. When we find more – which I hope we will – they will make us rich, and I shall be able to buy any clothes that take my fancy. Have you seen the girdles worn by the King's knights these days? They comprise a wide belt with the most *fabulous* buckles.'

Bartholomew took a sip of the wine, and was taken off guard when the taste summoned a vivid image of Matilde – it was identical to the brews she had prepared for him on cold winter nights. The intensity of the recollection took him by surprise, and he wondered whether he would ever stop thinking about her. He became aware that Agnys was staring at him.

'You have tasted its like before,' she said, while Michael struggled to drag her grandson's attention away from clothes and back to minerals. 'And it pains you. Shall I fetch you something else?'

'No,' said Bartholomew quickly. 'It is not an unpleasant memory.'

'A lost lover?' she asked sympathetically. 'You are a scholar, so it cannot have been a wife.'

Bartholomew did not often talk about Matilde, but he was seized by a sudden urgent and wholly irrational desire to do so now. While Michael did his utmost to learn about Joan, coal and Wynewyk – and Elyan regaled him with an analysis of courtly fashions instead – the physician told Agnys all about the woman he had loved. He was not

321

normally given to confiding in strangers, and could only suppose it was the result of a sleepless night and the shock of finding Kelyng. Agnys listened without interruption or comment, even when he described Matilde in the most impossibly eulogistic terms.

'You still hope she will return to you,' she said, when he eventually faltered into silence.

'Logic tells me she is gone for ever, but I cannot bring myself to believe it. However, I would settle for knowing she is safe and happy. The King's highways are dangerous places for lone women.'

'Your Matilde would not have let robbers best her,' said Agnys, patting his knee encouragingly. 'She will have arrived at her destination unscathed, never fear.'

Although she had no grounds for making such an assured statement, Bartholomew found her words oddly comforting; more comforting than reason dictated he should. He smiled, and when he took another sip of the wine, the experience was much less unsettling.

'You told me yesterday that you knew our colleague Wynewyk,' Michael was saying to Elyan. He sounded exasperated, and the physician could tell he was reaching the end of his patience.

'Actually, I did not,' countered Elyan. He also sounded irritable, indicating they had managed to rile each other. 'You asked if I knew him, but d'Audley started to gabble before I could reply.'

'Wynewyk said he knew you,' lied Michael. 'He told me you sold the best coal in Suffolk, and was pleased to have done business with you. He has been commending you to friends in other Colleges.'

'I very much doubt that,' said Elyan flatly.

Michael's eyes narrowed. 'And now we reach the crux of the matter. Your dealings with him were not honest – *that*

322

is why you sit there so certain he would not have mentioned you to anyone else.'

Elyan glowered in a way that made Bartholomew certain that Michael was right, but made no other reply. Agnys also noticed her grandson's reaction, and became sharp with him.

'Our manor has always held a reputation for fair dealing, Henry. If you have flouted that tradition, you had better speak now, so the matter can be rectified before any harm is done.'

Elyan tried to ignore her, but there was a steely glint in her eye that warned him to do as he was told. 'All right, I knew Wynewyk. But I did not sell him the coal I import from Ipswich – we had another arrangement.'

'He paid you eighteen marks,' stated Michael. 'He wrote it our account book.'

'Eighteen marks?' echoed Agnys, shocked. 'You did not tell me *this* when we enjoyed our pork and ale in the Queen's Head yesterday. Eighteen marks is a vast sum of money, and I might not have been so willing to agree to an exchange of information, had I known the stakes were so high.'

Michael grimaced. 'But you did not exchange information, madam – you promised to look into the matter of Wynewyk, but you had nothing to give us at the time.'

'Then we had better rectify the matter: an arrangement is an arrangement, and an Elyan's word is her bond.' Agnys turned to her grandson. 'Where is this eighteen marks, Henry? I hope you have not spent it on clothes.'

'Wynewyk gave it to me because he wanted a share in my mine,' said Elyan sullenly. 'To invest in its running in order to enjoy its profits. I did *not* spend it on clothes. Although, I admit there was a rather nice red tunic that just happened to be—'

'He *invested*?' breathed Michael, appalled. 'But your venture will founder, and eighteen—'

'I told you: it has yielded some excellent specimens,' interrupted Elyan tightly. 'And I used his money to pay guards and diggers, so do not expect it back. It is long gone.'

Bartholomew did not think he had ever seen Michael so full of rage. The monk leapt to his feet and treated Elyan to a stream of invective that would not have been out of place in a fish-market. Agnys's eyes grew wide with astonishment, and Elyan eventually put his hands over his ears. It was something Wynewyk did when he thought his colleagues were being unnecessarily bellicose, and it sent a pang of grief stabbing through Bartholomew. When Michael saw the gesture, he faltered, too.

'Wynewyk paid you with College funds,' he said, temper subsiding as abruptly as it had risen. '*Ergo*, this arrangement is with Michaelhouse, not with him, and you are legally bound to honour it. I want our money back. Now. I refuse to wait years for these so-called profits to materialise.'

'We signed no documents detailing our pact, and as he is dead, you cannot prove what he did or did not give me,' snapped Elyan. 'Your eighteen marks no longer exists, and neither does the seven he gave to d'Audley. Oh, damn it! Now look what you have made me say!'

Michael's expression was cold and angry. 'Tell me about d'Audley,' he ordered softly.

Elyan was clearly disgusted with himself, but also seemed to appreciate that the time for subterfuge was over. He sighed irritably. 'He had no spare cash of his own to invest in my scheme, so Wynewyk lent him some. In return, d'Audley was to supply him with free timber until the loan was repaid in full. Unfortunately for you, there is no written proof of his arrangement, either.'

'I will find proof,' warned Michael menacingly.

'You will not – and we could not repay you, even if we wanted to. The money is spent.'

'Squandered, you mean,' said Agnys, regarding her grandson in disgust. 'Joan was given pennyroyal for a reason, and I am beginning to think it is connected to this horrible mine.'

Elyan paled. 'No! I do not believe that. She was murdered, as I have said from the beginning, but it has nothing to do with my coal.'

'I imagine it has more to do with the fact that she was about to provide Elyan Manor with an heir,' said Michael, 'thus thwarting the hopes of three optimistic claimants. However, I understand the child may not have been yours.'

'How dare you!' shouted Elyan furiously. 'Of course it was mine!'

'You overstep the mark, Brother,' said Agnys warningly. Her face was a mask of anger, furious that a remark made in confidence should be so bluntly repeated.

Michael ignored her, focusing his attention on her grandson. 'You must feel vulnerable. Now she is dead and you are childless, d'Audley, Luneday *and* King's Hall all eagerly await your death.'

Elyan's expression was impossible to read. 'If you think that, then you are a fool. The situation with my estates is murky, and no one claimant has a better case than the others. Lawyers are needed to sort it out, so no one wants me dead before the matter is resolved. I am safe until the clerks have finished wrangling – which will not be for years yet.'

Michael regarded him dispassionately. 'You are the fool. Do you think a powerful foundation like King's Hall, which bursts at the seams with clever minds, is going to wait years for a decision? And do you think a sly, greedy man like d'Audley will sit back and wait for them to best him?'

'I disagree,' said Agnys coldly. 'Joan's death is connected to the mine, not the inheritance issue.'

Bartholomew wondered why an astute woman like Agnys could not see what was so obvious. 'But whoever wins the manor *will* get the mine,' he pointed out. 'The two are tightly interwoven. And Michael is right to warn you, Elyan: Neubold was involved in the case and he is murdered; Wynewyk invested in your mine and he is dead; Carbo advised you about coal, and he is stabbed – by someone from King's Hall; and your wife is poisoned.'

'You think I am in danger?' Elyan looked bewildered. 'But why strike now? I have been in this situation for years, and no one has tried to harm me before.'

'Clearly, someone is growing impatient,' replied Michael. 'The claims on both your manor *and* d'Audley's chantry are becoming more acrimonious, suggesting knives are being honed for battle.'

'You are wrong,' said Elyan unsteadily. 'No one will try to kill me. If they do, I shall take another wife. That will put an end to such nonsense.'

'Or result in another death from pennyroyal,' said Michael harshly. 'But why did Joan really go to Cambridge? She was heavily pregnant and not young. It was a risky thing to do, and I cannot believe she did it for ribbons.'

'It *was* for ribbons,' said Elyan firmly. 'She told me the ones in Haverhill were dull and she wanted brighter colours. She was going to buy me a new hat, too.'

Bartholomew studied him thoughtfully, and concluded that whatever the reason for Joan's sudden decision to travel, she had not confided it to her husband. She had invented an excuse she knew he would accept – inveterate clothes-lover that he was – and had pre-empted any objections he might have raised with promises of treats.

She had, however, taken care to leave at a time when Agnys was not there stop her. Why? Was it really because the old lady would have tried to dissuade her? Or was she running away from something in Haverhill, something Agnys knew all about? Agnys had denied knowing the cause of Joan's recent unhappiness, but who was to say she was telling the truth? He turned to look at the old woman, but could read nothing in her face.

'Perhaps she went to see the father of her child,' suggested Michael. 'Lady Agnys said she had been distant and distracted for a few weeks. Perhaps she wanted to tell him the good news.'

'The brat was mine,' said Elyan fiercely. 'And if someone else did step into the breach, then so what? It would still have been born to my wife, and raised as my heir.'

'D'Audley, Luneday and King's Hall would not agree,' Michael pointed out. 'They only lose their rights if *you* provide a child: another man's progeny does not count in the eyes of the law.'

'Who was it, Henry?' asked Agnys softly. 'Joan is dead, so breaking her trust cannot matter now.'

'I loved her,' said Elyan in a strangled voice. 'I will not . . .'

'I know you did,' said Agnys gently. 'But people are being murdered, and it is time to put an end to it. Who do you suspect of obliging Joan?'

Elyan sighed unhappily. 'Neubold said it was him. Joan claimed it was not, but I always assumed she lied because she did not want me to think less of her for selecting such a miserable specimen.'

'Neubold accompanied her to Cambridge,' mused Michael. 'And it was there that she died of—'

'Neubold would not have killed her,' interrupted Agnys with conviction. 'If he was the father, he would have wanted her and the baby alive, so he could reap the benefits. He would never have harmed her, not when there might have been profit in the situation.'

'But Michael is right in that the father may live in Cambridge,' mused Bartholomew. He thought, but did not say, that the University was awash with handsome men, most of whom would be only too pleased to provide their services to a desperate woman – Joan would have been spoiled for choice. 'Edith is wrong to think the solution to Joan's death lies here: it lies in the place where she died.'

It was mid-afternoon by the time Bartholomew and Michael left Elyan Manor, and the weather had turned chilly. It was not raining, but the clouds were low and menacing and it would not be long before there was another deluge. Michael complained bitterly, because it had been warm when they had set out on their journey, and he had not bothered to take his cloak. Now he was cold.

'I am more confused than ever,' he said, shivering. 'Did Elyan kill Neubold because he believed Neubold was his wife's lover? Personally, I doubt it was the case – I imagine she had more taste.'

'He was rather keen for a verdict of suicide,' replied Bartholomew. 'That is suspicious in itself. However, by killing Neubold, Elyan lost himself the services of a slippery lawyer.'

'He is not the only one,' said Michael, rather gleefully. 'I cannot imagine Osa Gosse will be pleased when he learns his legal adviser is no longer available.'

But Bartholomew's thoughts were still on Joan. 'The more I consider it, the more I am sure you are right about why she went to Cambridge – it *was* to see the father of her child.'

Michael sighed. 'To be honest, I only said that to shake a reaction from Elyan. It cannot be true, because we have been told – by several people, including your sister – that Joan had not been to Cambridge for years. *Ergo*, the babe must have been conceived in Suffolk. The father is not some willing scholar or burgess, but someone in *this* county. Or perhaps someone who visited Haverhill.'

'It cannot be Wynewyk,' said Bartholomew, seeing what the monk was thinking. 'It is one thing you cannot blame him for, because we both know his preferences. Although . . .'

'Although what?'

'Although Yolande de Blaston did say he hired her on occasion. However, I suspect Joan would have opted for someone more manly. Scholars from King's Hall must have visited Haverhill, too, to look at the Alneston Chantry and the manor they hope to acquire. Then there is Gosse. Joan knew him, because Edith was with her when she exchanged words with the fellow.'

Michael was shocked. 'But Gosse is a felon! A well-dressed, intelligent one, but a felon even so.'

'Perhaps she had no choice,' said Bartholomew soberly.

They were silent for a while, and the only sound was their footsteps on the muddy track and the distant bleat of sheep on the surrounding hills.

'Do you think Elyan was telling the truth about his arrangement with Wynewyk?' asked Michael at last. 'If so, we may never retrieve our eighteen marks.'

'Twenty-five marks,' corrected Bartholomew. 'Wynewyk lent d'Audley money for the venture, too. And yes, I think he was telling the truth. He is not clever enough to have deceived you.'

329

'What was Wynewyk thinking, to become embroiled with such people?' demanded Michael.

'I imagine he was thinking it offered an attractive long-term investment for Michaelhouse,' said Bartholomew, who had been relieved by Elyan's confession. 'He was not dishonest, as I have said all along. It was not a wise decision, given that the mine is unlikely to be profitable, but being a fool is not the same as being a thief.'

'We need to confirm this tale with d'Audley before we can be sure about that,' said Michael. 'And nor can we forget the five marks Wynewyk gave to Luneday, ostensibly for pigs.'

'What a coincidence – there is d'Audley,' said Bartholomew, pointing down the road to where a familiar figure could be seen riding towards them. 'On his way home from the market, I suppose.'

D'Audley saw the Michaelhouse scholars coming his way, and attempted to force his way through a hedge in order to avoid them. Unfortunately, the gap he had picked was not wide enough, and the nag panicked. It taxed even Michael's superior horsemanship to extricate them both unscathed.

'I saw a fox,' declared d'Audley, once he was free. 'And I wanted to see where it went. I have chickens, you know. A man with chickens cannot be too careful about foxes.'

'Speaking of foxes, I would like to hear about your arrangement with Wynewyk,' said Michael. 'Elyan has just informed us that Wynewyk lent you seven marks, to allow you to invest in his mine.'

'Damn him!' cried d'Audley furiously. 'He promised to keep the matter to himself. I should have known he could not be trusted!'

'The time for deceit is over,' said Michael, keeping a firm grip on the reins, lest his victim attempted to bolt.

'You have two choices: you can tell *us* the truth, or you can tell the King. However, I should warn you that His Majesty beheaded the last person who tried to cheat us.'

D'Audley regarded him in horror, and Bartholomew looked away, uncomfortable with the lie. But it had the desired effect, because d'Audley began to talk so fast that it was difficult to keep up with the stream of confessions.

'I should have followed my first instinct, and stayed well away from that wretched coal,' he gabbled, bitterness in every word. 'I knew it would be unprofitable, and we would all end up throwing away good money. So why did I weaken and let Elyan persuade me otherwise?'

'You tell me,' suggested Michael.

'He seemed so sure it would prosper, and I dislike the notion of neighbours growing rich while I remain poor. So I decided to accept his invitation to invest. Unfortunately, I had no free money of my own. Then I happened to meet your friend Wynewyk in the Queen's Head one night. I bewailed my plight to his sympathetic ear, and he gave me seven marks. I could not believe my good luck!'

'He *lent* you seven marks,' corrected Michael. 'He did not *give* it.'

'No,' agreed d'Audley tearfully. 'And the interest on the loan was free firewood for the next five years, plus a percentage of my profits from the mine. He was going to have a percentage of Elyan's returns, too, so it was a fabulous deal for your College.'

'In other words,' said Bartholomew quietly, 'he negotiated a perfectly legitimate transaction.'

D'Audley nodded miserably. 'But Elyan's mine has not yielded what was promised, and it is time to start sending firewood to Cambridge. Then I heard Wynewyk was dead, and as there was no written agreement between us, I thought – hoped – that your College would not know about it.'

331

Michael almost laughed. 'It did not occur to you that *he* might have kept records? Or that no foundation is likely to overlook such a large amount of money?'

'It did, but the others told me I was being unreasonably pessimistic.'

'What others?' demanded Michael. 'Your conspirators in crime? Luneday and Elyan?'

'We are not conspirators,' objected d'Audley, alarmed by the term. 'Nor have we stolen—'

'But not for want of trying,' interrupted Michael coldly. 'You have already confessed to attempting to defraud my College. The King will not like that.'

'Then you must tell him I made a mistake,' cried d'Audley. 'Please! If I am imprisoned, my manor will never produce enough firewood to appease you until I can repay back what I borrowed. It is in your own interests to be nice.'

'I shall think about it,' said Michael stiffly, knowing he was right. 'Now, if I draw up a written agreement of the transaction you arranged with Wynewyk, will you sign it?'

'Yes,' sighed d'Audley. He looked furtive. 'I always intended to do right by Michaelhouse, as far as I could. It was the others who wanted to renege, and they forced me to do likewise. Elyan is supposed to give Michaelhouse eighteen marks' worth of coal before the end of the year, and Luneday agreed to establish a fine herd of pigs at your manor in Ickleton.'

Michael was unimpressed. 'What are we supposed to do with that much coal?'

'It is a valuable commodity – I imagine Wynewyk planned to stockpile it, then release it when the price is highest. He was an astute man – too astute for us.'

'And what about the animals?' asked Michael in distaste. 'We are scholars, not farmers.'

'Yes, but you eat pork, and these are the best pigs in Suffolk. A herd of Withersfield beasts is an excellent bargain for any foundation. Of course, Luneday probably lied to you, and denied knowing Wynewyk. If he did, you should not be surprised. The man is a scoundrel.'

'Unlike you, I suppose,' murmured Michael in distaste.

'When did Wynewyk do all this?' asked Bartholomew. 'In the summer?'

D'Audley nodded. 'Late August. He must have heard about the coal from King's Hall, who were also invited to invest, and he came here to see it for himself.'

'Was he here earlier than that?' asked Bartholomew, thinking of Michael's contention that Wynewyk might be the father of Joan's child. He did some rapid calculations. 'February or March?'

'No. I had never seen him before August. And I wish to God I had not met him then, either.'

Michael released the reins, and the moment he did so, d'Audley jabbed his heels into his horse's sides and galloped away. Bartholomew felt happier than he had done in days.

'D'Audley's testimony exonerates Wynewyk,' he said, smiling. 'These arrangements are irregular, which is probably why he did not tell us about them, but he did not steal our thirty marks.'

'No,' acknowledged Michael. 'The whole affair is shabby, though. Langelee said Wynewyk was a scoundrel, and hoped he would use his unsavoury talents to benefit us. Well, he did.'

'We should speak to Luneday – make him sign a document to ensure he delivers these pigs to Ickleton. It may not be money, but at least we will have retrieved something.'

'We shall have eighteen marks in coal, too,' vowed Michael. 'And—'

He was interrupted by a sudden hiss, and an arrow thudded into the ground at his feet. The next one impaled the purse that dangled at his side.

Bartholomew grabbed Michael's arm and hauled him into the deep ditch that ran along the side of the road. The monk squawked as icy water seeped into his boots, and then released a string of pithy oaths when the arrow, still embedded in his scrip, poked through his habit and jabbed him in the leg.

'Quiet!' ordered Bartholomew urgently, peering through the long grass and trying to see where their assailant might be lurking.

'Easy for you to say,' muttered the monk. 'You are not soaking wet and grievously wounded.'

Bartholomew ducked when a third missile landed inches from his hand. From its angle, he thought the bowman was lurking behind the large beech tree on the opposite side of the road. Then another arrived from a different direction, and he realised there were two of them. He turned to Michael.

'We will have to escape by crawling along the ditch. We cannot stay here – it is only a matter of time before one scores a lucky hit. Can you do it?'

'Yes.' Michael sounded offended. 'I am not so portly that I cannot scramble along trenches to save my life.'

'You said you were hurt.'

Michael hauled up the voluminous folds of his habit, prudishly turning his back, so the physician should not see anything too personal. Then he presented a minuscule patch of bare white thigh – the rest primly concealed by material – to reveal a scratch that had barely broken the skin.

'It stings!' the monk protested, seeing from Bartholomew's

334

expression that it did not constitute being 'grievously wounded'.

'Follow me,' said Bartholomew. He winced when a fourth arrow soared into the drain, coming to rest in the space between them. 'And keep well down.'

Unfortunately, they had not gone far before the channel narrowed so much that even Bartholomew was unable to squeeze along it. And as arrows had followed them every inch of the way, it was clear the bowmen knew exactly how they were trying to escape. When the next quarrel hit his medical bag, Bartholomew knew time was running out.

'I cannot turn,' Michael hissed, when the physician indicated they were to go back the way they had come. 'I cannot even move – I am stuck. Which means you are trapped, too. Give me your bag.'

'What for?'

'I am going to leap up, holding it in front of me like a shield, so you can slither past. You should be able to make it to safety. Then you can fetch help.'

Bartholomew regarded him in horror. It was tantamount to suicide, and there would be no point in fetching help, because the monk would be dead.

'Can you see either of them?' asked Michael, ignoring his reaction. 'I should like to know the identities of the men who will kill . . . who are making such a nuisance of themselves.'

'They could abandon their hiding places and come to pick us off.' Bartholomew grabbed a stone and lobbed it towards the beech, more in frustration than in the hope of hitting anyone. 'But they prefer to remain hidden, presumably lest they are recognised but fail to dispatch us, and we—'

There was a yelp of pain, and he exchanged a startled glance with Michael. Wordlessly, he grabbed another missile

335

and hurled it as hard as he could. Michael did likewise, and for a few moments they managed an impressive barrage. The archers began calling softly to each other, then there were footsteps.

'They are coming for us,' said Bartholomew grimly. He drew his sword – the one he wore when he travelled but was not permitted to carry in Cambridge. 'We have driven them out of their cover. Still, at least we shall know who they are before they—'

Suddenly, there was a shout, followed by the thunder of hoofs. It was Luneday, William at his heels. Luneday's sword flailed and the steward held a crossbow. Bartholomew risked a glance over the top of the bank and saw the two archers thrusting through the hedge into the fields beyond. Both wore hoods, and there was nothing – in their clothes or gait – that would allow him to identify them.

'I will get the villains,' yelled William, yellow hair flying as he turned his horse.

Luneday stood in his stirrups to watch the chase. He was panting hard, and his eyes flashed. 'Sly bastards! They are making for the wood, where a mounted man cannot follow. William is going to lose them. Damn their black hearts!'

'Who are they?' demanded Bartholomew. 'Do you recognise them?'

'Not in those hooded cloaks,' replied Luneday. 'However, they are no one local – *we* do not attack unarmed monks on the King's highways. They must be robbers from another village.'

'You arrived just in time,' said Michael to Luneday, allowing Bartholomew to help him out of the ditch. His voice was unsteady. 'They were coming to kill us.'

'They were,' agreed Luneday, sitting back down when

William reached the edge of the trees and was forced to stop. 'You are doubly lucky, because I rarely travel this road – it leads to Haverhill, you see, and I do not want to run the risk of meeting my woman's husband.'

'So, why are you here now?' asked Michael. He rested his hand on Luneday's saddle, as if he did not trust his legs to hold him up.

Luneday did not reply, and when Bartholomew glanced up at him to see why, he saw tears glittering in the man's eyes. He gazed at the lord of Withersfield Manor in astonishment.

'I am sorry,' Luneday managed to choke out. 'But my woman has gone, and I keep being gripped by these overwhelming urges to weep. I cannot imagine why. I did not cry when my wife left me, and it is not as if Margery was much of a replacement.'

Bartholomew and Michael exchanged a quick glance. Was Margery's flight anything to do with the fact that she had distracted her gatekeeper husband while Neubold's corpse was toted to the chantry chapel? Or was she the killer and realised she was about to be caught?

'Gone where?' asked Michael.

'Not to Folyat,' said Luneday. 'She would not want to return to gatekeeping, not after the luxury she enjoyed at Withersfield. But you do not seem surprised by my news. Why not?'

'Because we think she knows more about Neubold's death than is innocent,' replied Michael.

Luneday's eyes narrowed, and Bartholomew braced himself for another skirmish, wishing the monk had phrased his remark in a more tactful manner.

'What are you saying?' Luneday demanded. 'That *she* dispatched Neubold?'

'Not without help,' said Michael baldly. 'However, it was

337

obvious that she hated him, and she did go out the evening he was murdered. We also know she led Folyat away from his duties at the gate, thus allowing someone to carry Neubold's corpse to the Alneston Chantry.'

Bartholomew expected Luneday to deny the charges, and was astonished when he closed his eyes in apparent despair. 'I should have guessed she intended mischief when she crept out that night – her grandchildren had spent most of the day at Withersfield, so she should not have needed to see them again so soon.'

'You did not mention this yesterday, when you found Neubold gone from the barn,' said Michael, rather accusingly.

'Why would I? I thought he had escaped to Haverhill, and only learned of his death later. The moment I did hear, I realised I would have to talk to my woman about it, but I have been busy. Then, when I returned from my piggeries this afternoon, I discovered her missing.'

'You do not think she has been harmed, do you?' asked Bartholomew uneasily, wondering whether her accomplice had decided it would be safer if she was permanently silenced.

'I might have done, had she simply disappeared. But she left with all her belongings, and some of mine. So no, I do not think she has been harmed. I think she realised the net was closing in around her, and has run for safety.'

'Why did she dislike Neubold so intensely?' asked Michael. 'I do not think I have ever seen more venomous looks than the ones they exchanged on Wednesday night.'

'For two reasons. First, he offered to fabricate writs of annulment – for her marriage and mine – which meant she could have wed me. She was eager for him to do it, because it would have made her a real lady of the manor.

338

Unfortunately, he wanted ten marks, which is beyond my meagre means.'

'Would you have paid, had he agreed to charge less?' asked Michael curiously. 'Bearing in mind that false annulments would not have made your union legal in any case?'

'Of course. We do that sort of thing all the time around here. Why do you think there is so much fuss about who will inherit Elyan Manor? Someone's nuptials were not all they should have been!'

'And the second reason?' asked Michael, declining to comment.

'Neubold told me she had commissioned him to create forged documents that would see *me* inherit Elyan Manor. She was furious with him for revealing what she had charged him to do – I want to inherit, but not by cheating. So perhaps she *did* kill him – she is a strong lass. She would have needed help to cart the corpse to Haverhill, though.'

'So what are you going to do about it?' asked Michael. He released his grip on Luneday's saddle and took a deep breath, nerves steady at last. 'Hunt for her, and demand an explanation?'

'She will be halfway to Paris by now. She has always had a hankering to see the place. There is no point mounting a search – the wretched woman has essentially escaped.' Luneday sounded bitter.

'She will not like Paris,' predicted Michael, although he had never been, so was hardly in a position to make such a judgement. 'And I have colleagues there – I shall write and warn them to be on the lookout for her. She will not escape, believe me. But enough of her. I have reason to believe you have misled us, Master Luneday.'

'Misled you about what?' asked Luneday. He sounded thankful to be talking about something else.

'Wynewyk, five marks and some pigs,' replied Michael coolly.

'We have just been chatting to d'Audley, who was rather more open than you have been.'

'Damn! I knew he could not be trusted. His big mouth has just cost me twenty pigs, and the best of Lizzie's litter. *And* a long and dangerous journey to your manor at Ickleton to see the herd settled.'

'You do not deny it, then?' asked Michael, taken aback by the abrupt capitulation.

'There is no point, not if d'Audley has blathered. I am sorry, Brother, but your Wynewyk struck a very hard bargain, and I was relieved when I heard he was dead. And you cannot blame us for trying to be as wily with you as he was with us. But we are caught, so we will all honour the debt.'

'You used the five marks to invest in Elyan's mine, too?' asked Michael.

Luneday spat. 'I would never waste good money on that foolish venture! No, I wanted it to buy new sows – Lizzie is not getting any younger, and it is time I experimented with fresh blood. A man cannot rest on his laurels where pigs are concerned.'

'Right,' said Michael. He gestured to Luneday's horse. 'You said Margery would be halfway to Paris by now, which means you are not looking for her. So, where *are* you going at such an hour?'

'To Elyan Manor. I have decided it is time to resolve this inheritance issue once and for all, because I am weary of the ill-feeling among us. I plan to ask d'Audley and Elyan to come to Cambridge with me and meet the scholars from King's Hall. Then we can review the documents like civilised men, and decide justly and truthfully what is to be done. If I lose my claim, then so be it.'

It was a noble idea, but Bartholomew foresaw problems. 'No one will accept anyone else's interpretation, especially if some deeds are missing or ambiguous. You will need to

340

appoint a mediator – someone to make fair decisions – but I doubt all three parties will agree on a candidate.'

'They will,' said Luneday with conviction, 'because I know the perfect man – someone with integrity and good judgement. In other words, your Master Langelee. You say he is blessed with outstanding wisdom, and he also knows pigs. I have never met a bad fellow who deals with pigs.'

Michael gaped at him. 'You want Langelee to decide the rightful heir to Elyan Manor?'

Luneday nodded. 'I will bide by his verdict, and I shall urge the others to do so, too.'

'See where your dishonest tongue has led us, Brother?' muttered Bartholomew, not liking to imagine what would happen when Luneday met the paragon of virtue that Michael had portrayed. 'We could have got away with Suttone or Thelnetham. But Langelee? What are we going to do?'

'When will you go to Cambridge, Luneday?' asked Michael uneasily.

'Sunday,' replied Luneday. 'I would say tomorrow, but we shall need a day to put our business in order. The road to Cambridge is long and dangerous, after all.'

'This is not a good idea,' said Michael desperately. 'Elyan and d'Audley are unlikely to—'

'They will come,' Luneday assured him. 'They are as tired of the uncertainty and growing mistrust as I am. D'Audley will agree to arbitration, and Elyan will agree to be there. I recommend you travel with us, given that there appear to be robbers at large.'

'If they *were* robbers,' said Bartholomew to Michael, watching Luneday ride away.

Michael nodded grimly. 'And we know they were not – they wanted our lives, not our purses.'

*   *   *

It was dusk by the time they reached Haverhill, and the first drops of rain were beginning to fall. They paid their toll to Gatekeeper Folyat, whose small house was full of roosting hens, and walked towards the Queen's Head. The tavern was busy when they opened the door and stepped into its stuffy interior, and there was a convivial atmosphere as men drank ale and devoured platters of roasted pork. The students were playing dice in a corner, and Cynric was regaling a small group of fascinated listeners with a colourful and not very accurate account of the battle of Poitiers.

'Perhaps we should do as Luneday suggests, and go with him on Sunday,' said Michael, when they were settled with cups of spiced ale. 'It may not be safe for us to travel in such a small group.'

'No,' said Bartholomew firmly. 'We have done what we came to do: cleared Wynewyk's name and located our thirty marks. You can draw up the legal documents tonight and d'Audley, Luneday and Elyan can sign them in the morning. Then we are going home.'

'Very well,' said Michael. 'I suppose we should tell Langelee what we have learned as soon as possible – about Kelyng, as well as about the money. And the Blood Relic debate is on Monday. I would hate to miss it – not to mention the fact that it is the Senior Proctor's duty to ensure Gosse does not burgle every College in Cambridge while it is under way. But what about Joan?'

'What about her?'

'Agnys said d'Audley was away from home when Joan was poisoned, and so was Margery. And both have good reason to want Elyan's heir dead. Meanwhile, we have missing pennyroyal here, as well as in Cambridge: Agnys, Hilton *and* Neubold all bought some.'

Bartholomew rubbed his eyes. 'Taking my students and

Cynric home is more important than catching Joan's killer – if indeed she was killed. Just because her unborn child stood between several claimants and a manor does not necessarily mean someone poisoned her. I still think she took her own life. Agnys said she was unhappy in the few weeks before she died—'

'Yes, but *why* was she unhappy, when she was pregnant with this long-awaited heir?'

'It was not her husband's child. Perhaps she was ashamed of having gone elsewhere for favours, and was afraid the child's birth might reveal the real father. Panic may have driven her to suicide.'

Michael tutted. 'I think we both know better than that. Of course she was murdered. But perhaps you are right in saying the answers lie in Cambridge. We shall soon find out, because we shall be there this time tomorrow.'

Bartholomew retired early, and was asleep the moment he lay down. Michael read for a while, then tossed and turned on his bed, his mind full of Kelyng, Wynewyk, Carbo, Joan and the forthcoming debate. He was not as convinced as Bartholomew that they had done all they could in Suffolk, and felt there were answers still to be learned.

He fell asleep eventually, but was woken abruptly by Tesdale, who was in the grip of a nightmare. It was a bad one, because he shrieked instead of moaned, and the howl was loud enough even to disturb Bartholomew, who raced into the adjoining room in alarm.

'Please, Master Wynewyk,' Tesdale was weeping. 'Do not die.'

'It is all right,' said Bartholomew, shaking him awake. 'It is only a dream.'

Tesdale looked around wildly, then dissolved into tears. Valence hurried to his side and put his arm around his shoulders, while Risleye glared at them, and made a show of turning over and trying to get comfortable again. When he saw there was nothing for him to do, Michael returned to his own chamber. Bartholomew sat next to Tesdale, speaking softly, so as not to disturb Risleye.

'What is wrong?' he asked kindly. 'You have been sleeping badly for weeks now.'

'I have always had vivid dreams,' sniffed Tesdale, struggling to bring himself under control.

'You did not have them when you first came to Michaelhouse. Or at least, you did not frighten us all out of our wits by screaming in the middle of the night. Tell me what is troubling you – I may be able to help. Physicians can do more than just devise horoscopes, you know.'

Tesdale shot him a weak smile. 'It is nothing. Really.'

'You should tell him,' advised Valence, his arm still about his friend's shoulders. 'He is good with difficult problems – look at all the murders he has solved with Brother Michael. Let him help you.'

'Are you worried about your debts?' asked Bartholomew, seeing Tesdale begin to weaken. 'Wynewyk told me they were upsetting you.'

Tesdale blinked back more tears. 'He was good to me – found me employment at King's Hall.'

'Employment?' echoed Valence, startled. '*You*? But you hate the duties you have at Michaelhouse, so why undertake extra ones in another College?'

'King's Hall?' asked Bartholomew at the same time, equally taken aback. 'How did he persuade them to hire you? They have their own students wanting to earn extra pennies.'

'I am not lazy,' said Tesdale stiffly to Valence. 'I just need more sleep than you. And I had no choice but to look for ways to earn more money, because I owe Michaelhouse a fortune in fees.' He turned to Bartholomew. 'I worked at King's Hall because Master Wynewyk fixed it up. His friend Paxtone agreed to hire me, as a favour.'

'Really?' Bartholomew was astonished to learn the relationship between Paxtone and Wynewyk had been so warm – that sort of good turn was not easy to arrange, so was usually reserved only for very close acquaintances.

Tesdale nodded. 'They were composing documents together, and became friendly by spending so much time in each other's company.'

'What sort of documents?' asked Bartholomew curiously. 'An academic project?'

Tesdale shrugged, wiping his nose on the back of his hand. 'Their labours revolved around rocks, although I am not quite sure how. They asked me not to say anything, and I *was* going to keep my word, but it cannot matter now Wynewyk is gone. I never saw what they were writing, but it was something to do with selling stones of one kind or other.'

Bartholomew regarded him unhappily. Could this relate to the letters Clippesby had discovered in Wynewyk's room, in which he had offered to hawk diamonds to certain nobles? Or was it connected to the pebbles he himself had found in Paxtone's cupboard – the ones Yolande said could help a woman in childbirth? But Wynewyk's activities were irrelevant to Tesdale's current troubles.

'There is more to your worries than your debt to Michaelhouse,' he said to the snuffling student. 'What have you done? Borrowed money from someone who has put undue pressure on you – either to pay it back, or pay in kind?'

'Christ!' Tesdale's expression was a mixture of fear and guilt. 'How do you know that? Is Isnard right, and you really can see into a man's soul?'

345

'It is a matter of logic, not sorcery,' said Bartholomew shortly. 'So, I am right?'

'Lots of us borrow,' said Valence, hastening to defend his friend. 'We are not all rich like Risleye. If we did not make use of moneylenders, we would starve.'

'Who did you borrow from?' asked Bartholomew, ignoring him and looking at Tesdale.

Tesdale looked as though he would refuse to reply, but saw the grim expression on his teacher's face and thought better of it. 'Osa Gosse,' he admitted reluctantly.

'What?' exploded Bartholomew. Risleye sighed angrily, annoyed to be woken a second time, while Valence looked stunned at the revelation. The physician lowered his voice. 'But Gosse is a criminal!'

'I *knew* you would react like this,' said Tesdale, bitterly unhappy. 'Why do you think I have been too scared to confide in you? I should have kept it to myself, because now you despise me.'

'I do not despise you,' said Bartholomew tiredly. 'But I did think you had more sense.'

'Gosse said he had just come into an inheritance, and had spare funds to lend students. Please do not look at me like that, sir! Nor you, Valence. I did not know at the time that he was a felon, and that his "inheritance" was probably the proceeds of his most recent burglary.'

'I suppose he offered you a better rate than the other moneylenders,' surmised Bartholomew. 'But you have since discovered that his interest accumulates faster than you can pay it off?'

Tesdale looked defeated. 'Wynewyk knew I was in trouble, which is why he got me the work at King's Hall. It was dismal pay, but enough to keep Gosse happy.'

346

'Go to sleep,' said Bartholomew. 'I will try to think of a way to extricate you from this mess.'

'Thank you,' said Tesdale, although he did not look very relieved, and Bartholomew supposed he thought Gosse was more than a match for a mere physician.

CHAPTER 10

Dawn came early, with streaks of pale blue sky showing through the clouds. Bartholomew woke determined to leave Haverhill immediately, but Tesdale proved difficult to prise out of bed. Cynric was about to resort to a jug of cold water when Luneday arrived. The Withersfield man grinned as he announced that Elyan and d'Audley had both agreed to his proposal concerning the disputed manor.

'Oh, good,' said Michael without enthusiasm. 'We are leaving today, so we shall warn . . . *tell* Langelee to expect you.'

Luneday's expression became sombre. 'I would not recommend that, Brother. Robbers struck again last night – either the ones who attacked you or others – and they killed a man. You should not travel in such a small party while they are at large. Wait until tomorrow, and come with us.'

'We cannot,' objected Michael. 'Important business clamours for our attention in Cambridge. Besides, an important debate is scheduled for the day after tomorrow, and I cannot miss it.'

'Well, it is your decision,' said Luneday with a shrug, 'but *I* would not want to meet these thieves with only three students for protection. Bartholomew and his servant may be able warriors, but what good will they be, once they have been dispatched with arrows?'

'Was he threatening us?' asked Michael uncomfortably,

348

when Luneday had gone. 'Because he does not want us to arrive first and inform Langelee that Michaelhouse is owed a herd of pigs?'

'I am not sure,' replied Bartholomew, unsettled. 'But perhaps we should wait until tomorrow.'

'I thought you were even more keen to leave than I am,' said Michael, turning to stare at him in astonishment. 'But now you advise kicking our heels in this miserable hole for another day?'

'I *am* keen to leave, but we were almost killed yesterday. We may not be so lucky next time, and I do not want Cynric or the students hurt, just because we want to go home. I think we should wait.'

While they spoke, Michael had been rifling through the blankets they had folded and piled at the end of the bed. 'I cannot find my cloak. Did I leave it at Elyan Manor?'

'You did not wear it there – you said you did not need it when we went out, then complained about being cold all the way home.'

Michael's expression hardened. 'Of course I complained about being cold – I was being forced to wallow in icy water. Still, at least I had the foresight to bring a change of clothes, unlike some I could mention. I did not bring a spare cloak, though, so you had better help me find it.'

But a search revealed that the garment was not in the bedchamber, and the landlord informed the monk that if it had been left in the tavern at some point, then it would be long gone. It was a fine item of clothing, he said, and it was not surprising someone had taken a fancy to it.

Michael exaggerated a shiver as they stood in the market-place. It promised to be warm that morning, and it was only later in the day that there was predicted to be a drop in temperature. 'We do not need to worry about being shot at – I shall freeze to death first.'

'There is Lady Agnys,' said Bartholomew, nodding to where the old woman was struggling to dismount her horse. 'Ask to borrow one of hers – she is large and favours sober colours.'

Michael shot him a nasty look, then grumbled at Agnys about the theft before she could say so much as good morning. She listened patiently.

'You and I had better ride to Clare this morning,' she said, as soon as she could insert a few words into the angry tirade, 'and beg one from the Austin friars. We cannot have you catching a chill.'

'If it is not safe to go to Cambridge, then it is not safe to go to Clare, either,' said Bartholomew, when he saw the monk seriously considering the offer.

'We shall take guards,' replied Agnys smoothly. 'And there is another reason for visiting the priory. I promised you information about your mysteries, and I have managed to find you some at last. An informant tells me that Carbo stayed with the Austins around the time when his mother died. Perhaps they can tell you what made him lose his mind.'

'This is too good an opportunity to miss, Matt,' said Michael in a low voice. 'We are sadly lacking in intelligence about Carbo, and I would like to help Shropham. We shall be safe enough with her guards, and Clare is only a fraction of Cambridge's distance.'

'A very big fraction,' Bartholomew pointed out unhappily. But he could see the monk's mind was made up. 'I will fetch the horses.'

'Actually, I have a different task for you, Doctor,' said Agnys, putting out her hand to stop him. 'D'Audley has changed his mind about going to Cambridge. He sincerely believes that Luneday killed Neubold, and claims he is too frightened to be in his company. You must persuade him that even the most brazen of murderers is not going to attack him in front of such a large deputation.'

'Why would he listen to me?' asked Bartholomew, not liking the notion that Michael was about to be whisked away without his protection – especially with Agnys, about whom his feelings were ambiguous. On the one hand, he liked her well enough to confide his feelings about Matilde, but on the other, he was unsure of her role in their various investigations.

'He is more likely to heed you than Brother Michael, whom he considers a bully,' replied Agnys baldly. 'If he refuses to come, no agreement will be reached, and we will be fighting each other and King's Hall for years. This is our one chance for a peaceful solution. Please help us.'

'Very well,' said Bartholomew reluctantly, feeling he had been skilfully manipulated. Why was Agnys so keen to get Michael alone? And surely d'Audley would not have the courage to refuse a direct order from her, so why did *she* not persuade him to go to Cambridge?

'Thank you,' said Agnys, smiling. 'And when you have done that, you can speak to Hilton about Joan. He said something last night that made me wonder whether he knows some secret about her death. I would ask him myself, but I suspect he will be more open with another man. He is always uneasy in my company – I frighten him, although I cannot imagine why. Hey, you! Come here!'

The last words were delivered in a bellow that brought the entire marketplace to a standstill, and several men raced towards her, not sure whether the remark had been directed at them but unwilling to run the risk of ignoring a summons. She selected three of the sturdiest and ordered them to lift her on to her horse. When she was up, she picked another half-dozen, and set off with Michael riding at her side. The 'guards' trotted behind them, delighted to be paid for a jaunt in the country, although Bartholomew wondered whether they would be quite so thrilled if they knew killers were at large.

'No,' said d'Audley firmly, when the physician had tracked him down and explained what he had been ordered to do. 'Luneday knows it was me who told you about our arrangements with Wynewyk, and he will kill me if I set off on an open road with him. He murdered Joan and Neubold, so he is getting a taste for dispatching those he thinks are in his way.'

'How do you know he murdered Neubold?' asked Bartholomew.

'Of course it was him! Neubold died at Withersfield, and you have already proved it was his woman who helped sneak the body into Haverhill. But to get back to the crux of our discussion, I am *not* going to Cambridge, and that is that.'

'But if you are not there to represent your interests, you may lose out. King's Hall has some very clever lawyers, and they may use your absence to disinherit you.'

D'Audley had started to stalk away, but Bartholomew's words made him pause. 'Then I shall travel a day later, with my own guards.'

'You may be too late,' warned Bartholomew, knowing Langelee was unlikely to waste too much time on a matter that was not going to benefit him or his College. 'Our Master is not a man to dither over a verdict. Indeed, I would be surprised if he took more than half a day.'

'Honestly?' asked d'Audley, narrowing his eyes. 'You are not making it up?'

'It is perfectly true. Have you ever heard of the Blood Relic debate? It is a scholastic dispute that has raged for centuries, involving some of the finest thinkers in history. But Langelee went to a lecture on the subject, and had what he claimed was a definitive answer within moments.'

'Lord!' exclaimed d'Audley, awed. 'He must be brilliant!'

'He makes quick decisions,' corrected Bartholomew. 'It is not the same thing.'

'I had better pack, then. But I shall rely on you to ensure Luneday does not stab me *en route*.'

'Ride behind him,' suggested Bartholomew. 'Then you will be able to see what he is doing.'

When d'Audley had hurried away to make preparations for his journey, the physician walked to St Mary's Church, where he found Hilton tidying up after his morning devotions.

'I thought you might visit today,' said the priest with a wry smile. 'I let slip something about Joan last night, and I had a feeling Lady Agnys would send one of you to ask me about it. She knows I am terrified of her, and I imagine she hopes I will be more forthcoming with a man.'

'Were you Joan's confessor?' asked Bartholomew.

'Neubold was, although he was not very good at keeping regular hours, and I was often obliged to help those of his flock in need of spiritual comfort. But I break no confidences by telling you that Joan was unhappy for a very long time. She desperately wanted a baby, not just to give Elyan an heir, but because she loved children. She became a different person once she conceived – joyous.'

'Agnys said she was despondent for the last few weeks. Do you know why?'

Hilton frowned. 'Yes and no. She was afraid for the safety of her child, and was terrified someone might harm it – a not unreasonable concern given the inheritance issues surrounding Elyan Manor. However, I was under the impression that something had happened recently to intensify her alarm. She never told me what, but it was almost certainly the cause of her sudden despondency.'

Bartholomew wondered how they could find out – it might answer a lot of questions about her death. *Did* Hilton know, and was lying when he said she had not told him? Bartholomew found he was not sure what to make of the priest's role in the affair. He turned to a slightly different subject.

'Do you believe Elyan was the father of Joan's child?' he asked.

Hilton grimaced at the blunt question. 'No. But I do not know who was, and I shall not speculate. However, it cannot have been anyone here. William of Withersfield is comely but coarse, Luneday would never dare betray Margery, and d'Audley made her skin crawl. There are others, but she had standards, and they were well below them.'

'Well, someone obliged her, because she was definitely pregnant.'

'Then you should look outside our villages. We get plenty of visitors, some from as far afield as Cambridge and St Edmundsbury.'

'Why does Agnys think you know some secret about Joan's death?'

Hilton stared at his feet. 'When I saw Joan in Neubold's cart and I learned where she was going, I tried to stop her – I was afraid for the baby. But she said she had vital business in Cambridge.'

354

'What do you think it was?'

'I cannot imagine what possessed her to take such a risk.' Hilton looked sincere, but Bartholomew was under the distinct impression that he was holding something back. 'I offered her some of my pennyroyal tonic, to strengthen her blood for the venture, but she told me that particular herb is bad for unborn children, although I have never heard of such a thing.'

When Hilton had left, Bartholomew stared after him thoughtfully. So, Agnys was right: Joan *had* known pennyroyal was something she should not have consumed – and she had refused some that had been offered kindly. Did that mean she would have rejected other offers, too, and was unaware that it was present in whatever she had swallowed before she died?

And what did Hilton know that he was keeping to himself? That his fellow priest had also bought pennyroyal oil and might have slipped it to his travelling companion? Bartholomew had no idea how to prise the truth out of Hilton, and could only hope that Michael would.

It was a pleasant journey to Clare, and Michael found himself enjoying it, despite his anxieties. The sun was shining, and the air bracing without being overly chill. The countryside was pretty, too, with little villages tucked among ancient woodlands, and a meandering river to keep them company.

'I have never been to Clare,' he said conversationally to Agnys, as they approached the place. 'Is that the Austin friary, below the castle?'

Agnys nodded. 'We shall go there first, and then I have something else I would like you to see. No, do not ask me questions. I shall show you in my own good time.'

355

'Very well,' said Michael, his interest piqued. Obligingly, he changed the subject. 'Have you thought any more about what might have happened to the pennyroyal you bought and lost?'

Agnys looked sharply at him. 'No. Why should I? I told you, it must have dropped out of my bag as I rode home. I am always losing items that way, because my grandson will insist on buying nags that are too lively for me, and they jostle me about. I almost had a nasty fall on Wednesday evening.'

'Did you?' asked Michael smoothly. 'You were out on the night Neubold was murdered?'

Agnys waved a dismissive hand. 'Perhaps it was Tuesday, then. At my age, days tend to merge together. Do not look at me like that, Brother – it is true. And do not expect me to be sorry that Neubold met such an end, either. He was a vile fellow, and had no business meddling in the matter of who owns Elyan Manor.'

'He meddled?' asked Michael innocently. 'I thought he had been asked to help decide—'

'He meddled,' said Agnys firmly. 'But here we are at the priory. You go in. I have other business, and will meet you in the garden when you have finished. Then I shall show you my surprise.'

The friars were hospitable, and it was some time before Michael remembered that he was not there to discuss Blood Relic theology, or to enjoy the delicious victuals that were supplied. The Prior was called John, a pleasant, intelligent man who was a distant relative of the Bishop of Ely.

'Carbo,' mused John sadly. 'When he was with us, his name was Roger. Roger Neubold. I heard he had changed it. Poor man! We did our best to help him, but some head injuries are simply too severe to cure – there is some

356

recovery, but not enough to allow the victim to return to his former life. Roger – we shall call him Carbo, if you prefer – was one of them.'

'He was here because of an injury?' probed Michael encouragingly.

John nodded. 'He was deeply insensible when his brother brought him here, and none of us expected him to live. To the surprise of all, he did. He stayed with us for several months, regaining the use of his limbs and his speech, but his mind was . . . changed.'

'The folk in Haverhill believe the death of his mother unhinged him.'

John frowned. 'She died several weeks *after* he was injured, and it was a bitter blow to him. But he was already "unhinged", as you put it.'

'Do you know how he came by this wound?'

John stared at the monk for several moments. 'Not for sure.'

'But you have your suspicions,' surmised Michael. 'Will you share them with me?'

John considered for a moment. 'Let me give you the facts first. Neubold brought Carbo to us in the dead of night, then left without waiting to hear our physician's diagnosis. It was clear he expected his brother to die without regaining his senses. He came back a week later with money for a burial, and was deeply shocked when I told him Carbo was still alive.'

'You think *he* hit Carbo over the head? That he tried to kill his brother?'

John hesitated, but then relented. 'Yes, I do. And then I think he experienced a surge of guilt, which he allayed by bringing his victim here. His relief when I told him Carbo had no memory of what had happened – and would never regain his full faculties – was palpable.'

'Do you know why he attacked Carbo?'

'Their mother told me of a vicious argument the night Carbo "went missing". Apparently, Carbo was appalled by Neubold's escalating corruption, and threatened to report him to the Dominican Prior General. I can only assume Neubold decided that was not going to happen. He took Carbo away from us as soon as he could, saying he would look after him. I doubt he did.'

Michael thought about Hilton's tale of Carbo wandering around half-starved, with no proper home. 'Why did you not stop Neubold? And why not tell someone of your suspicions?'

'Because that is what they are – suspicions. I have no evidence. And Neubold was a cunning lawyer, who would have inveigled his way out of any unsupported charges – and probably would have sued me for slander into the bargain. And we would rather spend our money on the poor.'

'Can you tell me anything else about Carbo?'

'Not really. About a year after Neubold took him away, I heard he tried to join the Dominicans. I cannot help but wonder whether memories of what had happened were beginning to resurface, and he had devised some wild plan to bring his brother to book from within the Order.'

'Do you think he was capable of developing and following through such a complex strategy?'

John shrugged. 'Look at his most recent actions – the ones you have outlined to me. He appeared in Cambridge at the same time as Neubold, even though Clare is the farthest he had ever travelled before his injury. He stole Hilton's spare habit, which was intelligent – he had no money and neglect had rendered him painfully thin; people were going to take pity on a skeletal friar

358

and give him alms. It seems to me there was method in his madness.'

'And then someone stabbed him,' said Michael heavily.

'Perhaps you should ascertain where Neubold was on the night of his brother's murder,' said John, meeting the monk's eyes. 'Because if Carbo really was regaining his lost memories, then Neubold almost certainly would not have liked it. The man you have in custody may be innocent.'

Michael grimaced. 'I am sure of it, but he will not speak to me.'

'Of course, Neubold is not my only suspect,' began John tentatively. 'There is a rumour . . .'

'Yes?' asked Michael encouragingly, when the Prior faltered.

'I do not know if it is true, which is why I hesitate to mention it. There is a tale that Carbo stole a sack of property from an infamous Clare felon named Osa Gosse.'

'I know – Hilton told me. And Gosse is in Cambridge at the moment, burgling my University.'

John raised his eyebrows. 'I wondered where he had gone. Anyway, when this sack went missing, Gosse was said to be furious. So, Brother, there is another man who may have meant Carbo harm.'

Michael accepted the cloak John pressed on him, then went in search of Agnys. She was waiting in the priory gardens, walking slowly as she savoured the peace and the beauty of the place. Fallen leaves formed a bright carpet of yellow and orange under her feet, and she was gazing up at a mighty elm, where a family of sparrows was twittering.

'Thank you for bringing me here,' said Michael, smiling

359

at her. 'It was very helpful. Now, what else did you want to show me?'

Agnys led the way along a riverside path. There was a bench under one of the trees, and a woman sat there, reading a book. Her hair was neatly bound under a coif, and she carried herself with a light grace that said she was a woman of breeding. Agnys retreated tactfully, leaving them alone.

'Matilde!' Michael managed to gasp, once he had recovered from his shock.

'Brother,' she replied, with the enigmatic smile he recalled so well. 'How are you?'

'I am well, but where have you been these past two and a half years?' Michael had so many questions, he barely knew where to begin. 'Did you not know that Matt has been scouring the civilised world for you?'

'Not until Agnys told me. The news I heard was that he had taken a sabbatical leave of absence, to visit the universities in Montpellier and Salerno.'

'He spent that time trying to learn where you had gone,' said Michael, trying to keep the reproach from his voice, but not succeeding. 'The tale about Salerno and Montpellier was one invented by me, to ensure he did not lose his University post if his hunt was unsuccessful – you may remember that scholars are not supposed to hare off after women.'

'Of course I remember,' said Matilde sadly. 'It made it difficult for Matt and me to be close.'

Michael looked into her face. She was pale, but still as lovely as ever. 'Langelee and Suttone think you fell prey to highway robbers, although Matt refuses to believe it.'

She winced. 'My original plan was to go to Norwich, but the roads proved too dangerous for a lone woman, so I decided to come here instead. I have friends in Clare, and they have been kind.'

'Matt will be delighted to hear you—'

'No,' said Matilde, lifting her hand to touch his lips. 'You cannot tell him I am here.'

'But he wants to marry you. He was going to ask you the morning you disappeared.'

'I did not know that.' Matilde turned away, so he could not see her face.

Michael grabbed her arm, and forced her to look at him. 'Well, you do now. Come with me to see him – today. It will grieve me to lose my Corpse Examiner, but his happiness will be worth it.'

'And that is why I cannot come,' said Matilde. There were tears in her eyes and her voice was unsteady. 'Matt will have to resign his Fellowship to wed me. He will not be able to teach, and he will be forced to take paying patients. And then what will happen to the Frail Sisters?'

'They will manage, and so will he. Besides, I suspect you are hardly poor.'

'On the contrary, I own nothing at all – you see, I *was* robbed as I travelled from Cambridge, and my attackers took everything. I am lucky my friends are charitable, or I would have starved.'

'Matt is used to having no money,' persisted Michael doggedly. 'He will not care.'

'But I will. His old patients will not accept that he needs to make a living, and they will expect him to continue to see them free of charge – and to provide their expensive medicines into the bargain. It will break his heart to refuse them.'

'You are resourceful. You will find a way around these problems.'

Tears began to fall in earnest. 'But it would make him so miserable! He would gain me, but lose the other things he loves – Michaelhouse, teaching, his patients and their horrible ailments, his colleagues. He will loathe preparing horoscopes for the wealthy, and I will not inflict that life on him. I want you to promise that you will not tell him I am here.'

'I shall do no such thing,' declared Michael indignantly. 'He has a right to know.'

'Then I shall have to leave Clare,' sobbed Matilde. 'And I have found a measure of peace and happiness here. Please do not take it from me, Brother.'

Michael regarded her unhappily. 'I wish Agnys had not thrown us together, because now I do not know what to do – and it is not often I am bogged down in moral quandaries.'

'She brought you because she suspected I was the woman Matt had told her about, but did not want to raise his hopes if she was wrong. She has agreed not to break my trust. Now you must do the same.'

'But I will never be able to look him in the eye again,' objected Michael, dismayed. 'Do you realise the enormity of what you are asking? You want me to betray my closest friend!'

'I know. But it is because I love him so very dearly that I will not condemn him to a life that will make him unhappy. You must see I am right. And if you love him, too, you will do as I ask.'

The journey to Cambridge the following day began long before dawn. It started badly, and went from there to worse. The wet weather of the past few days meant the road had degenerated even further since their outward journey, and was all but impassable in places. Progress was painfully slow, which was worrying when robbers were at large and determined to prey on the large party that straggled through their various domains. And it *was* a large party, because d'Audley, Elyan, Agnys, Luneday and even Hilton had brought all manner of servants and retainers. In fact, there were so many of them that Bartholomew wondered whether anyone was left in the two villages.

Their troubles began when Luneday had a brush with thieves as he made his way to Haverhill to meet the rest of the group, although he claimed to have driven the culprits off with no problem. Then the travellers were thrown into disarray when a volley of arrows was loosed at them near Hadstock. But Cynric, ever alert, quickly whisked them under cover, and so saved them from harm.

A little later, Bartholomew glimpsed someone wearing a scarf around his face lurking on the track ahead. Cynric was eager to stand and fight, but Agnys marshalled the party into a tight group, then led them in a furious gallop, so that any ambush that had been planned never had the chance to materialise.

'Lord!' breathed Cynric, regarding her in admiration. 'I shall have to remember that tactic.'

'I visited Essex once,' Agnys confided darkly, but did not elaborate.

When he was sure the danger was over, Cynric spurred his horse forward to ride next to the physician. 'I know we are unpopular in Suffolk – what with demanding thirty marks and exposing lies, deceit and murder – but I did not think the villains would go to these lengths to be rid of us.'

'What do you mean? These raids are the work of highway thieves – nothing to do with our investigations.'

'What makes you so sure?' asked Cynric. 'Or have you forgotten the murderous attack on us in Withersfield, and the ambush that drove you and Brother Michael into a ditch?'

'No, but—'

'The second incident was definitely sinister,' Cynric went on, getting into his stride. 'It would have been easy to incapacitate you and steal your purses, but the archers were more concerned with concealing their faces – until you provoked them to come out into the open. Now why was that?'

'In case they did not kill us, and we were later able to identify them?' suggested Bartholomew.

'Because you *knew* them,' corrected Cynric. 'And that means they want you dead for reasons relating to your enquiries. Now, some of these attacks today no doubt *have* been the work of common criminals, but not all. Do not relax your guard for an instant, boy.'

Bartholomew was not sure whether to believe him. 'Our Suffolk companions have managed to make us a very attractive target – Elyan's elegant clothes, Luneday's fine horses, d'Audley's fabulous amount of baggage. I imagine half the villains in the county cannot believe their luck—'

'Do not deceive yourself – someone wants you dead,' replied Cynric with absolute conviction. He indicated their fellow travellers with a flick of his dark head. 'And it may be one of this lot.'

'Then why did you recommend we ride with them?' asked Bartholomew uncomfortably.

'For two reasons. First, there *are* robbers along this road, and they have already killed a man, so being in a big group is definitely better from that standpoint. And second, if one of these lordlings is responsible, then it is better to

364

have him where we can see him. I have been watching them all very carefully, gauging their reactions.'

'And what have you deduced?'

'Nothing,' admitted Cynric, reluctantly. 'Yet.'

Uneasily, Bartholomew studied each rider in turn, to see if *he* could detect any hints of disappointment that the raids so far had been unsuccessful.

Luneday headed the procession and seemed to be enjoying himself – he kept stopping to point out 'interesting' features, such as lightning-struck trees or particularly well-made fences. Obviously, he was not the one who had ambushed Bartholomew and Michael by the ditch, because he had rescued them. Or had he? Perhaps the whole thing had been an elaborate hoax, in order to gain their confidence. Bartholomew could not imagine why Luneday should play such games, but that did not mean he had not done it. And what about Luneday's woman? Margery had not killed Neubold and taken his corpse to Haverhill on her own, so who had helped her?

Immediately behind Luneday, keeping a wary eye on his back, was d'Audley, nervous and unhappy in wrinkled, reddish-pink clothes that put the physician in mind of an earthworm. D'Audley hated the scholars for exposing his dishonesty regarding Wynewyk's loan. He also had good reason to hire assassins.

Michael was next, followed by the students and Hilton. Risleye, Valence and Tesdale had contrived to draw the priest into one of their interminable quarrels, and the four of them were arguing furiously over whether wet horse smelled worse than wet dog. Bartholomew stared at Hilton. He seemed a decent man, but what secret was he withholding about Joan? Would it be something that could solve the riddle of her death? Her *murder*, thought Bartholomew, finally acknowledging that Edith was probably right, and the sudden demise of her friend was indeed suspicious.

Elyan and Agnys brought up the rear, with the enormous gaggle of servants trailing at their heels. Elyan, immaculately attired in black tunic and cloak, was sombre and brooding. He was returning to the place where his beloved wife had died, so was that the reason for his bleak mood? Or was there more to it?

Bartholomew turned his attention to Agnys, but could gauge nothing at all from her bland expression. Moreover, he was no longer sure what to make of her. He had been inclined to trust her at first – he liked her common sense and pragmatism – but her dismissive attitude towards her lost pennyroyal bothered him profoundly.

When Cynric wheeled away to conduct one of his sporadic scouting missions the physician dropped back to ride with Michael, who had been oddly uncommunicative ever since he had returned from Clare the previous day. Bartholomew did not understand it: the monk claimed his discussion with the Austin friars had been fruitful, so why was he so morose?

'What is wrong, Brother?' he asked, growing tired of the tense silence. 'You have barely spoken to me since last night. Did you learn something to distress you in Clare yesterday?'

'No,' snapped Michael, regarding him intently. 'What makes you think that?'

Bartholomew was taken aback. 'Your manner, for a start. You keep barking at me.'

The monk sighed, and Bartholomew saw lines of weariness etched into his face. 'I am sorry; it is this damned case. We know a lot more about Carbo, but have no real evidence that Shropham did not kill him – and nor will we, unless he breaks his annoying silence and talks to us.

366

Meanwhile, you still have no idea who poisoned Joan, although we have suspects galore to present to Edith.'

'But we proved Wynewyk's innocence,' said Bartholomew, who was more than happy with the outcome. 'He should not have dabbled in money-lending, but Michaelhouse will not emerge the loser from the arrangements he made.'

'I am not so sure about that,' said Michael. 'Once Langelee is forced into deciding who should inherit Elyan Manor, the disappointed parties may refuse to honour the debt. Our money could be tied up for years while lawyers wrangle. Moreover, Elyan has already said that he does not have eighteen marks to give us, and I am not sure we should accept that low-grade coal in its place.'

Langelee *would* be disappointed when presented with promises of pigs and fuel instead of coins, but it could not be helped. Personally, Bartholomew was more concerned with what the Suffolk men would say when they met Langelee, and was sure King's Hall would refuse to bide by any decision made by the head of a rival foundation. The physician did not blame them: Langelee was hardly noted for his sagacity, unless it was in assessing camp-ball strategies.

'And to make matters worse, there is no way we will reach Cambridge today,' Michael went on gloomily. 'Not unless we travel after dark, which would be tantamount to suicide, given the number of arrows that have been let loose of late. I shall miss the Blood Relic debate.'

'You will not. It is not until tomorrow afternoon – we will be home long before then.'

'But we shall have these Suffolk people to entertain,' complained Michael bitterly. 'Do you think they will let us abandon them while we attend an academic extravaganza?

They will expect us to stay with them, talking about pigs, coal and boring deeds of ownership.'

Bartholomew could have said it was the monk's own fault for telling lies about Langelee, but he held his tongue. Michael was in an unfathomable mood, and he did not want to make it worse.

Just as the day was beginning to fade, Cynric spotted lights gleaming through the trees. Bartholomew estimated it was still at least another six miles to Cambridge, and recommended they find lodgings for the night. The mood of the party had soured during the afternoon; there had been no further ambushes, but the miserable weather and difficult travelling conditions had taken their toll, and everyone was tired and irritable. It was certainly time to stop.

'But that is Babraham,' declared Risleye in distaste. 'I am not staying *there*. I visited it once before – when I saw Wynewyk and he bribed me to say nothing about it – and it is a horrible place. There is only one inn, for a start, and there will not be enough room for all of us.'

Tesdale shot Elyan, d'Audley and Luneday a black look. 'And it will not be our wealthy friends who are expected to sleep outdoors,' he muttered resentfully. 'It will be the poor students.'

'The lady seems tired, sir,' whispered Valence to Bartholomew, nodding towards Agnys. 'She tries to hide it, but I think riding hurts her ancient joints. It would be a kindness to stop here.'

Michael agreed. 'And it would be foolish to travel through the dark anyway, much as I would like to reach Michaelhouse tonight. We shall stay here.'

They followed Cynric along a track that led to a small church and a moat-encircled house; the village huddled between them. Risleye was right about there being only one inn, and it did not take long to learn it only had three rooms. Luneday earned himself the best one by gifting the landlord a piece of smoked pork. D'Audley paid handsomely for the second. And because it was polite, Michael and Bartholomew insisted Lady Agnys take the last; she agreed to share with her grandson and Hilton. Meanwhile, the servants wasted no time in claiming the few dry spots in the stables and barn.

'I told you we should not have stopped here,' said Risleye bitterly, a look of disgust on his face. 'What do we do now? Sleep under the stars? In the rain?'

'We could try the manor house,' suggested Valence. 'My grandfather used to bring me here, and I know for a fact that it has been abandoned since the Death. It is derelict, but there will be some corner that still owns a roof, and we can light a fire.'

'Then lead on,' said Tesdale with a huge yawn. 'Or I shall fall asleep on my feet.'

Valence was right – the mansion was one of many houses that had been left to rot after the plague had claimed its owners. It was accessed by a wooden bridge so dangerously ruinous that crossing the moat was an adventure in itself. Michael squawked in alarm when his foot plunged through a decayed plank, and he fell so heavily that he demolished the rickety handrail as he went.

'Whose idea was this?' he snarled, as Bartholomew and Cynric struggled to drag him upright.

'Valence's,' replied Risleye, making no effort to hide his amusement at the monk's predicament. 'You should fine him for making the Senior Proctor flail about like a landed whale.'

'Sorry, Brother,' said Valence, shooting Risleye a venomous look; he could ill afford a fine. 'I did not know the bridge was in such a state. Perhaps we should take our chances in the stables.'

'With the servants of men who might be eager to kill us?' muttered Cynric. 'I do not think so!'

'We are all safely across now, anyway,' said Tesdale. 'And I jarred my knee when I dismounted from my horse – I cannot go traipsing about in the dark. I need to sit down and rest.'

Cynric regarded him askance. 'I cannot imagine him as a physician,' he muttered to Bartholomew. 'He is so lazy that he will never manage to get out to tend his patients.'

Bartholomew suspected he might well be right, but the rain was coming down harder now and it was no time to stand and debate the matter. He began to explore. The manor's main hall was roofless and sodden, but the kitchen was relatively intact; its door was missing, but it had a functional fireplace. He and Valence scoured the outbuildings for dry wood to burn, Michael and Cynric found straw and set about preparing crude mattresses, and Risleye laid out bread and dried meat for supper. While they worked, Tesdale sat by the hearth and made a half-hearted attempt to light a fire.

'With killers at large, we must keep watch,' said Cynric, elbowing Tesdale out of the way and igniting the kindling on his first attempt. 'Valence and I will take the first turn, then Doctor Bartholomew and Tesdale, and Brother Michael and Risleye can see us through until dawn.'

'Me?' asked Tesdale, horrified. 'But I have a bad knee. I cannot spend the night working.'

'Do you see with your legs, then?' demanded Cynric. 'A sore limb will prevent you from sitting up and keeping guard? Or do you *want* a killer to slit your throat while you slumber?'

Tesdale shot him an unfriendly look, then began a sniping argument with Risleye about which mattress each should take. While they quarrelled, Michael claimed the best one for himself, moving it so close to the fire that he risked setting himself alight, not to mention hogging most of the heat. Grinning at the students' stunned disbelief, Bartholomew lay next to the monk and closed his eyes.

The physician did not think he would sleep – the 'bed' was hardly comfortable, and his damp cloak was no protection against the cold – but he fell into a doze almost immediately, and was hard to wake when Cynric decided it was time for him and Tesdale to stand guard duty. Afraid he might drowse if he sat, he went to stand by the door. Tesdale opted to remain near the fire.

'You will sleep again if you stay there,' Cynric warned the student. 'It is better to prowl.'

'I cannot prowl – I have a bad leg,' retorted Tesdale. 'And how can I sleep when I am hungry and freezing cold? Do not worry, Cynric. I can keep a perfectly efficient watch from here.'

Bartholomew listened to them argue as he stared into the darkness outside. It was still raining, and he could hear water splattering through a broken roof somewhere. Wind hissed in the nearby trees, and he heartily wished he was back in Michaelhouse, safe, warm and dry in his own bed.

'It is too dark to see, and impossible to hear over the racket the wind is making,' he whispered to Tesdale after some time had passed. 'It would not be difficult for someone with evil intentions to sneak up, no matter how vigilant we are.'

He glanced around when there was no reply, and

rolled his eyes when Tesdale issued the kind of snort that told him he was fast asleep. He was about to wake him when he heard a noise coming from the direction of the bridge. It sounded as though an animal – a deer or a fox – had been startled from its lair. Why? Had the storm made it skittish, or had something else frightened it? He strained his ears, listening for any other misplaced sounds.

'I heard it, too,' came Cynric's voice in his ear, making him jump. White teeth flashed in the darkness as the Welshman grinned. 'I did not trust Tesdale, so I decided to watch with you.'

'Shall we wake the others?' asked Bartholomew anxiously.

Cynric shook his head. 'Not yet. We shall mount a little foray first, to see what is out there.'

It did not seem like a good idea to Bartholomew, but Cynric was an old hand at such matters, so the physician deferred to his expertise. He followed the Welshman out of the comparative shelter of the doorway and into the blustery night, trying to tread softly.

'One of them just came out,' hissed a voice from the shadows, far too close for comfort. 'The book-bearer, probably. Sneaking around.'

'Nonsense,' said a second voice. 'They have no idea we are here, and will not have set a guard. We shall dispatch them quietly, as *you* should have done in Withersfield and in the Haverhill ditch.'

'That was not my fault,' said the first, indignant and angry. 'The alarm was raised before I could do it. And do not berate me for ineptitude, not after your disastrous ambushes on the road today.'

'I cannot see them,' whispered Cynric in Bartholomew's ear. He sounded frustrated. 'And they—'

He stopped speaking abruptly when footsteps sounded

near the bridge. Someone else was coming – not stealthily, but openly and boldly. Bartholomew swallowed hard. How many of them were there? The newcomer paused for a moment, perfectly silhouetted against the light from the fire in the kitchen. It was a large figure wearing a familiarly voluminous cloak.

'Brother Michael!' exclaimed one of the whisperers.

'Where did he come from?' Cynric murmured to Bartholomew. 'He cannot have—'

There was a flurry of movement and two figures broke cover. It was too dark to see anything other than that they were converging on Michael. There was a startled shout, followed by the sounds of a struggle. Bartholomew raced to the monk's rescue, but tripped over the handrail Michael had broken earlier and went sprawling. Cynric surged past him. Then there was a high-pitched squeal of pain.

Bartholomew scrambled to his feet and darted forward. But he did not get far before colliding so heavily with one of the skirmishers that he was knocked clean off his feet. He fell backwards, and felt himself begin to slide down the rain-slick bank towards the moat. He scrabbled frantically, trying to gain purchase on the grass before he reached the water. But the vegetation came away in his hands. Then, just when he had resigned himself to a ducking, he managed to grab a bush. One foot dipped into the agonisingly icy water, but the rest of him came to a halt.

Above him, all was quiet.

'Cynric?' he called tentatively. 'Michael?'

For a few unsettling moments, there was no reply, but then a silhouette appeared. Without a word, Cynric extended his hand, and it was not many moments before Bartholomew was off the bank and on level ground.

One leg was soaked below the knee, but he was otherwise unscathed.

'What happened?' he whispered. 'Have they gone?'

'Yes,' replied Cynric. 'I would have given chase but I was afraid you would drown.'

'Who were they?'

'I could not see.' Cynric sounded disgusted. 'I could not even tell if there were two or three of them, and they did not speak long or loudly enough for me to identify their voices.'

'Where is Michael?'

Cynric grabbed his arm and pulled him towards the bridge, where a dark shape lay unmoving. Bartholomew's stomach lurched as he ran towards his friend. One rotten plank crumbled beneath his feet, but he ignored the danger as he dropped to his knees beside the prostrate figure.

But it was not Michael who gasped and cursed from the pain caused by a dagger wound in the groin. It was Luneday's woman Margery.

Bartholomew had no idea what was going on, but it was no time for questions – Margery was losing a lot of blood. Cynric lit a candle, shielding the unsteady flame from the wind and the rain as best he could with his hat, and the physician began the battle to save her life.

The wound was deep, and had sliced through a major blood vessel. It needed several layers of sutures, but she was a hefty lady and the fat in her leg was making it difficult for him to operate. His task was not rendered any easier by her writhing, and even Cynric, who was strong for his size, was unequal to holding her still. Bartholomew yelled for Michael or the students, but there was no response, and he knew that if he left to rouse them Margery would die for certain. He had no choice but to press on alone.

It was not long before she became weaker and struggled less. It made Bartholomew's work more straightforward, but it also meant she was slipping away from him. He tried to work faster. He ordered Cynric to press as hard as he could just above the injury, while he himself wrestled with slippery needle and thread, squinting to see in the unsteady light.

'You are probably wondering what I am doing here,' Margery said in a soft voice.

'Lie still,' ordered Bartholomew urgently. 'Do not speak.'

'Why not?' she asked in a gasp. 'I am dying anyway. And it hurts, so I shall not mind the release. I should have known better than to meddle.'

Bartholomew thought he had finally succeeded in stemming the flow of blood, but when Cynric lifted his hands, the wound spurted again. It was hopeless – the injury was too deep, too wide and the conditions appalling. Margery was right: she was going to die. However, Bartholomew refused to give up. He indicated Cynric was to push down again, and began inserting more stitches.

'They wanted to kill Brother Michael, not me,' she whispered. 'But it was my own fault. I stole his beautiful cloak and they mistook me for him in the dark.'

'Who mistook you?' asked Cynric, ready with questions, even if Bartholomew was too distracted.

'I could not see, although they have been following you ever since you arrived in Suffolk. I thought they had decided to spare you when we reached this village unscathed. But I was wrong.'

'Luneday said you had run away from him,' said Cynric. 'Is it true?'

Margery nodded weakly. 'I decided to stay with a friend

when you guessed how I distracted my husband the gate-keeper. But I wanted to hear what Master Langelee decides about Elyan Manor . . .'

'You rode after us alone?' asked Cynric disbelievingly. 'With robbers and killers at large?'

'No, I rode *with* you.' The ghost of a smile played around Margery's lips. 'There were servants from three different estates . . . it was easy to hide among them. I kept my face hidden . . .'

'Enough,' said Bartholomew sharply to Cynric. 'Let her rest.'

'I shall rest soon enough,' whispered Margery. 'And I want to talk. When I left Luneday, I stole his documents. That is why I am here now . . . I was bringing them to you.'

'What documents?' asked Cynric, watching Bartholomew take more thread and bend to his sewing again. The physician's hands were red to the wrists, simultaneously slick and sticky.

'I do not know – I cannot read. But they relate to Elyan Manor. I want you to give them to Master Langelee. You say he is a good man . . . he will see justice done . . .'

Cynric stopped pressing on Margery's leg to grab a leather satchel that lay not far away. It was embossed with a pig. He opened it, and began leafing through its contents.

'Cynric!' hissed Bartholomew angrily, indicating the book-bearer was to replace his hands.

The bleeding was sluggish now, but the physician suspected it was nothing to do with his efforts to save her, and more to do with the fact that she was almost drained. He glanced at her face. It was deathly white, and there was a sheen of sweat on her forehead. He flexed his cramped fingers as he inspected his handiwork. The wound was oozing badly. The situation was hopeless, but he pressed on anyway.

'You think Elyan Manor is just farmland,' Margery was gasping to Cynric. 'But it is more. Why do you think everyone wants to inherit it?'

'Because of the coal,' replied Cynric promptly. 'It tends not to occur in this part of the world, so whoever owns the seam will enjoy a monopoly.'

Margery shook her head. 'People do not resort to killing and treachery over fuel.'

Cynric frowned. 'Then what—'

'The mine holds a secret. Your Wynewyk knew it . . . It is why he came in August.'

'What secret?' demanded Cynric.

But Margery's expression was distant, as if she no longer heard him. 'He sent a boy to spy . . . Gosse stabbed him. Carbo was a fool . . . should have kept his discovery quiet . . . but he told Elyan . . . and the evil was released.'

'Evil?' asked Cynric uneasily, removing one hand from her leg to grab one of his amulets. 'You mean a curse?'

'Cynric!' snapped Bartholomew again. Reluctantly, the book-bearer replaced the hand.

'It has led me . . . led *us* to terrible things,' gasped Margery.

'Like hanging Neubold?' asked Cynric baldly.

'No! I did not kill him . . .'

'Then who did?' demanded Cynric. 'Mistress? Tell me who murdered the priest.'

'She cannot,' said Bartholomew, sitting back on his heels, defeated. 'She is dead.'

Bartholomew knelt next to Margery for a long time, wondering whether there was more he could have done to save her. Eventually, Cynric indicated he was to move. Then, while the physician scrubbed the blood from his hands in a ditch, Cynric wrapped Margery in her stolen cloak. When both had finished, Cynric went to ensure the killers were not still lurking, while Bartholomew returned to the manor house to tell Michael what had happened.

He tiptoed carefully across the floor, so as not to wake the students, not even Tesdale. Nothing would be gained from alarming them with tales of stabbings and murder. The monk was dreaming when the physician touched his shoulder.

'Matilde?' Michael blurted blearily, before he was quite in control of his wits.

Bartholomew regarded him askance. 'You dream about Matilde?'

The monk scowled. 'Of course not. You misheard. What do you want? Is it time for me to keep watch? It does not feel late enough.'

Bartholomew gave him a terse account of the attack on Margery, and her subsequent confession.

'Why pick now to hand us these documents?' asked Michael when the physician had finished. 'Surely, there were safer opportunities on the road? In daylight?'

'Not when she knew we suspected her involvement in Neubold's murder. I imagine she planned to leave the satchel for us to find anonymously. Shall we tell Luneday what has happened?'

'Absolutely not. He may think we had something to do with her death, and we have enough problems without adding him to our list of enemies.'

'He is already on mine. And do not say he would not hurt his woman, because it was too dark to see who was stabbing whom. Of course, *any* of our travelling companions could have been responsible – or their servants. But what shall we do with her? We cannot leave her here.'

'We must. She will be safe enough in the woods, wrapped in my cloak. We shall collect her later, when assassins are not dogging our every move.'

Bartholomew stared at the satchel with its embossed pig. 'I suppose we had better read these documents – find out why she thought they were important enough to risk a nocturnal wander.'

'Not now, Matt. The light is too poor. Hide them in your bag – we shall study them tomorrow.'

Bartholomew's thoughts were a chaos of confusion and distress. 'Do you believe what she said about Kelyng? That Gosse killed him?'

'There is no reason not to – her tale fits the few facts we have. However, while Gosse may have wielded the blade, I cannot forget that Wynewyk was the one who took Kelyng to Suffolk, into a situation he knew was dangerous.'

'There is no evidence to suggest he knew any such thing,' objected Bartholomew hotly. 'And—'

'Of course there is,' snapped Michael. 'Cynric is right: Wynewyk wanted Kelyng to act as his guardian, because the boy was good with weapons. And I imagine he sent Kelyng to spy on the mine because he was too frightened to do it himself. He *is* responsible for Kelyng's murder.'

Bartholomew put his head in his hands, unable to think of a reply.

'I am sorry,' said Michael, speaking gently when he saw the extent of his friend's anguish. 'I know you were fond of Wynewyk – we all were. But—'

'Where is Valence?' said Bartholomew suddenly, seeing one of the pallets was empty.

Michael sat up. 'I did not hear him leave . . . ah, here he is.'

'Call of nature,' said Valence with a smile, going to his

makeshift mattress and settling down again. 'How much longer until dawn?'

'Too long,' muttered Michael. He turned to Bartholomew, and lowered his voice. 'Are you sure those villains killed Margery because they thought she was me? You cannot be mistaken?'

'We heard them say your name, and she was wearing your cloak. There was no mistake.'

'Then you can sleep while I keep watch. Knowing there are men itching to slide a dagger into your innards is hardly conducive to restful slumber, anyway.'

The rain stopped during the night, and the following day saw a dawn with clear skies and the promise of sunshine. Bartholomew had woken chilled to the bone, and could not stop shivering as he waited for Cynric to saddle the horses. Tesdale, Risleye and Valence came to stand next to him.

'What a miserable night,' said Tesdale, yawning. 'I did not sleep a wink. Still, at least nothing terrible happened, and we are all alive and well. I could have told Cynric that no self-respecting villain would strike in such grim weather.'

'It was horrible,' agreed Valence. 'I do not think I shall ever be warm again.'

'I am all right,' said Risleye smugly. 'I have some strong wine in my saddlebag, and it served to banish the cold nicely. I would offer to share, but I might need more of it myself later.'

'We should still ride with the main party,' whispered Cynric to Bartholomew and Michael. 'As I said yesterday, it is better to have them where we can see them. Them *and* their servants. Besides, it would look odd to abandon them here.'

380

As it transpired, their companions were waiting for them on the main road, all claiming they had slept poorly. Various reasons were offered – lousy beds, noisy wind and rain, saddle sores – and there was not a single traveller who did not seem weary and heavy eyed. It meant Bartholomew was unable to tell whether one – or more – was involved in the previous evening's dark business.

They made good time once they were underway, and it was not long before they began the long, slow climb up the Gog Magog hills. Luneday gave a delighted yell when he reached the top, and reined in to admire the view.

The Fens were veiled by a pall of mist to the north, and Cambridge was a huddle of spires, towers and roofs amid a patchwork of brown fields and leafless hedges. But Bartholomew was more interested in the undergrowth surrounding the road, because he thought he had glimpsed movement there. The woods lay thick around that section of the track, and they were eerily silent. He could see the ramparts of the ancient fortress to his right, vast, mysterious and shrouded in weeds.

'We are being followed,' whispered Cynric.

'I know,' said Bartholomew, twisting to look behind them. The manoeuvre almost unseated him, for his horse objected and he was not a good enough rider to control it when it bucked.

'Shall we find out who it is?' asked Cynric. 'For some reason, we have fewer Suffolk servants in tow than yesterday. Perhaps they have been detailed to finish what was started last night. We can ride down this small path and come out behind them before they realise what is happening.'

'There are fewer servants because Valence told Agnys and d'Audley that rooms are expensive in Cambridge,' explained Bartholomew. 'The dispensable retainers have been left in Babraham.'

Cynric shot him the kind of look that said he was a fool for believing such a tale. 'Here is our chance to see whether we can learn who is behind these attacks. Are you ready?'

'We are almost home.' Bartholomew was still troubled by his failure to save Margery, and did not feel like a foray into the undergrowth that might prove dangerous. 'And then it will not matter – Michaelhouse will keep us safe.'

'I am not so sure about that,' said Cynric. 'And it is always better to attack than defend. Come.'

'Yes, but—' Bartholomew swore under his breath when the book-bearer wheeled away, clearly expecting him to follow. He jabbed his heels into his horse's flanks, but the beast snickered malevolently and immediately shot off in the opposite direction. He managed to turn it, then was obliged to cling on for dear life as it started to gallop.

'Hush!' hissed Cynric irritably, when he caught up. 'I said we were going to spy on them, not stampede them.'

He dismounted, so Bartholomew did likewise. The horse clacked its teeth at the physician when he tied its reins to a tree, then lurched sideways and almost knocked him over. Irritably, he shoved it back, and it released a high-pitched whinny of annoyance. He glanced at Cynric and saw that the book bearer's expression was one of weary disgust. Then the Welshman disappeared into the trees so abruptly that Bartholomew was not quite sure where he had gone. It took several moments to locate him, by which time Cynric was muttering testily about thinking his master had abandoned him.

'That is not a good idea,' whispered Bartholomew. 'It is too—'

But Cynric had slid off into the undergrowth again with

all the stealth of a hunting cat. The physician followed rather more noisily, and was treated to several long-suffering glares when he trod on sticks that snapped underfoot or rustled the vegetation.

Eventually, they reached the clearing in the centre of the ancient earthworks. Osa Gosse stood there, hands on his hips. His sister was with him. They were both angry, and even from a distance Bartholomew was aware of the cold malevolence that emanated from them both.

Bartholomew's first instinct was to back away and leave the pair well alone, but Cynric gestured that they should edge closer, to hear what was being said. With considerable reluctance, and no small degree of unease, the physician did as he was told.

'How much longer do we wait?' Idoma was demanding. Her fine clothes were rumpled and the veil that covered her jet-black hair was askew. The dark rings beneath her shark-fish eyes gave them a decidedly sinister cant, and her fury was palpable. She was sitting on a tree stump, rubbing her leg.

'A few more moments,' Gosse replied. 'We cannot risk being seen and recognised. We had a narrow escape last night – that book-bearer almost unmasked us.'

'And I was gashed, into the bargain.' Idoma flexed her knee. 'Damned villain!'

'But Brother Michael lives to tell the tale,' Gosse went on sourly. 'The physician must have saved him, although I cannot imagine how. I struck hard and low, and the wound should have been—'

'None of it would have happened if we had attacked when I said,' Idoma snapped. 'They would be quietly dead and we would have been back in Cambridge by now – unscathed.'

Gosse was struggling for patience. 'We needed to wait until the book-bearer slept. He thwarted me in Withersfield with his vigilance, and he thwarted *you* on the road near Hadstock yesterday.'

'He was not there when we had the monk and the physician pinned in the ditch, but they still escaped.' Idoma's voice was a low, angry growl. 'Some demon is watching over them, keeping them safe. By rights, they should be in their graves.'

Bartholomew had heard enough. 'It is not the Suffolk people trying to harm us,' he whispered to Cynric. He took a deep breath, to summon his courage, and started to stand. 'It is them – and it is time they answered for their crimes.'

Cynric yanked him down again, sharply. 'We cannot tackle them alone.'

Bartholomew stared at him in surprise. Cynric was not usually a man to shrink from a fight. 'Of course we can. They are two, and so are we.'

'But Idoma is a witch,' objected Cynric, pale-faced. 'I do not mind spying on her, but we cannot fight her in open combat. She will summon denizens from Hell and then she and her brother will have what they want: us dead and Brother Michael unprotected.'

'They murdered Kelyng.' The disquiet Bartholomew had felt when he had first seen Gosse and his malevolent sibling in the clearing was giving way to anger. 'And Margery, too.'

Urgently, Cynric indicated he should lower his voice. 'They are talking again. Listen – see what can be learned.'

'Will they still pay us?' Idoma asked, continuing to rub her leg. 'Even though the scholars live?'

'Oh, yes,' said Gosse quietly. 'They dare not break an agreement with Osa Gosse.'

Bartholomew had been in the process of shaking off Cynric's hand and going to confront the pair on his own, but their words stopped him in his tracks. He sank down again, aware that Cynric was regarding him triumphantly.

'See?' the book-bearer murmured. 'You would not have known they were only *hired* to kill you, if you had charged up to them with your blade whirling. In other words, they are only instruments, and someone else is behind the raids. I doubt they will be very forthcoming if you rush in demanding answers, so let them be, and see where they lead us.'

Bartholomew rubbed a hand through his hair, confused and uncertain. 'They are killers, and you advocate letting them go? What if they harm someone else?'

'It is a risk we will have to take. I will watch them when we reach Cambridge, see where they go and who they meet.'

It was not an ideal plan, but Bartholomew could think of no better way to discover who had paid the pair to kill – and Cynric was doubtless right in saying they were unlikely to answer questions if he stormed up to them. But Idoma was speaking again, and he strained to hear what she was saying.

'So who has our property?' she was asking. 'We should have retrieved it by now – you have searched all the University's most likely buildings.'

'Removing a little something for my pains at each one,' said Gosse with a grin. Then the smile faded. 'But I have no idea where it might be. King's Hall and Michaelhouse seemed the most likely candidates, but it is not in either of them – of that I am certain.'

'Carbo should rot in Hell for laying sticky fingers on our things,' Idoma snarled, her face dark, vengeful and dangerous. 'He had no right!'

'I wish Neubold had not stabbed him, though.' Gosse was more meditative than irate. 'I know we questioned him at length and his answers made no sense, but I am sure we could have broken through his mad ramblings eventually.'

'And do you know *why* Neubold killed him?' Idoma's voice was pure acid. 'To save himself! He was afraid Carbo was going to run to the Dominican Prior with tales of his venality.'

'Neubold was a fool,' said Gosse dismissively. 'The Prior would never have believed the likes of Carbo.'

'And Carbo's death means we are left with *no* clue as to where our property might be,' added Idoma bitterly. 'Are you sure it is not at the mine?'

Gosse nodded. 'I spent days watching and searching it when I first realised what he had done. You know this – I told you about the boy I was obliged to stab, who almost caught me. Thank God for Elyan, who buried the corpse because he did not want Suffolk's Sheriff sniffing around.'

'And thank God for Neubold, too,' added Idoma caustically, 'for inventing the tale that put Carbo in line to take the blame, should word of the murder slip out.'

Gosse's expression was oddly unreadable. 'He was a decent lawyer in many ways. It is a pity his crimes caught up with him and took him to a premature end. But it is more of a pity that he did not use his sharp wits to find our property.'

'What are they talking about?' whispered Cynric. 'What property?'

Bartholomew shrugged. 'Something they think went from Haverhill to the University, which explains why they have only burgled scholars' homes.'

'I never thought I would say it, but it is a pity Wynewyk is dead, too,' Gosse was saying. 'His role has been ambiguous,

386

to say the least, and I never did trust him. But I am sure *he* knew where it is.'

'What about his friend Paxtone? Is it worth questioning him?'

'It would be more trouble than it is worth.' Gosse squinted up at the sky. 'I think enough time has passed now – the travellers are unlikely to see us if they happen to glance back. Can you walk?'

Idoma nodded. 'We should not waste more time here, anyway, or we will be too late to put our plan into action – and there will not be another chance like this, with all the scholars crammed into the Blood Relic debate. I cannot wait to show them what happens to folk who take what is ours.'

She laughed softly, a sound that made Bartholomew shudder; when he glanced at Cynric, the book-bearer was crossing himself with one hand and clutching his amulets with the other.

'We will show them,' Gosse said in a voice that was pure malice. 'Today shall be a day none of them will ever forget.'

CHAPTER 11

'I recommend you stay at the Brazen George,' said Michael briskly, when the party finally reached Cambridge and the town's guards had allowed them through the Barnwell Gate. 'I shall escort you there, and arrange for you to meet Langelee later. It will mean him missing the Blood Relic debate, but I doubt he will mind.'

Bartholomew was sure Langelee would be delighted to be provided with an excuse to escape a lot of theologians pontificating. The Master had never been very keen on public disputations.

'No,' said Luneday firmly. 'We shall go to Michaelhouse now, and ask him for his verdict. We will not deprive him of a chance to display his razor-like wits to his admiring colleagues.'

'But this great philosopher may be otherwise engaged.' Elyan pulled distastefully at his travel-stained clothes. 'And we do not want to meet him looking like peasants.'

'He probably *is* busy,' agreed Michael, eager to brief Langelee before the claimants descended on him. 'And he will want time to prepare a proper welcome for you.'

'But that will inconvenience him, and we would not do that for the world,' argued Luneday. 'The sooner we all state our cases, the sooner we can go home. So lead on, Brother. You said he is known for speedy decisions, and I miss Lizzie already.'

'But not Margery,' muttered Cynric. 'His woman of several years. His *dead* woman.'

'If he gives too swift a verdict, King's Hall will accuse him of not assessing all the evidence,' said Michael warningly. 'So do not expect a decision today. And if the answer to this case were simple, your priests would already have devised a fair and legal solution.'

'It *is* complex,' agreed Hilton. He glanced at Risleye, Valence and Tesdale. 'But not as complex as the arguments surrounding whether wet dog is more unpleasant than wet horse, apparently.'

'Then let us go to Michaelhouse, and have an end to it once and for all,' said Elyan with a petulant sigh. 'Master Langelee will just have to accept that no man looks his best after enduring the King's highways. And if we hurry, there may be time to buy some new clothes before we return home.'

Bartholomew's attention was elsewhere. 'There is Paxtone,' he said, spotting his colleague's impressive bulk and tiny ankles.

He dismounted, eager for news of his patients, but Michael coughed meaningfully, and shot him a look that said he would need the physician's help when the Suffolk men met the Messiah of Arbitration. The encounter was going to need some skilful manipulation if the visitors were not to know they had been shamefully misled.

'Is he from King's Hall?' asked Agnys, narrowing her eyes. 'I heard they all wear blue tabards.'

'Yes. Have you met him?' asked Michael, making polite conversation. 'He is one of their Fellows, and might well have journeyed to Haverhill to inspect Elyan Manor and the Alneston Chantry.'

'No,' said Agnys sharply, cutting off some reply her grandson started to make. 'I imagine they took care to avoid our company, given that they are trying to disinherit honest Suffolk folk.'

'What is happening?' asked Paxtone of Bartholomew,

intrigued by the cavalcade. The physician thought his gaze lingered slightly longer on Agnys than the others, but could not be sure. Perhaps it was because her veil was comically awry from the ride and her heavy boots looked incongruous against the fine cloth of her kirtle.

'These are claimants against King's Hall for Elyan Manor,' Bartholomew explained. 'They want Langelee to pass judgement.'

'Langelee?' Paxtone started to laugh, but stopped when he saw Bartholomew was serious. 'Lord! I doubt Warden Powys will agree to that. I mean no disrespect, but Langelee would not be my first choice of men to adjudicate complex legal disputes.'

'The other litigants want a quick decision,' warned Bartholomew. 'So you had better arrange for someone to represent King's Hall as soon as possible. Who will it be? You?'

'Our best lawyer is Shropham, but he is in gaol. Perhaps Powys will represent us himself – he is not as good as Shropham, but he has an astute legal mind. I had better go and tell him at once.'

Bartholomew watched him waddle away, then caught up with the others. 'When will you release Shropham?' he asked of the monk. 'Or are you inclined to dismiss what Gosse said – that Neubold was Carbo's killer?'

Michael shook his head slowly. 'The news of Shropham's innocence comes as no surprise; you know I have never really been convinced of his guilt. But why did he not *tell* me he was blameless in the affair? It makes no sense. So, call me callous, but Shropham can stay in his cell until I know why he would rather hang than tell the truth.'

Bartholomew and Michael led the visitors along the High Street and down St Michael's Lane. The College looked the same as always, and the physician felt a profound sense of relief when he saw its sturdy yellow walls. Walter opened the gate, peacock tucked under his arm.

'Where is the Master?' demanded Michael without preamble. 'Will you tell him he is needed? Now?'

While Walter went to do as he was ordered, Bartholomew heard Thelnetham holding forth in the hall, entertaining his colleagues with one of his witty lectures.

'I should check on my students,' the physician said, keen to see his class and find out what they had learned in his absence. He found he was looking forward to the questions they would have on the texts he had set, and it made him realise how important they were to him.

'No, you should not,' hissed Michael, grabbing his arm. 'You are going to stay here and help me out of this mess. It was not my idea to go to Suffolk in search of coal, timber and pigs.'

'But it was your idea to lie about Langelee's integrity,' countered Bartholomew. 'You are reaping the wages of your deceitful ways.'

Michael started to respond with a curt remark, but Langelee had heard the commotion by the gate and was striding across the courtyard to see what was happening. Michael gaped at him, while Bartholomew struggled not to laugh.

The Master had been with Agatha, being fitted for new clothes. Because money was tight, she was using an altar cloth that had been rendered unsuitable for its original purpose by moths and wine-stains. It was draped across his shoulders, and fell in folds to his feet. The damage had been disguised – although not very skilfully – with motifs cut from a fox pelt.

'By heaven!' breathed Luneday. 'Is *this* him?'

'I am afraid so,' replied Michael wearily.

'Fashions change so fast these days,' said Elyan, glancing down at his own black garb. 'And it is difficult to keep up when you live so far from court. But, if this is what is in vogue, then this is what we must wear. I had better purchase some of that cloth while I am here.'

'It is very fine,' declared Luneday. 'Exactly what a man of honour and intelligence might select.'

'Gentlemen,' said Michael, as Langelee approached. Agatha was behind him, trying to keep the fabric from dragging in the mud. 'This is Master Ralph de Langelee, Michaelhouse's finest philosopher and a man of great wisdom.'

Bartholomew was amused to note that Langelee did not seem at all surprised or discomfited by the grand introduction. He effected an elegant bow, and Agatha swore under her breath when some of her pinning slipped and material cascaded to the ground.

'I am deeply honoured, noble sir,' said Luneday, stepping forward to make a low and very sincere obeisance. Langelee frowned a little, but took it in his stride.

'There is an inheritance dispute over Elyan Manor,' Michael started to explain. Bartholomew could see faces pressed against the windows of the hall, as students strained to see what was going on. 'King's Hall is also involved. You have been chosen to preside over a discussion of the business, to decide who has the strongest claim.'

'All right,' said Langelee amiably. 'I am always pleased to voice an opinion, even if it is on affairs I know nothing about.' He guffawed heartily, and Michael winced.

'Will you hear us now, my lord?' asked Luneday politely.

'He will not,' growled Agatha. 'He is busy, and I had him first.'

'You heard the lady,' said Langelee, with a wink. 'She has first claim on my person, and I need this cloak finished, because the other slipped off and fell in the latrine during a careless moment. Come back later – preferably during the Blood Relic contest.'

'Oh, no!' objected Luneday, chagrined. 'We would not deprive the University of your wisdom for the world – especially as I am told you have solved the matter.'

'Well, perhaps not *solved*,' hedged Langelee, aware that he was in the presence of Michael, a talented theologian. 'But I certainly have views. However, the reason I asked you to come this afternoon is because there is a camp-ball game later, and I shall be able to take part in it if you give me an excuse to miss the debate.'

Bartholomew ran after him when he started to walk away. 'Do you not want more of an explanation?'

Langelee shrugged. 'Here are folk in need of a decent mind to resolve a long-standing problem. What other explanation is needed? Besides, I suspect it has something to do with our missing thirty marks, and I am willing to do just about anything to retrieve that.'

Bartholomew's pleasure at being among the safe, familiar things of home did not last long. The moment he had finished talking to Langelee, Deynman approached, his expression troubled. He began speaking without preamble.

'Master Paxtone came to borrow poppy juice when you were gone. I gave him the whole jar, but he brought it back and said it contained nothing of the kind. I had a sip, and he was right. Someone had swapped it for water.'

Bartholomew knew there was no point in remonstrating with Deynman for tasting something that might have been dangerous. 'Are you saying Paxtone exchanged an expensive medicine for—'

'Oh, no! He was simply drawing attention to the fact – someone else is responsible. The culprit probably changed the pennyroyal for water, too, because it certainly did not put a shine on my hasps.'

Bartholomew was sceptical of Deynman's claims, but obligingly followed him across the yard to the storeroom. Once there, it did not take him long to see the Librarian was right. He was aghast.

'My God!' he breathed, sinking down on to a bench. 'Who would do something like this?'

'Poppy juice is both costly and difficult to come by,' replied Deynman. 'So perhaps a student took it, in readiness for when he becomes a physician. Who do you know who is interested in money?'

'Not Tesdale or Valence. They may be poor, but they—'

'I said someone *interested* in money, not someone without any,' interrupted Deynman. His curt tone suggested he had already given the question considerable thought, and had reached a conclusion.

'Risleye?' asked Bartholomew. Was that why Paxtone had declined to teach him, even though the lad was a decent student – he objected to having his supplies pilfered? And had Paxtone borrowed poppy juice to see whether Risleye had resumed his tricks with a new master? 'No, I do not believe—'

'Then who?' demanded Deynman. 'Because there are two facts you cannot escape here. First, the poppy juice is gone and water has been left in its place. And second, it did not happen by itself. So, who else might it have been? Valence? Tesdale? Me?'

'Of course not,' said Bartholomew. 'But Risleye . . .'

Risleye was one of few lads who had official access to his storeroom, came a clamouring voice in his head. And Risleye was secretive and sly – he kept his possessions locked in a chest, whereas everyone else left theirs for others to share. Bartholomew put his head in his hands, overwhelmed by the betrayal. Then he stood abruptly, not sure how he would start his interrogation of Risleye but determined it would be at once.

'Where is he?' he asked.

Deynman shrugged. 'He was here a moment ago, talking to that Dominican priest about wet horses. Perhaps he went to the hall. Thelnetham is lecturing, and you know he is an entertaining—'

Thelnetham looked up questioningly when the physician burst in, but Risleye was not there. Without so much as a nod to his bemused colleague, Bartholomew ran back to his room, wondering whether the students were lying down after the journey. It was empty, so he tore up the stairs to talk to Michael.

The monk was studying the documents from Margery's travelling bag, treating Langelee to an account of his experiences in darkest Suffolk at the same time. The Master was still draped in his altar cloth, and Agatha had resumed her pinning. Bartholomew paced back and forth in agitation as he told them about the missing poppy juice and his prime suspect.

'Valence and Tesdale are just walking past,' said Langelee, peering through the window into the yard. He leaned out and ordered the students to get themselves up the stairs in a bellow that would have been heard on the High Street. 'Perhaps they know where Risleye has gone.'

'He went out with the Haverhill priest, sir,' supplied Valence, when the Master demanded the whereabouts of their classmate. 'And will drag him from stable to stable until the poor man is forced to admit that wet horses smell worse than wet dogs.'

'Did you know he has been stealing medicine?' asked Langelee baldly.

Tesdale's jaw dropped. 'How do you . . . He is not . . . Lord Christ!'

'No!' cried Valence at the same time. 'I do not believe you!'

'I should have been more careful,' said Bartholomew bitterly. 'Then it would not have happened.'

He thought about the stain on his workbench, which had reeked of poppy juice. He should have known it was a new mark, and that he would not have overlooked it when he had been cleaning the day before. He rubbed a hand through his hair, feeling his stomach tie itself in knots.

'Do not blame yourself, sir,' said Valence, still struggling to control his shock. 'It is not your fault he took advantage of your trust.'

'Meanwhile,' added Tesdale, 'you have the evidence to confront him, so make him pay you back and then dismiss him. Meanwhile, we will all learn from this and make sure it never happens again.'

'It is good advice, Matt,' said Michael soberly. 'Be more vigilant in future, but do not hold anyone but Risleye responsible for what *he* has done.'

'I am sorry to change the subject,' said Tesdale tentatively. 'But Isnard sent word: he was very drunk last night and needs a tonic. Shall Valence make it and take it to him?'

'*You* do it,' ordered Langelee, while Valence rolled his eyes at his classmate's brazen idleness. He held up a thick forefinger when Tesdale started to object. 'No excuses. I am tired of seeing you foist your duties on to your friends, and unless you change your ways, you can look for another College.'

Bartholomew handed over the key to the storeroom and watched his students leave, his thoughts in chaos. It was all very well for Valence and Tesdale to dismiss so blithely the actions of a classmate they had never liked, but Risleye's actions would bother their master for a long time to come.

'I need to find him,' he said, trying to imagine which stables Risleye might have elected to visit. 'I cannot just wait here for him to show up.'

'You can – and you should,' said Michael. 'You run the risk of missing him if you dash off on a wild goose chase. He will not be long. Just be patient.'

'Clippesby has not been himself since you left,' said Langelee, deciding the physician needed a diversion. 'Wynewyk's treachery hit him hard, and I have never seen him so unhappy. He has not even found solace in his animals.'

Bartholomew regarded him in alarm. Clippesby did not forsake his furred and feathered friends lightly, and when he did, there was usually something seriously wrong. 'Has he been . . . unwell?'

'You mean has he been more lunatic than usual,' translated Langelee. 'No – quite the reverse, in fact. He seems as sane as any of us, except when you actually listen to what he is saying. Then you realise he is raving. He keeps claiming that Wynewyk took poison because he was unable to live with his remorse.'

'Fortunately, we know that is untrue,' said Michael. 'Wynewyk made these business arrangements in good faith, and we were wrong to have suspected him of dishonesty.'

'Yes and no,' said Langelee. 'He may not have stolen from us, but he had no right to give our money to these Suffolk lords, no matter what the returns. It has left us all but destitute – and we will remain destitute until we have these pigs, wood and coal. I am not forgetting that he tried to kill me, either. He may be innocent of cheating, but he was definitely guilty of that.'

'He took Kelyng to Suffolk, too,' added Michael. 'And must have known some harm had befallen the lad when he failed to return from the mine. Then to pretend to be worried . . . it beggars belief!'

'Are you sure it was Wynewyk who tried to kill you, Master?' asked Agatha conversationally. 'Only Idoma Gosse likes to ambush men in the dead of night. Incidentally, I heard her brother bragging the other day in the Cardinal's Cap. He claims to be on the verge of acquiring wealth that will see him established in the finest house in Cambridge.'

'Did he say how?' asked Michael nervously.

'No,' replied Agatha. 'But you can be sure it will not be legal.'

'Arrest him, Brother,' said Langelee promptly. 'Now. Today. Before he earns these riches.'

'I shall,' vowed Michael. He turned to Agatha. 'So you had better tell me exactly what you overheard in the Cardinal's Cap.'

'Unfortunately, he declined to give details, and none of us liked to press him,' replied the laundress apologetically. 'Well, he said one thing, but I do not see how it can be relevant.'

'What?' demanded Michael.

'He said his fortune is closely tied to that of a Fellow, and that they have great plans together.'

'Not Wynewyk?' asked Langelee heavily.

'No. It is someone from King's Hall – and from his description, I would say it is Paxtone.'

'Damn!' muttered Michael, standing wearily. 'I thought I would have a few quiet moments to study my Blood Relic texts, but it seems I must go to interrogate King's Hall scholars instead.'

'You planned to *study*?' asked Langelee incredulously. 'I thought you would have been deploying your troops to hunt down Gosse. Or, if he proves elusive, to prevent him from doing any mischief during this tiresome debate.'

'Junior Proctor Cleydon has that in hand,' said Michael coolly. He disliked it when people questioned the way he ran his affairs. 'I trust him.'

'Then you can help me read Margery's documents,' said Langelee, waving the monk back down again. 'You volunteered me as arbitrator, so it is only fair that you help me prepare, and you can talk to King's Hall when we have finished. Meanwhile, you can visit Clippesby, Bartholomew. It will take your mind off Risleye – until he comes home.'

Bartholomew found the Dominican in his room. Clippesby was reading a book on Blood Relics, and the physician sincerely hoped he did not intend to take part in the debate: he might claim animal sources to prove his points, and lead the rest of the University to assume Michaelhouse was full of lunatics.

'Langelee said you have concerns about Wynewyk,' said Bartholomew, going to stand by the window so that he would see Risleye return. His thoughts were more on his student than his colleague.

'The Master does not believe me,' said the Dominican softly. 'But I *know* Wynewyk poisoned himself deliberately because he was ashamed of what he had done.'

'You are wrong,' said Bartholomew gently, hearing the distress in his friend's voice and turning to face him. 'Wynewyk was not dishonest – we proved it in Suffolk. He made some unorthodox arrangements, but none of them were detrimental to the College.'

'I wish that were true,' said Clippesby fervently. 'I really do. But it is not, and I can prove it.'

Bartholomew frowned. It was rare that Clippesby did not

399

bring animals into a discussion, and the grave, intense expression on his face was unnerving.

'Langelee charged me with packing up Wynewyk's personal effects,' Clippesby went on. 'I was going through a box of documents, throwing away laundry lists and the like, when I found a letter from his father. It reminded his son never to eat nuts, because he had an unusually strong reaction to them. And it said never to let a poultice of foxglove near an open wound for the same reason.'

'I knew about the nuts,' said Bartholomew. 'Meanwhile, foxglove is a potent herb, and if Wynewyk was sensitive to it, then even a small dose might have brought about his death. However, it is rarely prescribed for—'

'I have been thinking hard about his manner of death, trying to recall all that happened,' interrupted Clippesby. 'And my ponderings told me that he consumed *four* pieces of cake. Obviously, I did not realise then that he had an aversion to nuts, or I would have stopped him. I remember him gagging several times, but he did not stop eating.'

Bartholomew frowned. 'Tesdale says he drank more than usual, which may have made him incautious. However, there was no foxglove—'

'There *was* foxglove!' Clippesby spoke sharply. 'I use it to kill the fleas I catch from the hedgehog, so I am familiar with its smell. When I was cleaning up the hall after Wynewyk's body had been taken away, I found an empty pot of it. It meant nothing to me at the time, so I threw it away. But then I discovered the letter from Wynewyk's father, and all became clear.'

It was not clear to Bartholomew, and he struggled to understand what Clippesby was telling him.

'There is more,' said Clippesby, when the physician made

no reply. 'I told you about the copies of letters written to powerful men, offering to sell them precious stones. Do you remember? We decided he did not have any, so we dismissed the matter. But he did.'

'Did what?' asked Bartholomew, mind spinning.

'He *did* own diamonds,' said Clippesby. He reached into his purse and withdrew a handful of stones. 'I found these under a loose floorboard in his room. Langelee said they are just rocks.'

Bartholomew took them from him. 'But they *are* just rocks, John. Wynewyk carried another one in his purse, and Paxtone has a whole bag of them in his room. Tesdale said they pored over documents about stones together, so these are probably a charm against sickness. Or perhaps bad luck. But they are not diamonds, because diamonds are smooth and shiny, and these—'

'They are raw,' snapped Clippesby, uncharacteristically curt. 'Diamonds look like this in their natural state, and only appear jewel-like when they have been cut and polished. If you do not believe me, rub one on this piece of glass. Diamonds scratch glass, as you know.'

'So do many other things,' said Bartholomew doubtfully. 'Sapphires, rubies, even rock crystal.'

Clippesby slapped the glass into his hand. 'Just do the experiment.'

Bartholomew did as he was told, and gazed at the mark the stone left behind. He looked more closely at the rock, and supposed Clippesby might be right. He had never seen diamonds straight from the ground, so it was hardly surprising that he did not know what they looked like.

'I have no idea where these stones came from,' said Clippesby quietly. 'But the sly letters to the nobles suggest something untoward. So, you see, no matter what you discovered in Suffolk, I am afraid Wynewyk *was* embroiled in something shameful. And it led him to take his own life.'

Bartholomew grabbed Clippesby's arm and hauled him across the yard, so the Dominican could tell Michael what he had surmised. They met the monk coming from his room, having read more of the documents Margery had given them. He started to speak at the same time as Clippesby.

'Me first,' insisted Michael. 'Most of Luneday's records are irrelevant to who should have Elyan Manor – they pertain to the sale of pigs – but two are vital.' He brandished them.

'What are they?' asked Bartholomew. He was distracted, more concerned with Risleye and Wynewyk than with Haverhill's problems. The door to his storeroom was open, and Tesdale was there, working on Isnard's remedy. Bartholomew stepped inside to stare at his empty poppy-juice jug again. The student glanced up and smiled absently at him.

'The first is the will of Alneston – the fellow who founded the chantry and who was a past owner of Elyan Manor,' replied Michael. 'In it he leaves his estate to King's Hall, on the grounds that he disliked his children.'

'So King's Hall does have a valid claim?' asked Bartholomew flatly. 'That will please them.'

'I have not finished. This deed was clearly written when Alneston was angry, but he later made peace with his sons and there is a *second* will that favours them.' The monk waved it in the air. 'It proves King's Hall does *not* have a claim on the manor, and I shall tell them so when I speak to Paxtone, and demand to know why he has dealings with Osa Gosse.'

402

'I thought something odd was going on in that College,' mused Clippesby. 'Wynewyk spent inexplicable amounts of time there, with Paxtone and the Warden; Shropham stands accused of murder; they associate with felons; they stake dubious claims to distant manors; and Matt tells me Paxtone owns raw diamonds, just like the ones I found hidden in Wynewyk's room.'

Michael's eyes narrowed – he was never quite sure what to make of Clippesby. 'What diamonds?'

While Clippesby regaled Michael with his theory, Bartholomew's attention wandered to his storeroom. How much time had Risleye spent there, stealing and hiding evidence of his crimes? How many patients in desperate pain had been given water?

As his mind filled with dark thoughts, he happened to glance at Tesdale. The student was listening to Clippesby telling Michael about the foxglove and was going through the motions of preparing the tonic for Isnard, but he had just added too much charcoal. It took a moment for Bartholomew to recognise the curious expression that filled the young man's face, but when he did, his stomach lurched. It was guilt.

'Oh, no,' he whispered softly. '*You* gave Wynewyk the foxglove!'

'What?' asked Tesdale. He laughed his disbelief at the accusation, but not before the physician had caught the flash of panic in his eyes.

'You are one of few people who have access to this room,' Bartholomew went on. 'He asked you for foxglove and, eager to help a man who was kind to you, you let him have it.'

Tesdale shook his head. 'I did not give him anything. I swear!'

But Bartholomew was wise to the pedantry of students.

'You did not give him anything,' he repeated heavily. 'So what did you do? Open the door and look the other way while he took what he wanted? I thought Risleye was the thief, and you let me.'

'But Risleye *is* the thief,' cried Tesdale, beginning to be agitated. 'Perhaps I did help Wynewyk once when he asked, but he did not take the poppy juice – Risleye did. Risleye is always accusing us of stealing from him, but all the while *he* was the thief.'

Bartholomew sat heavily on the bench, and regarded Tesdale with haunted eyes. 'Why did you not tell us you let Wynewyk in here when we were trying to understand how he died?' he asked, not sure whether he was more shocked by Risleye's pilfering or Tesdale's complicity in a colleague's demise. 'It would have answered so many questions.'

'I wanted to, but I was afraid you would expel me,' said Tesdale, tears welling. 'It has not been easy, wondering whether I helped a man to suicide. I realise now that I should have refused when he asked to be allowed in, but it is easy to be wise after the event.'

Michael was angry. 'You are a fool, Tesdale! However, you may be able to redeem yourself.'

Bartholomew was not so sure about that, but Tesdale looked up with hope in his eyes. 'How?'

'You can tell me about King's Hall. Something untoward is happening in that place and I want to know what. You were employed there, so you can provide me with some answers.'

Tesdale was horrified. 'But I worked in the kitchens, Brother! I do not know anything that will—'

'Then you had better start looking for another master,' said Michael, beginning to walk away. 'Because you are finished at Michaelhouse.'

'Wait!' shouted Tesdale, flustered and frightened. 'I can tell you one thing you might find interesting – although Paxtone paid me to keep quiet about it. On the night Carbo was murdered, Paxtone went out. He came back covered in blood. Shropham saw him, too.'

'You thought Paxtone killed Carbo?' Bartholomew was aghast. 'But that is—'

'Then why did he buy my silence?' cried Tesdale. 'He must have had something to hide.'

'This explains why Shropham will not speak to you,' said Clippesby to Michael. 'He worships Paxtone, but believes him to be guilty of murder. So, he decided to take the blame instead.'

'Why would he do that?' demanded Michael suspiciously. 'It makes no sense.'

'Perhaps not to sane men like us,' said Clippesby. 'But Shropham once told me that Paxtone was King's Hall's most valuable asset – for his noble character *and* the revenue he brings from teaching.'

'Loyalty,' said Tesdale in a small voice. 'Shropham will do anything for his College, even go to the gallows to ensure another Fellow is spared.'

'You will have to release Shropham now, Brother,' said Bartholomew. 'We already knew he did not stab Carbo, but Tesdale's evidence explains his suspicious silence, too. He is innocent of everything, even concealing murder, because Paxtone did not kill Carbo – Neubold did.'

But Michael's expression remained grim. 'Perhaps so, but he can still stay in his cell until we are certain.' He fixed the hapless Tesdale with a stern glare. 'Are you willing to tell me anything else?'

'I do not *know* anything else,' said Tesdale in a wail. 'I would have told you already, if I did. I am not such a fool as to stand by while another College breaks the law.'

'You had better be telling me the truth,' growled Michael. 'Or there will be trouble such as you have never seen.'

Bartholomew could not escape the unsettling sense that time was running out, and that unless they found answers to their various mysteries fast, someone else would die. And, as he and Michael had been targeted several times already, he had the feeling that they might be among the next victims.

'I am going to interrogate Paxtone about his shady association with Gosse now,' said Michael, as they left the physician's storeroom. Tesdale skulked away towards the hall. 'I do not want you there, though. You are friends, so it will be painful for you.'

Bartholomew was worried. 'It is not a good idea to go to King's Hall alone—'

'I will not be alone. I shall take beadles and Cynric.'

Bartholomew regarded him unhappily, suspecting it would not be easy to march into King's Hall and leave with one of its Fellows. Tesdale was right about the depth of devotion some members felt for their College, and they might well prove it with their swords.

'Then be careful. Meanwhile, I had better visit Isnard. I would send Tesdale, but he might see it as a sign that he is back in my favour – and he is not. And then I will deal with Risleye.'

Bartholomew walked to Isnard's house with a heavy heart, barely acknowledging the greetings of people he knew. He found the bargeman mostly recovered from his drunken revelry, but did not feel like lingering to chat. He mumbled something about preparing for the Blood Relic debate, and made his escape, leaving Isnard staring after him in bewilderment; the physician was never usually too busy to spend a few moments nattering with an old friend.

Bartholomew wanted to be alone, to consider Wynewyk's death afresh, so he took the towpath route home, on the grounds that he would be less likely to meet anyone. As he walked, he berated himself for thinking nuts could kill a man so quickly, and for even entertaining the possibility that Wynewyk might have laughed to death. But foxglove would certainly explain what had happened – he had seen chickens die within moments of ingesting the stuff.

But why had Wynewyk killed himself? Because of the Suffolk business, or the diamonds Clippesby had found? Bartholomew was so immersed in his thoughts that he did not notice who was coming towards him until it was too late.

'Not so fast, physician,' said Idoma, reaching out to grab his arm.

He knocked the hand away and continued walking, loath to engage in a confrontation with her when Cynric had been too frightened to do it. He stopped abruptly when Gosse emerged from the bushes ahead, blocking his path. The thief carried a long hunting knife. Bartholomew turned quickly, intending to shove his way past Idoma before she realised what was happening, but she was similarly armed. With a pang of alarm, he saw he was trapped between them.

'What do you want?' he demanded, sounding more composed than he felt. He started to reach for his sword, before remembering that he no longer had it – scholars were not allowed to carry weapons in the town. He had nothing but his birthing forceps and some small surgical knives.

'To kill you,' replied Idoma evenly. Her cold, flat eyes were fixed unblinkingly on him and he realised he was in serious trouble. 'We know you eavesdropped on our discussion in the hills, because we saw you creeping away.

I doubt you have put all the pieces together yet, but it is only a matter of time before you do, and we cannot allow that. Not when we are on the verge of being rich.'

'Rich?' asked Bartholomew, wondering what they thought he knew. *He* did not feel as though he was close to a solution, and was as perplexed now as he had been when the business had first started.

'Kill him,' called Gosse softly. He was standing well back, watching the lane that led to the main road. 'The longer you chat, the greater are our chances of discovery.'

'Is stabbing me wise?' Bartholomew edged away from Idoma, while inside his medical bag his fingers closed around the birthing forceps. 'Michael will guess who did it, and you will hang.'

'We will not,' predicted Idoma smugly. Bartholomew tried to stop himself shuddering as her shark-fish eyes bored into his. 'There are no witnesses, so no one will ever be able to prove anything.'

'Idoma!' snapped Gosse urgently. 'You said you could do this better than me, so prove it. Stop chattering and dispatch him.'

'I *can* do better,' said Idoma. 'Your mistake was putting too much emphasis on keeping your face hidden, lest your attack failed. But mine will *not* fail, so it does not matter if the physician sees me.'

'It *will* matter if you do not hurry,' retorted Gosse. 'You cannot kill him with witnesses watching – and this is a public footpath. So get a move on!'

Idoma ignored him, relishing the opportunity to gloat. 'Incidentally, your student told us you would be coming this way, *and* that this path was likely to be deserted. You should not have exposed his treacherous activities, because he is spiteful when crossed. And we should know – we are long-term friends of his family.'

408

'You have seen Risleye? Where is he?'

'Risleye?' Idoma sneered. 'You mean Tesdale! He is the one who raided your stores. He blamed Risleye, did he? Sly lad! Risleye accused him of essay-stealing, and it was quite true – Tesdale always did have sticky fingers. He has a vicious temper to go with them, too – you and Risleye would both have done better to stay on his good side. Not that it matters to you now.'

She raised her knife, and Bartholomew glanced at the river behind him, assessing his chances of jumping in and swimming to the other side. But it was fast, brown and swollen with recent rains – he would drown. He hauled the birthing forceps from his bag, determined not to make his murder too easy for her. But the implement was no kind of defence against daggers, and he could tell from her grimly determined expression that there would be no escape for him this time.

Suddenly, there was an agonised yell, followed by a thud. Bartholomew risked glancing away from Idoma and saw someone lying on the ground. Gosse stood over the figure, holding a bloody blade.

'I told you to hurry,' he snapped at his sister. 'Now look what you made me do. Finish the physician quickly, before anyone else comes.'

Idoma resumed her advance, but there was another commotion from Gosse's direction. Bartholomew knew better than to take his eyes off the enemy a second time but fortunately for him, Idoma was less prudent and he was able to take advantage of her momentary lapse of concentration by hitting her with the forceps. She staggered away with a howl of pain, and it was then that Bartholomew saw the riverfolk were emerging from their houses. Isnard was among them, lurching along on his crutches.

'Leave him alone!' the bargeman bellowed. 'Damned felons!'

'Felons, are we?' snarled Idoma, turning to face him. 'You will pay for that remark, cripple!'

'We must kill them all,' shouted Gosse urgently. 'Or they will tell—'

He stopped yelling when one of Isnard's crutches cartwheeled towards him. It missed, but startled him into dropping his dagger. He bent to pick it up, but the riverfolk surged towards him, far too many to fight. He backed away fast, then turned to shoot up the alley that led to Milne Street, howling for his sister to follow.

'Do not think you have won, physician,' Idoma hissed, also backing away. 'We have something planned for you – for all of you. Your debate will be talked about for years to come, but *you* will wish it never happened.'

Aware that the riverfolk were closing in on her, she turned and fled, moving surprisingly swiftly and lightly for someone her size. The riverfolk waited until she had gone, then went back inside their houses without a word. One lingered long enough to raise his hand in salute, and then he disappeared, too, leaving Bartholomew alone with the bargeman.

'Thank you, Isnard,' said Bartholomew unsteadily. 'They would have killed me for certain this time.'

'The hero of Poitiers?' demanded Isnard scornfully. 'Do not make me laugh! We all know Cynric's tales of your military prowess.'

'Unfortunately, they are untrue.'

Isnard did not believe him. 'Well, regardless, my neighbours would not have let any harm come to you. You are their physician, and all that free medicine you dispense has some rewards.'

'I see,' said Bartholomew. His heart was hammering, and

he took a deep breath, in an attempt to calm himself. He glanced at Isnard, balanced precariously on his one leg. 'Let me help you home.'

'I can manage, thank you, which is more than can be said for him.' Isnard pointed, and Bartholomew turned to look at the person Gosse had felled. It was d'Audley.

'What happened?' asked Bartholomew, kneeling next to the Suffolk lordling. There was too much blood, and when he put his ear to d'Audley's chest he detected an unnatural gurgle. A lung had been punctured, and there was nothing he knew that could be done to save him. He glanced anxiously towards the alleys that led to Milne Street. He did not think Gosse would return, but Idoma was unstable enough to be unpredictable.

'He stabbed me!' gasped d'Audley, his face white with pain. 'Why? All I wanted was to talk to you. Brother Michael told me you had come this way, so I followed.'

'Could it not have waited for—'

'No!' D'Audley grabbed the front of Bartholomew's tabard. His grip was strong for a man with such a serious wound. 'We need to talk *before* the arbitration. I tried to bribe the monk but he would not listen, and you are the only other scholar I know. I will give you six marks if you back my claim to Elyan Manor – concoct some legal nicety that will see me win.'

'This is not the time to discuss such matters,' chided Bartholomew. 'You are—'

'But it *must* be now,' snapped d'Audley. He coughed wetly, and for a moment could not catch his breath. 'King's Hall cannot have a legitimate claim, and I am damned if Luneday will get the place.'

'You need a priest,' said Bartholomew. 'You should not be thinking of earthly concerns now.'

411

D'Audley stared at him. 'I am dying?' He began to shiver.

Bartholomew removed his own cloak and spread it over him. 'Do not try to speak.'

D'Audley swallowed hard. 'Oh, sweet Christ! I shall go to Hell! I have committed terrible sins. I thought I would have time to make amends – that future good deeds would . . .'

'I will fetch a friar,' said Isnard practically. He hobbled off to collect his crutch, but he moved slowly, and the physician knew he was going to be too late. So did d'Audley.

'You must hear me,' the Suffolk man gasped. There was panic in his eyes. 'I will confess to you, and you can tell the priest that I repented, so he can pray for my soul.'

'No,' said Bartholomew uncomfortably. 'I am not qualified—'

'Where to start?' whispered d'Audley. The grasp on the physician's tabard intensified, and Bartholomew felt himself dragged downwards, better to hear the words that began to pour from the landowner's lips. 'I seduced Margery away from Luneday – took her to Sudbury two weeks ago. Luneday thinks one of us was in Cambridge, killing Joan, but he is wrong. We were cuckolding him together.'

'I see.' Bartholomew tried to free himself from the man's fingers, but could not do it without using force – and no physician liked to be rough with the dying.

'I made her see *I* was the better proposition,' d'Audley gabbled on. 'I promised that if she stole all his documents, I would marry her, and she would share my estates *and* Elyan Manor. She brought them to me last Friday, and was with the party travelling from Suffolk, pretending to be a servant.'

Friday, Bartholomew recalled, was the day Margery had fled Withersfield Manor, after feeling the net closing in

412

around her. So, d'Audley was the 'friend' with whom she had taken refuge.

'Did you tell her to pass the documents to us, so they could be delivered to Langelee?' he asked.

D'Audley nodded weakly. 'I could not give them to Langelee myself – Luneday would have known who was behind the theft. But Margery has disappeared – and the documents with her.'

Bartholomew was not sure what to say; he did not want to distress d'Audley by telling him Margery was dead. Fortunately, though, d'Audley did not see him as someone with answers.

'I honestly believe Alneston's records will end King's Hall's claim,' he went on softly. 'But Luneday would never let anyone see them – he distrusted Haverhill's priests, while Withersfield's is a bumpkin, barely literate. Luneday and Margery cannot read . . . neither can I . . .'

'Hush,' said Bartholomew, seeing the desperate flood of words was taking its toll. 'The priest will be here soon. You can make the rest of your confession to him.'

D'Audley's expression was haunted. 'He will be too late, and I have not finished . . . the worst is yet to come.' He closed his eyes and took a deep breath. 'I murdered Neubold.'

'Yes,' said Bartholomew quietly. 'I know.'

D'Audley stared at him. 'How? I thought I was careful.'

'You were. I would never have known, had you not mentioned your relationship with Margery. But she was your accomplice in stealing the documents, so it stands to reason she was your accomplice in killing Neubold, too. She told you he was locked in the barn – you hanged him there.'

'Yes,' whispered d'Audley. 'I wanted Luneday blamed because I hate him – and because it would eliminate one

413

of Elyan Manor's claimants. Then it would just be me and King's Hall.'

Bartholomew was beginning to understand at last. 'You took Neubold to Haverhill, because it is what Luneday might have done – he would not have wanted Neubold dead in Withersfield. And you hoped a week in the Alneston Chantry would destroy any evidence that you—'

'Yes, God forgive me!'

'But *why* kill Neubold? Was it just to make trouble for Luneday?'

D'Audley closed his eyes. 'No – it was also for his corruption, for befriending the thieving villains at King's Hall, for making the inheritance issue more complex than it is . . . He was a bad man.'

Bartholomew resisted the urge to point out that it still did not give anyone the right to murder him, then use his body to see another man accused of the crime.

'So, there are my sins,' breathed d'Audley. 'I cannot say more now . . .'

He slipped into the kind of drowse from which Bartholomew knew he would never wake. All the physician could do was make sure he was comfortable, and sit with him until his ragged breathing faded into nothing.

Isnard had known d'Audley would die before he returned and, coolly practical, had brought two Michaelhouse servants and a bier, as well as Clippesby. The compassionate Dominican did not waste time with questions, but promptly dropped to his knees and began to pray. While he muttered his devotions, Bartholomew helped the servants load d'Audley on to the stretcher. They carried it to the nearest church together, after which Bartholomew hurried back to the College.

'Risleye is not the culprit,' he said when he met Michael

in the yard. He darted into his room, but it was empty, and there was no sign of any of his students. 'It is Tesdale, and he sent Idoma and Gosse after me on the towpath. Gosse killed d'Audley, so he would not be a witness to my murder.'

'What?' Michael was shocked. 'But I thought—'

'Tesdale was lying,' said Bartholomew, going to the chest where the lad stored his possessions. It was empty, and a glance inside some of the other students' boxes told him Tesdale had not confined himself to his own belongings when he had packed. 'He knew we would realise the truth as soon as we spoke to Risleye, so he escaped while he could.'

'After sending Gosse in your direction, to repay you for seeing through his nasty little game.' The monk's face was white with anger. 'We must find him. He cannot have gone far yet.'

'King's Hall,' said Bartholomew. 'They are the only friends he has left now. He will have gone there, in the hope that they will lend him a fast horse.'

'He has not – I have just come from there. They must have gone early to the Blood Relic debate, because there was no reply to my knock. I considered going to St Mary the Great and hauling Paxtone outside, but the church is already packed and there would have been a riot. The atmosphere is uneasy – our colleagues are honing their tongues for some serious invective.'

'But King's Hall has porters,' said Bartholomew, alarmed. '*They* will not be at the church – and if they failed to answer the door, then it means something is wrong. I will go there. But Idoma said again that something is going to happen during the debate, so you should be at St Mary the Great.'

'I *have* been at St Mary the Great. But short of dressing up as a scholar and expressing a controversial opinion, there is nothing she can do to disrupt the proceedings. Besides, my beadles have been charged to arrest them on sight. They will not remain free for long.'

'I hope not – they are cold-blooded killers. There was no need to harm d'Audley.'

'Well, at least we know it was not him who hired them,' said Michael. 'They would not have killed the man who paid their wages. That leaves Elyan, Luneday and Hilton.'

'And Agnys,' added Bartholomew, making for the door. 'But now is not the time for talking. I am going to King's Hall.'

'I had better come, too, because you are right – it *is* odd that the porters did not answer my knock, and Tesdale will be desperate. Who knows what he might do?'

Bartholomew did not wait to hear more. He set out for King's Hall, running as hard as he could. The streets were oddly empty, and he supposed everyone had gone early to the debate to ensure themselves good places.

Michael panted along behind him, shouting about waiting for beadles, but Bartholomew did not stop. Nor did he aim for King's Hall's front, but instead raced to the back, where a gate led from the towpath into the grounds. Then he sprinted across the vegetable plots, aware of Michael falling farther behind with every step. Only when he neared the main courtyard did he reduce his speed.

The College was indeed deserted. The only sign of life was a cat washing itself. He crossed to the porters' lodge, then backed out sharply when he saw the carnage within. Tobias had fought hard, but it had not saved his life.

Michael was still lumbering through the gardens when Bartholomew dashed up the stairs towards Paxtone's room. He heard voices and slowed down, treading softly in the hope that the wooden steps would not creak and lose him the element of surprise.

'I will not do it,' Paxtone was saying. 'I thought you were just a lad in debt when Wynewyk asked me to help you, but you are a criminal. Kill me if you must – as you slaughtered Wynewyk and Tobias – but I will *not* forge you a graduation certificate, and nor will I give you one of our horses.'

'Then you can die,' came Tesdale's furious voice.

Bartholomew abandoned stealth and tore up the last few stairs. The racket he made alerted the student to his approach, and he only just managed to avoid the swipe that aimed to disembowel him. Tesdale lunged again and Bartholomew stumbled backwards, tripping over something that lay on the floor. It was Risleye, clutching a wound in his stomach. Paxtone was kneeling next to him, trying to staunch the flow of blood.

Bartholomew's brief moment of inattention almost cost him his life, for Tesdale attacked with such ferocity that the physician was hard-pressed to defend himself. He was astounded by the speed and force of the assault – it was wholly unexpected from so slothful a lad. Absently, he recalled Risleye once praising Tesdale's skill with knives, and supposed the remark should have warned him that there was another, darker side to the indolent student.

He forced himself to concentrate, pushing all else from his mind. Tesdale held a blade in either hand, and was clearly adept at using both. Bartholomew winced when one tore through his sleeve, but managed to grab the young man's wrist, twisting it hard and forcing him to let go of one weapon. But Tesdale still had another, and the vengeful, furious expression on his face told Bartholomew that the student intended to see him dead. He jerked backwards as the blade sliced towards him.

417

Then Michael staggered in, puffing like a pair of bellows. Without missing a beat, the monk grabbed one of Paxtone's books and lobbed it with all his might. It was dead on target, and Tesdale crashed to the floor, clutching his head.

'See to Risleye, Matt,' ordered Michael, retrieving the knives Tesdale had dropped and walking to where the student was trying to struggle to his feet. 'This little toad will not be going anywhere.'

'Risleye was Paxtone's spy,' Tesdale said, ignoring the monk and addressing Bartholomew. 'Paxtone urged you to teach him, just so he could report on you. I dispatched him for *your* benefit.'

'Do not lie,' said Bartholomew shakily, still shocked by the lad's murderous attack. 'It is not—'

'It is true,' said Paxtone quietly. There were tears in his eyes, and Bartholomew saw Risleye had died while he had been skirmishing with Tesdale. 'I did recruit Risleye to watch your College.'

'I knew it!' muttered Michael. 'I *knew* there was something suspect about that arrangement!'

'But why?' Bartholomew asked Paxtone, bewildered and hurt. 'I would have told you anything you wanted to know. I *like* discussing medicine.'

'It was not about medicine,' said Paxtone tiredly. 'And it was not about you, either – I wanted to know what Wynewyk was doing. He was an enigma, and Warden Powys and I were afraid he might damage King's Hall. Risleye was loyal, and volunteered to find out . . .'

'Wynewyk would never harm King's Hall,' objected Bartholomew, stunned by the accusation.

'I disagree,' said Paxtone in the same weary voice. 'He was embroiled in some very unsavoury business, although Risleye learned very little about it. His life has been squandered . . .'

'Let me go,' said Tesdale softly. 'Risleye was the spy, and I have exposed him. He—'

Bartholomew dragged his attention away from Paxtone, recalling what had been said as he had crept up the stairs. He looked hard at Tesdale. 'Did you really kill Wynewyk?'

'Yes, he did,' said Paxtone, before Tesdale could deny it. 'He knew Wynewyk was sensitive to foxglove, because Wynewyk told me and I mentioned it in a class – to make a point about the hidden dangers of potent cures. Tesdale was there. So he added foxglove to the Fellows' claret: not enough to harm anyone else, but enough to kill a man who could not tolerate it.'

'So the tale you spun earlier was untrue?' asked Bartholomew of Tesdale. 'Wynewyk did not demand access to my storeroom? You took the foxglove yourself?'

'He was going to kill himself anyway,' said Tesdale defensively. 'He ate the cake, knowing it was full of nuts. I *helped* him – gave him an easier death.'

'But why?' cried Bartholomew, appalled. 'Most people would have stopped him.'

'He was damaging my College,' snarled Tesdale. 'And I was afraid the nuts might not work. He had swallowed almond posset a few days earlier and lived to tell the tale. So I decided that this time there would be no mistakes. I did the right thing.'

'You fed poison to a man in the process of committing suicide?' said Michael, shaking his head in disbelief. 'If it were not so tragic, it might be funny.'

'I thought you liked Wynewyk.' Bartholomew was lost and confused. 'You said he was kind to you, and you seemed genuinely distressed by his death.'

'No – he was a bad man,' said Tesdale angrily. 'He got me a job at King's Hall, but he was always asking me questions; he thought finding me employment put me in his debt.

He was harming our College with his crafty dealings, so I pretended to befriend him. But it was really to learn what he was doing and stop him. I did it for Michaelhouse – for all of us.'

Michael regarded him with loathing. 'You do not care about the College! What annoyed you was that Wynewyk's financial games were resulting in dismal food. The rest of us can afford commons, but the meals in the hall are all you get. You blamed him for subjecting you to them.'

Tesdale raised his hands in piteous entreaty, trying a different tactic when he saw righteous indignation was not going to work. 'It was not only that – it was Gosse. He kept demanding more and more money from me, making me poorer than ever. None of this is my fault. I am a victim.'

'Of course you are,' said Michael harshly, while Bartholomew sank down on a bench and put his head in his hands, repelled by the lad's transparent efforts to worm his way out of trouble.

'Gosse said he would forget my debt if I got rid of Wynewyk,' Tesdale went on. 'I was frightened, and had no option but to do as he ordered. You must see I was out of my depth. Terrified and—'

'You were not terrified,' said Michael disdainfully. 'You are adept with knives, and know how to look after yourself. Besides, you were reluctant to travel to Suffolk with us. If you were frightened of Gosse, you would have relished the chance to be away.'

'He did not want to go, because he is lazy,' said Paxtone, regarding Tesdale with a mixture of shock and revulsion. 'I hired him to work in our kitchens because Wynewyk asked me to – and I did not dare decline a request from *him* because he unnerved me so with his capacity for sly dealings – but it was almost impossible to get Teasdale to do any work, and we were on the verge of dismissing him.'

Tesdale pounced on the physician's words. 'Did you hear that? Well, I did not dare decline Wynewyk, either. And he *did* demand access to your storeroom. I admit he did not take foxglove, as I led you to believe. What he actually stole was pennyroyal, but I did not tell you because I was confused by all that was—'

'More lies,' said Michael in distaste. 'Deynman took the pennyroyal – he has admitted it.'

'But he also said it did not shine the metal on his books as it should have done,' argued Tesdale. 'And that was because Wynewyk had replaced it with water. Where do you think I got the idea? Wynewyk did not say why he wanted it, but he stole most of the bottle.'

'No wonder you have nightmares,' said Michael in distaste. 'Your lying conscience plagues you.'

'It is not his conscience that gives him bad dreams,' said Bartholomew. 'It is the poppy juice he has been swallowing. It makes him lethargic, too, which is why we all think he is lazy. I should have known there was something wrong about a young man who was quite so sluggish.'

'Poppy juice can induce night-terrors?' asked Tesdale, uneasily. 'I did not know that. Is it—'

'Enough of this,' interrupted Michael, taking a firmer grip on the dagger. 'The Blood Relic debate will be starting soon and I have more important things to do than listen to your nasty tales. Start walking. We are going to the proctors' prison.'

'We are not,' said Tesdale, backing away. 'I know too much – especially about King's Hall. If you arrest me, I will reveal all.'

'No,' cried Paxtone. 'You cannot repay our kindness to you with—'

'Ask the Warden why he is so eager to own Elyan Manor,' crowed Tesdale, seeing the King's Hall physician's distress. 'And question him about *his* relationship with Osa Gosse.'

'I really do not care,' said Michael coldly. 'At the moment, I am only interested in locking you away, you poisonous little rat.'

'Then I will tell everyone about Wynewyk's crimes,' declared Tesdale, eyes flashing with malice. 'And Michaelhouse will be disgraced. But if you let me go, I will start a practice in some distant city and we need never see each other again.'

'We will take our chances,' said Michael. 'Come.'

Tesdale hesitated, then sagged in defeat. Michael lowered the dagger, but before Bartholomew could yell a warning, Tesdale had shoved past the monk and dived towards the window.

'Go to Hell!' the student yelled, as he clambered on to the sill. He stood and reached up, intending to scramble across the roof and make his escape. He moved so confidently that Bartholomew was sure he had done it before. Or was it poppy juice that gave him a sense of wild recklessness?

Unfortunately for Tesdale, he had reckoned without the constant rain of the past few weeks. The tiles were slick, and he immediately lost his balance. Bartholomew darted forward and managed to grab a corner of his tabard, arresting the young man's fall with such a violent jolt that it almost pulled him out, too. Tesdale hung three floors up, with only Bartholomew's fingers between him and oblivion. Then the material began to slide out of the physician's hand.

'Help me!' Tesdale screamed, struggling frantically as he tried to gain purchase on the smooth stones of the wall. Bartholomew fought to retain his grip, feeling the muscles in his arm burn from the effort.

'Do not squirm,' ordered Michael urgently, leaning out of the window as far as he could, and straining to reach the terrified student. 'I am almost—'

But more of the cloth tore through Bartholomew's fingers. He tried to lift the dead weight, so Michael could catch Tesdale's desperately flailing hand, but it was a manoeuvre beyond his strength. The last fragment of tabard ripped free, and Tesdale dropped with an ear-splitting scream.

'Is he dead?' asked Michael, deliberately not looking at the shattered figure on the ground below.

Bartholomew could only nod.

CHAPTER 12

Michael wasted no time in summoning some of his beadles to remove the bodies from King's Hall. Junior Proctor Cleydon was with them, and was instructed to return to St Mary the Great and discreetly invite Powys to walk outside for some air. The monk needed to talk to the King's Hall Warden urgently, but did not want to do it in such a way that several hundred scholars would wonder what was going on. Fortunately, the debate had started, so he hoped attention would be on the disputants, not on what was happening in the audience; the last thing he needed was a contingent of outraged King's Hall students rallying to their Warden's side.

'I was looking forward to today,' he said bitterly. 'I was going to dazzle everyone with my incisive analyses, to remind men of influence that I would make a good bishop. Instead, I am forced to explore Tesdale's sordid accusations against King's Hall. And when that is done, I am obliged to help Langelee resolve the dispute surrounding Elyan Manor. Sometimes I hate being a proctor!'

'You need to arrest Gosse and Idoma, too,' added Bartholomew, who felt missing an academic discussion was the least of their worries. 'They are killers, and we *must* thwart whatever they are planning to do during the debate.'

'Then we had better not waste any more time,' said Michael, beginning to stride to where Paxtone, white-faced and tearful, was sitting on a bench in King's Hall's well-appointed yard.

Bartholomew grabbed the monk's arm and held him back. 'He was protecting his College, Brother. Do not tell me *you* have never recruited spies to combat a threat to your home?'

'You are too willing to see the good in people,' said Michael, freeing himself impatiently. 'I saw Paxtone myself, laughing and joking with Wynewyk, pretending to be his friend. At best he is duplicitous, and at worst . . . It does not bear thinking about.'

'Paxtone did not harm Wynewyk, though,' Bartholomew pointed out reasonably. 'Tesdale confessed to that – along with Wynewyk's own efforts to kill himself.'

'Then what about Agatha's claim – that Paxtone is in league with Gosse?' demanded Michael. 'Or Tesdale's similar allegation against Powys? And do not forget the diamonds.'

'Diamonds?' Bartholomew was not sure how they fitted into anything.

Michael made an exasperated face. 'Wynewyk carried an uncut gem in his purse, and had others hidden under the floorboards in his room – and Clippesby found letters in which he had offered them to wealthy nobles. Meanwhile, what does Paxtone have in his cupboard, that he snatched away from you when you happened across them? Uncut diamonds! Do not tell me that is coincidence.'

'No,' agreed Bartholomew cautiously. 'But I still cannot see the significance.'

'Has it occurred to you that Paxtone may not have been spying on us to protect King's Hall, but because Wynewyk had something King's Hall wanted? He made Wynewyk the villain, but who is to say he is telling the truth?'

Bartholomew was confused. 'But Tesdale told us that

425

Wynewyk and Paxtone discussed and wrote about stones together – he did not mention any antagonism between them. They were more likely to have been working jointly to—'

'No. King's Hall is not the sort of foundation to share that sort of thing, and neither, frankly, was Wynewyk. They may have maintained a veneer of co-operation, but the intentions of each of them would have been to best the other.'

'Really, Brother,' said Bartholomew in distaste. 'Not everyone is base, greedy and corrupt.'

'I think you will find they are,' countered Michael. 'Especially where lots of money is concerned. But let us take a moment and review what we know of these diamonds.'

'They came from Neubold,' obliged Bartholomew. 'Yolande de Blaston told me Neubold gave Paxtone these stones because they can help women in childbirth. She stole one from him.'

'Paxtone lied to her.' Michael took up the tale. 'He fabricated a tale, so a prostitute would not spread the story that King's Hall owns a lot of uncut diamonds. I imagine Wynewyk's stones came from Neubold, too. But why would a Dominican priest be dispensing such things?'

'He dispensed them to men who were going to invest in Elyan's coal seam,' said Bartholomew.

Michael gaped at the implications. 'You think Elyan's colliery is actually a diamond mine?'

'Of course not, but that is not the point – which is what *other people* believe. Precious stones discovered on Elyan land explain a lot of things. For example why Wynewyk made his secret journey to Suffolk in the summer. Why King's Hall, d'Audley and Luneday are so eager to inherit Elyan Manor. And why Elyan pays vigilant guards.'

Michael was thoughtful. 'It also explains why Wynewyk

426

sent Kelyng to watch the place: he wanted to know if the tale was true.'

Bartholomew rubbed a hand through his hair, as various clues snapped together in his mind. 'Margery said the mine held a secret. This must be what she meant. But Elyan said his mine is not producing what was expected. We thought he referred to coal, but he must have meant diamonds.'

'Which were numerous to begin with – hence the free samples to investors – but which quickly petered out,' finished Michael. 'Wynewyk probably intended to repay Michaelhouse without us being any the wiser, and keep the fabulous profits for himself – profits earned by selling these uncut diamonds to wealthy nobles.'

'No,' said Bartholomew stubbornly. 'He would have shared them with Michaelhouse.'

Michael ignored him. 'But when the promised returns failed to materialise, he realised he had "borrowed" too much. We began to feel the pinch, and he knew it was only a matter of time before his colleagues started to wonder why. He began to grow desperate—'

'No,' insisted Bartholomew. 'He is not a thief.'

'He would not have tried to kill Langelee if his intentions had been honest, nor would he have kept the whole thing secret – he would have solicited our help. But we do not have time for protracted deliberations here. I cannot escape the feeling that something terrible is about to happen, and while it is good to have answers to some of our questions, too many still remain.'

'Such as who killed Joan, why she came to Cambridge—'

'Such as what King's Hall is doing with Gosse,' corrected Michael. 'That is far more pressing.'

'Here is Powys,' said Bartholomew, as the Warden of King's Hall entered the College at a run. The Junior

427

Proctor was behind him. 'You can demand answers from him, as well as Paxtone.'

'I dare not linger,' gasped Cleydon, pulling Michael to one side. 'Thelnetham has just made a highly inflammatory declaration, and the Franciscans are howling heresy. One of us needs to be there to keep the peace, or there will be bloodshed for certain.'

'Do you need more beadles?' asked Michael. 'If so, we can use the ones I sent to arrest Gosse and Idoma. Laying hold of felons is not nearly as urgent as preventing a riot.'

'I have already redeployed them,' replied Cleydon, his face taut with worry. 'It seemed reckless to squander resources on a manhunt when we are on the brink of serious trouble.'

'Send word to Constable Muschett,' ordered Michael. 'His soldiers can deal with Gosse.'

'I *have* told him, Brother. But he has locked himself in the castle and informs me that he does not intend to come out today. This would not be happening if Sheriff Tulyet were here.'

'Gosse and Idoma are planning something terrible,' said Bartholomew, horrified to learn they were still free. 'We must stop it – whatever it is.'

Michael turned to Cleydon. 'I will make enquiries about Gosse's plans while you return to the church. Keep everyone calm and prevent a riot at all costs.'

It was a tall order, and Cleydon did not look happy as he hurried away.

Bartholomew's mind was spinning as he and Michael walked towards Paxtone. The King's Hall physician was in urgent conference with his Warden, but they stopped speaking abruptly when the Michaelhouse men came within earshot.

428

'You owe us an explanation,' said Michael coldly.

'There is nothing more to say,' replied Paxtone, exchanging a brief and rather furtive glance with his colleague. 'I encouraged Matthew to accept Risleye as a student because we needed to know what Wynewyk was doing. And you heard Tesdale: Wynewyk was in such deep water that he tried to kill himself, so our qualms were certainly justified.'

'I was not referring to that,' said Michael icily, 'although sending spies to other foundations is unsavoury, and is a matter that will be aired at greater length later. I refer to the rumours that say you have been doing business with Gosse – that he expects to share a considerable fortune with you.'

'With us?' asked Paxtone, startled, while the Warden gaped at the charge. 'I cannot imagine—'

'Do not play games,' blazed Michael, patience at an end. 'Men are dead, and there is something rotten going on that involves your College. You *will* tell me what.'

'I have no idea what you are talking about,' said Paxtone, alarmed.

'You can start by explaining why you came back to King's Hall covered in blood on the night that Carbo was murdered.' Michael's expression was glacial.

'What is wrong with you today, Brother?' cried Warden Powys. 'You cannot come here and start issuing wild accusations! You already have Shropham in your clutches. Is that not enough? Or do you intend to persist until you have all my Fellows under lock and key?'

Paxtone had looked confused when Michael mentioned the night of Carbo's death, but suddenly his expression cleared. 'You refer to the occasion when I left Matthew reading in my room, while I went to bleed Constable Muschett?'

Events suddenly made sense to Bartholomew, too. 'You

were wiping your hands when you came back, and said you were grateful you had worn an apron.'

'I am not good at phlebotomy,' said Paxtone sheepishly. 'And it is not unusual for veins to spurt at me. I went to the kitchens to wash and Tesdale was there. I was embarrassed by my ineptitude, and paid him not to say anything – I suppose he put his own inimical twist on the incident. I do my best with these nasty techniques, but I do not own your skill with them, Matthew.'

Bartholomew ignored the barb and saw that Paxtone might well be telling the truth: Muschett's summons had been unexpected, and Paxtone *was* notoriously bad at anything that involved cautery.

'Then what about the diamonds?' demanded Michael.

'Diamonds?' echoed Paxtone, jaw dropping. 'What in God's name are you talking about?'

'The bag of stones I found in your cupboard,' explained Bartholomew. 'They are uncut gems.'

Paxtone continued to gape. 'They are rocks to help a woman through childbirth. Even you, despite your unorthodoxy, must know certain minerals have the power to alleviate specific conditions.'

Bartholomew was uncertain what to think – Paxtone was convincing – but Michael was less credulous. 'Tesdale said you and Wynewyk worked together on a project involving rocks,' the monk said accusingly. 'And he also said you took care to keep it away from him.'

'Of course Paxtone did not let Tesdale know his business,' snapped the Warden, before Paxtone could answer for himself. 'We were wary of the lad – doubting the wisdom of hiring him – so naturally we made sure he saw nothing of our affairs.'

'That does not tell us what you were doing with Wynewyk,' said Bartholomew.

Paxtone sighed. 'We were discussing Elyan Manor, if you must know. Wynewyk had purchased a share in the mine, and was concerned about who would eventually inherit. He supported our claim, because he knew we would treat fairly with him. We did not discuss *rocks* – we discussed *coal*.'

'We dealt honestly with him, but our decency was not reciprocated,' added the Warden bitterly. 'I never trusted him, although we maintained a veneer of friendship. And if you say I malign him, then you are fools. I could not believe it when Langelee gave him free rein with the Michaelhouse accounts, and if you do not find inconsistencies in them, I will dance naked in St Mary the Great.'

'Something malevolent is at work here,' said Michael, declining to discuss a colleague, even a treacherous one, with members of a rival foundation. 'It has already resulted in the deaths of Joan, Carbo, Neubold, Margery and her paramour d'Audley, Wynewyk and Kelyng, and attempts have been made on my life and Matt's. It is time to bring an end to it. You *must* help me.'

'But we have no idea what you are talking about!' cried Paxtone. 'Who is Margery?'

'Neubold is dead?' cried the Warden. 'How?'

'It would take too long to explain,' snapped Michael. 'So, for the last time, what is going on?'

'Nothing is going on,' declared Powys angrily. 'At least, nothing involving King's Hall. You say Gosse claims an association with us, but he is lying. Your accusations are outrageous – and offensive to a foundation that enjoys the patronage of the King.'

Bartholomew recalled what Michael had said about Powys – that he was unlikely to do anything without royal approval. Did His Majesty know that precious stones might be being unearthed in a quiet corner of his realm, and had he charged the Warden of his favourite College to ensure he did not lose out? Bartholomew's stomach churned at the implications of the remark.

Michael also seemed to accept that the interrogation was going no further now such a powerful player had been introduced. 'We should all go to Michaelhouse,' he said coldly. 'Langelee will be making his decision about Elyan Manor soon, and someone needs to represent King's Hall if you think you have a right to the place.'

'We do have a right,' asserted Powys, equally icy. 'Far more so than the other claimants.'

He gestured that Michael was to leave his domain, and with no alternative but to do as he was bid, the monk complied. Bartholomew followed, and the two King's Hall men brought up the rear.

Michael, glanced around uneasily as they walked. 'Idoma said you have all the pieces of the puzzle now, and I suspect she is right. We just need to put them together and find answers before anyone else dies.'

'But you heard Powys,' said Bartholomew, coils of unease writhing in his stomach. 'The King—'

'I do not believe that – he is just trying to frighten us. He is involved in something dark, and I can think of no better way to make him show his hand than to take him to Michaelhouse and see what happens when he learns his College has no right to inherit Elyan Manor.'

'Are you sure?' asked Bartholomew uneasily. 'It is not dangerous?'

'Oh, it is dangerous,' said Michael. There was a gleam in his eye that said he was looking forward to outwitting his enemies. 'But so are we.'

When Bartholomew and Michael arrived at Michaelhouse, Paxtone and Warden Powys in tow, the deputation from

432

Suffolk was already there. Langelee was entertaining them in the hall, empty of scholars because they were all at the debate, and had donned his ceremonial robes for the occasion.

He was regaling them with details of a camp-ball game he had enjoyed the previous week. Luneday listened with rapt attention, his eyes never leaving Langelee's face, and Lady Agnys interrupted with several astute observations. Hilton was more interested in the library, while Elyan was covetously fingering the half-finished cloak Agatha had left hanging over the back of a bench.

Michael began to make introductions. Elyan was pleased to meet the King's Hall men, and began talking about the arrangements Neubold had made on his behalf. Agnys was polite but strangely subdued, especially towards Paxtone, while Luneday was bluff, hearty and insincere.

'Where is d'Audley?' asked Langelee. 'We are all busy men, and cannot wait for him to—'

'Dead,' interrupted Michael. 'Gosse killed him.'

There was a startled silence.

'Are you sure?' asked Agnys eventually, the first to recover her composure.

'Quite sure,' replied Michael tersely. The confrontations with Tesdale and the King's Hall men had unsettled him, and made him disinclined to mince words.

'It is probably good news for me,' said Elyan, ignoring the warning glare his grandmother shot him. 'He wanted me dead, because he was so sure *he* was going to win my estates. I shall sleep easier in my bed knowing he is not after my blood.'

'We had better make a start,' said Langelee briskly. 'I understand that Gosse and his hell-hag sister have something deadly in mind for later, so it is in all our interests to get a move on.'

433

'Something deadly?' asked Hilton, turning white at the prospect. 'What?'

'We do not know yet,' replied Michael coolly, looking around at each of the gathering in turn. Bartholomew did likewise, but could read nothing in anyone's expression – could not tell if he was among friends or in the presence of people who were in league with some very deadly criminals.

'Do you think this "something deadly" will happen here?' asked Elyan, tugging his cloak around him as if he found the hall suddenly too cold. 'I thought we would be safe inside these thick walls.'

'We are secure enough,' said Langelee. He grinned rather diabolically as he patted the sword he wore at his side; it was incongruous against his academic garb. 'But if not, I can wield a blade with the best of them. I skewered many a villain when I worked for the Archbishop of York.'

'Did you?' asked Luneday, impressed. 'You are indeed a man of many parts, Master.'

'I am,' agreed Langelee smugly. He took his sceptre and gave the table several enthusiastic raps to indicate business was under way. 'This meeting will take the form of all College proceedings: we shall begin with a prayer, then discuss the matter in hand. I will hear all sides of the argument, and then make my decision. Do you all consent to bide by it?'

'Only if you find in our favour,' said Powys. 'I cannot stand by and see King's Hall dispossessed.'

'That is not how these things work,' argued Luneday. 'You either agree in advance to accept whatever Master Langelee decrees, or you do not – in which case we may as well go home.'

The Warden stood. 'I do not approve of the way this is being rushed, and you have King's Hall at a disadvantage.

All our colleagues are at the Blood Relic debate, while our most skilful lawyer is in prison. I demand an adjournment until such time—'

'In prison for what?' asked Luneday curiously.

'For something he did not do,' replied Powys before Michael could speak.

'We know he did not murder Carbo,' acknowledged Michael. 'But there are other matters with which he might be able to help us. So he will stay where he is until I have answers.'

'I say let him out,' said Luneday. He shrugged when everyone regarded him uncertainly. 'Just for an hour. He can represent King's Hall, and then everyone will be happy – they will have their best lawyer, and we shall have our decision. Afterwards, you can lock him away again.'

'No,' demurred Warden Powys, looking uneasy. 'He will not be himself after all this time in a cell, and this is too important a matter for errors. I object most strongly.'

'You cannot object,' said Agnys. 'Your basis for demanding a delay is the lack of a good lawyer. But once Shropham is released, that no longer holds. Or do you have other reasons for wanting this to drag on for years – such as your case not being as strong as you would have us believe?'

'Well, Powys?' demanded Michael archly, when the Warden opened his mouth to argue, but no words emerged. 'Lady Agnys makes a good point.'

Paxtone saw they were cornered, even if Powys was not ready to admit it.

'Very well,' he said, ignoring Powys's immediate scowl of disapproval. 'Bring Shropham. A respite from that dank gaol will do him good anyway.'

'I shall fetch him at once,' said Michael.

'Good,' said Paxtone. 'It means I am not needed, for

435

which I am grateful. The events of the day have distressed me, and I feel the need to rest.'

'What events?' asked Agnys immediately.

Paxtone's smile was pained. 'College matters, madam. You would not understand.'

Bartholomew followed Michael outside and across the yard, aware that they had left behind them a very unhappy group. Luneday and Langelee were the only two who seemed to be enjoying themselves, although even they were showing signs of strain: Langelee was itching to be done so he could attend his camp-ball game, while Luneday's jovial bonhomie was beginning to sound forced. Meanwhile, Elyan was growing increasingly uneasy; he kept going to the windows to look out. His grandmother watched him with wary eyes, Hilton played nervously with pen and ink, and Powys was white with barely restrained fury.

'There goes Paxtone,' said Michael, stepping outside the gate and pointing to where the King's Hall physician was waddling briskly towards the High Street. 'I would have thought he would be eager to ensure King's Hall is as well represented as possible, yet he cannot wait to leave.'

'He explained why – he is not needed if Shropham is here. Besides, Risleye just died in his arms. I do not blame him for being loath to think about legal matters now.'

Michael frowned anxiously as they walked along the lane. 'I was hoping Langelee would deliver one of his instant decisions, and we would be done with the matter. We do not have time to race back and forth with incarcerated felons.'

'Langelee will not dally,' said Bartholomew. He increased his stride. 'But we should hurry, anyway. You are right – we do *not* have time for this kind of errand.'

The streets were strangely empty of scholars, and

Bartholomew imagined St Mary the Great must be bursting at the seams. There was a distant roar of applause as a disputant made a clever point, although it was immediately followed by an equally loud chorus of boos and hisses.

'I would not want to be in Luneday's shoes,' mused Michael, breathless from the rapid pace. 'With Elyan's heir and d'Audley dead, he is all that stands between King's Hall and the inheritance.'

'He does not seem concerned, though,' said Bartholomew, wondering whether it was significant.

'Damn it all!' cried Michael. 'We have murder and deception taking place right under our noses but we do not have enough clues and evidence to stop it. I cannot recall when I have ever felt so helpless in a tide of unfolding events.'

A roar of clamouring voices told them someone had just made another contentious point, and Bartholomew knew from experience that when the disputants issued statements that induced that sort of reaction, tempers ran very hot.

Michael was becoming exasperated. 'We have solved a number of murders – Gosse killed Kelyng, d'Audley dispatched Neubold, Neubold stabbed Carbo, and Tesdale killed Wynewyk – but there are still far too many questions. This is not like other cases – there is not one culprit this time, but several, all with their own distinct agendas.'

There was a third roar from St Mary the Great, angry and clamouring. It was followed by the kind of jeers that were intended to be provocative.

'Get Shropham, Matt,' ordered Michael abruptly. 'And take him to the College. I think I had better check Cleydon does not need me.'

Shropham, pale and heavy-eyed, said nothing when the physician told him he was going to represent King's Hall in a legal dispute, and meekly followed him out into the High Street.

'Shropham,' said Paxtone warmly, stepping in front of them and forcing them to a sudden standstill. Bartholomew frowned, because Paxtone appeared to have come out of St Michael's. It was not a church he usually frequented, and Bartholomew was not sure why he should start now. Moreover, Paxtone said he had escaped from Langelee's impromptu court because he needed to rest, so why was he not at home, lying down?

'Paxtone!' cried Shropham, his face lighting up with genuine pleasure.

'I have many things to tell you,' said Paxtone. He glanced at Bartholomew. 'Perhaps you would give us a moment alone together? God knows, we deserve it, after all we have been through.'

'No,' said Bartholomew, not sure what Paxtone intended by the odd request, but determined he would not be party to it. 'Langelee is waiting.'

'I am only asking for a few moments. Surely, you will not begrudge me that? You are my friend.'

Bartholomew was suddenly seized with the absolute conviction that Paxtone was nothing of the kind. He took a firmer hold of Shropham's arm, and tugged him away. He was aware of Paxtone following, and it was not easy pulling Shropham in a direction he did not want to go, but the increasing sense that something was horribly amiss gave him the strength to do it.

'You should not rile him,' said Shropham, trying to look over his shoulder. 'He is dangerous when crossed. I do not condemn him, of course. Great men are bound by different rules from you and me.'

Bartholomew regarded him blankly, then realised what he meant. 'You think Paxtone stabbed Carbo because you

438

saw him covered in blood on the night of the murder. But you are wrong: he was summoned to bleed Constable Muschett and he cut too deeply. He killed no one.'

Shropham gaped at him. 'Are you sure? Only—'

'Only what? Tell me, Shropham. You cannot harm Paxtone with anything you say – his innocence of that particular crime is incontrovertible.'

'Only I saw him in the vicinity, and his knife was in Carbo's body,' whispered Shropham, hanging his head. 'Oh, sweet Jesus! What have I done? I thought I was protecting him, but instead I have maligned him with false assumptions!'

'His knives are standard equipment for anyone who needs small, sharp blades,' said Bartholomew. 'Lots of people own them, including me. Were you really prepared to hang for him? I know King's Hall men are loyal, but . . .'

'My College needs him,' said Shropham softly. 'More than it needs me. So it was a case of expediency. King's Hall is the only home I have ever known, and I will do anything for it.'

Bartholomew was too agitated to tell him he was insane. 'So what *did* you see that night?'

'Paxtone covered in blood. Carbo with one of those little knives in his stomach. Beadles coming. I knew they would catch Paxtone unless I acted, so I sliced my own arm to distract them.'

'Then what?'

'You know the rest – the Junior Proctor was so certain I was the culprit that he did not notice Paxtone disappearing around the corner. The only other person in the vicinity was another Dominican, who left as soon as the commotion started.'

Bartholomew groaned. 'You are a fool, Shropham! That was Neubold, who had ample reason to want his brother dead. If you had spoken out, we would have resolved all this days ago.'

He turned at a sound behind him, and realised that while they had been talking he had slackened his pace, and Paxtone had caught up. With a shock, he saw that the King's Hall physician held one of his little phlebotomy blades.

'I want to inspect his wound,' said Paxtone, holding the implement as if he intended to use it to cut away Shropham's bandage. 'It was inflamed yesterday, and I should examine it again. You do not need me to tell you the importance of monitoring cuts, Matthew. Let me see him.'

Bartholomew tugged Shropham away a second time. Was Paxtone using Shropham's injury as an excuse to get him alone because he wanted to coach him about Elyan Manor? Or was his intention more deadly? Bartholomew did not wait to find out, and once again left the portly physician behind.

When Shropham saw Warden Powys sitting at the table in Michaelhouse's hall, he darted towards him and dropped to his knees, sobbing. Bemused, Powys rested his hand on his colleague's head. Suffolk eyebrows shot up in astonishment, although, politely, no one made any comment.

Powys tried to pull Shropham into a corner so they could speak undisturbed, but unfortunately for him, the visitors were interested in the newcomer, and followed. They all turned sharply when there was a thunder of footsteps on the stairs, accompanied by heavy breathing. It was Michael.

'What are you doing here?' demanded Bartholomew worriedly. 'You should be at St Mary the Great, preventing a brawl – and protecting our colleagues from Gosse.'

'Cleydon has the situation under control,' panted

Michael. 'And my presence transpired to be inflammatory, because people started howling at me over contentious theological points I have made in the past. It calmed somewhat when I left.'

'Right,' said Langelee, rubbing his hands together when he saw that all the participants were present at last. Powys grimaced when the Master indicated they were to take their seats: he still had not managed to speak to Shropham alone. 'We should begin. *Benedic nobis. Domine.* That should do for a starting prayer. Now, who wants to go first?'

'You do not tarry, do you?' said Hilton in awe.

'No,' agreed Langelee amiably. 'Luneday, tell me why Elyan Manor should be yours.'

'I once had documents to prove my case,' said Luneday ruefully. 'At least, I assume I did – I cannot read, so it is difficult to be certain. But my woman made off with them.'

'We retrieved them,' said Michael, placing the bundle on the table. 'Do not ask how.'

'I *like* Michaelhouse!' exclaimed Luneday approvingly. 'You are amazing men, and I wish we had invited you into our affairs years ago. It would have saved a lot of trouble.'

Powys's expression was unreadable. He leaned towards Shropham and tried to mutter something, but Langelee was speaking again and Shropham did not notice his Warden's attempts to pass him a message. He merely lent his undivided attention to what the judge was saying, like any good lawyer.

'Your claim, Luneday,' prompted Langelee. 'Outline why you should have the manor.'

'Now d'Audley is dead, I am Elyan's closest blood relative,' replied Luneday. 'Not counting his grandmother. We share a great-great-uncle.'

'Fair enough,' said Langelee. He looked at Powys. 'What does King's Hall have to say?'

441

'We were left Elyan Manor by a man named Alneston,' replied Powys, also setting a pile of writs on the table. Bartholomew recognised one as a copy of the early will. 'Alneston's son claimed it illegally after his death, and so the occupation by his descendants is similarly illegal.'

'I have seen that particular will,' said Hilton. 'Lady Agnys has a copy of it, too. But I am sure there are more recent codicils that would—'

'If they exist, then no one has found them,' interrupted Powys smoothly. 'And my inclination is to believe that they are figments of hopeful imaginations. Alneston's will is unambiguous: Elyan Manor belongs to King's Hall, and so does his chantry chapel.'

'It is true,' said Shropham with a shrug, picking up the relevant document. 'As a lawyer, I would say this deed is as straightforward as any I have seen.'

Warden Powys beamed at his colleague. 'Does anyone have anything else to add?' he asked smugly. 'Because if not, perhaps we shall have this speedy decision, after all.'

'I cannot believe Alneston lived another fifty years without making some amendment to his testimony,' said Hilton unhappily. 'I have long wanted to peruse Luneday's records, but—'

'But I was not having Haverhill men poking about in my personal affairs,' said Luneday firmly.

Powys continued to look smug. 'And as no one can produce such a document, I submit it does not exist. The case is closed, and you may pass judgment, Langelee.'

Michael started to rummage through Margery's pile, aiming to present the later deed and wipe the smile from Powys's face, but Shropham was there before him. With a lawyer's consummate interest, he had taken a handful of the deeds, and was leafing through them. When he reached Alneston's second testament, he went still.

Powys noticed his reaction, and tried to see what he had found.

'The priest is right,' said Shropham, passing the deed to his Warden. 'Alneston did make a—'

'No,' said Powys, screwing the parchment into a ball and tossing it over his shoulder. 'This is a forgery, and prison has addled your mind.'

Shropham cringed, and looked as if he wished the floor would open and swallow him up. 'Yes,' he said in a small voice. 'I am not well. It must be a fake, or it would have come to light before now.'

'Not necessarily,' said Hilton, retrieving the document and reading it for himself. 'And it looks authentic to me – I am familiar with Alneston's seal.'

Langelee was also rifling through the pile. 'And here is a writ drafted by King's Hall and signed by your predecessor, Powys. It relinquishes all claims on Elyan Manor *and* the Alneston Chantry in exchange for the sum of forty marks, which was paid in full twenty-five years ago.'

'No!' cried Powys. 'That is a forgery, too. We must have what is rightfully ours!'

'Must?' pounced Michael. 'That is a powerful sentiment, Warden.'

Powys reddened and turned away. 'You know what I am saying.'

'I am beginning to understand. You are interested in what the mine can offer. Not coal, but—'

'Coal is a valuable commodity,' snapped Warden Powys. 'Of course we are interested.'

'*I* do not care about the coal,' said Luneday. 'And if Elyan Manor comes to me, I shall fill in the mine and turn the land over to grazing for pigs.'

'Then sell that particular wood to us,' said Powys eagerly. 'King's Hall will take the coal.'

Elyan laughed softly. 'I do not plan on dying very soon, Warden Powys. Do you think my mine will still have anything to interest you years in the future?'

Powys regarded him strangely. 'I imagine it will. Why? Do you know different?'

Elyan shrugged. 'I have spent more than fifty marks on the place – d'Audley and I borrowed twenty-five from Michaelhouse and twenty-five from you – and I have been digging for almost three months now. Something should have been unearthed in all that time.'

'Diamonds,' said Bartholomew, leaning against the wall as he gauged Powys's reaction. 'That is what you were expecting to find.'

'Diamonds?' echoed Agnys, regarding her grandson in stunned disbelief. 'You have been mining for *diamonds*? You ridiculous boy! Diamonds do not occur in England.'

'Carbo found them,' said Elyan. 'He showed me where he had prised them from the seam.'

'You did not mention this the other day, Elyan,' said Michael accusingly. 'You only said your minerals were exceptionally hard and pure.'

Elyan looked shifty. 'Diamonds *are* hard and pure. And it was none of your affair, anyway.'

Powys was glaring. 'Are you telling me you have excavated nothing since August? That was not what Neubold told us. Only last week, he said the work was proceeding apace and that King's Hall would soon begin to enjoy the profits from its investment.'

Langelee was growing bored with a discussion he did not understand. 'You can chat about this nonsense later,' he said. 'Meanwhile, I have reached my decision: King's Hall has no grounds to press its claim and d'Audley is dead. *Ergo* I declare Luneday to be the rightful heir.'

Luneday beamed at him, while Powys gaped in horror

444

and Shropham looked as if he was ready to cry. Shropham tried to apologise, but his Warden was too angry to listen. He surged to his feet and left without another word, Shropham scurrying at his heels. Langelee raised his eyebrows, but did not seem overly concerned that he might have made an enemy of King's Hall.

'I *knew* a man who professes skill with pigs would see justice done,' declared Luneday, tears in his eyes as he shook the Master's hand. 'Put your decision in writing, if you please. And while we wait, you can tell me more about this game of camp-ball. You say a pig is on one team?'

Pleased the matter had been resolved before his camp-ball game was due to begin, Langelee became magnanimous. He fetched wine from the kitchens, and began to pour generous measures into goblets. Elyan swallowed his thirstily, clearly glad the business was over, and held out his cup for more before the Master had finished distributing them around his other guests.

'I was going to propose a toast,' Langelee said, shooting Elyan an admonishing look for his greed. He pressed a goblet into Bartholomew's hand, although the last thing the physician felt like doing was drinking in cosy bonhomie with the visitors from Suffolk.

'To justice and pigs?' suggested Luneday, raising his vessel.

'And camp-ball,' added Langelee with a grin, returning the salute.

The others raised their goblets obligingly, and everyone was in the process of putting them to their lips when Elyan gave a cry and gripped his throat. The cup fell from his hand, and he dropped to his knees.

'What is wrong with him?' cried Agnys, hurrying to his side.

Bartholomew was there before her. He tried to hold Elyan still, but the lord of the manor was thrashing about violently. It did not need a physician to know he had been poisoned.

'But this wine came from the kitchens,' shouted Langelee defensively, when everyone looked at him. 'It was delivered earlier today – a gift from Bartholomew's sister.'

'My sister is not in the habit of providing us with wine,' said Bartholomew, struggling to keep Elyan still so he could examine him. 'Only cakes.'

'Gosse,' muttered Michael grimly. 'Is this what he meant when he said he had something planned for us? I assumed he had set his sights on St Mary the Great.'

'Do something,' cried Agnys, gripping Bartholomew's shoulder hard. 'Help him!'

But Bartholomew was already thrusting fingers down Elyan's throat to make him vomit up what he had swallowed – he had watched Margery, d'Audley, Risleye and Tesdale die within the past few hours, and had had enough of feeling helpless in the face of death. He was not losing anyone else.

Elyan retched violently, and when he leaned back, exhausted by the effort, Bartholomew made him sick again. And again. Eventually, when he thought all or most of the toxin had been expelled, he wiped Elyan's face with a clean cloth and helped him sit comfortably.

'It is a pity to die now,' rasped Elyan, tears flowing down his cheeks. 'Just when everything is going my way. Wynewyk dead, Luneday to inherit my manor – *he* will not harm me for a few gems.'

But Bartholomew knew, from the colour that was beginning to trickle back into Elyan's face, that the worst was over. 'You are not going to—' he began.

'It is ironic to die of poison left by Gosse,' interrupted

446

Elyan, with a weak but bitter smile. 'You see, Carbo found the diamonds in my mine, but Gosse said they were his – stolen from him by Carbo when he lived in Clare. He was very insistent, but I did not believe him. Perhaps I should have done.'

Bartholomew recalled that both Hilton and Prior John had mentioned Gosse's purloined sack, the contents of which Gosse had declined to reveal. 'You are not going to—'

Elyan cut across him a second time. 'I told Neubold to pass some to potential investors. Namely Wynewyk and King's Hall. But I kept most – the biggest and best – for myself.'

'You kept precious stones that Gosse thinks are his?' asked Hilton uneasily. 'That was reckless.'

Bartholomew tried a third time to tell Elyan he was going to recover, sure he would not be baring his soul if he knew he would live. 'The poison is not—'

But Michael jabbed him in the ribs. 'We need answers,' he hissed urgently.' Do not interrupt him – lives depend on it.'

'It would only have been reckless if Gosse *knew* I kept them,' Elyan was rasping to Hilton. 'But he does not. I told him they had all been given to scholars in Cambridge. So he came here to find them. But then someone pilfered the sack from me.'

'So you were right, Matt,' murmured Michael. 'Gosse and Idoma really were asking for the whereabouts of something specific. I thought it was a ruse, to confuse me.'

'Joan!' exclaimed Hilton, somewhat out of the blue. '*She* took them! She told me she had vital business in Cambridge – important enough to risk her child on a journey. She must have realised these stones were going to cause trouble, so she brought them here.'

'Why would she do that?' demanded Luneday. 'Why not keep them for herself – for her child?'

'Because she was a sensible lady,' replied Hilton softly. 'She would not have been so credulous as to believe that Carbo had found diamonds in Haverhill – she would have been sceptical. Opportunities to travel are few and far between in our village, so she took advantage of the only one available: she came to Cambridge with Neubold, intending to hide them here.'

'That explains why she chose this town,' acknowledged Agnys. 'It also explains why she was unhappy these last few weeks – it would have been a terrible burden, knowing Henry had property belonging to Gosse and that these stones might urge powerful foundations and greedy men to desperate measures to acquire them. But not why she felt compelled to transport the wretched things in the first place.'

'It is obvious,' said Michael. 'The mine has produced no gems, and getting rid of the ones Carbo "found" – the big ones Elyan kept for himself – means Haverhill has none left. She probably had a plan to show King's Hall and Wynewyk that Elyan Manor has nothing worth fighting for – and therefore nothing worth harming her child for, either. Unfortunately, her plan misfired.'

'Oh, Henry,' said Agnys, gazing at her grandson with sad eyes. 'How could you have been so foolish? All these deaths – including Joan's – and for what? Jewels stolen from the Gosses, that were never on Elyan Manor in the first place!'

'They were!' asserted Elyan weakly. 'Carbo would not have lied to me.'

'Not lied, no,' agreed Agnys. 'He did not have the wit. But that does not mean his tale was true.'

But Elyan was not listening to her. His gaze was fixed on Bartholomew. 'Wynewyk was an evil man. He sent his student to spy on the mine, and someone killed the boy. God forgive me, I buried his body in the woods. But worse than that, Wynewyk killed Joan. I have thought long and hard, and I understand what happened now. *He* poisoned her.'

'No!' said Bartholomew, ignoring Tesdale's tale about Wynewyk taking pennyroyal from his storeroom. 'You have no evidence to make such a terrible accusation.'

'Actually, he might have,' said Langelee quietly. 'Because of something *I* saw on the day she died – namely Wynewyk giving her a phial and telling her it would make her baby strong. I had forgotten about it until now. He was congratulating her, saying what a bonny child it would be, but there was a certain look in his eye . . . It was one I have often observed in men about to commit a crime.'

'There!' exclaimed Elyan weakly. 'I knew it! You see, you were right – her child was *not* mine. But Wynewyk met her when he came to buy pigs . . .'

'He did visit me in February,' acknowledged Luneday uncomfortably. 'But I had no idea he went to Haverhill and seduced Joan at the same time.'

'He flirted outrageously with her in the Market Square,' added Langelee. 'As your sister will attest, too. He preferred men, but he knew how to charm the ladies, as well.'

'Enough!' cried Bartholomew, when Elyan opened his mouth to say something else. 'You are not dying. There is no need to pursue this horrible matter any further.'

Michael grimaced his annoyance that the discussion was to be cut short, while Elyan just stared at the physician. Bartholomew braced himself for anger at the deceit, but instead the Suffolk lordling's eyes filled with tears. He groped for Agnys's hand, and gripped it hard, and Bartholomew indicated the onlookers were to move away, to give them privacy.

'You cannot wait any longer to hunt down Gosse, Brother,' Bartholomew said exhaustedly. 'He might have killed the entire College. And he is a danger to every scholar in Cambridge as long as he is free.'

There was a distant roar as someone in St Mary the Great made a contentious point, and it was followed by the kind of yells that had no place in an academic dispute.

'You are right,' said Michael, hurrying towards the door. 'But my first responsibility is to help Cleydon. I have wasted enough time here.'

The monk began to run towards St Mary the Great, Bartholomew at his heels. The clamour of angry voices grew louder as they drew closer, and they saw that a number of townsfolk had gathered to stand outside. Some looked concerned at the sounds of discord within, but most were openly delighted that the hated University sounded as if it was tearing itself apart. Cynric emerged from behind a buttress.

'I have been watching them,' he explained, nodding towards the crowd: 'A stone through a window now will be enough to spark a huge riot inside.'

'You said you would follow Gosse and Idoma when they arrived back in Cambridge,' said Bartholomew accusingly. 'It was why we did not challenge them in the hills.'

'We did not challenge them in the hills because they outmatched us,' corrected Cynric. 'And they managed to give me the slip once they reached town. I cannot imagine how – witchcraft, probably.'

He winced when there was another howl of fury from the debating scholars, then darted forward when two apprentices bent to prise rocks from the ground. Several beadles joined him in hustling the would-be offenders away, but the remaining townsfolk objected to their cronies being arrested before they had committed a crime. There was a rumble of anger and some serious jostling.

'Your men have their hands full here, Brother,' said Bartholomew. 'Which means they cannot be watching the back of the church. Gosse might—'

But Michael was already hurrying towards the graveyard. Bartholomew followed, and they had completed almost a full circuit of the building before the physician skidded to a standstill.

'There!' he shouted, pointing to where a fold of material and the tip of a shoe poked from behind a bush. Idoma was simply too large to conceal herself in undergrowth. Michael powered towards her and ripped away the branches.

'Good afternoon, Brother,' said Gosse mildly, not at all discomfited to be caught. 'Why are you not at the debate? I thought you were an accomplished theologian. Or are you afraid to take part, lest you are found wanting?'

From somewhere on his ample person, Michael produced a cudgel. 'You have plagued my town long enough. Will you come peacefully to my prison, or must I force you?'

Idoma regarded him in disbelief, then issued a low, deep laugh. It was an unpleasant sound, more demonic than human. Her eyes seemed especially cold and shark-like that day, and she exuded an aura of deadly malice. Was Michael making a terrible mistake in tackling her, when not even the bold Cynric would do it? Trying to prevent his hands from shaking, Bartholomew reached into his bag and withdrew his birthing forceps, although the implement was no match for the knives both Gosse and Idoma produced at the same time.

'You are dead men,' hissed Gosse. 'Your University stole a fortune from us – made it disappear as though it never existed. But we shall have our revenge. You will not be alive to see it, though.'

451

'We found your poisoned wine,' said Michael, standing firm. 'Elyan swallowed some, but no scholars fell victim—'

Idoma sneered. 'Good! It serves him right for giving away our property. We would have killed him, anyway, for the inconvenience he caused. Now we do not need to bother.'

'No more talking,' said Gosse sharply. 'There is no time.'

He lunged at Bartholomew with his knife, leaving Michael for his sister. The physician was unprepared for the viciousness of the attack, and was forced to retreat fast. The defensive blows he struck with the forceps went wide, and only succeeded in throwing him off balance. He went down on one knee. Gosse moved in for the kill, and, too late, Bartholomew knew Cynric had been right – they were more than a match for him.

Suddenly, there was a yell of fury, and the book-bearer appeared. He carried his long Welsh hunting knife, and when he saw Gosse's blade begin to descend towards the physician, he lobbed it. Gosse screamed as it tore a gash in his arm. Before the felon could recover, Bartholomew leapt to his feet and knocked the weapon from his hand. Cynric darted forward, drew back his fist and punched Gosse on the point of the jaw. He went down as if pole-axed.

Bartholomew spun around to help Michael. Idoma had dropped her blade, but had both hands wrapped around the monk's throat. Michael was a strong man, but it was clear he was losing the battle, because his face was scarlet. He rained blows on her head and shoulders, but she seemed oblivious to them, and Bartholomew wondered whether she really was imbued with some diabolical energy. He raced towards them, and tried to prise the powerful fingers loose, but they were like bands of steel. He saw the desperate terror in Michael's eyes.

Knowing Michael was going to die before he could lever

her fingers away, Bartholomew took several steps back, put his head down, and charged at the struggling pair with all his might. All three went flying. There was a sickening crack as Idoma's head struck the buttress.

'Well,' said Cynric, looking at the two insensible villains with enormous satisfaction. 'Perhaps I was wrong about their military prowess. We bested them with ease.'

But Bartholomew was not so ready to gloat. And there had been nothing 'easy' about their victory, anyway – he and Michael had come far too close to losing the fight.

'Now we cannot ask what they have plotted,' he said, alarmed. 'Their plan may yet succeed.'

'How?' asked Michael hoarsely, rubbing his throat with one hand and holding out the other for Bartholomew to help him up. 'They are hardly in a position to act now.'

'They were not here to "act",' shouted Bartholomew, heart pounding. 'They were here to watch what happened – to enjoy the spectacle. Oh, no!'

'What?' asked Michael fearfully, leaning against the buttress to catch his breath.

'Wine,' said Bartholomew, white-faced. 'Will some be provided at the end of the debate? For every scholar in the University?'

Michael gaped at him in horror, then whipped around and began running towards the church door. Bartholomew followed, stopping only to order three beadles to help Cynric secure the Gosses.

Inside, the clamour of discordant voices was loud enough to hurt the ears. The refreshments sat on a table in the north aisle. Bartholomew aimed for them, but Michael found his way barred by a horrified Junior Proctor.

'Thank God you are here, Brother,' gasped Cleydon.

453

'The two sides are on the verge of a huge fight and I am powerless to stop it.'

'There he is!' cried a familiar voice. It was Warden Powys, and he was pointing at Michael. 'There is the man who prefers to let College business take precedence over his University duties. He has been in Michaelhouse, drinking claret with his Master, when he should have been here.'

'Is this true, Brother?' asked Chancellor Tynkell nervously. He was a timid nonentity, wholly incapable of calming the anger that was erupting all around him.

'Of course it is not true,' bellowed Deynman indignantly. 'King's Hall is just trying to make trouble for Michaelhouse.'

As he headed for the north aisle, Bartholomew saw the scholars had arranged themselves into two distinct factions – those who sided with Michaelhouse, and those who preferred King's Hall. He knew from past experience that it was bad news when a debate moved from academic topics and began to air other grievances. It meant the audience was itching for a fight. Powys seemed to know it, too.

'Michael should resign,' he shouted provocatively. 'He has accrued too much power, and I have no confidence in his rule. I demand he steps down as Senior Proctor.'

There was a cacophony of yells, some howling support for Michael and others bawling that Powys made a very good point. The clamour was deafening.

'Powys is right,' hollered Eltisle of Bene't College, who had never liked the monk. He had a shrill voice, and it carried over the others. 'We have all been burgled over the last few weeks, but Brother Michael has made no effort to catch the culprits.'

'On the contrary,' boomed Michael, scrambling on to the dais next to the Chancellor. He held an imperious hand aloft, and such was the force of his personality that

454

it immediately quelled the din. 'I have just arrested Gosse and his sister on charges of theft and murder.'

His words were met with a startled silence, which was followed at once by a clamour of questions and cheers. Bartholomew reached the refreshments and looked at the three large casks of wine that were sitting ready to be poured. Had Gosse poisoned them all, or just one?

He could not afford to take risks with his colleagues' lives, so he pulled the stoppers from all three and watched their contents splatter to the floor. Fortunately, the rumpus caused by Michael's declaration drowned the sound it made. By the time the din subsided, the kegs were virtually empty.

'You have Gosse in custody?' It was Powys asking, and he sounded worried.

'They are being taken to my prison as I speak,' affirmed Michael haughtily. 'Of course, I was *deeply* disappointed to miss the debate, but sacrifices must be made. I have always put duty before pleasure, and catching criminals who have harmed my University is a sacred responsibility, as far as I am concerned.'

'I am glad you have him, Brother,' called Rougham of Gonville Hall warmly. 'He stole three gold candlesticks from us.'

'And a silver paten from us,' added Master Wisbeche of Peterhouse.

'I shall do my utmost to see they are returned to you,' promised Michael. 'Meanwhile, I insist you all return to your debate, and leave the unpleasant work to me.'

Deynman released a sudden cheer, which was taken up by other Michaelhouse men, and soon the whole church resounded with it. Friends surged forward to clap Michael on the back, although no one from King's Hall was among them.

Bartholomew shook the barrels, to make sure they were drained to the dregs, then backed away and edged towards the door. The gathering could turn against him just as quickly as it had turned to favour Michael – no scholar liked to be deprived of free wine.

'You transformed yourself from villain to hero,' he remarked, when the monk's path crossed his own. 'It was cleverly done.'

Michael preened. 'And Powys is furious. Look at his dark face!'

'It will not stay dark for long,' warned Cynric worriedly, appearing beside them. 'Idoma recovered her senses as we were taking her to the cells. We could not hold her, and she has escaped.'

EPILOGUE

Two weeks later, Bartholomew and Michael were again travelling the road that led to Suffolk. The physician was reluctant to leave his pupils a second time, but Deynman had managed a surprisingly good job of supervising them during the earlier jaunt, and had offered to do it again. And it would be the calm before the storm as far as the students were concerned, because Bartholomew intended to keep them so busy for the rest of the term that no one would have time to think, let alone indulge in spying or stealing his medicines.

It was a pretty day, with the crisp scent of late autumn in the air. The trees were red and gold, and showers of leaves drifted across the road each time the wind blew. A pheasant croaked from deep in the woods, and a cow lowed in a nearby meadow. Bartholomew tipped his head back and took a deep breath, savouring the smell of damp leaves and freshly tilled soil. Unfortunately, his horse objected to the movement, and skittered sideways.

'Grip with your knees,' said Michael automatically. 'And shorten the reins.'

'I was wrong,' said Bartholomew, when he had regained control of the beast. He noticed Cynric and the beadles were riding well back, partly to give the scholars the opportunity to talk without being overheard, but mostly to stay away from the menace the physician represented while on horseback. 'About Wynewyk.'

'We all were,' said Michael softly. 'It just took you longer to accept the truth.'

'He was a thief and a murderer,' said Bartholomew, still barely able to believe it. 'I kept thinking there would be an innocent explanation for the wrong he did, but there was not.'

'Poor Joan,' said Michael. 'If Carbo had not made his so-called discovery of diamonds, she and Wynewyk would probably never have met again. Their affair would have been forgotten – Joan would have given Elyan his heir, and Wynewyk would never have known about the child.'

'So what happened?' asked Bartholomew tiredly. 'What made him poison her?'

'I suspect he saw her in Cambridge, and assumed she was there to make trouble for him – to reveal that he, a scholar, had fathered a child. In other words, he judged her by his own rotten standards. But, of course, she would have been as eager as he to conceal what had happened.'

Bartholomew closed his eyes. 'So he gave her pennyroyal, and he did it without compunction.'

Michael nodded. 'Valence told me he heard Wynewyk and Tesdale discussing that particular herb the day before Joan died. Tesdale almost certainly told him what to use.'

Bartholomew kept his eyes closed. 'It *was* my supply that killed Joan. Edith will never forgive me.'

'She knows it was not your fault, Matt,' said Michael kindly. 'She liked Wynewyk, too, and was appalled when she heard how he deceived us.'

'Did he deceive us? He borrowed money to make arrangements with Luneday, d'Audley and Elyan, but there is no proof that he intended to keep the proceeds for himself.'

'Actually, there is. Clippesby discovered more hidden documents in Wynewyk's room, in the chimney this time. There were arrangements to buy a big house in London, fine new clothes and deposits to be left with a moneylender

– a kind of pension. Apparently, he had a lover who was going to join him there, because there are several fond references to a man named Osa.'

Bartholomew's eyes snapped open. 'Not Osa Gosse? But Wynewyk talked about him the night he was ill – when the almond posset upset him – and he did not describe him in very flattering terms.'

Michael ignored him. 'Apparently, Wynewyk and Osa met in February, when Wynewyk travelled to Suffolk to inspect Luneday's pigs – and impregnated Joan, into the bargain – and they embarked on a relationship. He always did have a weakness for ruffians, but the correspondence indicates he was deeply in love this time.'

Bartholomew frowned. 'But the night he was unwell, he told me he had only met Gosse the previous week. He said Gosse had accused him of seduction, and was offended by it.'

'He was lying. Reliable witnesses have since informed me that he and Gosse were often together. And the night he misled you was his first attempt at suicide. Tesdale said so, and I think he was telling the truth about that. You see, there is some indication in Wynewyk's letters that Gosse had recently spurned him – that he was refusing to go to London.'

Bartholomew tried to recall what else Wynewyk had said. 'He told me he and Gosse had some sort of spat that turned violent. Gosse's servant was killed when daggers were drawn.'

'The Carmelite novices saved him from a trouncing and there *was* a fatality – you gave me a verdict, if you recall. But I suspect Wynewyk had realised by then that he was on a slippery slope to nowhere: he was *sans* lover, he had taken too many liberties with the College accounts to put right, he was responsible for our Bible Scholar's death . . .'

459

'Gosse killed Kelyng,' said Bartholomew stubbornly. 'They fell over each other when they were spying on Elyan's mine.'

'But who ordered him there?' demanded Michael harshly. 'Wynewyk was a villain, Matt. He even tried to kill Langelee, and when that failed and he knew his game was over, he ate nuts in earnest. But Tesdale got him first.'

'But *why* kill himself? Why not go to London?'

'I think he could not bring himself to leave Cambridge in the end,' replied Michael. 'But it was all for greed. For these wretched diamonds – Carbo's so-called magic stones.'

'And the irony is that the whole thing was a hoax. First, diamonds do not occur in England – and they certainly do not appear in seams of coal in Suffolk. And second, the rocks in the bag Carbo stole from Gosse were not diamonds anyway.'

The last point was news to Michael. His jaw dropped. 'They were, Matt! They were raw diamonds – uncut, and so unfamiliar to most of us. But they scratched glass, and everyone knows—'

'Many minerals scratch glass, Brother.'

Michael regarded him thoughtfully. 'What about the sack of pebbles Joan buried in Edith's garden?' Edith had noticed freshly turned soil, and asked Bartholomew to investigate, although he and Michael both knew what they would find. Joan had buried it there, in the hope that its disappearance would prevent men like Wynewyk, Paxton, Warden Powys and d'Audley from harming her child.

'Poor Joan,' said Bartholomew. 'No wonder she was distressed for the last few weeks of her life. She knew she had to dispose of the "diamonds" – the ones the husband she loved hoped would make him rich, and that she knew really belonged to Osa Gosse. It cannot have been an easy decision to make.'

But Michael was more interested in the physician's claim

that the precious gems were a hoax. 'Can I assume from your remarks that you performed some kind of experiment on them?' he asked.

'I borrowed a real diamond and a ruby from Edith, and both scratched what Joan had buried – which means Elyan's stones are softer. I did some reading, and deduced that they are actually rock crystal, which is quarried by the bucket-load in Greece.'

Michael sighed. 'I should not be surprised, given that the originator of the tale was Carbo – a madman. Elyan was a fool for believing him, and everyone else was a fool for believing Elyan.'

'According to Sheriff Tulyet, who returned today, a box of rock crystal was stolen from a Suffolk jeweller last summer. Clearly, Gosse is the culprit, and no doubt he intended to pass them off as raw diamonds at some point in the future. Just as Wynewyk tried to do.'

'But Carbo found them first, and told Elyan they had come from his mine.'

'I doubt Carbo lied – he probably believed it himself. Poor Carbo! It is a pity, because in other ways he was regaining his wits – he came to Cambridge to expose his felonious brother. And Neubold killed him for it.'

'Elyan is no innocent, either,' added Michael. 'He told Gosse the "diamonds" had been distributed around the University, so Gosse would leave him alone and pick on someone else. Did I tell you he has gone on a pilgrimage to Walsingham, to atone for all his sins?'

Bartholomew nodded. 'The whole affair was horrible. It led Gosse to kill Kelyng, Margery and d'Audley; Wynewyk to kill himself – with Tesdale's help; and d'Audley to hang Neubold. It brought Wynewyk into fatal contact with Joan; and induced Gosse and Idoma to try to poison the entire University.'

461

'And Risleye was killed by the duplicitous Tesdale,' finished Michael. 'Incidentally, in an effort to save himself, Gosse became very verbose. He told me King's Hall had hired him and his sister.'

'Hired them to do what?'

'To break into Michaelhouse and retrieve documents about the diamonds from Wynewyk. But they could not find any, so they made off with the Stanton Cups instead. He also said they were paid to follow us to Suffolk and dispatch us there, because King's Hall was worried that we planned to take up where Wynewyk had left off.'

Bartholomew regarded him in horror. 'Do you believe him?'

Michael was silent for a long time. 'Gosse also said that King's Hall promised him a lot of money – enough to buy a decent house in our town and enjoy a life of luxury. Powys assures me that his College does not have that sort of cash to hand. But who knows the truth? I do not.'

Bartholomew shook his head, sickened. 'So King's Hall tried to murder us? Paxtone and Powys? I thought they were our friends!'

'They were not friends once the prospect of diamonds appeared,' said Michael bleakly.

'But they must have been aware that we knew nothing about these wretched gemstones – they had a spy in our midst, after all.'

'Risleye. But we were suspicious of him – or I was, at least – and took care never to say anything we did not want him to hear. He was next to useless to King's Hall.'

Bartholomew thought about his student. 'I should have known something was amiss when he and Paxtone remained on friendly terms. How could I have been so blind?'

'Because you are too willing to see the good in people,

as I have told you before. You need to develop a more cynical attitude to your fellows – present company excepted, of course.'

'Did Shropham know about the diamonds?' asked Bartholomew, not wanting to think too much about his colleagues' shortcomings. He had liked the men from King's Hall and was shocked by what the investigation had taught him about them.

'No – just Powys and Paxtone. Did I tell you Powys has resigned as Warden? And Paxtone plans to leave Cambridge and practise medicine in Lincoln?'

Bartholomew nodded unhappily, but made no other reply.

'Gosse also claimed it was King's Hall's idea to poison the wine at the debate, but I know he was lying about that. Powys turned out to be corrupt and greedy, but he does not bear a grudge against the entire University. That particular piece of nastiness belonged to Gosse and Idoma alone.'

'Good,' said Bartholomew bleakly, supposing it was some comfort.

Michael tried to lighten the mood. 'However, one good thing came out of this wretched affair: I was spared taking part in the Blood Relic debate.'

Bartholomew regarded him askance. 'I thought you were disappointed about that? You wanted the chance to show everyone that you are bishop material.'

'I did – but I would have failed. Thelnetham was ruthlessly savaged by the Franciscans, and he is better versed in the dispute than me. I had a very narrow escape.'

It was late by the time Bartholomew and Michael arrived in Suffolk. They stopped in Haverhill first, to visit Agnys, and found her entertaining Luneday. Both were lonely, with Margery dead and Elyan on pilgrimage, and had taken to keeping each other company of an evening. Agnys was teaching Luneday how to cheat at dice, and she was learning a great deal about pigs in return.

The next morning, she took the scholars to the mine, where Kelyng was excavated and placed in a chest, ready to be carried home. Then Bartholomew went to inspect Lizzie: her humours were awry, and Luneday would not let the scholars leave until the physician had examined her.

Bartholomew did not mind. The loans Wynewyk had made to d'Audley and Elyan had been less than scrupulous, but the deeds in Margery's satchel revealed that the one to Luneday was perfectly honourable. And Michaelhouse, not Wynewyk, had stood to profit from it. The physician wondered whether Wynewyk had negotiated it out of guilt – that he had wanted his College to have something after he had disappeared to London with the riches arising from the diamonds he had planned to sell.

While Bartholomew and Luneday were busy, Michael went to Withersfield's quiet churchyard. He found Carbo's grave – Agnys had arranged for his return to the village of his birth – and scraped a hole in the freshly turned soil. Then he reached into his saddlebag and extracted the stones that had caused so much trouble. He dropped them into the hollow and replaced all as he had found it, hoping they would never resurface to cause trouble in the future.

'Are you sure you should go to Clare, Brother?' asked Agnys, while she and the monk waited for Bartholomew to finish with Luneday's pig. 'Is it the best thing you can do?'

'I have given it a lot of thought, and I think it is,' replied Michael, watching Bartholomew walk towards them, Luneday jabbering at his side. 'Besides, we need to retrieve the Stanton Cups, and Gosse tells me they are in Clare.'

464

'I took care of that for you,' said Agnys. 'I almost forgot. I sent word to Prior John, and he found them. Here are your silver-gilt chalices.'

She handed over a bundle of cloth, which Michael snatched eagerly. He unwrapped it, and ran loving fingers over Michaelhouse's most precious heirlooms.

'One is dented,' he said. 'But it can be repaired, and they are otherwise unharmed. Thank you.'

Neither heard the faint rustle of leaves as the person in the bushes shifted positions. Cynric's head snapped up, but there was nothing to see, and he soon turned his attention back to the horses.

As soon as Cynric was occupied, Idoma eased forward again. She regarded the monk with a glittering hatred. The Stanton Cups were all that was left of the riches her brother had acquired in Cambridge, because the rest had been seized and returned to its rightful owners. She had intended to grab them and go to London, which the foolish Wynewyk had said was a good place for anyone wanting to disappear – huge, sprawling and transient. But she had left it too late. She felt like killing someone, so hot was her rage, and it was all she could do to stop herself from racing out and tearing the scholars apart with her bare hands.

'You have no reason to go to Clare now,' Agnys was saying to the monk. 'You can stay with me again tonight, and return to Cambridge tomorrow. There is nothing for anyone in Clare.'

'You are wrong,' said Michael evenly, aware that Bartholomew was listening now. 'I found a great deal to interest me there, and I believe Matt will, too.'

They were going to Clare? Idoma's heart quickened. She knew the road well, and there were plenty of places for an ambush. Two well-placed arrows would take care of the book-bearer and the physician, and the beadles would mill around in panic. And then she would kill the monk with her knife, and the cups would be hers – along with vengeance for her losses.

But Agnys was arguing with the Benedictine. 'I disagree. Strongly. But Matthew is your friend, so I suppose you must decide what is best.'

Bartholomew looked from one to the other, bemused. 'I thought Clare was just a pretty village with a castle and a priory. Is there something—'

'Nothing that will benefit from unannounced visits,' interrupted Agnys. She looked at Michael. 'Well? Will you listen to the advice of a wise old woman?'

Go, thought Idoma fiercely, fingers tight on the hilt of her dagger. Ignore the meddling old woman and go to Clare.

Michael rubbed his chin. 'I am thinking about it.'

HISTORICAL NOTE

Twenty-first century Haverhill is a thriving market town with a population that expanded radically after the Second World War, and fires – particularly one in the seventeenth century – have robbed it of much of its medieval heritage. Although considerably smaller than today, it was still a bustling village in the Middle Ages. It was located on a major road, and tolls probably added to its wealth. It had a huge triangular marketplace, with shops that sold meat, cloth, fish and fancy goods. Archaeological investigations have also found animal bones in the kind of number that might suggest some serious slaughterhouse activity.

Two churches were extant in Haverhill in the 1350s. One was St Mary the Virgin, which still stands in the market-place today. Adam de Neubold and John de Hilton were both priests appointed shortly after the plague. The second church was earlier, and was also dedicated to St Mary, although reference to 'Bovetownchurch' (meaning 'upper church', probably because it was on a hill) has led some sources to speculate that the dedication might have been to St Botolph. The Alneston Chantry was mentioned in later wills, and its location is uncertain.

Haverhill boasted several manors, too. The main one was called the Castle, and was owned by the de Clare family until the early fourteenth century, when it passed to the Earl of Gloucester (Hugh d'Audley). A sub-manor of Haverhill was Helions (also spelled Elyan or Helyan). It was in the hands of Henry de Elyan and his wife Agnys in 1332.

Then it passed to their son John, and to John's son Henry. Folyat is another name that crops up in contemporary records of the area.

Pretty Withersfield, just a couple of miles north-north-west of Haverhill, had one manor, which was owned by the Luneday (or Loveday) family. A William of Withersfield lived in the village just before the plague.

Meanwhile, back in Cambridge, historical records show that King's Hall purchased timber and coal (or possibly charcoal) from Haverhill in the fourteenth century. Its Warden in 1357 was Thomas Powys, who had earned his Master's degree by 1333. He died in 1361. Thomas Paxtone was a Fellow of King's Hall by 1342, and went on to take posts in Lincoln, Chichester and Hackney. Their colleague John de Shropham was Powys's successor as Warden.

The Master of Michaelhouse was Ralph de Langelee, who remained in post until 1366. Michael de Causton was a contemporary, as were John Clippesby, Thomas Suttone, William de Thelnetham, and Simon Hemmysby. John Valence and William Risleye were members of Michaelhouse in the 1400s. John Tesdale, who was a Fellow in the 1380s, bequeathed the University library a large number of books. John Wynewyk was an early benefactor of Michaelhouse, whose name was included in the list of people for whom prayers were to be said.

The College's founder, Hervey de Stanton, left Michaelhouse two silver-gilt chalices when he died, which were said to be among its most valued possessions.

TO KILL OR CURE

The Thirteenth Chronicle of Matthew Bartholomew

Susanna Gregory

Cambridge University is in dire financial straits: the town's landlords are demanding an extortionate rent rise for the students' hostels and the plague years have left the colleges with scant resources. Tension between town and gown is at boiling point and soon explodes into violence and death.

Into this maelstrom comes a charismatic physician whose healing methods owe more to magic than medicine but his success threatens Matthew Bartholomew's professional reputation, and his life . . .

'Her intimate understanding of the period shines through'
Historical Novels Review

978-0-7515-3545-7

A CONSPIRACY OF VIOLENCE

Chaloner's First Exploit in Restoration London

Susanna Gregory

The dour days of Cromwell are over. Charles II is well established at White Hall Palace, his mistress at hand in rooms over the Holbein bridge, the heads of some of the regicides on public display. London seethes with new energy, freed from the strictures of the Protectorate, but many of its inhabitants have lost their livelihoods.

One is Thomas Chaloner, a reluctant spy for the feared Secretary of State, John Thurloe, and now returned from Holland in desperate need of employment. His erstwhile boss, knowing he has many enemies at court, recommends Chaloner to Lord Clarendon, but in return demands that Chaloner keep him informed of any plot against him.

But what Chaloner discovers is that Thurloe had sent another ex-employee to White Hall and he is dead, supposedly murdered by footpads near the Thames. Chaloner volunteers to investigate his killing: instead he is despatched to the Tower to unearth the gold buried by the last Governor. He discovers not treasure, but evidence that greed and self-interest are uppermost in men's minds whoever is in power, and that his life has no value to either side.

'Immaculate research, a well thought-out plot, and a sense of drama' *Choice*

978-0-7515-3758-1